A SINGLE
TO FILEY

A DCI Tony Forward Novel

Michael Murray

CONTENTS

CHAPTER ONE

Detective Chief Inspector Tony Forward checked his watch. He noted there were only twenty-five minutes to go until midnight and reflected, not for the first time that evening, on the perils of staging amateur theatricals.

Owing to various delays, the Sandleton-on-Sea Players' dress rehearsal of *The Cherry Orchard* had only progressed as far as the Third Act. It was initially delayed because Fred Bright, who played the key role of Lopakhin, had missed his train from Luffield and arrived an hour late. Then there'd been all the usual problems with lighting, scenery changes and actors' entrances. These were expected as it was the first opportunity the Players had had of running the play through in its entirety on the Sandleton High School stage and there'd been no time for the usual technical rehearsal. However, it was now nearly midnight; they hadn't even started the Fourth Act; and the first performance of the play was due to take place the following evening at seven thirty.

As the play's director, Forward could have

instructed the cast to speed things up, but he was too scrupulous to do that. This was Chekov they were playing: a playwright who achieved his most intense dramatic effects through the creation of atmosphere. Forward knew that if he forced the actors to rush the great man's lines they would lose all the nuances they'd created during weeks of rehearsals. It just wasn't on, even though it probably meant he'd be writing up his report on the Attridge case at three o'clock in the morning.

Forward sat at the back of the hall watching the action unfold painfully slowly, and conceded that perhaps his colleagues at Sandleton Police Station had a point when they told him, as they often did, he was mad to take on these extra commitments. But the Chief Inspector was a positive man by nature and he immediately put an end to such thoughts. In all other respects the dress rehearsal was going quite well: everyone knew their lines; all the props had been in the right places; the scenery hadn't collapsed; and even Nina Spillers, the dental assistant who was playing the leading role of Madame Ranyevskaya, was at last sounding like a Russian landowner instead of a Sandleton-on-Sea social climber whose elocution teacher had had a faulty ear.

Forward knew he had to decide whether to end the dress rehearsal there and then, and resume the following day when Act

Four could be run prior to the opening performance. Of course, if they'd been working in the professional theatre he'd have insisted on the cast and crew continuing until the dress rehearsal was finished, even if it meant working on into the early hours. But the Sandleton-on-Sea Players were all amateurs who had other lives outside the theatre to return to. And he could tell already that some were getting decidedly anxious about missing their last bus or train home.

On an impulse, Forward reached into his jacket pocket and took out a ten pence piece. Deftly he flipped the coin a short distance into the air, caught it and closed his hand over it.

If it's 'heads', we'll press on and I'll drive home all those who've missed their buses and trains, he vowed to himself.

He slowly opened his fingers. The coin nestling on his palm showed 'heads'. He was delighted: they would press on.

The unmistakable figure of Charlie Adams, Sandleton High's cantankerous schoolkeeper, suddenly appeared in the aisle to Forward's left. Forward couldn't see the expression on Adams' face because the hall was almost in darkness, but he didn't need to. The schoolkeeper's body language communicated with wordless eloquence that he was impatient for everyone to leave. Forward cursed quietly and tried to ignore the schoolkeeper's intimidating presence by concentrating harder on the rehearsal. They'd now reached the climax of the Third Act. Fred Bright was well into the long and emotional speech in which Lopakhin, a successful businessman, announces to the impoverished owners of the cherry orchard that he has bought their estate at auction: the very estate where he'd once been a serf. This speech was a particular favourite of Forward's. Before he'd become a policeman he'd been an obscure professional actor and had often used the same speech as an audition piece. He was glad that Fred wasn't gabbling it as usual.

"The hall's only been hired until eleven thirty, Mr Forward," said the schoolkeeper, aggressively. During the course of Lopakhin's speech he had moved along the row of hard, straight-backed chairs and sat himself down next to Forward. "I don't get paid a penny after that, y'know."

Forward kept his eyes on the stage. "I'll make sure you get your money."

"It's not just the money. I want an early night for a change."

A telephone started ringing somewhere at the back of the building.

"Who the bloody hell's this now?" Adams whined. He sighed, got slowly to his feet and went off muttering.

The Third Act was drawing to a close.

Madame Ranyevskaya was being consoled on the loss of her beautiful cherry orchard by her daughter, Anya, played sensitively by Luffield bank clerk, Audrey Ticehurst. Forward wondered if the telephone call was from Audrey's possessive mum, demanding to know what time her daughter would be arriving home.

The Act finished and the curtain came down. Forward got to his feet and clapped enthusiastically, but his lone applause in the vast, empty hall seemed inadequate, almost mocking.

"Well done everybody," Forward shouted towards the stage, where a working light had appeared behind the curtain. "Straight on with the last Act please. And make this scenery change a quick one, for heaven's sake."

"Mr Forward!"

The schoolkeeper was calling him from the back of the hall. Forward turned.

"There's a Sergeant Wilmott on the phone for you."

Forward groaned. Now what?

Adams directed Forward to the school secretary's office, where the telephone was located. The Chief Inspector picked up the receiver and said curtly, "Forward."

"Wilmott here, sir. Sorry to bother you."

There was an unusual agitation in the sergeant's normally calm East Yorkshire tones.

Forward prepared himself for trouble.

"I'm at Flamborough Head, sir. Monks Bay. A body's been found. A male with severe head injuries."

"I see," said Forward, his mind pitching wildly as it sought to readjust to sordid reality after a surfeit of theatrical illusion. "Why are you calling me? Hoggart can deal with it, surely."

"He's not available, sir. He's out at a farm near Wold Newton. Suspected arson attack."

"Who's there with you, then?"

"Diane Griffiths and the local PC from Flamborough. SOCOs and uniform are on their way."

"What about Marston?"

"He's arriving right now."

"Where did you say you were?"

"Monks Bay, sir."

"All right. I'll be there in about half an hour," said Forward, grudgingly.

"Just one thing, sir. The body was partly submerged in the sea. It's been moved up the beach. The tide's coming in."

"Right, don't forget to call out the coastguard."

There was an antagonistic silence at Wilmott's end. "Of course, sir. I've already done that."

Forward replaced the receiver, visualising the affronted look on Wilmott's face. Despite the inconvenience, he had to smile. As he left the secretary's office and made his way back to the school hall, a picture postcard image of Monks Bay was already forming in his mind. It was a narrow inlet squeezed between towering chalk cliffs and had a gently shelving beach of that fine sand for which the East Yorkshire coastline is renowned. In the days before their divorce, he and Mariane had spent many pleasant hours in the bay: she'd loved to sketch the chalk stacks at the northern end and to photograph the seabirds that colonised every square inch of the cliffs.

Forward put aside these memories as he passed through the double fire doors and entered the hall. The Fourth and final Act of *The Cherry Orchard* was in progress. He stood at the back and watched the characters as they prepared for the final departure from their beloved home. He observed with simple satisfaction that his choice of gel colours for the floodlights and spotlights was just right. They combined perfectly to produce the exact atmosphere of melancholy intended. How he wished he could watch the Act through to the end.

"I'm sorry everyone. I'm going to have to stop you there."

Forward's clear, resonant voice cut through the auditorium and stopped the actors dead in their tracks. Blinking fiercely and narrowing their eyes against the direct beam of the stage lights, they switched their attention away from the stage and peered into the darkened hall, seeking out the reason for the interruption.

Forward snapped on the hall lights and walked down the aisle towards the stage. When he reached the front row of the auditorium, he said, "Well done everyone. Despite the many problems we've had, you've coped magnificently. If you perform as well as this tomorrow night the audience are going to be delighted. It's a lovely production."

"Why have you stopped us then, darling? Is the hall on fire or something?"

The enquiry was put by Irene Babcock who was playing Charlotta Ivanovna, the governess. By common agreement she was regarded as the most theatrical and affected of the Players.

Forward smiled. "Police business, I'm afraid, Irene. I've been called away on a case. Sorry but the dress rehearsal will have to stop."

At this news the schoolkeeper looked gleeful, and several members of the cast, particularly those with the smaller parts, appeared quite relieved. However, the leading actors were all for continuing Act Four to the end without their director. They had a very good reason: they'd never managed to get to the end of the play before. As Forward left the school hall they were still arguing. The schoolkeeper had also joined in.

CHAPTER TWO

As Forward stepped through the school's main doors and went out into the night his nostrils were instantly confronted with the unique smell of freshness that comes after a sudden, heavy shower of rain. He splashed through puddles to his BMW, and then drove towards Sandleton's outskirts through wide, deserted streets. Substantial detached houses with immaculate front gardens and driveways crowded with expensive vehicles lined these avenues. They belonged to Sandleton's most exclusive residents. To Forward's certain knowledge three of the biggest villains in the North had owned houses there at one time. Unfortunately, the police had never been able to pin anything on them.

Forward switched on the car radio to catch the midnight news headlines. Apparently, pressure was mounting to end the Waco siege; leading economists were predicting that Britain would be out of recession by the middle of 1993; and it had been confirmed that the Grand National, which had been abandoned in chaotic circumstances, would not now be re-run.

Forward rarely listened to the whole of the news bulletin. He cut the radio and focussed entirely on the narrow, single-track road which illuminated by his main beam was rushing towards him out of the rural darkness.

Monks Bay, Forward's ultimate destination, lay four miles to the north east of Sandleton. On the map, the sweep of the East Yorkshire coastline strongly resembles an old man's face seen in profile. The most prominent feature of this image is the old man's nose: formed by the headland that juts out into the North Sea and comes to a point at Flamborough Head. Over aeons, the wind and waves have sculpted numerous bays and inlets out of the three-hundred-foot cliffs that dominate all sides of this promontory. Monks Bay was an example of such ceaseless erosion. It lay on the northern side of Flamborough Head, smack on the bridge of the Old Man of Yorkshire's nose.

It was shortly after midnight when Forward turned off the B1229 into the narrow, unlit road that was eventually to peter out on the clifftop overlooking Monks Bay.

He had barely straightened up after the turn when a rabbit appeared in his main beam. Forward automatically rammed his feet down hard and the car stopped just inches from the petrified animal.

He waited for the rabbit to move. It didn't. It had been hypnotised by the headlights. Forward cursed and switched off all the car's lights, thinking that would de-mesmerise the creature. Immediately, he was engulfed in that intense darkness familiar to remote country dwellers the world over. It was as though all the light had drained from the world.

But not quite all. Suddenly, behind him, far down on the point of the headland, the Flamborough Head lighthouse opened its brilliant eye and gave him the full benefit of its formidable candle power. Then, just as abruptly, the light was gone. The darkness was again palpable. A few seconds later, on came the lighthouse beam again. Forward forgot all about the corpse that was waiting for him at the end of the road. Like the rabbit, he was mesmerised by the alternating darkness and light. Then, remembering where he was and the danger he presented to other vehicles, he switched on his lights again. The rabbit had gone.

Forward drove on. The narrow band of road in his headlights looped without any apparent logic through open fields for about three quarters of a mile. Then, just before Monks Bay, bungalows and holiday chalets appeared. This was the tiny hamlet of Monkhouses. Lights were on in several of the buildings, and outside, in their front gardens and on the pavement, people were standing about, mostly in groups, staring down the road at the flashing lights of the police vehicles parked on the cliffs overlooking Monks Bay.

Forward continued on until he reached these vehicles and parked his BMW next to one of the SOCO vans. To his right was a clifftop parking area for tourists which his colleagues had completely roped off. A solitary car, a Vauxhall Astra, was in the parking area. It was at the cliff edge, facing out to sea, and looked incongruous under its tent of waterproof sheeting erected by the SOCOs to safeguard evidence. A mobile floodlight mounted on one of the police vehicles illuminated the whole scene in a ghostly orange glow. SOCOs were already going over the Astra and taking samples of the soil around it.

As Forward got out of his car, he saw the blonde, bare headed figure of Sergeant Wilmott standing by his own car which was parked next to the steps that descended into the bay. Next to him was a slight, stooped man in a flat cap. He had a small Jack Russell terrier with him on a lead. Wilmott said something to the other man and then left him and came towards Forward. He walked with some difficulty because he was big and physically awkward and the clifftop was uneven.

Forward nodded at Wilmott. The sergeant immediately informed him of the urgent need to obtain as much evidence from the crime scene as possible before the sea covered it. Meanwhile, one of the SOCOs provided Forward with a white protective suit like those being worn by Wilmott and themselves. As Forward pulled it on, Wilmott said, "A helicopter's been despatched to airlift the body out of the bay. It'll be a close thing: the tide's about in."

Forward glanced meaningfully at a large Mercedes parked alongside one of the police Land Rovers.

"Is that why Sir Andrew's arrived early?"

Wilmott grinned. The eminent pathologist was notorious for his lateness.

"He couldn't escape this time, sir. He was at a big dinner in Sandleton. A black tie do. He's not very pleased about being dragged away from it."

"He has to earn his keep occasionally," said Forward. "Well, what have we got?"

Wilmott went over to the SOCO van and returned with two polythene evidence bags.

"The dead man's name is Coulson. Mark Coulson. He's the Headmaster at Melthorpe Primary School."

He offered Forward one of the transparent bags. Forward took it and saw it contained a carefully folded piece of paper.

"That's a letter addressed to him at the school. It's from the National Association of Headteachers reminding him to pay his subscription."

Forward handed the bag back to Wilmott without comment.

"What's the other thing?"

"It's a railway ticket. A single to Filey."

Filey was a fishing village and holiday resort nearly fifteen miles north of Flamborough Head.

Forward took the ticket, and holding it up to the beam of the arc lights peered at it closely. "It's got today's date on it."

"Yesterday's date, sir. It's past midnight now."

Forward handed the polythene bag back to Wilmott. "Is that all he had on him?"

"Yes, sir. Whoever did it went through his pockets and took everything else. They probably missed these because they were in his back trousers pocket."

Forward considered this, then he pointed towards the Vauxhall Astra in the car park. "Is that Coulson's car?"

"Aye, it seems to be. The registered keeper is a Mrs Sheila Coulson. She's at a Melthorpe address."

"Pretty little village, Melthorpe. Got a very nice pub."

"Yes. We've played them once or twice in the pub league." Wilmott was a keen cricketer and a regular member of the team fielded by his village local.

A sudden movement caught Forward's eye. The little man with the dog was approaching. "Who's that?" Forward asked.

"Horace Sissons. He found the body while he was out walking his dog."

Sissons shuffled nearer and Forward could see that he was very old. Well up his seventies. A white scarf was tied as tight as a tourniquet around his neck and he was wearing a dishevelled Barbour that gleamed with a greasy iridescence in the police lights.

"Have you done with me tonight, Sergeant?" Sissons enquired, irritably.

"Have you got his statement?" Forward asked.

Wilmott nodded.

"I understand you found the body, Mr Sissons."

Sissons pulled a face. "That's right. Right bloody mess it was."

"I'm going to see it now," said Forward. He opened one of the rear doors of the BMW. "I wonder if you'd mind sitting in here for a while until I get back. I may have one or two important things to ask you."

"I'd rather sit by me own fireside," said the old man. He gave no sign of moving towards the car and stared at Forward defiantly. "This cold's no good for me rheumatism. And Toby needs his drink. He always has a drink after his walk."

"Mr Sissons lives just up the road," said Wilmott.

Forward sighed. "All right. We'll call in on you later, Mr Sissons."

"Not too late if you don't mind," said Sissons, moving off.

Forward slammed his car door. "A real character!"

Wilmott smiled. "Aye, they're a funny lot out here."

"Strikes me," said Forward, "They're a funny lot in Yorkshire, period."

The two men caught each other's eye. Their respective origins were often the basis of their banter. "Come on," said Forward. "I want to see what remains of Mr Coulson."

They set off towards the cliff edge. Suddenly, from far away, came a faint pulsing sound, as though in the distance the sky was being beaten by tiny iron wings.

"I hope that's our chopper," said Wilmott.

"Bound to be."

Collins, a uniformed constable from Sandleton, was barring the way at the top of the steps. He'd been assigned to keep members of the public away from the crime scene. It was not unknown for the perpetrator of a crime to return to the scene to discover what progress was being made with the investigation.

"Anyone been nosing about, Collins?"

Forward asked.

"No, sir." Collins stood aside and allowed them through.

Forward and Wilmott each pulled on the hoods of their protective suits and began to descend the steep wooden steps that led down to the shore. Three hundred feet below them, in the orange glare of the portable arc lights, Forward saw a group of surreal figures that seemed to be engaged in some bizarre ritual. They were all clothed in white and were gathered around another figure lying prone on the sand a short distance from the bottom of the steps. Each appeared to be engaged in some absorbing task at which they worked hurriedly. Occasional snatches of their conversations floated up from the bay on the wind, but were rendered incomprehensible by the crashing of the waves below.

"How's the play going?" asked Wilmott, as they continued downwards.

"I'm not sure," said Forward. "I was dragged away before I could decide whether it was going to be a triumph or a disaster."

"Marjorie's really looking forward to it. She always enjoys your shows."

"She's evidently got good taste."

"I'll tell her that."

"Not that excellent though. After all, she did marry you."

"I'll tell her that too."

Forward laughed. Marjorie, like Wilmott, was in her late twenties. She'd once been a WPC at Sandleton and Forward had regarded her work highly. Now she stayed at home looking after the Wilmott offspring, and wasn't, from what Forward had gathered, too pleased with the arrangement.

They neared the bottom of the steps. A protective waterproof sheet had been draped over the final two or three of them. It also covered the handrails.

Forward recognised most of those gathered around the body, which was lying just a yard or so from the steps. There were half a dozen uniformed men and women from Sandleton and several Scenes of Crime Officers, one of whom, Grice, was taking photographs. Diane Griffiths, a DC who was a recent addition to Forward's team, was also there, deep in conversation with a young police constable Forward had never seen before. Probably the local bobby. Less than twenty feet away, near the sea's edge, Skipsea, the senior SOCO, was down on his knees examining something on the beach. Huddling over the body was the massive corpulence of Sir Andrew Marston.

"We'll have to avoid the last few steps, sir," cautioned Wilmott. "There's a lot of blood and gore on them. The sand around them is covered in it too."

Forward stopped. He turned and stared up

at Wilmott who was just one step behind him. "It's a good thing I've had some ballet training, then."

Wilmott looked uneasy. It amused Forward that any direct mention of his artistic past always made the sergeant embarrassed. He was sure that Wilmott, like most of his beer drinking, cricket playing colleagues, had certain stereotyped notions about ex-actors.

Like a limbo dancer, Forward squeezed his body athletically under the handrail and dropped down onto the sand beside the steps. Less elegantly, Wilmott followed suit. His feet were almost on the sand, when he lost his grip on the handrail and fell in a heap at Forward's feet.

"Bugger!"

There were smiles on all the watching faces.

"You're out of training, Sergeant," said Forward.

"Too many pork pies."

Forward went over and joined Sir Andrew Marston, who had now risen to his feet and was returning a thermometer to his bag. Like all the others, the pathologist was wearing a white, one-piece protective suit. It was slightly open at the neck, revealing a glimpse of white evening shirt and black bow tie. His large, light blue eyes bulged even more irritably than usual behind lenses as thick as the bottoms of milk bottles.

"Why is it, Forward, that murders always seem to happen at the most inconvenient times?" Marston demanded, brusquely.

Forward stared down at the body on the sand. "I expect the victims usually find it fairly inconvenient too."

"Yes, but this one has deprived me of an excellent golf club dinner and dance."

Forward would have found Sir Andrew's remark unacceptably callous had he not heard its like expressed in similar situations many times before. He'd long ago decided that Marston's predictably unpleasant manner was some kind of defence mechanism which he'd developed to help him deal with horrific sights, such as the one which presently lay on the sand between them. For what Coulson had originally looked like it was impossible to say. His face and scalp had been pulped into a congealed mess of blood and brain tissue. His head was unrecognisable as the head of a human being at all.

"Not the neatest method of despatch I've seen," said Marston, "but certainly effective. Died of a fractured skull I should think. Wouldn't you?"

"How long has he been dead?"

"Judging by the body temperature, a couple of hours at the most. Perhaps not even that. Between ten and eleven p.m., if you must have a time."

The dead man was clad in a knee length anorak with a hood. Underneath it he was wearing a dark suit. Conservative brogues were on his feet. In accordance with standard forensic practice, polythene bags had been placed over his hands and taped at the wrist to preserve any evidence under the fingernails.

Forward ducked down and looked beneath the waterproof sheet that covered the bottom of the steps. He saw dark stains on them and tiny fragments of something which gleamed.

Forward turned to one of the SOCOs. "Been over these steps yet?"

"Yes, sir. There's blood and brain tissue on them. I've got lots of specimens."

"Is it possible he could have simply fallen off the cliffs?" Forward asked Marston.

The pathologist snorted like a pig. "With head injuries like those! The man's been struck at least half a dozen times with a heavy object."

"But that could have happened on the cliffs. He could have been bludgeoned up there and his body thrown over."

"In which case he'd have sustained many other serious injuries. Broken his pelvis or back. Certainly an arm or a leg. Apart from the head injuries and some defensive wounds, he has only a small, deep cut on his left hand. Besides, there's blood spatter and brain tissue all around us. I'm positive he was battered to death right here by these steps."

Forward's gaze took in the furrow in the sand that ran from the bottom of the steps straight down the shore and disappeared into the sea. Alongside it, another furrow emerged from the water and ran back up the beach and ended at Coulson's feet.

"Looks like he was killed at the bottom of the steps and then dragged down to the surf," said Forward, thinking aloud. "I suppose whoever killed him hoped the sea would cover him for a while."

"Aye. Or wash him away," said Wilmott.

"Any ideas about the weapon?" asked Forward. The question was directed at Marston.

"All around us," said Marston, indicating with a plump hand the many chalk boulders that lay about the shore. "I'd say he was attacked with a rock the size of a small melon."

"We'll have to check every stone on the beach," groaned Wilmott.

"Yes," said Forward. "We'll organise a fingertip search."

"What's the point?" said DC Griffiths. "Even if the murder weapon's still in the bay, the tide will have washed all traces of blood off it."

Griffiths was a tall, striking woman of twenty-seven who commanded instant attention whenever she spoke. If her long, blonde, curly hair hadn't been covered by the hood of her protective suit it would have gleamed like gold under the arc lights.

"No, you're wrong there," said Wilmott. "If the chalk's got blood on it, the lab will find it."

Griffiths looked sceptical. "Oh?"

"The sergeant's right," said Marston. "The victim was struck repeatedly with great force. Blood and other fluids, probably brain tissue, will almost certainly have impregnated the murder weapon. If you can find it, even if it's been immersed in sea water, forensics have sophisticated chemical techniques for identifying it."

There was a pause. Marston had addressed Griffiths pompously, almost condescendingly.

"Fancy me not realising that," she said.

Forward laughed. "No problem, then. It's just a question of finding the right lump of chalk."

"If it was chalk," said Griffiths. She moved off and went over to speak to the PC from Flamborough.

Marston's gaze followed her disapprovingly. He had not come across her much in the ordinary course of his duties and her manner obviously irritated him. He was therefore unaware of the hostile attitude she took towards anyone whom she thought was patronising her because of her gender. She was a serious young woman who carried out her duties with diligence and commitment. She'd had an early association with policing through her father who'd been a Special Constable.

Following in his footsteps, she'd become a Special Constable too. After university and Police College she'd joined the uniformed branch in her home city of York. Having always wanted to be a detective, she'd transferred to Sandleton CID just a couple of months earlier. Although she considered herself the equal of any man, Forward knew her to be self-critical and reflective: he was sure she was already berating herself for her flippant remark. He could have explained to Marston the reasons for Griffiths' truculence, but chose not to. There were more pressing matters on his mind. The helicopter sounded a lot nearer now, but if it didn't get there soon the body and those protecting it were going to be caught by the rising tide.

"Who are we looking for?" asked Forward. "A man or a woman?"

"Either," said Marston. "The severity of the injuries suggest a man. Equally, a strong woman could have inflicted them. Whoever it was though, was right-handed. The bulk of the injuries are to the left side of Coulson's head and face. His left arm bears most of the defensive wounds too, indicating that the blows were inflicted by a right hander. The cut on his left hand also lends strength to that conclusion."

DC Griffiths and the local PC laughed suddenly. The sound echoed around the bay like a profanity.

Forward went over to them. "Why weren't screens placed around the victim?" he demanded, addressing Griffiths directly.

Griffiths looked sheepish. "Sergeant Wilmott didn't think it was worth it, sir."

Forward stared at the young, uniformed PC. "And you are?"

"PC Reynolds, sir. Flamborough."

"Were you the first officer on the scene?"

"Yes, sir. The body was nearly covered by the tide when I got here. I had to drag it up the beach a bit."

"Was it head first or feet first in the water?"

"Feet first, sir."

"You'd better go and make out your report. I want it on my desk first thing in the morning."

"Yes, sir," said the officer. He immediately made for the steps.

Forward turned to Griffiths. "You can stand down now. I don't think there's anything further you can do here."

Griffiths looked surprised. "You don't want me to come with you to Melthorpe to break the news to Coulson's wife?"

"No. A WPC can do that. You go home and get some sleep."

The set of Griffiths' face told him she was not best suited but she did not argue. She wished him goodnight. Skilfully avoiding the crime scene, she started to ascend the steps leading out of the bay.

"All right. I'm finished here," Marston called loudly to the SOCOs. "You can bag him up now." Looking directly at Forward, he said, "Not a moment too soon with that tide coming in. I'll do a post-mortem sometime tomorrow."

"And when will we have your report?" asked Forward. It was not an entirely innocent question.

Sir Andrew chose to ignore the implicit reproach. "As soon as it's ready, of course. Now, if you'll excuse me, I have to go back and collect my wife. The golf club president has probably bored her to death by now."

Sir Andrew civilly wished everyone a goodnight. He fastened his bag and handed it to Wilmott, saying, "Pass me this when I get on the stairs, will you, Sergeant." Then slowly and heavily he moved towards the steps. He placed one foot on the outside edge of the third step and then took hold of the handrail and hauled his massive bulk up. Both feet were now on the step. He then swung one leg over the handrail, sat on it with feet dangling either side, and then, with some effort, swung the other leg over and got himself into a standing position. Wilmott passed Marston the bag. Marston started to ascend and then stopped suddenly and turned to address those below who had been watching his exertions with some amazement.

"By the way, Forward, I gather you're producing *The Cherry Orchard*."

"That's right."

"Excellent. It's about time Sandleton experienced some culture. I look forward to it."

Sir Andrew turned and went up the steps, panting heavily.

"He wants to watch his heart," said Wilmott. "When I stand next to him, I feel slim."

The helicopter was obviously very close now, no more than a mile off. The rumbling revolutions of its rotors seemed to be making their bodies vibrate.

Forward and Wilmott strolled together down the tiny strip of fore-shore that was all that remained now between the cliffs and the sea. Just visible to the right of them were the two furrows made by Coulson's body when it had been dragged down to the sea by whoever had killed him, and then rescued from the incoming tide by Wilmott and the bobby from Flamborough. They were criss-crossed with a jumble of footprints and scuff marks. Skipsea was crouched over these, hurriedly taking impressions with a quick setting solution: preserving as many as he could before the tide eradicated them forever.

"Found anything useful, Dave?" Forward asked.

Skipsea stood up and stared at the area he'd been working on. "Not a lot. As you can see there's plenty of impressions. But most of them were made by Mr Sissons and his dog and those who moved the body. The others are of very poor quality. It looks as though they've been deliberately scuffed over to obliterate them. Whoever did it hasn't been entirely successful though. In one or two cases, despite the moisture, I've managed to get some quite detailed casts. This one here, for instance."

Skipsea bent down and retrieved an impression from the sand and showed it to Forward.

"You see. There's a fair bit of sole here. Enough for identification purposes anyway."

"Good man. Found many as fine as that?"

"A few. If it wasn't for this tide, I'd have got a lot more."

"You'd better get on with it then," said Forward. "Canute, my name isn't."

The Chief Inspector and the Detective Sergeant stared at the sea in silence. Light spilling off the arc lamps was turning each wave into a tongue of flame.

"What makes a man come out to a remote spot like this so late at night?" Forward wondered aloud.

"To meet someone?" suggested Wilmott.

"A woman, you mean?"

"It has been known, sir."

"Perhaps he just wanted a bit of solitude. A bit of peace and quiet. I understand that teaching in these village schools can be quite stressful."

"No place is safe from muggers, though."

"You think he was mugged?"

Wilmott looked surprised. "Almost everything on him was taken. Robbery can't be ruled out."

"In which case why didn't they go the whole hog and take his car? They must have got his keys. Why leave it up in the car park?"

Wilmott thought for a moment. "Any number of reasons. They might have panicked. Or they might have had their own car. Perhaps they couldn't even drive."

Forward nodded. He was about to explain why he still didn't think robbery was a plausible motive, when night suddenly turned to day.

They both turned and looked up. Hovering just yards out from the edge of the clifftop was the chopper: an Air Sea Rescue Sea King. Its powerful searchlights were sweeping the bay, illuminating everything in it with the greatest clarity, particularly the white suited figures who were struggling to insert Coulson's corpse into its body bag. The big side door in the helicopter's fuselage had been flung open, and the crew, silhouetted against the interior lights, were standing ready to winch the body out of the bay.

For a moment or two the machine hovered

unnaturally above them, looking like a bloated metal locust, too deep bodied and heavy for its frail, rotating wings. Then, slowly, it began to descend.

"About time too," said Wilmott. "Now we can go and break the good news to Mrs Coulson."

"First I want a word with Horace Sissons."

CHAPTER THREE

When Forward and Wilmott arrived at Sissons' terraced cottage in Monkhouses they experienced some difficulty in gaining admittance. The moment they knocked, Toby went berserk and created a tremendous commotion behind the stout, whitewashed front door. After much cursing and scuffling, Sissons was eventually able to restrain his fierce little terrier and open the door. He stood framed in the doorway for a moment, holding Toby in his arms. Then, without a word to Forward or Wilmott, Sissons turned on his heel and carried the dog back down the short, dimly lit passage. The two detectives exchanged looks and stepped inside the house. Wilmott closed the front door and then he and Forward went after Sissons and located him in a small, back sitting room. All the while, Toby continued to growl softly in Sissons' arms. Finally, the old man placed the dog down on the pitted and worn linoleum.

"Basket!" Sissons commanded.

The Jack Russell stopped growling and obediently went over to a well gnawed wicker dog basket. He got into it and settled himself down on a grubby cushion that was covered in his own hairs. Sissons then closed the sitting room door and eased himself into a clean but battered armchair in front of a coal fire that was almost out. He was wearing striped pyjamas underneath a tartan dressing gown that had seen much better days.

"I'd given up on you," said Sissons. "Still, now you're here you'd better sit down." He indicated the two ancient oak dining chairs drawn up under an equally ancient oak dining table.

Forward and Wilmott took their seats and found them to be as uncomfortable as they looked.

"Mr Sissons, please think very carefully about the questions I'm going to ask you. I'd like you to answer them as fully as you can," said Forward, speaking slowly and precisely as though to one who was deaf. "What might seem unimportant to you might prove vital to us."

"Nay, you don't have to talk to me that way. I'm not senile y'know," said Sissons. "Not yet, any road."

Wilmott put a hand to his mouth to suppress a laugh.

Forward was tired and irritable and in no

mood for jokes. "You say you took Toby for a walk at five to eleven. How can you be sure of that?"

The old man reached for the poker and began to jab at the fire's spent embers. "Easy. I always take Toby out after News at Ten."

"The News at Ten finishes at ten thirty, not five to eleven," said Forward.

"Of course, it does. I was coming to that."

"Go on," said Forward. He gave Wilmott a weary look.

"When I opened the front door at ten thirty it were pouring with rain. So I had to wait till the shower gave o'er. Which it did at five to eleven." Sissons pointed to a clock in a handsome walnut case on the mantelpiece. "That clock's never wrong. I always set it by Big Ben."

"All right. While you were waiting for the rain to stop did you hear any cars outside or see any headlights?"

"No. Nothing. I wouldn't have anyway. I was in here all the time watching television."

"But you must have looked out of the window to see if it had stopped raining?"

"No."

"Perhaps you went to the front door?"

"No," said Sissons, adamantly. "I were checking on the rain through the back kitchen window. There's nothing but fields behind the house. I wouldn't have seen a thing."

"All right, so you walked the dog from here straight down to the bay. Is that right?"

"That's it. Just like I always do."

"You didn't take him along the cliffs in any direction?"

"Only to the place where he does his business."

"Where's that?"

"Just by the car park."

"So, you must have noticed the car that was parked there. The Vauxhall Astra."

"Of course I did. I'm not blind y'know."

"Didn't you think that was a little unusual?"

"To see a car there? Well, it is a car park."

Wilmott snorted.

Forward made a mental note to control his rising anger. It was one o'clock in the morning and they still had to go over to Melthorpe and remove all hope from a woman that her missing husband was still alive. It was going to be a long night and he needed to conserve all his resources.

"I meant: did you think it unusual to see a car there at that time of night?"

"No, there's often cars parked there. Sometimes two or three on a night." Sissons' grey eyes twinkled and became unexpectedly youthful. "It's only lads and lassies out for a bit of fun."

"Courting couples, you mean?"

"Aye." Sissons grinned suddenly, revealing

almost toothless gums. "But they don't call it courting these days, do they? They call it bonking."

This time even Forward had to smile. "I believe they do, Mr Sissons. So, was there anyone in the car?"

"Not that I saw," said Sissons. "But then I wouldn't see anyone if they were bonking, would I? They'd be more likely lying down on the back seat." He chuckled quietly.

"Had you ever seen the Astra parked there before?" Wilmott asked suddenly.

"I couldn't say."

"Try," said Forward.

Sissons tried hard to remember. The strain on his memory showed clearly in his face. "I don't think so," he said.

"All right," said Forward. "Then what happened?"

"Same as always. I took Toby halfway down the steps in the bay and then let him go the rest of the way himself. He likes to have a good run along the beach when the tide's out."

"You didn't go down with him?"

"Not at first. I never do. I usually sit on the steps, smoke a pipe, and then when I've finished, I whistle him and he comes straight back up. He's very well trained."

"Yes. I can see that," said Forward. "Bit late to be taking a dog for a walk though, isn't it?"

"Have you ever owned a Jack Russell."

Sissons didn't express this as a question, rather as a statement of the obvious.

"No. It's a pleasure I've denied myself," said Forward.

"They can be a very funny breed," said Sissons. "Him particularly."

He nodded in the direction of Toby who was by now snoring in his basket. "He don't get on with other dogs. He attacks 'em. Even Alsatians. So, I can't let him off the lead and have a run when other dogs are about. That's why I take him out so late."

"OK. So, you were sitting on the steps. What happened then?"

"I finished me pipe and whistled up Toby."

"How long were you sitting on the steps?"

"Not that long. Just a couple of minutes."

"And you didn't see anyone, or hear anything?"

"Not a thing."

"How did you find the body?"

"Well, as I were saying, I whistled up Toby. He didn't come, so I went down the steps after him whistling and calling all the time. When I got near the bottom, I could see he were interested in something by the water. He were growling and pulling at it with his teeth. I got to the bottom step and me foot slipped on something. If it hadn't been for the handrail, I'd have gone flat on me back. Anyway, I picked meself up and went over to the dog. At first, I thought he'd got his teeth into an old lobster pot or something. But when I got close up to him, I could see he were tugging at someone's arm. He had their sleeve in his mouth." Sissons' voice faltered and an expression of nausea came over his sharp, grey features. "I could see they were dead. Their 'ead had been all bashed in."

"How far away from the steps was the body?" Forward asked.

"I'm not much good at distances. Could 'ave been thirty feet. Could 'ave been forty. I'll tell you one thing though, the tide were coming in fast and there weren't much beach left."

"Was all of the body in the water?"

"No. Just the feet and ankles."

"So, the body's feet were pointing out to sea?"

"That's right. At first, I thought it were a fisherman. We've 'ad one or two of them washed up here in the past. But when I saw the state of 'is 'ead, I knew something wasn't right. I got Toby back on 'is lead and phoned the police as soon as I could from the phone box in the car park."

"You did the right thing, Mr Sissons. If it wasn't for your swift action a lot of valuable evidence would have been lost."

At this Sissons visibly inflated with pride.

"How long have you lived in Monkhouses?" Forward asked.

"I were born 'ere," Sissons replied. He gave

Forward a long look. "Unlike some."

Forward suspected the jibe was intended for him but ignored it. "Tell me frankly, Mr Sissons, is there anyone in Monkhouses who might have been capable of killing that man?"

Sissons' facetious air suddenly vanished. Looking Forward directly in the eye, he said, "No. Not a soul."

Forward held the old man's gaze. "Certain?"

Sissons shrugged uncomfortably. "There's a few funny buggers round 'ere, for sure. But none of 'em are so cracked they'd do summat like that." He looked genuinely concerned. "What's the poor sod's name?" he asked. "Do you know who he is?"

There was a long pause, during which an image appeared in Forward's mind of his lonely bed, which now seemed unbelievably attractive. He side-stepped Sissons' question by saying, "As you've lived here so long, Mr Sissons, you must be very familiar with the bay."

"Aye," said Sissons, suspiciously, as though every word he now said might incriminate him.

"Is there anything special about it?"

"Special? It's a bay. Like loads round here."

Forward knew when he was being stonewalled. Sissons was obviously trying to work out what was being inferred.

"I mean, is there any reason someone would

wish to go there late at night?"

Sissons gave him a sudden, toothless smile of recognition. "For bonking, you mean?"

"Something like that."

"It wouldn't be somewhere I'd take a lass."

The thought of Sissons scrambling down the steps into Monks Bay for a clandestine tryst greatly amused Forward. Trying not to smile, he said, "Why?"

"Too uncomfortable."

Wilmott laughed. "And you like your comfort, don't you Horace?"

"I certainly do. And it's dangerous. It's only a small bay and when the tide turns it comes in so fast you can easily get caught. Especially with your trousers down."

"How long does it take for the bay to fill with water, would you say?"

"That depends. Usually just a couple of hours at the most."

Forward stood up. "Thank you, Mr Sissons. You've been most helpful. Now, just one more thing. I see you've changed. I wonder if we could have a look at the clothes and shoes you were wearing when you found the body."

Sissons looked surprised. "What, everything?"

"If you don't mind."

"Do you want to see me underpants?"

Wilmott laughed loudly.

"Just the outer clothes, please," said Forward.

Sissons went out. They heard him go up the stairs and then shuffle across the room directly overhead.

Forward and Wilmott both eyed the sleeping Toby warily.

Wilmott's eyes looked up to indicate the ceiling. "He's a real card," he said softly, with an affectionate grin.

Forward nodded, and also grinned but not affectionately. Then his expression changed completely. "It's a pity he didn't see anyone though."

Sissons returned with various garments stuffed under his arms. A shoe was suspended by its laces from each hand.

Wilmott examined Sissons' things carefully.

"Here we are, sir," said Wilmott, holding out a shoe for Forward's inspection.

"What's that?" asked Sissons.

"Blood, Mr Sissons," said Forward. "Dried blood. Here, on the sole."

"How did that get there?" Sissons demanded.

"There was a good deal of blood on the bottom steps," said Forward. "That's what probably caused you to slip."

"There's more on the trouser turn-ups," said Wilmott.

Forward looked closely at the old man's crumpled, slightly damp, grey trousers. "I'm afraid we're going to have to take the clothes and shoes away with us for examination."

Sissons looked shocked. "What do you want them for?"

"It's possible it wasn't only the dead man's blood on those steps. We have to be sure. We also need to distinguish your footprints from others we found on the beach. Tomorrow we'll take your fingerprints for the same reason."

There was no need at this stage to tell the old fellow that those who discover bodies are not themselves above suspicion.

"Have you got another pair of trousers?" asked Wilmott.

"Well, I should bloody well hope so!" said Sissons.

****

Forward removed one hand from the steering wheel and rubbed his eyes. Wearily they re-focussed on the rear lights of WPC Turner's Ford Escort. Forward and Wilmott were following it to Melthorpe. They'd collected the WPC from Sandleton Police Station fifteen minutes earlier. Carol Turner was a warm, understanding sort of woman in her mid-thirties. Yet, as well as her obvious sensibility, there was a clear headed, practical side to her nature. Just the sort of person you needed when you had to break the news to a wife or husband that their partner was no more.

The blonde nape of Carol's neck gleamed in

Forward's headlights. Of course, he reflected, if he hadn't been such a coward about these occasions there'd have been no need to drag her along at all. But he was a coward and that was that.

He gave a short, sideways glance at Wilmott who was sitting next to him. Then he said, "Something tells me this isn't going to be a straightforward case."

Wilmott gave a low murmur of agreement. The sound was as earthy as the darkened fields that rushed past on either side.

"Take that railway ticket, for instance."

"What about it?" said Wilmott, and immediately followed this with a yawn.

"It was purchased on the same day Coulson died."

"I'm sorry, I don't follow you."

"Well, it is well past one in the morning," said Forward. "Look, we know he had a car. It was parked in the car park on the cliffs. So why did he need a railway ticket to Filey? And why a single, not a return?"

"Perhaps his car was being serviced or repaired at Filey and he went by train to collect it."

"Perhaps," said Forward, without conviction. "But if he was on his way home from Filey, why did he stop at Monks Bay? Ah well, Mrs Coulson should be able to enlighten us."

Melthorpe village was some twelve miles

west of Sandleton, high up in the Yorkshire
Wolds. It was a typical Wolds ribbon village:
ancient red brick cottages with roofs of orange
pantiles picturesquely lined the roadside,
occasionally interrupted by the barns and
outbuildings which belonged to the village's
various working farms. The only other
buildings were a Norman church, a pub and the
primary school.

The police turned into the unlit side road in
which the school was located. Like all the other
buildings at that time of night, the school was
in complete darkness. However, by contrast,
every window of the little schoolhouse next
door was ablaze with light.

In front of the schoolhouse was a small,
walled garden. The two police vehicles pulled
up in front of it. WPC Turner was out of her
car first. She reached the garden gate before
Forward and Wilmott. As they followed her,
the front door of the schoolhouse was flung
open and a slim, frantic figure shot out and
rushed down the short garden path towards
them.

"No! Please! Oh no!" she screamed.

CHAPTER FOUR

Wilmott and WPC Turner took control of the situation immediately. They ignored Mrs Coulson's hysterics and the wails of the two little girls who'd followed her, and concentrated on getting them all back into the house. Once inside, they eventually managed to get Mrs Coulson to calm down sufficiently to sit in an armchair. Carol Turner tried to take the children out of earshot but Mrs Coulson was having none of that. "If it's what I think it is, I want them to hear it too," she insisted, keeping an arm firmly clamped around each little girl's waist.

It had been pre-arranged that Wilmott would break the devastating news. After introducing himself and his colleagues, he turned to his unpalatable task. He broke it to her straight, in the gentlest tones he could muster.

"We've bad news for you, Mrs Coulson, I'm afraid. I'm sorry to tell you your husband has been killed."

Mrs Coulson closed her eyes. The muscles in

her face contorted as she fought to control her emotions. Her head went down until her chin was touching her chest. She clutched at her children so tightly it seemed she was physically trying to return them to the safety and comfort of her womb. The two little girls were burrowing their faces into their mother's neck, and all three were wracked with prolonged and pitiful sobbing.

Mrs Coulson suddenly looked up at the police officers beseechingly. "Where did it happen? I must see him! I must go to him!" Her voice was so distorted by grief her words were barely recognisable.

"Mrs Coulson, it really would be much better if we talked to you about this alone," said Wilmott quietly. He threw Carol Turner an imploring look.

Carol went to the armchair and put her hand on Mrs Coulson's shoulder. "Is there anyone who could come round and be with you?" she asked. "Your parents, perhaps?"

Mrs Coulson made an attempt to gain control. "Both my parents are dead," she said. "There's only my sister but she lives in Chester." Immediately she cried out, "Norman! Oh my God! Norman! He'll be devastated!"

"Who's Norman?" Carol asked.

"Mark's father. This will kill him."

"Does he live nearby?" asked Wilmott.

"No. He lives in Derbyshire."

"Is there someone who lives closer?" asked Carol, calmly. "A friend? Someone who could come over?"

"There's Audrey, the vicar's wife. But I can't disturb her at this time of night."

"I'm sure she won't mind," Carol assured her. "Not when she realises what the situation is. I'll phone her if you like. What's her number?"

"It's in the address book next to the phone. Her name's Audrey Jennings."

"Audrey Jennings. Right, I'll give her a ring," said Carol. "But first I'll take the girls off to the kitchen." She took each child by the hand. "Come on. You can show me where the tea things are and we'll make mummy a nice cup of tea. You can see she needs it."

Reluctantly, Mrs Coulson relaxed her grasp on her daughters. "Go on girls," she said. "Go along with the nice policewoman. Mummy's got a lot of things to do."

Understandably, both girls were reluctant to leave their mother, but, after much persuasion, Carol was able to get them to accompany her to the kitchen. For this she received a heartfelt look of gratitude from Wilmott.

As Carol and the girls left the room, Mrs Coulson stood up. She waited until the door had closed and then said, bitterly, "Mark was always a terrible driver. So impatient, you see. I always worried that something might…" Her voice tailed off and a hand flew to her face as the tears started to come again.

Up until now Forward had stood apart from the others, towards the back of the room, near the window. He did this not out of awkwardness but because he wished to be a detached observer of the scene. He knew that murder victims were much more likely to have been killed by those well known to them rather than by a complete stranger. That's why it was vital to observe the reactions of close relatives when they were informed of the victim's death. People received the news in different ways: some said nothing, were quietly stunned; others screamed and bawled like babies; some refused to believe it; others turned in on themselves, were full of blame and guilt. Whatever the reaction, Forward relied on his own instinct and the experience he'd acquired in life, the force and the theatre to tell him when someone's grief wasn't entirely authentic. Right now, all he saw was a beautiful woman in her early thirties in the deep shock of sudden bereavement.

"Your husband wasn't involved in a car accident," said Forward, moving towards the centre of the room. "He was found at Monks Bay, Flamborough Head, with fatal head injuries. We're treating his death as murder."

Mrs Coulson stared at him, uncomprehendingly.

"Murder?"

"I'm afraid so, yes."

She looked as though she was going to faint. Forward and Wilmott rushed to support her. Slowly, they eased her onto an armchair.

"Are you all right?" enquired Wilmott.

"Of course, I'm not all right," she cried, "you've just told me my husband's been murdered!"

She went to jump up from the armchair but the two men carefully restrained her. "Poor Mark!" she wailed. "Poor, poor Mark!"

It took a good deal of time, but, eventually, Mrs Coulson was able to calm down sufficiently for Wilmott to explain to her the exact circumstances in which her husband's body had been discovered, and why they'd been able to identify him so quickly.

This gave Forward an opportunity to observe Mrs Coulson further. She was dressed only in jeans, trainers and a blue and white striped sweatshirt; yet the string of pearls at her neck and the handsome bracelet she wore loosely on her wrist combined with her casual clothes to convey an impression of effortless chic and elegance. This was enhanced by the stylish cut of her dark brown hair which was swept back off her face in layers. She wore little make-up apart from the faintest touch of pale pink lipstick. Her high cheekbones and delicate facial features suggested that she was a person of intelligence, sensitivity and discernment.

She wasn't local to the area; Forward was convinced of that. He had a good ear for accents and it was telling him that Mrs Coulson's origins lay not in East Yorkshire but the North West. He watched her as she listened with total absorption to Wilmott, and he observed the genuine distress in her limpid, green eyes.

Wilmott brought his unhappy account to a close by looking intently at Mrs Coulson and saying, "There's never an easy way to break this sort of news. I'm very, very sorry, believe me." Then he took a step backwards, reached into his pocket and took out his notebook. It was Forward's turn now.

Mrs Coulson said nothing. She looked completely crushed. Dazed and uncomprehending, she sank back into her chair and folded her arms consolingly around herself. Suddenly, she sat up animatedly, as though rejuvenated by sudden hope. "Where did you say they found Mark?"

"Monks Bay, out on Flamborough Head," said Forward.

"Then the man you found can't possibly be him. Why would he go there? I've never heard of it before."

"Neither you nor your husband have ever been to Monks Bay?"

"Never."

"You have no idea why your husband was at Flamborough Head? What he might have been doing there?"

"None. Why would he go to a place like that tonight? No, you must have the wrong man."

Forward asked Mrs Coulson if she owned a blue Vauxhall Astra. She nodded and he quoted the registration number. "Is that yours?"

"Yes."

"And as far as you know it hasn't been stolen?"

"No."

"Well, as the sergeant just told you, it was found in the car park at Monks Bay. I think it's reasonable to assume that your husband drove it there." Forward watched her expression closely. "The car is registered in your name. Didn't he have his own car?"

Her eyes darkened. "He did at one time. But it became too expensive to run both of them so we had to sell his."

"I see. And he drove yours?"

"We shared it."

The look of desperate hope came back into her eyes again. "But it could have been stolen, couldn't it? Maybe the man you found dead in the bay is the one who stole it?"

"Show Mrs Coulson the letter, Sergeant."

Wilmott produced the polythene evidence bag containing the letter found in Coulson's back pocket. "This was found on the body."

Mrs Coulson stared at the letter for a long time. "Yes, that's his. He received it a couple of days ago. I remember him carrying on about it." She smiled, indulging a fond memory. "He was hopeless with money. Never paid his subscriptions on time." She stared up at Forward and held his gaze for what seemed forever. Her eyes were like moist opals. "You're right," she said. "It must be him. But why was he there? He was supposed to be at a meeting."

"What meeting was that?"

"It was at the Teachers' Centre in Sandleton. A meeting for headteachers and chairmen of school governors." She surprised Forward by suddenly slapping her wrist in self-admonition. "Chairs of school governors, I mean," she said, emphasising the 'chairs'. She gave Forward a pained, explanatory smile. "Mark was always telling me off for making that mistake. He was very anti-sexist you see." Her lip trembled. "And the Chair of Melthorpe School Governors is a woman. Lady Fernshawe."

A packet of cigarettes and a lighter were on the occasional table beside Mrs Coulson's chair. She reached for the packet, took out a cigarette and lit it, inhaling deeply.

Forward said, "This Lady Fernshawe, would she have gone with Mr Coulson to the meeting?"

"Presumably. But he wouldn't have given her a lift. She would have met him there."

"When was the last time you saw your

husband?"

"This afternoon, just after school ended. He popped home to tell me about the meeting. County Hall had rung and asked him to go at the last minute."

"And what time was this?"

"When he came home?"

"Yes."

"About twenty to four."

"How did he seem?"

"Seem?"

"Yes. What sort of mood was he in?"

"I couldn't say. I didn't take much notice. I was too busy getting the girls' tea ready. I think he was a bit more stressed than usual. He hadn't bothered to read a document that was to be discussed at the meeting and he was busy speed reading it."

"What time did he leave for the meeting?"

"That's the awful thing. I can't even remember him going. I was too busy giving the girls their tea." Her voice faltered. "It was the last time I saw him and we didn't even say goodbye properly. And now I'll never see him again." She burst into tears and her slender, petite frame was again wracked with sobbing.

Her distress affected Forward deeply. This was the worst part of the job. Finding villains and banging them up was the easy part compared to dealing with the carnage they left in their wake.

He waited until she composed herself and then said, "What time was the meeting at the Teachers' Centre? Do you know?"

"Four thirty, I think."

"So, Mark would have left here about what time? Four?"

"Yes. Probably around four."

"And this was a meeting for headteachers and chairs of governors?"

"Yes."

"Do you know what time the meeting was supposed to end?"

"They usually finish about six o'clock."

"So, you'd have expected him home by what time? Half six?"

"Yes. Half six, seven at the latest. He knew I had to go to my flower arranging class at seven and I couldn't leave the children by themselves."

"What did you do when your husband didn't come home?"

"Do? What could I do? I just waited. I assumed he'd gone to the pub with the other heads. He sometimes did after those meetings."

"But he knew you were expecting him at seven?"

"That's right. And it made me very annoyed when seven o'clock came and he wasn't home. He knew how important it was for me to be at the flower arranging class. Of course, none of that's important now."

Mrs Coulson inhaled deeply on her cigarette and exhaled the smoke on a sigh.

"But I soon got over my anger and started to think rationally. It was unusual for Mark to break a promise, so I assumed that something must have happened to prevent him from coming home. I wondered if the car had broken down or if he'd had to go back to the Hall with Lady Fernshawe. He sometimes did that when they needed to discuss school matters."

Forward and Wilmott exchanged an almost imperceptible look.

"Did you ring Lady Fernshawe to see if Mark was there?"

"No."

"Why not?"

"Because it was gone seven, and she was supposed to be at the flower arranging class by then. She's an instructor, you see."

"So, what did you do?"

"When it got to half past seven and Mark still hadn't come home, I rang our regular babysitter and asked her if she could look after the girls for the evening. She said she would, but she was in the middle of eating her supper so she didn't get here until eight o'clock."

"I see. And that's when you left for your class?"

"Yes."

"And was Lady Fernshawe able to give you any idea what happened to your husband?"

"No. When I got to the class she wasn't there. The other ladies told me she'd looked in, but had left early with a headache."

"Did you stay at the class?"

"Yes."

"Even though there was no instructor?"

"Lady Fernshawe's not the only instructor."

"I see. What time did the class end?"

"Ten o'clock."

"And you came straight home?"

"Yes, but there was still no sign of Mark. That's when I began to get really anxious. It was so out of character for him to be that late. I sent the babysitter home and rang Lady Fernshawe to see if she'd been at the meeting in Sandleton and could give me some idea where he might be. But all I got was her answering machine. I knew she had a headache so I assumed she'd gone to bed."

"Did you ring anyone else?"

"Not at first. But when it got past midnight and Mark still hadn't come home, I called the police. I didn't want to dial 999 in case they thought I was an hysterical woman whose husband had gone for a night on the tiles. So, I rang the station at Sandleton and asked if Mark had been involved in a road accident. They said they'd investigate and ring me back. I waited and waited but they never did. And then you came." She paused and tried to continue, but was prevented by grief. When she finally spoke, a sob had again entered her voice. "I knew then that something terrible had happened."

"Mrs Coulson. Does your husband have any connection with Filey?"

"Filey?"

"Yes. It's a resort up the coast."

"I know where it is. We've taken the children there several times."

"Has your husband any friends or relatives there?"

"Not that I know of. Why?"

"He had a rail ticket to Filey in his pocket."

Mrs Coulson stared at Forward in amazement. "To Filey?"

"Yes."

"But why should he want to go there?"

"We were rather hoping you'd be able to tell us,' said Forward. "The ticket had today's date on it."

"Yesterday's," Wilmott corrected. "It's Tuesday now."

"I beg your pardon. Yesterday's. Was your husband at school all day yesterday?"

"Yes."

"You're quite sure?"

Mrs Coulson explained that if her husband had not been in school she would have known. He taught a class all day and her eldest daughter was in it.

"So, there's no possibility he could have gone out of school yesterday?" Forward asked.

"And gone to Filey? None at all. He could only have gone to Filey after school had ended. This is unbelievable. I can't think why he'd want to go to Filey. Or to Flamborough Head." She shook her head despairingly. "I can't think why he'd want to go anywhere when he promised to be home at seven o'clock."

"This may sound like a stupid question," said Wilmott, "but can you think of a reason why anyone would want to kill your husband?"

She dismissed the suggestion immediately. "No. None at all. Mark was the kindest of men. Of course, you can't be the Headteacher in a village school without making some enemies amongst the parents. You can never satisfy everybody. But I hardly think any of them would have been annoyed enough to kill him."

There was a slight evasiveness about the way she said this that made Forward suspect, for the first time, that a sub-text had entered the conversation. He had the distinct feeling that something was being hidden.

"Inspector, when can I see my husband?"

"You can make a formal identification later today."

"But where is he? Where is he now?"

Forward told her that her husband's body was at the mortuary and was now the responsibility of the Forensic Pathologist; but even as he said this, he knew it was not the answer to the question she really sought. The husband who had been so real and familiar to her was no longer there. He was no longer anywhere. So where was he? Really?

"There'll have to be a post-mortem and an inquest you see," he said lamely.

Mrs Coulson nodded.

"The letter and the ticket to Filey were the only things found on your husband," said Forward. "What else did he usually carry?"

She stubbed out her cigarette, thoughtfully. "A wallet with a picture of us in it. Another smaller wallet for his credit cards. You know, the type banks give you. And his keys. His own keys and the keys to the school." She sat up suddenly, her eyes widening. "Do you think he was killed for just those things?"

"It's a possibility."

Her jaw clenched angrily. "How despicable! To kill a man for that. He wouldn't have had more than ten pounds on him. What bastards!"

"It's only a possibility, Mrs Coulson."

"But what other reason could there be?"

"Hopefully we shall find out. Now, I think it's time you went and telephoned your sister and father-in-law."

Mrs Coulson stood up and started towards the hall.

"Mrs Coulson!"

She stopped and turned.

"Do you have any recent photographs of your husband?"

"Yes, I think so."

"Could we borrow them? We'll need photographs for our enquiries."

She nodded sadly, and went out.

Wilmott replaced his notebook in his pocket. "That didn't tell us a lot."

"There's not much we can do here tonight," said Forward. "It's not the time anyway. After she's identified the body, I'll come back and go through Coulson's things. You never know, something might turn up."

"Where are we going to direct the investigation from?" said Wilmott. "Sandleton?"

"Yes, but we'll be relying on a lot of local information. Monks Bay and the surrounding area will have to be searched. We'd better establish an incident centre at Monkhouses. I'll get Hoggart onto that." He checked his watch. "Christ. It's twenty to three. God knows what time I'm going to get some sleep. Carol can hang on here for now."

CHAPTER FIVE

Monkhouses village hall had been chosen as the site for the incident centre. It was a single storey, prefabricated building on the village's main street and had received its annual coat of whitewash only a few weeks previously. As Forward approached it in his BMW just before nine a.m., he saw that several police vehicles were already parked outside and officers were unloading furniture from a large transit van.

Forward gave a wave but did not stop. He drove straight on to Monks Bay. At the approach to the bay, he was prevented from going any further by police tape. He got out of the BMW and saw that an extensive area, which included the car park and the surrounding cliffs on either side of the bay, had now been completely cordoned off. Uniformed officers were deployed at intervals along the cordon to ensure that the crime scene was protected from the attentions of a small but growing number of curious bystanders. In the clifftop car park Coulson's Vauxhall Astra was being winched onto a vehicle transporter to be taken to the forensics lab in Hull; meanwhile Skipsea and a number of officers from Sandleton were down on their knees conducting a fingertip search.

On seeing Forward get out of the BMW, Skipsea stood up, called out a greeting and with a sweep of his arm indicated the area of the car park by the vehicle transporter.

"You're all right to walk on that bit. We've already searched it."

Forward ducked under the tape and, moving cautiously, crossed the parking area and joined Skipsea on the cliff edge overlooking the bay. It was a beautiful, bright morning and the towering chalk cliffs and stacks gleamed unnaturally white in the sunlight. To Forward's right the cliffs extended majestically for nearly two miles, until they ended at the dazzlingly white cylinder of Flamborough Head lighthouse at the extreme point of the headland. Forward turned to his left, and his gaze followed the cliffs back down the headland for another couple of miles until they gradually lost height and gave way to the long sweep of Filey Bay. At its northern end the seaside town of Filey was clearly visible.

Forward then stared directly below him into Monks Bay, a considerable area of which was still exposed and not yet covered by the morning tide. The sea was as calm as a still water lake; the waves hardly bigger than ripples. The beach was liberally strewn with hundreds of chalk boulders of all shapes and sizes, and only now, in the daylight, was it possible to appreciate the magnitude of the task confronting those looking for the murder weapon. Seven or eight figures were already on their knees in the bay, meticulously searching the area surrounding the steps where Coulson had been murdered. Waterproof sheeting completely covered the bottom of the steps now, and ladders had been erected and attached to either side of them to provide access to the beach without further disturbance or contamination of the crime scene. Forward found it hard to believe that this quiet, tranquil spot had been the scene of such violence and drama the night before. He mentioned this to Skipsea, and then said, "Found anything?"

"One or two suspect lumps of chalk. Otherwise just litter."

"What about the car?"

"It's covered in prints, but, of course, it's a family car."

"Any tyre prints?"

"That's looking more hopeful. The ground was quite soft last night. We've found tracks from several different vehicles apart from the Astra. Got some good casts too."

Something in Skipsea's tone told Forward that the senior SOCO was clearly frustrated.

This was unusual. He was hugely experienced and normally imperturbable. After a career in the RAF, as a technician, he'd taught physics and chemistry in a rough Hull comprehensive before becoming a Scenes of Crime Officer.

"What's the matter, Dave?" asked Forward. "You look pissed off."

"I am. You can see for yourself the size of the task. And the changing tide is a bloody nuisance. It was at its lowest at seven this morning and they've all been hard at it since then."

Forward assured Skipsea that officers from all over the county were being deployed to assist in the search. Skipsea looked pleased. "Good. We need to get a move on, though. The bay will be full of water again around one. That doesn't give us much time."

They discussed various aspects of the case, and Forward told Skipsea he required him to be present at the briefing that was to take place at the incident centre at ten a.m.

Forward left Skipsea to his work and drove back into Monkhouses. As he approached the entrance to the village hall, he was gratified to see that a police notice giving information about the killing had already been appended to the Parish Council's notice board. The photograph of Mark Coulson, which was supplied by his widow, had been cropped and incorporated into the leaflet. It showed a good-looking man in his forties, with even features and a clean-cut appearance. Forward lingered over Coulson's image for some time, speculating on the secrets it might have concealed when the man was alive.

When Forward entered the incident centre he found a scene of great activity. All available space had been sectioned into a number of separate areas and a desk placed in each of these. Extra telephone lines had been installed: and, in addition to various telephones, a couple of computers and a fax machine had been connected. A blown-up photograph of Mark Coulson was prominently displayed on a large pinboard. Next to the photograph, also enlarged, was a copy of the ticket to Filey found in Coulson's back pocket. Both the photo and the ticket were clearly labelled in thick, black felt pen. Attached to the pinboard was a large map of East Yorkshire showing its coastline, with the locations of Sandleton, Monks Bay, Filey and Melthorpe boldly labelled, and the distances between them indicated. To the right of the pinboard was a flipchart mounted on an easel: the kind of oversized notepad beloved by college lecturers. Blackboards had also been set up at various points around the room. On one of the desks a computer printer was in operation, emitting a characteristic whine. A portable photocopier was making a further contribution to the decibel level by noisily churning out leaflets. Forward was impressed: the transformation of this relatively empty community space into a fully operational incident centre had been achieved by Inspector Hoggart in the space of just a few hours.

Hoggart was working at a desk at the far end of the room. Forward went over to him, and, as they exchanged "Good mornings", he noted the Ordnance Survey map of Monks Bay and its surrounding area spread out in front of Hoggart. Using a grid system, the map had been divided into search areas, and Hoggart was in the process of allocating the names of officers to each of these from a list beside him. Forward profusely congratulated Hoggart on his rapid establishment of the incident centre; which the DI received with perfunctory thanks and an expression that suggested it was no more than his due.

Hoggart briefed Forward on the fire which had destroyed a barn near Wold Newton. The Chief Fire Officer had originally determined it to be suspicious, but had now decided it was accidental. It was then Forward's turn to brief Hoggart on every aspect of the Coulson investigation, and discuss with him the modus operandi for searching the bay and the cliffs, as this was Hoggart's responsibility. Discussions with Hoggart were never easy for Forward. Relations between the two men were strained, and had been so for the past two years: ever since Forward had been preferred over Hoggart for promotion to the rank of Detective Chief Inspector. This had been a severe blow to Hoggart's esteem. Aged forty-six at the time, he was nine years older than Forward, and his service in the force had been much longer. Yet the younger man was preferred because the senior officers responsible for promotions had decided that Forward's communication skills were greater, and he was able to empathise more effectively with colleagues and members of the public.

During Forward's conversation with Hoggart, DC Griffiths appeared. She ignored the two senior detectives, whom she observed to be in discussion, but greeted her other colleagues, and then moved all round the room, inspecting the set-up. She'd then gone and sat at one of the computer terminals. She was dressed in a dark blue business suit. Under the jacket she wore a white top: her skirt was knee length, and the overall effect was completed with blue tights and black, high heeled shoes. Her hair looked as though it had been freshly washed and was full of blonde bounce and vitality. Looking at her made Forward feel middle-aged and jaded. It occurred to him that despite being intently engaged in conversation with Hoggart for several minutes, he'd still no idea what the DI was wearing, yet had noted every feature of Diane's appearance. If she'd known this, given her acute antipathy to exhibitions of predatory male behaviour, she might well have taken it as evidence of his latent sexism. But it wasn't sexism: it was sexual attraction.

Forward excused himself and went over to Griffiths.

"Someone looks as though they've had a good night's sleep," he said.

She smiled broadly, showing straight, white teeth. "I did, as it happens. What time did you finish?"

"It was after four when I crawled into bed."

"I'm glad you sent me home early, then. What about Mrs Coulson? Was she any help?"

Forward briefed Griffiths on his interviews with Sheila Coulson and Horace Sissons. He'd just finished when Wilmot appeared. From his appearance, Forward deduced that he too had spent a sleepless night but not from mental hyperactivity: Wilmott had a young baby that frequently interrupted his sleep patterns.

Forward smiled at Wilmott. "Morning. You're early."

Sarcasm was wasted on Wilmott. "I know. I sacrificed my cornflakes to be here."

"Very noble." Forward turned to Diane. Of the three of them who'd attended the crime scene in the early hours, she looked the most energetic. "Liaise with Drinkwater and McIntyre when they arrive, and do a house-to-house in the village. There aren't many houses here so it shouldn't take long. See if anyone noticed any strangers about last night or any strange vehicles. Try and get us a fix on the earliest sighting of Coulson's Astra. Someone might have seen it in the car park before Horace Sissons did."

Forward produced a photocopy of the railway ticket that was found in Coulson's pocket. The original had already been sent to forensic in Hull. He handed the photocopy to Wilmott. "See if you can find out who issued the ticket to Coulson. Start at Sandleton Station and then go on to Filey. If he got off there someone must have seen him. Find out why no-one collected his ticket at the end of the journey. Did he buy another single back to Sandleton? Check out the cabbies that work the stations. Maybe he got a cab out here to Monks Bay from Filey or Sandleton."

"I'll ring round the local cab firms first," said Wilmott. "But first I need a cup of coffee."

"He looks dreadful," said Griffiths, as Wilmott moved off. "Thank God I don't have any kids."

Forward chatted briefly to Griffiths, and then rang Sir Andrew Marston in order to organise Mrs Coulson's formal identification of the body. In the course of this conversation, he learned that Marston was absolutely convinced Coulson's head injuries were made with a chalk boulder. Certainly, the evidence for this now seemed indisputable. After speaking to Marston, Forward contacted Mrs Coulson to tell her he would collect her at eleven o'clock to attend the mortuary in Sandleton for the identification of her husband's body.

Whilst Forward was engaged on the phone, the village hall had been slowly filling up with detectives from Sandleton CID and their uniformed colleagues from all over the county who'd been drafted in for the search of Monks Bay and the cliffs. Skipsea and his team of SOCOs had also arrived.

At exactly ten a.m. Forward took up a position in front of the pinboard and asked for everyone's attention. "OK," he said, "we all know why we're here so let's make a start. First, I'd like to thank you all for your assistance. I'd also like to express my gratitude to your senior officers for releasing you for this vital search. I'll begin by giving you a résumé of the events in this case so far." He turned and pointed to Coulson's photograph. "This man is Mark Coulson, aged forty-four. Until yesterday he was the Headteacher at Melthorpe Primary School. At around twenty-seven minutes past ten last night, he was brutally murdered at the bottom of the steps that lead down into Monks Bay. He sustained fatal head injuries in what appears to have been a frenzied attack. We can be quite precise about the time of death, because Coulson's watch appears to have been badly damaged as he tried to ward off the attack, and it stopped at ten twenty-seven p.m.

"After Coulson was killed, it looks like his murderer - or murderers, at this stage we're not sure how many were involved - dragged his body down to the sea and left it there, presumably hoping it would be covered by the incoming tide.

"Coulson's body was discovered just after eleven p.m. by Toby, a Jack Russell owned by Horace Sissons, a Monkhouses man. When the tide's out, Sissons allows Toby to exercise by himself down in the bay. When he realized Toby had found a body, Sissons contacted the police. The first officer on scene was PC Reynolds. He was concerned that forensic evidence on the body might be contaminated by the waves which had already reached Coulson's legs, so he dragged the body back up the beach. The next to arrive were DS Wilmot, DC Griffiths and some SOCOs. The tide was advancing, so they helped PC Reynolds move Coulson's body higher up the beach until it was adjacent to the bottom of the steps. The place where the pathologist, Sir Andrew Marston, is convinced Coulson was originally killed.

"All this has implications for our search of the crime scene. Marston is convinced Coulson was killed on, or by, the bottom of the steps in the bay. The forensic evidence he's already established, strongly indicates that the murder weapon was a medium size chalk boulder. Heavy enough to have smashed Coulson's skull several times, and yet light enough for the assailant to raise above his head and bring down with some force."

Griffiths' hand suddenly went up.

"Yes?"

"What makes you certain the assailant was a man, sir?"

"I'm not," said Forward. "I was using the term 'he' inclusively to cover male and female."

Griffiths nodded. She seemed satisfied to have made the point.

Forward was disconcerted by the interruption to his flow. He took a moment or two to collect his thoughts, and then went on, "Marston thinks the lump of chalk was probably about the size of a small melon or pineapple. It's quite likely that after dragging Coulson down to the sea, the perpetrators may have thrown the murder weapon some distance into the water, gambling that the blood on it would be washed off. This means that while the tide is at its lowest point, the whole of the lower strand at Monks Bay must be searched."

At this point Hoggart interrupted. "As one chalk boulder is just like another it might be helpful, sir, if you could explain to the men what exactly they're looking for."

There you go, stirring again, thought

Forward. Immediately, he castigated himself for being so uncharitable. After all, Hoggart was simply making a perfectly reasonable request for clarification. Wasn't he? It was just that Hoggart was so calculating. Forward had learned long ago not to trust him. Everything Hoggart said or did was usually disingenuous. He may have looked like a portly character with the fat man's jolly disposition, but that belied the reality: behind the bespectacled, genial image was a thin skinned, prickly individual who went out of his way to be unco-operative. His reference to the 'men', despite several of the officers present being women, was deliberate. On several occasions Hoggart had voiced his strong objections to women working on the front line alongside the male officers. Women, he believed, should be confined to back-office duties. Consequently, his intense loathing of DC Griffiths was returned mutually.

"Thank you, Reg, that's an excellent point," said Forward, more than getting his own back. Hoggart was an old-fashioned stickler for rank, and hated being addressed familiarly in public by his first name. Forward turned his attention back to his audience. "Sniffer dogs will, of course, be assisting in the search. Look out for boulders that have obviously been disturbed. The lump of chalk you're looking for will probably be lying loose on the surface of the beach. Any boulder that's half buried in the sand or is covered by a thick layer of bladder wrack needn't concern you. These chalk boulders would normally have exceptionally smooth surfaces caused by the constant action of the sea and tides. What you're looking for is a boulder where this smoothness has been disturbed by violent trauma. Perhaps the chalk is pitted, cracked, scratched or striated in some unusual way. Perhaps it has small craters on it. Or a chunk has been taken out of it. It might even be discoloured. But anything that's about the right size and looks suspicious should be bagged and handed over to the SOCOs. Just use your observation and apply your own judgement." Forward stopped and took in the faces of the officers, sweeping his head from left to right and back again as though he was at a tennis match. "All right?" he said. "Clear enough?" There was a general murmur of assent. "Any questions, so far?" he asked.

PC Sanders, who had recently transferred to Sandleton from the Met, raised his hand. "Yes, sir. What's bladder wrack?"

DI Hoggart shot Sanders a contemptuous look. "Seaweed!"

Hoggart's reaction was so characteristic, it struck everyone from Sandleton as immensely funny. There were gales of laughter. Sanders looked surprised at the reaction.

"The Yorkshire coast is full of it," Forward told Sanders. "Now, let's move on. SOCOs, assisted by a small team of officers from Sandleton, have been searching the bay since low tide this morning. I understand that one or two boulders have been identified as suspicious."

Forward caught Skipsea's eye. "Is that right, Dave?"

"Yes, sir."

"Found any others?"

"None yet."

"Of course," Forward went on, "it's possible that the perpetrator may have actually removed the murder weapon from the bay and discarded it somewhere on the cliffs. That's why the cliffs around the bay and the tourist car park will have to be thoroughly searched too. Our biggest problem is that the tide changes every six hours or so, and because the bay is relatively small, it fills up quite quickly. Therefore, to optimise our resources everyone will be deployed to search the bay when the tide's out: when the tide's completely in everyone will search the cliffs and roadside verges."

Hoggart spoke again. "I'm wondering why you're so certain that the murder weapon was a large lump of chalk. Couldn't it have been something else? A brick? A baseball bat?"

"It's the pathologist who's certain the murder weapon was a big lump of chalk. When I spoke to him earlier, he told me that several fragments of calcium carbonate, which is chalk, have been found in the wounds to Coulson's skull and embedded in his scalp. Chalk's also been found in the defensive wounds to his left hand and wrist; on the sleeve of his anorak and on his broken wristwatch. That's why Marston's convinced we're looking for a chalk boulder. He assures me that if the murder weapon is found, despite having been immersed in sea water, forensics have chemical and ultra violet tests that will detect whether it has been in contact with human blood or tissue. But I'll also tell you this. We're looking for another weapon that was used in the attack. It's a knife. Coulson had what looked like a defence wound on his left palm. It was so deep it severed an artery. It was made with a very sharp knife that had a narrow blade. The wound was barely an inch wide. This is curious because there are no other stab wounds on the body. But it's not the only curious aspect to this case. Coulson's wife, or rather widow, told me that her husband normally carried a money wallet, and a smaller wallet for his credit cards, around with him. Also, car keys, house keys and the keys to Melthorpe Primary School. None of these items were found on Coulson's body, so obviously a robbery motive can't be ruled out. Finally, I want to remind you to bag up anything that wouldn't naturally occur on the beach or on the cliffs. In other words, litter. Empty cans of drink, magazines, newspapers, cigarette packets, cigarette butts. Anything that shouldn't be there, should be collected. This is not a waste of time. In the last murder investigation I was on, we bagged up over three hundred and fifty items of litter, and two of them were instrumental in proving that the murderer had been in the vicinity.

"Now, there are one or two very puzzling aspects to this case. Coulson's car was found in the clifftop car park here at Monks Bay." Forward pointed to the map. "Yet, according to Mrs Coulson, her husband shouldn't have been anywhere near here last night. He had to be at a meeting here" - he pointed again to the map - "in Sandleton at four thirty p.m." Forward's finger moved on to Melthorpe. "And he was expected home here, in Melthorpe, by seven. But even more strange is that in his back pocket we found this," - his finger was now pointing to the pinboard. "It's a rail ticket to Filey. A single, not a return. It must have been issued sometime on Monday afternoon or evening, because Mrs Coulson is certain that her husband was at school all day until he left for the meeting in Sandleton. She has no idea why he would want to go to Filey either. I've asked Sergeant Wilmott to find out everything he can about this ticket. If Coulson's car was parked in Monks Bay, why was it necessary for him to go to Filey by train? Obviously the most important task is for us to establish Coulson's exact movements on Monday night. I've asked DC Griffiths to organise a house-to-house here in Monkhouses. Someone might have seen Coulson's car arriving in the car park, and might even recall the time. Temporary murder notices with Coulson's photo have been photocopied, and one, as you're probably aware, has already been displayed at the entrance to this incident centre. I want to see as many handed out and put up in the immediate vicinity and surrounding villages as possible. Communications have promised to have the proper posters with more detailed information available by this evening, in time for the press conference which will be held here at five p.m." Forward paused and gave the assembled officers an encouraging smile. "Right. I think I'll now covered everything. I'll now hand you over to DI Hoggart who will assign you to the areas of the beach and cliffs you are to search. As you can see, he's drawn up a very impressive grid."

Forward moved away and allowed Hoggart to take his place. Hoggart attached his own map to the pinboard and began reading out a list of officers, assigning them to various areas of Monks Bay, the car park and the cliffs.

While this was going on, Forward went over and joined Wilmott and Griffiths. He said, "Try and get me something to feed to the vultures at five. Apparently, the press office is under siege: there's nothing like a potential scandal involving a Headteacher to get the hacks' macabre imaginations working overtime."

"Where will you be? Melthorpe?" Wilmott asked.

"Yes. Marston says he'll have Coulson presentable enough for a formal identification by mid-morning. So, when that's over and done with, I'll take Mrs Coulson home and go through her husband's things. You never know, something amongst his personal papers might throw up a connection with Filey or Monks Bay. After that, I'll have a word with Lady Fernshawe. She was probably one of the last people to talk to Coulson. She may be able to give us some idea where he was going after the meeting at Sandleton."

"You're going to have a long day," said Griffiths. "All this and the first night of your play too."

****

Despite the unpleasantness of his forthcoming task, a feeling of deep satisfaction invaded Forward as he drove across the Wolds towards Melthorpe. The cloudless sky was an azure mirror for the sun's radiance. Spring, which a week before had only hinted at a presence in hesitant shoots and buds, was now in rampant efflorescence. Trees and hedgerows were burgeoning into full leaf; crocuses, primroses and daffodils thronged the verges of the narrow lanes that meandered between the hills. Not that the Detective Chief Inspector could have named any of the flowers he saw, for he was no countryman. Nevertheless, this didn't prevent him from enjoying their beauty. He felt so exalted: spring was in the air; there was the first night of *The Cherry Orchard* to look forward to; and he also had a challenging and intriguing murder case to untangle. At once, he recalled the pitiful expression on Mrs Coulson's face when she'd learned that her husband had been murdered, and he castigated himself for his thoughtless insensitivity.

The door of the schoolhouse was opened by a woman whom Forward didn't recognise. She was in her early forties with greying, dark hair and features that were vaguely familiar.

"I'm Catherine, Sheila's sister," she informed him, after he'd introduced himself. "You'd better come in. They're waiting for you."

Forward followed her across the tiny hall and into the sitting room.

There were two people in the room: Mrs Coulson and a grey-haired man in his late sixties.

Mrs Coulson was sitting on a straight-backed, wooden chair. She was dressed in a black jacket and skirt and a black polo neck jumper. Her tights were also black, as were her very shiny shoes. She was smoking. "Hello,

Inspector," she said jumping up. "I was getting a bit anxious. I thought you might have forgotten. I couldn't remember if you said ten thirty or eleven. And people do sometimes forget. I was in half a mind to ring you. Anyway, you're here now."

Forward could see she was still in a state of shock. There was a tremor in her voice and she spoke unnaturally quickly, uttering her thoughts the instant they occurred, as people do when their emotions are in turmoil.

"I think I said I'd collect you about eleven," said Forward. He looked at the elderly man who was sitting on the sofa. Then he looked back at Mrs Coulson, quizzically, to indicate that he was expecting an introduction.

But Sheila Coulson was too distracted to observe the social niceties. Her sister realised this. "This is Norman Coulson, Mark's father. He drove all through the night to be here," said Catherine.

The elderly man's knees made a faint cracking noise as he stood up. "How d'you do," he said. "I was wondering if I might come along with Sheila to identify Mark. I haven't seen him for so long and ..."

He couldn't continue; all he could do was shake his head in disbelief.

"Of course, you can," said Forward. He wondered why he hadn't had the good sense to delegate this task to someone else.

"Thank you," said Coulson's father. His light blue eyes were moist. "Thank you."

Mrs Coulson was taking quick, darting little puffs at her cigarette, as though terrified of it. "My sister's taking the children away with her for a few days," she said.

"Good." Forward turned to Catherine and nodded at her encouragingly. "I think that's a very sensible idea."

"How long do you think we'll be at the mortuary, Inspector?" Mrs Coulson asked. She pronounced the word mortuary very carefully and self-consciously, as though it was an unfamiliar word in a foreign language.

"It'll take the best part of an hour."

Mrs Coulson extinguished her cigarette, turned to her sister and gripped her hand tightly. Now they were standing together, side by side, it was obvious they were close relatives and Sheila was clearly the younger by a good ten or twelve years. She was the more striking too. Both sisters had regular, finely chiselled features, but Sheila's were keener, like something more cleanly pressed from the mould. Her hair was darker than her sister's and retained the vigour of its natural colour. Catherine's eyes were an insipid brown, but Sheila's, even though dulled by tragedy, were the kind of rare green you saw on exotic birds and insects. As she stood there, dressed in black, her eyes moist and vulnerable, communing in sorrow with her sister, grief seemed to rise off her like a vapour.

"This has been a terrible year, Inspector," said Norman Coulson. "First my wife and now this." He stopped and swallowed hard. Then he burst out, "Who would want to murder my boy? It's so unreal!"

"When did you last speak to Mark?" Forward asked.

"Just a few days ago. Last Wednesday."

"And did he seem all right?"

"Yes, perfectly all right."

"As far as you're aware nothing was troubling him?"

"No. No more than usual."

"More than usual? How do you mean?"

"Well, you know. Coping with a difficult job. Finding enough time to do everything. That sort of thing."

"No money worries? No arguments with anyone about anything?"

"No. And if there were, I'd have been the last to know. I brought him up to stand on his own two feet and not burden other people with his troubles."

"And he never mentioned to you anything about going to Monks Bay or Filey?"

"No. Nothing."

"Can you think of any reason why he'd want to go to either of those two places?"

"None at all. It's a complete mystery to all of

us."

The clock on the mantelpiece was showing five past eleven.

"I think we'd better make a start," said Forward.

"Yes," said Mrs Coulson. She turned to Catherine. "You'd better take the girls away from here before I get back. I'll go up and say goodbye to them now." She looked appealingly at Forward. "Have I time to say goodbye to the girls?"

"Go ahead."

Mrs Coulson moved towards the door.

"I'll come with you," said her father-in-law, and followed her out.

When they'd both gone, Catherine went quickly over to the door and closed it. "I couldn't say this in front of them but I think I know what Mark was doing out at Monks Bay."

"Oh?"

"I think he was with a woman."

Forward was intrigued. "Really. Who?"

"I don't know. But I think it's the most likely reason."

"Why do you say that?"

"I've never trusted him where women are concerned. Oh, it's easy to see why they liked him. He was handsome and charming. Clever too, of course. But he wasn't honourable in my book. He left a wife and two children for Sheila. Did you know that?"

"No."

"I don't think that's very responsible, do you?"

"Sheila is his second wife?"

"Yes. She's been married to him for six years." She pursed her lips tightly. "Both girls were born out of wedlock, of course."

She paused and waited as though she expected him to agree that this was a terrible thing. Forward said nothing.

"Mark was the Deputy Head of a school in Chester," Catherine went on. "Soon after Sheila joined the staff, as a probationary teacher, he started an affair with her."

"Is that so unusual?"

"I suppose not in today's world, but if you'll do it once you'll do it again. That's what I say."

"And that's why you think he was at Monks Bay? To meet a woman?"

"It's the only explanation."

"Then why was he murdered?"

"Perhaps he and the woman were followed there by the woman's husband. When Mark and the woman went down into the bay, the husband attacked him."

"Did Mark ever try it on with you?"

"Certainly not. And if he had, I'd have given him short shrift."

"You'd have told Sheila immediately?"

"Of course." She looked deeply affronted. "What are you suggesting?"

Forward ignored her question. "Mark's two former children, how old would they be now? Any idea?"

"They're teenagers. The boy's eighteen. The girl's sixteen."

"Is Mark still in contact with them?"

"He saw the daughter from time to time, I believe."

A sudden thought occurred to Forward. "Has Sheila told them their father's dead?"

"No. She couldn't face it, so I had the pleasure. Utterly harrowing. You can imagine what a shock it was for them."

There was the sound of footsteps on the stairs. "I'd better have your address and telephone number," said Forward. "I may need to talk to you again later."

"Very well."

Catherine sniffed and wrinkled her nose. "This place stinks like an ashtray. Smoking is such a disgusting habit. You'd think being a teacher Sheila would know better, wouldn't you?"

****

The mortuary at Sandleton Hospital was located in the recesses of the Pathology Department. Forward led Mrs Coulson and her father-in-law down a corridor and into the gowning-up area. There, they each put on a green gown and passed on through to the labs where they were met by Sir Andrew Marston.

"I'm afraid you'll have to prepare yourselves for a shock," said Marston. "Mr Coulson sustained extensive injuries to his head. We've cleaned him up somewhat but it's still not a pleasant sight."

Without another word Marston led the way through the labs and into the mortuary. This was a very long, cold room, the walls of which were lined with rows of large refrigerated drawers. Some of the drawers had the name and date of birth of their occupant chalked on them. Forward found himself shivering involuntarily at the sudden drop in temperature.

Sir Andrew gestured for them to hold back; then he went over to the drawer with Mark Coulson's name chalked on it. He pressed a lever on the drawer and it slid smoothly and quietly out from its mounting, like the drawer of a filing cabinet. Mrs Coulson and her father-in-law both tensed as they watched it.

Coulson's body was covered by a green sheet. Sir Andrew beckoned them to approach the drawer, and as they did so he lifted the sheet and drew it back.

Forward could see that Marston had done an excellent job of minimising the horrific impact of Coulson's injuries. Coulson's head was completely enclosed in a green skullcap and so no sign of his multiple fractures was visible.

His face, although purple with bruising and slightly swollen, was still recognisably human and bore some resemblance to his photograph. Even so, it was not a pretty sight for his nearest and dearest.

Mrs Coulson gasped and immediately started to whimper. Coulson's father clamped his arm tightly around her shoulders. Was it to comfort her or to comfort himself? Forward wondered.

"Is it your husband?" Forward asked gently, but he already knew from her reaction that the question was unnecessary.

Mrs Coulson looked at him and tried to speak but her face was twisted in grief. All she could do was nod.

"Yes, that's him, Inspector," said Coulson's father, still clinging to her. "That's my lad."

"I'd like you to identify Mark's clothes as well, Mrs Coulson," said Forward. "It's all part of the procedure."

Marston led them out of the mortuary and into a much smaller room adjoining it. This was full of filing cabinets. Marston went over to a drawer with Coulson's name on it, pulled it out and produced several items of clothing. Each item was in a polythene bag and labelled. He showed them to Mrs Coulson one by one. She nodded her recognition of each in turn.

"That's not Mark's," said Mrs Coulson suddenly. Marston was holding a large, yellow anorak.

A quiver of excitement passed through Forward. "Are you certain?"

"I'm positive. Everything else is his but not that. Mark's never worn anything like that."

"He was wearing it when we found him," said Forward.

"I don't understand!" Mrs Coulson cried. She turned to her father-in-law. "I don't understand any of this, Norman!"

"I'm sure there's a good explanation," said Forward reassuringly. He nodded at Marston, and taking his cue, Marston returned the clothes to the filing cabinet.

"Can't I take his clothes home with me?" asked Mrs Coulson.

"I'm afraid not," said Forward. "They have to be sent on for forensic tests."

"I wish I could take them home with me," she said. Her tone was plaintive. "They're the last things he wore."

****

Neither Mrs Coulson nor her father-in-law spoke much, at first, on the drive back to Melthorpe. Forward assumed they were too preoccupied with their grief and their memories. The sombre silence, punctuated only by intermittent messages on the car's short-wave radio, made him grow philosophical. What was it he'd read somewhere about the true horror of death? It marked the end of all lost opportunities, that was it: the Christmas card you'd always meant to send; the apologies you'd always promised to make; the wrong you'd always intended to set right. And then, before you could get round to it, the person had died. They'd entered the realm of no more second chances. That's what you really grieved over. That was the true nature of your loss. And nothing brought home the finality of it more than their body lying dead in a drawer in a freezing morgue.

Suddenly, Norman Coulson said, "When will we be able to have Mark's body for cremation?"

"Not until after the inquest," said Forward.

Norman shuffled in his front seat, looking vexed. "But why do you need an inquest? You know what the cause of death was. He was murdered."

"Only the coroner can determine that."

Forward explained that in order to bury or cremate a body a death certificate was needed; and that when someone died in a violent or unexplained way it could only be granted after an inquest.

"Then when will the inquest be held?"

"As soon as we've finished the examination of your son's body."

"But I thought they'd done the post-mortem."

"There may be the need for further

investigations." Forward adopted a quiet, conciliatory tone. "In a murder case the body of the victim is a major source of evidence, so, often, it's not possible for it to be released to the relatives for some time."

Norman Coulson nodded but made no other reply. He just sat there staring through the windscreen into the distance. He looked as though all of the stuffing had been knocked out of him.

Forward debated with himself whether or not this was an appropriate moment to bring up the subject of Mark Coulson's first marriage. He found it curious that Mrs Coulson had failed to mention it when she'd been interviewed. Shock, was it? Possibly. He'd intended to ask her about Mark's former wife and children when they were alone; but he had a hunch that if he asked her about them in the presence of her father-in-law, particularly so soon after they'd seen Mark's body, it might be revealing.

Casually, he said to Norman, "I understand Mark has teenage children from his first marriage."

The older man stared at him. "That's right. Philip and Rachel. They're devastated by all this, as you can imagine. So is Helen."

"Helen?"

"Mark's first wife," put in Sheila from the back seat.

There was a long pause.

"Was Mark in frequent contact with them?" Forward asked.

Norman cast a quick glance behind him at Sheila. "Frequent? No."

"Where do they live?"

"In York."

Forward was surprised. "Not Chester?"

"No. Helen got a new job and moved them all to York."

"So, they're relatively near then?"

"Yes."

"I'll need their address."

"Why?" Sheila asked.

Forward glanced at her reflection in his rear mirror. "It's a murder investigation. I need to speak to anyone who may have been in contact with Mark recently."

Norman said, "Mark only spoke to Rachel."

"He didn't speak to his son?"

"No."

"Why was that?"

Norman looked uncomfortable.

"They were estranged," said Sheila Coulson. "Philip never forgave him for leaving his mother and marrying me."

There was another long pause.

Forward said, "What about Mark's ex-wife, Helen? Was Mark still in contact with her?"

"No. At least I don't think so," said Sheila.

Forward brought the car to a stop at a temporary traffic light that was at red.

"Why didn't you tell us all this before, Mrs Coulson?" he asked sharply. Again, he observed her expression in the rear mirror.

"I didn't think it important."

Her father-in-law snorted, contemptuously.

Quickly, Mrs Coulson said, "I didn't mean to suggest they're not important." She paused, and then went on, "I'm sorry, Inspector, I should have mentioned I was Mark's second wife. But when I heard he'd been murdered it was such a shock I couldn't think straight."

Forward decided to ease off her. He'd found out a lot more than he'd expected.

The traffic light turned to green. He drove on pondering the significance of what he'd discovered.

****

When they got back to the schoolhouse, Forward asked Mrs Coulson for permission to go through her husband's personal papers. He told her he was hoping to find something amongst them that would explain Mark's association with Filey and Monks Bay.

"I don't think you'll find anything," said Mrs Coulson, "but I've no objection to you having a look. I'll show you his study."

She led Forward upstairs to a small room containing several bookcases, a two-drawer filing cabinet, a desk and a single chair.

She pointed to the filing cabinet. "Mark kept

all our personal stuff, insurance policies and that kind of thing in there."

"Was your husband well insured?" asked Forward.

"Amazingly, yes."

"Why amazingly?"

Mrs Coulson sighed heavily. "Mark wasn't very good with money, Inspector. It always seemed to slip through his fingers. But fortunately for us, about two years ago he had the foresight to take out some life insurance."

"May I ask how much for?"

"You'll see it anyway. It was for about fifteen thousand pounds. He was older than me, you know. By about thirteen years." Her face began to contort helplessly again, and there was a catch in her throat, as she said, "He always thought he'd die before me."

Mrs Coulson started to go and then turned back. "It was Catherine who told you about Mark's first marriage, wasn't it?"

"Yes."

"She'd have enjoyed that."

Her frankness encouraged him to be equally frank. "Well, I did get the impression she didn't like him very much."

"She thought he was completely unsuitable for me."

"I'm sorry, I have to ask you this. Have you ever suspected Mark of having an affair?"

"Never. But often the wife's the last to know,

isn't she?"

So is the husband, Forward reflected grimly.

"I'll be downstairs if you need me," Sheila Coulson said.

Forward spent nearly half an hour examining every letter and document he could find but there was nothing to connect Coulson with Filey or Monks Bay. There were, however, many examples of unpaid bills and several letters from irate tradesmen demanding payment of small sums. These confirmed Mrs Coulson's view that her husband wasn't very good at handling his finances. Forward considered whether or not this was relevant to the enquiry and decided that it probably wasn't. Tradesmen didn't murder their debtors for a few pounds.

Just as Forward finished his search, Mrs Coulson appeared carrying a tray on which there was a mug of tea and a sugar bowl.

"I thought you might welcome this," she said. "Do you take sugar?"

"No thanks."

She handed him the mug. "Have you found anything useful?"

"No. Nothing." He sipped his tea and then said with a smile, "You were right about one thing though. Your husband wasn't very good with money."

"All those unpaid bills, you mean?"

Forward nodded.

"Well, the insurance will take care of those now."

There was a long pause.

"Are you all right?" Forward asked.

"No. Not really. I keep thinking about that anorak. Can't get it out of my mind. Why was he wearing it? Where did he get it from?"

"You're positive you've never seen it before?"

"Yes. It's not something I'd have forgotten."

"Perhaps he kept it in school."

"In school? Why?"

"To wear on educational visits. School journeys, that sort of thing."

"But I've been with him on trips and school journeys so I would have seen it. I'm sure he's never owned an anorak like that."

Forward sipped his tea again. A sudden idea had occurred to him. "Was your husband an angler?" he asked. "A sea angler?"

Mrs Coulson looked surprised. "No, he wasn't interested in anything like that. Why do you ask?"

"I have an old friend who's an angler. He's got the bug so strongly that even when he can't fish because of the weather or the time of year, he still travels to his favourite spots. He says it keeps him close to the fish."

For the first time since he'd met her, she smiled broadly. It was a wonderful, transforming smile that liberated her beauty from its absorbing sadness.

"That's a lovely story. But I don't think Mark would have gone to Monks Bay to be near the fish, if that's what you're getting at. He wasn't very keen on the great outdoors. He was essentially a mind man."

Forward went silent and concentrated on his tea.

"You're as bewildered by Mark's murder as I am, aren't you?" said Mrs Coulson suddenly.

Forward was unsure how to reply. He didn't want her to lose confidence in him.

"It's perplexing, certainly," he said. "But I have all the resources I need to get to the bottom of it."

CHAPTER SIX

It was shortly after one when Forward left the schoolhouse. He drove a short distance down Melthorpe's main street and then stopped to consult his map. He was looking for the exact location of Melthorpe Hall, Lady Fernshawe's residence. He discovered it was situated a couple of miles outside the village on a large country estate.

Forward drove on for about a mile until he found the gravel drive leading to the Hall. He continued on down it for a further half mile until he was eventually stopped by a set of high, black, metal gates that were closed against him. He got out of the BMW, inspected the gates and found them to be locked. An entry phone was positioned on one of the gate posts. He placed his thumb over the button marked 'Call' and pressed it down firmly for several seconds. There was a sudden click, a crackle and then a man's voice which said faintly, "Yes?"

"Detective Chief Inspector Forward, East Yorkshire Police. I wish to speak to Lady

Fernshawe."

"Is Lady Fernshawe expecting you?"

"No. But I think she'll see me."

There was a pause at the other end. Then, "Have you any proof of your identity, Inspector?"

"Yes. I have my warrant card."

"Very good. On the gatepost immediately to your right there's a surveillance camera. Do you see it?"

"Yes."

"Would you mind holding your warrant card up towards it please?"

Forward complied with the request.

"Thank you, Inspector. I'll see if Lady Fernshawe is available."

Forward had to wait for several minutes, until, without any prior warning, the gates swung silently open. He got back into his car and drove on. He passed through the gates and watched them close behind him in his rear mirror. The gravel drive curved sharply to the right, and Forward found himself motoring through lush parkland that rolled on and on and was dotted with many mature, spreading trees. He came over a rise, and there, directly ahead of him, about a quarter of a mile distant, lay Melthorpe Hall. He instantly recognised it as Queen Anne. As he neared the house the open parkland gave way to formally laid out gardens. The gravel drive went over a stone bridge which separated two large and grandiose lakes. On either side of the bridge, in the centre of each lake, was a working fountain from which spumes of water cascaded.

After the bridge, Forward drove on between two large parterres, until the road entered a square courtyard and ended in a turning circle at the front of the house.

Forward parked the BMW, got out and stared up in admiration at the imposing edifice, built in grey stone. Then he climbed a set of steps and stood before the massive double doors. Immediately, he heard bolts being shot back and both doors were opened by a tall, fair haired young man. His formal butler's uniform of black jacket and grey striped trousers was in ludicrous contrast to his youthfulness. He looked like a young boy at a society wedding.

Forward stepped into a vast vault of an entrance hall that was nearly two storeys high. Confronting him was a wide, wooden staircase. Forward followed the butler up this to the first landing. The butler then went left down a long gallery until he came to a set of double doors which he opened for the Chief Inspector.

Forward found that he'd entered a magnificent library. It was an immensely long room and three of the walls were lined entirely with dark bookshelves that went from floor to ceiling. These were mostly crammed with antique books bound in various hues of brown, gold and green leather. One set of bookshelves had, however, been reserved for books of more recent publication. The floor was completely covered by a sumptuous Axminster carpet dominated by a design of huge circles and other, smaller, geometrical motifs in red and cream. Around the edges of the room were a number of antique tables on which stood either an elaborate flower arrangement or a vase of cut flowers. Forward glanced up at the ceiling and caught his breath. It was in gilded stucco and inset with circular paintings of Greek Gods.

"Detective Chief Inspector Forward of the East Yorkshire Police," announced the butler.

The woman who rose from the high-backed, Louis XIV chair to greet Forward was some twenty years younger than the aged worthy of his imagination. She was slim and nearly as tall as he was, which meant she had to be at least five foot ten. She was dressed in a black jacket, jodhpurs and black riding boots. Her dark brown hair was pulled tightly back off her face and ended in a short plait at the back of her neck. This gave her classically beautiful features a severe aspect which vanished as soon as she spoke. Her manner conveyed a seriousness appropriate to the gravity of the situation.

"Good morning, Chief Inspector," she said. "I was expecting you to call on me at some point.

What a dreadful business. Do come and sit down."

She led Forward towards the room's main focus: a stunning chimney piece with a marble fire-surround above which hung a mirror in the Rococo style. Three gilded sofas were arranged at right angles to each other around this fireplace. Lady Fernshawe sat on one of them and Forward took his seat opposite her. From this position he was able to observe her features more closely. Her nose was aquiline and aggressively aristocratic; yet her countenance was saved from total harshness by her wide forehead and fine, dark brows under which were eyes of startling and changeable iridescence. Were they blue or violet? It was hard to decide.

She smiled. "Would you like some coffee? Or perhaps you would prefer tea?"

"No, thank you," said Forward.

"You can go now, Wending." The barely perceptible lift of the head and the casual assumption of automatic obedience revealed Lady Fernshawe's breeding. This, it appeared, was a woman who'd been giving orders to servants since childhood.

Lady Fernshawe waited for the butler to leave the room. Then she said, "As you can probably imagine, the news of Mark's death has given me a terrible shock. I called on his wife early this morning to offer my condolences.

Poor Sheila, she's inconsolable."

"Understandably."

Lady Fernshawe picked up a cigarette box from a side table and offered it to him. He shook his head. She lit a cigarette and then continued, "I feel so guilty you see. I only realised that something might be wrong when I heard her message on the answerphone this morning. She sounded so desperate. If only I'd been available last night when she needed to speak to me."

"You were out?" Forward enquired lightly.

"No. I was asleep. I had a migraine so I went to bed early."

"I understand you attended a meeting with Mr Coulson in Sandleton yesterday."

"That's right. The meeting was called by the Local Education Authority. It was to consider the new legislation regarding school governors. That was why I was there. I'm the Chairman of Melthorpe School Governors."

'Chairman' seemed such an incongruous term for the attractive woman sitting opposite him that Forward suddenly understood why Coulson had insisted people used the term 'Chair' instead. Yet apparently Lady Fernshawe had no objection to being described as 'Chairman'. Forward resisted the temptation to ask her if this was because she had an aversion to feminism. "Did Mr Coulson give you a lift to the meeting?"

"No, I went separately in my own car."

"What was Mr Coulson's demeanour at the meeting?"

"I'm not sure what you mean."

"Did he behave normally?"

She reflected for a moment and then said, "Perfectly normally."

"He didn't appear agitated or anything like that?"

"Not as I recall."

"What time did the meeting end?"

"About six, I think."

"Did you and Mr Coulson leave together?"

"Oh no. He stayed behind to chat to some colleagues."

"So, you couldn't say what time he left the meeting?"

"I'm afraid not."

"Could you give me the names of any of the people he was talking to when you left?"

Lady Fernshawe placed one long, sensitive finger thoughtfully to her forehead. "Let me see. The only one I could actually put a name to is Mr Burn. He's the Headmaster at Danewold Primary School."

Forward recorded this information in his notebook. "Did Mr Coulson give you any idea what he was going to do after the meeting?"

"None at all. But I wouldn't have expected him to. Our relationship was professional, not social."

"You didn't mix socially?"

"Only on rare occasions."

"And on those occasions was his wife present?"

She frowned and looked bemused. "I'm not sure I like the implication in that."

"I'm not implying anything. I'm merely trying to establish whether he might have privately mentioned anything unusual to you, anything that was troubling him."

"Occasionally I would invite him back here for a sherry after official meetings. But I assure you that all he ever spoke about was his school. He was rather a boring man, Inspector." She laughed, throatily. "The last sort of man I would think of having an affair with."

Forward responded with a perfunctory smile. "So you wouldn't know if Mr Coulson had any enemies?"

Lady Fernshawe silently stubbed out her cigarette. Then she said, "I'm not sure I ought to mention this."

"If you think it's relevant, you must," said Forward.

"I can't believe this has any bearing on Mark's death but I do know he was having problems with Mrs Dangerfield's son."

"Mrs Dangerfield?"

"She's the infant teacher at Melthorpe School. I'm sorry to say that she and Mark didn't get on professionally. He was much younger than her and she considered he had too many modern and progressive ideas. There was a lot of friction between them. Apparently, it all came to a head when Mark tried to get Mrs Dangerfield to change her teaching methods. Quite forcefully, I understand. Anyway, her son, he's called Richard by the way, told Mark to leave his mother alone. There was a particularly unpleasant scene one evening in the village pub. Richard was drunk and he made certain threats to Mark."

"What sort of threats?" asked Forward.

"I believe he said he'd give Mark a good hiding if he didn't stop harassing his mother."

"Mark Coulson told you that himself?"

"That's right. He thought matters were getting out of hand and that I, as Chairman of Governors, ought to know."

"When was this exactly?"

"Months ago." Again, the elegant and sensitive finger went to her forehead. "Let me see now. Why yes, it would have been sometime in December of last year. But I wouldn't read anything sinister into it. It was merely a storm in a teacup. These kind of petty disputes are always breaking out in villages. They're the bread and butter of village life. Do you live in a village, Inspector?"

"No, I live in Sandleton."

"A fascinating place." Her tone was just the right side of patronising.

"Did these threats disturb Mr Coulson?" Forward asked.

"Naturally they were unpleasant but I wouldn't say that Mark was really disturbed by them. Before he came here, he was the Deputy Head of a particularly difficult school in Chester. He was quite used to people acting aggressively towards him."

"And did they?"

"Did they what?"

"Did the people in the village usually act aggressively towards him?"

"Oh no, certainly not."

"He was generally well liked?"

"Absolutely. Both liked and respected. His death is not only a personal loss. It will be a great loss to the community. He was an excellent headmaster and very active in local affairs. Very generous with his time. Before his death he was helping me organise an evening of music and poetry involving local people and children from the school. In view of what's happened I considered cancelling, but as it's an annual event here at the house I'm sure Mark would have wanted us to go ahead. What do you think?"

"It's not for me to say," said Forward.

"You're very welcome to come," said Lady Fernshawe. "It starts at eight o'clock next Monday. Tickets will be available at the door. Usually, the proceeds go to charity, but in the circumstances, I think we ought to use them to provide some sort of memorial."

"I'll make a note in my diary," said Forward. He stood up and looked around the room in admiration. "What a delight it is to see a room so full of flowers."

Lady Fernshawe rose, smiling. "Another of my passions, Inspector. I adore flowers. I have to be surrounded by them at all times. I had my own market garden, you know." She spread her arms out widely. "Until I inherited all this."

"Hence your interest in flower arranging?"

Lady Fernshawe looked at him curiously for a moment. "Oh, I suppose Sheila told you that."

"Yes. I wouldn't mind trying my own hand at it but it looks very difficult."

"Nonsense. Anyone can do it. I only learned myself by attending the flower arranging class in the village. In fact, I was there last night." She smiled. "Until, that is, I was stricken with a beastly migraine."

"I'm glad to see you're feeling better," said Forward, feigning solicitude. "Thank you for giving up your time. I don't think we'll need to bother you again except to sign a statement."

Lady Fernshawe beamed. "Not at all, Inspector. I'm only upset we should have met in such distressing circumstances. It's rare to meet a policeman of such sensitivity as yourself."

Lady Fernshawe fixed him with a stare. In

the brief time that her eyes held his, something warm and beckoning was transmitted in her look. In other circumstances he would have said she was flirting.

Lady Fernshawe looked away and walked elegantly across the vast Axminster carpet to the window. She felt behind the curtain and pressed something.

Forward assumed she was summoning the butler. "By the way," he said, "I should have asked you this before. Do you know of any connection Mr Coulson might have had with the East Yorkshire coast? Filey for example. Or Flamborough Head?"

Lady Fernshawe looked perplexed. "No. None at all."

"He never mentioned either of these places?"

"Not that I recall."

"You do know his body was found at Monks Bay?"

"So I gather. Sheila told me. She hasn't the faintest idea what he was doing there. She said he had a rail ticket to Filey in his pocket too."

"Yes."

"Extraordinary!"

The door opened and Wending appeared.

Lady Fernshawe bestowed on Forward a charming smile. "Goodbye, Inspector. And do try to come to our little concert if you can."

"I'll do my best," said Forward. He followed Wending out of the room, through the house and down the stairs. As Wending opened the heavy entrance doors, Forward stopped suddenly. Wending waited, deferentially.

"Do you have your own accommodation here, Wending?" Forward asked.

He seemed surprised. "No, sir. I have a flat in York."

"That's unusual, isn't it? I thought butlers lived in."

"Not so much these days, sir. Besides, I'm not just a butler. My duties are more general."

"What time do you normally finish work?"

"I'm usually on duty until after dinner."

"Until about eight thirty. Something like that?"

"Yes, sir."

"And then you drive back to York?"

"Yes, sir."

"What time did Lady Fernshawe arrive back from the village hall last night?"

"I wouldn't know, sir. I wasn't here. It was my day off."

"Would any other servants have been here?"

"No, sir."

"Would you mind telling me where you were last night?"

"Certainly not, sir. I was at the theatre in York. A performance of *The Rivals*."

"Ah. A theatre buff, are you?"

"Yes, sir."

"That's a coincidence. I'm producing *The*

Cherry Orchard at Sandleton High School. Our first performance is tonight. It runs until the end of the week. If you're interested."

Wending hesitated, as though preparing himself to say something impolite. "I doubt I would be able to get the time off, sir. In any event I rarely go to amateur productions. I usually find them deeply unsatisfying."

"Do you!" said Forward. He brushed past Wending and walked down the steps to his car.

CHAPTER SEVEN

The village of Danewold lay about six miles east of Melthorpe on the York road. Forward arrived at Danewold Primary School shortly after two. The school secretary, a stout, maternal looking woman, told him that Mr Burn was teaching and wasn't available until the afternoon break, which was at two twenty. Forward agreed to wait and the secretary went off to inform Burn of the Chief Inspector's presence.

The secretary returned and resumed working at her desk. Forward sat in the tiny office and listened to her fingers scuttling over her typewriter whilst long forgotten smells of paint and clay and chalk came wafting in through the open door. These aromas, mingling with the low murmur of children's voices, evoked in Forward memories of his own childhood. How, he wondered, had he progressed (if that was the word) from that blissful innocence to the awful knowledge he now possessed of human beings, their motives and their capacity for evil?

Dead on twenty past two the secretary got up and pressed a button on the wall. A bell sounded. "I'm off to get a cup of tea," she said. "You can get one for yourself in the staffroom if you like."

"No thanks," said Forward.

"I'll remind Mr Burn you're here. He'll be with you in a minute."

From the classroom next to the office came sounds of chairs scraping and children speaking in the sort of loud and excited tones which indicate the sudden relaxation of a strict regime. A few moments later a short, powerfully built man wearing tortoiseshell glasses entered the room. He was carrying a polythene lunchbox.

"Inspector Forward? I'm Alex Burn. Sorry I couldn't see you earlier but I was teaching. One of the penalties of being the Head of a small primary school. You have to teach full time as well."

"That's quite all right. I understand," said Forward.

Burn sat down and took the lid off his lunchbox. "I hope you don't mind but I'm going to have to eat while we talk. I had no time at lunch time, you see."

"Feel free," said Forward.

"Obviously you've come to see me about

Mark's death. It's been a terrible shock. The phone hasn't stopped ringing. People just can't believe it." He took a bite out of his sandwich. "The circumstances, I mean. Murder. It's extraordinary."

"I understand that you and Mr Coulson were at a meeting in Sandleton yesterday."

"That's right. I must have been one of the last people to speak to him."

"What did you talk about exactly?"

"The government's latest educational reforms. It's what we always talk about."

"Anything else?"

"Not really. We talked a bit about various plans we had for the cluster, that's all."

"The cluster?"

"Yes. Small village schools often work together in cluster groups. We share teachers and other resources. Melthorpe School and this one are in the same cluster."

"What sort of emotional state would you say Mr Coulson was in yesterday?"

Burn scratched his greying head and smiled.

"Emotional? Now that's a word I wouldn't apply to Mark. He was very detached, you know. A clinical sort of character. Rather dry."

"All right, I'll put it this way. Did he seem himself?"

"Yes, I think so."

"Nothing unusual about his behaviour?"

Burn took another bite of his sandwich and

munched on it thoughtfully. "I suppose you might say this was unusual, although I hardly think it very significant. Normally after a meeting Mark would join the rest of us in the cluster for a drink or two. But last night he didn't."

"Did he say why?"

"He said he was taking his wife out for a meal."

Forward tried hard to conceal his surprise. "Did he say where?"

"No. Just said he was taking her out for a meal. There isn't a restaurant at Monks Bay, is there?"

"No."

"But that's where he was found, wasn't he?"

"Yes."

"Then what was he doing there?"

"I was hoping you might be able to tell me."

"Me? Why should I know?"

"No reason. I just thought you might know of some connection he had with Monks Bay."

Burn shook his head. "No, I don't. Sorry."

"What about Filey? Did he ever mention Filey for any reason?"

Burn stared at him nonplussed. "No."

"Can you think of any reason he might have wanted to go to Filey last night?"

"None at all. Except for a meal."

"A meal?"

"Yes, to take his wife for a meal."

"Oh, yes," said Forward. "The meal. I was thinking of another reason. An educational reason, perhaps."

Burn shook his head doubtfully. "I wouldn't have thought so. Filey's not in our education authority. Anyway, I think he would have said."

"Let's go back a bit," said Forward. "Did he leave the Teachers' Centre at the same time as you and the others?"

"No. He left before us."

"So, he left on his own?"

"I think so, but I couldn't swear to it."

"What time was that? Do you know?"

"I should say about ten past six."

"You're sure of that?"

"Absolutely. The meeting ended dead on six. I know that because there's a clock in the Teachers' Centre. It was right above the speaker's head. He was a dreadful speaker and we were all relieved when he finished on time. Afterwards, Mark stayed around to chat for about ten minutes, so he couldn't have left much later than ten past six."

"And Lady Fernshawe left before him?"

"That's right." Burn's eyebrows rose almost to his hair line. "Surely you don't suspect her?"

"I suspect everyone and no-one, Mr Burn. At the moment I'm simply trying to establish the sequence of events prior to Mr Coulson's death."

"I see. Sorry."

"I need the names of everyone who was at the meeting. Can you provide me with that?"

"No. Heads and their chairs of governors came from all over the Authority. But the information will be available from the Education Department at County Hall. A clipboard was passed around before the meeting started and everyone present signed it."

"Good." Forward made a note of this. "Lady Fernshawe mentioned that Mr Coulson had had some trouble with Mrs Dangerfield's son, Richard. Did you know about that?"

"Yes, I did. It's no secret Mark and Mrs Dangerfield didn't get on. Richard got it into his head that Mark was trying to get rid of his mother, force her to retire or some such nonsense. So, he made a few stupid threats when he was drunk one night."

"What sort of threats?"

"I think he told Mark he was going to remove his head from his shoulders. Something like that. He could have done it too. He's a big lad, by all accounts."

"Do you know if Mr Coulson ever received threats from anyone else?"

"Not to my knowledge."

Burn started on his second sandwich. Forward left him to finish his lunch in peace and, wondering when he was going to find time to get some lunch himself, he drove back to Melthorpe.

****

The *Blue Boar Inn* on Melthorpe's main street was a black and white timber framed building with a slate roof. Forward had to pound on the stout, oak door several times before it was opened. When the door eventually swung back, the man who stood before him completely filled the doorway. Despite being six feet tall, Forward felt dwarfed by him. The man was five inches taller at least, and had a straggling black beard that would not have looked out of place on a nineteenth century whaling ship.

"Yes?" said the man in an unexpectedly light voice. "If it's a drink you're after, we're closed."

"No, I don't want a drink," said Forward. "Are you the landlord?"

The man looked at him quizzically. "I am."

Forward introduced himself, displayed his warrant card and asked if he might have a word.

"You can," the landlord said. He led Forward into the pub and once they were both inside, he closed the door and bolted it. "People are always turning up thinking I'm open in the afternoon," he said, "walkers and such like. If I leave the door unbolted, they're straight in." He offered Forward his massive hand. "I'm Ray Dobson, by the way." After Forward had shaken hands, he was relieved to find he still had all his fingers.

They were standing in what looked like the pub's main and only bar. The beamed ceiling was so low it forced the immensely tall landlord into an uncomfortable stooping position. Glancing around, Forward had a favourable impression of much wood: low wooden beams on the ceiling; gleaming wooden floors; wooden furniture. There was also a lovely long wooden bar with hand pumps like big upturned skittles. What a delight it was to walk into a pub that had retained so many original features. There were no horrible quiz or games machines, not even a television; just some nineteenth century photographs and a range of burnished horse brasses mounted on one wall. It was a perfect example of an old country pub that looked as though it hadn't altered since the day it was built.

"I'm investigating the death of Mark Coulson, the Headmaster," said Forward.

Mr Dobson stared back at him gravely. "Terrible business."

"Yes, it is. Do you know Richard Dangerfield?"

The landlord frowned suspiciously. "Of course."

"I understand that one night, last December, Richard threatened Mr Coulson in here. Do you recall the incident?"

"I certainly do. Incidents like that are very rare."

Forward could certainly understand why. The landlord was such a big, intimidating presence and so obviously capable of taking care of himself, it would be a brave man indeed who went out of his way to upset him.

"So, you've got Richard in the frame for Coulson's murder, have you?" asked Mr Dobson.

"No-one's in the frame," Forward said firmly. "Now, would you like to tell me exactly what happened?"

"Sure. It happened about nine o'clock. Mr Coulson and some of the school governors had come in after one of their meetings. Richard were drinking on his own in the small bar down here." Dobson pointed towards the end of the pub and instantly set off in that direction. Forward followed him, until at the end of the bar they came to a small room set at right angles to it. The landlord stepped into the tiny room and at once his massive, stooping frame seemed to occupy every inch of space in there. Forward squeezed in beside him. The room was snug and cosy with long plush seats around the walls and a few tables and chairs. The sort of place you'd expect to find courting couples. It had its own short bar too, from which you could have a good view of the serving area and the main bar.

Mr Dobson stared down at Forward and said,

"Do you mind if I sit down? Standing under this bloody low ceiling for any length of time gives me a terrible pain in the neck."

"Of course not, I understand."

With obvious relief the middle-aged giant eased himself down onto a seat by one of the tables. Forward took a chair opposite him."

"Have you ever thought of having the ceiling raised?" Forward asked, only half humorously.

Mr Dobson scoffed. "Cost a fortune. Anyway, my son's nowhere near as tall as me and he's to inherit, so it'd be a waste of time as well as money."

Forward nodded. "Anyway, you were saying?"

Dobson indicated the room with his big, open palm. "Richard were sitting in here drinking whisky and bitter chasers for over an hour before Mr Coulson came in."

"Would you say he was drunk?"

"No, not drunk. Richard could hold his drink better than anyone. All I'd say is, he weren't as in control of himself as he is when he's sober. His tongue were starting to get a little bit loose."

"What about?"

"Oh, nothing in particular. This and that. But it were unusual for him. Normally he's quite tight lipped."

"All right, go on."

"There's nothing much to say really. Mr

Coulson and some of the governors were in the other room having a drink. Richard came up to the bar in here and called across to Mr Coulson, 'Coulson, I want a word with you!' Mr Coulson excused himself from the people he were with and went and joined Richard in here. I were pulling pints so I got a good view of what were going on. I couldn't hear what were being said though."

"Why was that?"

"The pub were full and it were very noisy. But from their body language and the way they were glaring at each other, I could tell they were having an argument. Then, suddenly, their voices became really raised. Richard grabbed Mr Coulson by his lapels and stuck his face right into Mr Coulson's. Well, I knew what would happen next and I weren't having any of it. I left off serving and shot in here. Just in time too. Richard had shoved Coulson hard up against the wall. If I hadn't intervened and separated them, I think he'd have done Mr Coulson some serious damage."

"I see. What happened then?"

"I told Richard to get lost."

"Did he go?"

"Like a lamb. Left straight away."

"Presumably, Mr Coulson was quite shaken?"

"Oh, aye. Very. I asked him if he wanted to take it any further, you know, call the police in. But he weren't very keen. He just said Richard had drunk too much and got a bit upset. No, he didn't want the police involved."

"Did he say what the row was about?"

"No. He just went back and joined the people he were with."

"And you heard nothing that Mr Coulson and Richard said when they were scuffling?"

"Only one thing." The landlord raised his head slightly and looked into the distance. "As I came in here Richard were forcing Coulson against the wall and shouting 'She's not on her own, you know. She's still got me to defend her'." Mr Dobson returned his gaze to Forward. "He were shouting it right in Mr Coulson's face."

"Was anyone else in this little bar when it happened?"

"No. It were empty. Richard and Coulson were the only ones in here."

"But people in the other bar could see what happened?"

"Oh sure. Those that were standing at the bar could, anyway. They've got a clear view into here, as you can see. Mind you, by closing time, everyone in the pub were talking about it. It were that unusual. And, of course, it were all over the village the next day."

"What did people think was at the bottom of it?"

"The word were Coulson were bullying Richard's mother. She's the infant teacher in the school, you know."

"Yes."

"They said Richard had decided to put his foot down and make it clear he weren't going to stand for it."

Forward dropped his voice and spoke almost confidentially. "Tell me about Richard Dangerfield. How did he get on with people generally?"

The landlord looked non-committal. "He's a pleasant enough lad. But more popular with the women than the men, I'd say. He's had a good education but he's certainly not stuck up. Yes, overall, he's not a bad sort."

"Had you ever had any trouble with him before? I mean before the night he had a go at Mr Coulson?"

"No."

"And what about Mr Coulson. What sort of a bloke was he?"

"Now there I don't think I can help you very much. He rarely came in here. Just occasionally for Sunday lunch with his family and after the school governors' meetings, which, of course, don't happen very often. He were always polite and pleasant enough, mind. But always the Headmaster: you know, always on duty. It's hard for those sort of people in a village, professional people I mean. Always got to be on their guard. Can't seem to be letting their hair down. Everyone's watching them, see. Bit like policemen, I suppose."

Forward laughed.

"Funnily enough, the only long conversation I had with him were about fruit machines."

"Fruit machines?"

"Aye, he were trying to persuade me to install one. He said it would be good for business. People enjoyed playing them. Having a little flutter. That sort of thing."

"What did you say?"

"I told him I wouldn't give them house room. Can't stand the horrible, noisy things."

"Well, Mr Dobson, I'm very glad you did."

Forward went on to trenchantly express his objections to the modernisation of old pubs, and was delighted to find that the landlord's views were completely in accord with his own. They then discussed the range of ales available from the hand pumps at the bar, many of which were brewed relatively locally. One called *Troll's Delight* particularly caught Forward's eye.

"Would you like a quick half on the house?" Mr Dobson asked.

"It's very tempting but I have to say no. Not when I'm on duty."

"You do right. I never touch a drop meself. This pub's been in my family for four generations and all of us have been teetotallers. You have to keep a clear head when you're running a pub. Too many temptations. Our ale's very strong too. It's so strong that by the end of the night men's tongues are glued to the roofs of their mouths and they can't get their words out."

Forward laughed. "Then I certainly won't be having a half. By the way, on the night Richard went for Mr Coulson, was Lady Fernshawe in the pub?"

The landlord laughed incredulously. "Lady Fernshawe? She's never once set foot in here. That'll be the day when her ladyship comes in for a pint." His eyes narrowed suspiciously. "Why do you ask?"

"No reason." Forward stood up. "Well thanks, Mr Dobson, you've been very helpful."

From his sitting position, Dobson reached out and touched Forward's arm. "Just a minute, Inspector. I've thought of something." He looked at Forward frankly. "I've spent all me life in pubs. Seen plenty of barneys, one way or another. Men arguing over cards and thumping each other. Even over dominoes. Women coming in and catching their husbands out with other women, and then going at it like fishwives. But this thing between Coulson and Richard were different. When I separated them, there were a look went between 'em like I've never seen before. Pure hatred it were. I think if I hadn't stopped them, they would have killed one another."

****

"I didn't expect to see you again today, Inspector," said Mrs Coulson when she eventually answered the door of the schoolhouse. She was still wearing her black sweater, but had taken off her suit and had changed into a pair of black stretch pants.

"One or two things have come up that I need to discuss with you," said Forward.

He followed her into the living room. "My father-in-law's gone for a walk," she said. "Poor man. He doesn't know what to do with himself."

Forward could understand why. He'd learnt from Norman Coulson that he'd spent his entire life working as an accountant, and he and his wife, Linda, had eagerly anticipated the day when he would retire, and they would move to rural Derbyshire. But just a month after they'd realised their dream, Linda had died suddenly of a heart attack. And now, to top it all, Norman's only son had been brutally murdered. "If I was in his position," said Forward, "I wouldn't know what to do with myself either."

They both sat down: she on the high-backed chair, he on the sofa facing her.

"I've been to see Lady Fernshawe," said Forward. "She tells me that Mrs Dangerfield's son, Richard, threatened your husband a few months ago."

She looked surprised. "That's right."

"Why didn't you mention this when I asked you if your husband had any enemies?"

Her hands fluttered apologetically. "I'm sorry. I never thought of Richard as an enemy."

"If someone threatened me with violence, I'd consider them an enemy. A potential enemy at least."

She gave a fatalistic shrug. "Richard was drunk. He often behaves badly when he's had too many."

"Did your husband tell you why Richard threatened him?"

"It had something to do with Richard's mother." Mrs Coulson leant towards the coffee table and picked up her cigarettes and matches. "She worked with my husband and Richard thought he was giving her a hard time."

"And was he?"

Mrs Coulson lit a cigarette. "Not really. He was just trying to improve the school's organisation and she was obstructing him. That's how Mark saw it, anyway."

"Was your husband bothered by Richard Dangerfield's threats?"

She smiled faintly. "Not at all. It would have been a different matter if Richard had actually hit him, of course, but it soon blew over. Richard apologised to him the next day. All part of the rich tapestry of village life, Inspector."

"Richard never threatened him again?"

"No. When he's sober Richard's very nice."

"You know him well, do you?"

Mrs Coulson shook her head. "Not really. But when you live in a small community like this, you soon find out who's nice and who isn't."

"I also spoke to Mr Burn. Do you know him?"

"Yes. The Headmaster at Danewold. Mark often spoke about him."

"He was at the meeting your husband attended at Sandleton yesterday. He says Mark told him he was going to take you out to dinner last night. Does that surprise you?"

She stood up astonished. "Mark was going to take me out to dinner?"

"Yes. Apparently, it was the reason he gave for not going to the pub with the rest of them."

Her eyes were full of bewilderment. "He never said anything to me about it!"

"Perhaps he was planning to give you a pleasant surprise?"

She dismissed this with a shake of her head. "Mark didn't like surprises. They upset his routine. Besides, he knew I was cooking dinner."

Forward adopted a soft and tactful tone. "Look, I'm sorry to ask you this again. Was Mark having an affair with someone?"

"No. No, he wasn't." Her look told him she was amazed he hadn't believed her the first time. "He wasn't the type, Inspector. His whole world centred on his work and his family."

"From what I gather he spent a good deal of time with Lady Fernshawe up at the Hall."

Her eyes widened. "You're not suggesting he was having an affair with her, surely?"

Forward said nothing.

"Mark did spend a certain amount of time at the Hall but it was always to do with school matters. They were organising the annual village concert. There was nothing more to it than that. Isabella is happily married."

"But why should your husband have told Burn he was taking you out to dinner, when he wasn't?"

"I don't know. But then I don't know what he was doing at Monks Bay either." She sat down heavily. "I don't know anything anymore!"

CHAPTER EIGHT

A large crowd had gathered outside Melthorpe Primary School. They were parents and other relatives who were waiting to collect their children at the end of the school day. Some with simple curiosity, others with obvious suspicion - even downright hostility - watched Forward leave the schoolhouse and cross the road to his car. Once seated inside it, he contacted Sandleton on the radio to request a previous convictions check on Richard Dangerfield.

He'd just finished this, when the entrance doors to the school opened and the children started streaming out, hurrying down the path and through the school gates towards the waiting adults.

After some delay, Sandleton came back to tell him that Dangerfield was 'clean'.

Forward was glad to see the milling throng had now mostly dispersed. He got out of the BMW and was locking it when a large coach drew up and parked behind him.

Forward crossed the road and passed

through the school gates just as a tubby, middle-aged man came out of the building. The man was followed by a rather ragged crocodile made up of about a dozen children. The man stopped, turned back to face his charges and ordered them to keep together. "I'm warning you," he said firmly, "no-one's going on the bus until you're all behaving sensibly." The children immediately went quiet and stood stiffly to attention.

Forward went over and introduced himself.

"I'm Eric Haynes," said the man. "Peripatetic Headteacher. I've been assigned here until a new Head is appointed."

"I wonder if I could have a word with Mrs Dangerfield?" asked Forward.

"Certainly. Why don't you go inside and wait? I'll be with you in a moment." He smiled broadly. "I've got to get these little devils safely on the coach."

Forward went inside and stood waiting in the school's tiny entrance hall. About five minutes passed and then he heard the coach's engine start up. A minute or so later Haynes appeared.

"Sorry about that, Inspector. I have to make sure those children get on the coach at the end of the day. They're the ones that live miles away. There'd be hell to pay if they missed it."

"I'll bet," said Forward.

Haynes led him into a large classroom.

"Everyone's pretty shell-shocked here, as you can imagine," he said. "I'm only just getting over the news myself. Mark was the last person I thought would be murdered."

"You knew him?"

"Yes. Fairly well. In a rural community like this, virtually all those in education know each other. You wanted to speak to Mrs Dangerfield, you said?"

"That's right."

Haynes nodded towards a door at the far end of the room. "Her classroom's through there."

"Was this Mr Coulson's classroom?" asked Forward.

"Yes." Haynes looked around sadly. "It's been very hard explaining to the children what's happened to him. They're devastated, as you can imagine. He was a very popular Head."

"When I've finished with Mrs Dangerfield I'd like to come back in here and have a look around, if you've no objection," said Forward. "I'm hoping to find something that might assist the investigation."

"I've no objection. I'll be on hand if you want me. I won't be leaving for at least an hour."

Haynes led Forward through the classroom and into the adjoining one. Seated at a desk covered with piles of exercise books was a grey-haired woman in her mid-fifties. She looked up from the book she was marking and took off her glasses.

"Maureen, this is Chief Inspector Forward," said Haynes. "He'd like a word with you." He started to back out through the doorway. "I'll be through here if you need me."

After Haynes had left, Forward closed the door and went and sat down on one of the desks in front of Mrs Dangerfield.

"You seem to have a lot of marking," he said.

Mrs Dangerfield sighed. "Yes, it never ceases. But that's a good thing in a way. It helps to take my mind off things."

"Yes. I know what you must be feeling," said Forward, quietly. "Unfortunately, I have my job to do. It often involves ignoring people's feelings and asking rather insensitive questions. I hope you'll understand."

"Of course."

Forward decided to come straight to the point. "From what I've gathered, you didn't get on particularly well with Mr Coulson."

Mrs Dangerfield visibly bristled. "I don't know who's told you that but they obviously didn't work in this school. Mr Coulson and I got on quite well personally. Professionally, we didn't see eye to eye all the time, but anyone who's had experience of schools or teachers wouldn't find that unusual."

"But it was unusual for your son to threaten him, surely?"

An anxious look came into her eyes. "That was unforgivable. I made sure Richard apologised to Mr Coulson the next day."

"I understand your son did it because he was concerned at the way Mr Coulson was treating you. Is that right?"

She hesitated. "Yes."

"So, in a way, it was understandable. Would you like to tell me about it?"

She sat up and straightened her back. "There's very little to tell. I came home one evening after a rather heated discussion with Mr Coulson and burst into tears in the living room. Unfortunately, Richard happened to see this and he wanted to know what was wrong."

"When was this exactly?"

"Several months ago. Sometime in early December."

"Go on."

"Well, naturally I tried to make light of it, but Richard got into a raging temper. He was convinced that Mr Coulson was trying to get rid of me and replace me with someone younger."

"Was this true?"

"No, I'm sure it wasn't. But for some reason Richard thought it was."

"What happened then?"

"We were both in such a state we ended up having an enormous row ourselves." Her mouth tightened. "Richard stormed out and went straight to *The Blue Boar*. Unfortunately, there was a governors' meeting that evening at the school and Mr Coulson and several of the governors came into the pub afterwards. By then Richard was quite drunk, and he insulted Mr Coulson in front of the governors and some of the parents. It was terribly embarrassing."

"Richard threatened to harm Mr Coulson, didn't he?"

"It was the drink talking, Inspector. Richard is not a violent person."

"Nevertheless, he did threaten him?"

"Yes. When he came back and boasted about it to me, I was appalled. As I said, I made sure he went and saw Mr Coulson the following day and apologised."

"And he did this willingly?"

"I wouldn't say willingly. Really, he did it for me. But, deep down, I believe he did regret what he'd done."

"To your knowledge did he ever threaten Mr Coulson again? Or even consider it?"

"I've told you, Inspector, Richard isn't a violent person." She gave him a hostile look. "You think he killed Mr Coulson, don't you? That's why you're asking me all these questions!"

"Quite the contrary. I'm trying to eliminate him from the enquiry. In an investigation like this every lead, however slender, has to be followed up." Forward took out his notebook. "Now, could you tell me where Richard was last night, particularly between ten o'clock and midnight?"

She shrugged unhappily. "I'm sorry I can't. I didn't see Richard at all last night. But he was at home this morning. He must have come in very late when I was asleep."

Something in Forward's look must have unnerved her because she immediately said, "It's not unusual, Inspector. Although Richard lives under my roof we often don't see each other. He quite frequently stays out till all hours."

"I see."

She brightened at a sudden thought. "But I can tell you that he did come home at some point yesterday evening because he'd eaten the dinner I'd left him. Yesterday, you see, I went to have tea straight after school with a friend of mine who lives in the village. So I told Richard I was leaving him an oven ready meal to cook in the microwave. After tea, my friend and I went to the flower arranging class in the village hall."

"The one attended by Mrs Coulson and Lady Fernshawe?"

"Yes."

"Lady Fernshawe left early, didn't she?"

"Yes. She had a migraine coming on."

"That must have caused some problems as I gather she's the instructor."

Mrs Dangerfield smiled patronisingly. "No problems at all, because I was there. You see I'm the senior instructor. Lady Fernshawe's the junior instructor. I was the one who originally trained her in flower arranging. Mind you, she picked it up enormously quickly. She had the perfect background for it, of course. She owned her own market garden, you know, before she inherited her title."

Forward listened while Dangerfield's mother talked on, extolling the virtues of Lady Fernshawe. The infant teacher appeared to be easily impressed by wealth and privilege and was obviously something of a snob.

Interrupting her, Forward said, "And Mrs Coulson arrived at what time?"

Mrs Dangerfield considered. "Shortly after eight, I think."

"I see. And what time did you leave the flower arranging class?"

"Just after ten."

"And you went straight home?"

"Yes."

"And when you got home Richard wasn't there?"

"No. I told you, I didn't see him at all last night. But I saw that he'd cooked the meal I'd left for him."

"What time was that?"

"What time did I get home?"

"Yes."

"About twenty past ten."

"Do you have any other members of the family living with you?"

"No. My husband died years ago when

Richard was just a toddler. I have an older daughter but she works in Plymouth." She sighed and smiled sadly. "So, there's just Richard and myself."

"Really you've no idea what time Richard got home last night then?"

"No. But it was probably well after midnight." She looked vexed. "It usually is."

"Does Richard have a job?"

"Yes." She looked down at the table. "He's working for a building firm on a site in Sandleton. They're converting the old vicarage in Church Lane into flats." She looked up again. Bitterness and disappointment showed in her eyes. "Not a very prestigious occupation, I admit, but he's better off doing that than being unemployed, as so many youngsters are."

There was a solemn, unforgiving cast to Mrs Dangerfield's countenance. Nothing comes easily, her expression said. Life's a struggle and you mustn't give in. Forward suspected she was the sort of teacher who shouted at you when you got your sums wrong, and made you write things out at playtime again and again. He was glad he hadn't been in her class.

"How old is Richard?" Forward asked.

"Twenty-five. With all his intelligence I'd hoped he'd be doing something better than working on a building site. He's been quite a disappointment to me."

"What time does he usually finish work?"

"Around six. Unless he's asked to do overtime." She regarded Forward apprehensively. "Are you going to see him?"

"As his whereabouts last night are uncertain, we'll have to. You'd better give me your address in case we don't catch up with him at the building site."

Mrs Dangerfield dictated her address and Forward wrote it down in his notebook.

"Just one more thing," said Forward. "Did you ever hear your son speak of Filey or Monks Bay for any reason?"

She immediately looked wary. "Monks Bay. That's where they found Mr Coulson wasn't it?"

"Yes."

"I've never heard Richard mention it. And he hasn't been to Filey since he was a little boy and I used to take him on the sand."

"What about Mr Coulson? Do you know if he was connected in some way with either of those two places?"

"I'm afraid I don't."

Forward left Mrs Dangerfield and returned to Coulson's classroom. Haynes was still in there, pinning up some children's work onto one of the many display boards.

"Can I use your phone?" asked Forward.

"Sure. It's in the office."

Forward dialled the number of the incident centre at Monkhouses. DC Griffiths answered. He gave her the address of the building site Richard Dangerfield was working on and told her to go round there right away and establish what Dangerfield's whereabouts were on Monday night, and whether or not they could be verified.

Griffiths started to tell Forward about the results of the house-to-house, but he cut her short. "Fill me in on it when I get back to Monkhouses."

The frosty silence at the other end made him immediately regret what he'd said. Griffiths was very sensitive to any implication that her contribution wasn't appreciated.

"I'm at Melthorpe School, and rather busy at the moment," he said as justification. "By the way, it turns out that Coulson was previously married and has a family living in York." Forward took out his notebook, opened it and read out the address of Coulson's ex-wife. "Can you ask one of your friends in York CID to get round there and find out what she and her two kids were doing last night?"

Griffiths' tone was almost impudent. "Do you want me to do that before or after I speak to Dangerfield?"

"After Dangerfield. He's the priority."

Forward spent the next half an hour searching Coulson's classroom. He went through the drawers of Coulson's desk and all his box files but found nothing of any significance. When he'd finished, he sat down heavily behind the teacher's desk, looking somewhat defeated.

"Any luck?" Haynes asked, walking towards him.

Forward shook his head. "Only what you'd expect to find in a teacher's classroom." He stopped and stared at a cupboard that was set in one of the walls of the room. "What's in there?"

"School stock, that's all. Exercise books, pencils, that sort of thing. I'd let you have a look inside but it's locked. Mr Coulson had the only key, apparently, and it's vanished. It's a damn nuisance. The school's involved in a concert up at Melthorpe Hall next week, and all the props and costumes are in that cupboard. Fortunately, there's ample amounts of school stock lying around in the classrooms. I've informed the council that we need the lock changing, but you know how fast they work."

"If Mr Coulson had all the keys, how did you manage to open the school today?" asked Forward.

"No problem. The schoolkeeper has a door key."

Forward spent several minutes probing to see if Haynes had any useful information about Coulson, particularly his connection to Filey and Monks Bay. But it soon became clear that Haynes knew Coulson only in a professional capacity.

Forward stood up. "Thanks for all your help, Mr Haynes. I'll be in touch if there's anything else."

"Will you want to have a look in the stock cupboard when I manage to get it open?"

"No, I don't think so," said Forward. "I've seen all I need to."

As he left the school and approached his car, Forward caught sight of Mrs Coulson. She was staring at him out of the kitchen window of the schoolhouse. Her eyes met his, and she smiled wanly and gave him a pathetic little wave. Forward returned the wave and then got into his car. He looked at his watch. It showed four fifteen and the press conference had been called for five. He would have to go straight to Monkhouses. On the drive over, he tried to make sense of all the confusing information he'd gathered so far. By the time he'd parked outside Monkhouses village hall, he could feel his mind rebelling at the strain he was inflicting on it.

CHAPTER NINE

The Monkhouses village hall was packed with people waiting for the press conference. Television and radio reporters were there; so too were reporters and photographers from the regional and local press. Every CID officer from Sandleton had also turned up.

Hoggart was talking to a well-known, local TV reporter. Forward went over and, drawing Hoggart aside, asked if the search of the beach and cliffs had produced any results.

"Nothing significant," said Hoggart. "But we haven't covered half the ground yet." His look became questioning. "Have you had any success over at Melthorpe?"

Forward provided a quick account of what he'd discovered.

"Coulson was obviously up to no good," said Hoggart. "Otherwise he wouldn't have made up that story about having to take his wife out to dinner. But where does this Dangerfield lad fit in?"

"I may be able to tell you in a minute," said Forward, noticing that DC Griffiths had just walked into the incident centre. He immediately waved her over.

"Well, did you get anything?" he asked.

"I certainly did. A load of sexual harassment from all those horny labourers!"

Hoggart looked stern. "You should have taken another officer with you."

Griffiths gave Hoggart a look that could have melted glass. "A male officer, you mean? Why? They soon changed their tune when I showed them my warrant card."

"Excuse me," said Hoggart sullenly, and went back to talk to the TV reporter. Bemused, Forward watched him go and then turned his attention back to Griffiths.

"Did you speak to Richard Dangerfield?"

"Yes. He said he was at the *Drovers Inn* in Luffield from eight until ten on Monday night. After that he went for a Chinese meal at the *New Friends*. He returned home to his mother's place in Melthorpe some time after midnight."

"Was he drinking alone or in company?"

"Alone. But he says he can produce witnesses to confirm he was in the pub until ten."

"Anything else?"

"No, that's all there is. But he was adamant he had nothing to do with Coulson's death."

"Right. We'll check out his alibi, but it sounds as though Mr Dangerfield's a blind alley. He's got no pre-cons, I've checked." He glanced at her quickly. "What about your house-to-house?"

Griffiths consulted her notebook. "Several people saw Coulson's Vauxhall Astra at various times in the car park last night. The earliest sighting was made at six forty-five p.m. That was by a Mr Fergusson. He was out walking his dog."

Forward laughed. "Is that all they do in Monkhouses?"

Griffiths grinned.

"Don't tell me," Forward went on, "the dog was a Jack Russell?"

"Actually, sir, it was a Labrador."

Forward's tone became serious. "Six forty-five. I hadn't expected the Astra to be there that early. Did this chap Fergusson see anyone in the car?"

"No. In fact, no-one reported seeing anyone in or near the car."

"That's strange," said Forward.

The tall, thick set figure of Sergeant Wilmott entered the hall, grimacing at the din and the crush. He saw Forward and made a bee line for him.

"It's like a bear garden in here," complained Wilmott.

"Never mind that," said Forward. "What have you found out about that ticket?"

Wilmott sat down wearily on one of the desks. He brought out his notebook. "The ticket was issued to Coulson yesterday at around seven fifteen. It was actually issued on the train from Sandleton to Filey."

"On the train?"

"Yes."

"At seven fifteen in the evening?"

"That's right. The booking office at Sandleton closes at six thirty. After that you have to get your ticket from the conductor-guard on the train. His name is Peter Sygrove. He recognised Coulson from the photograph. He clearly recalls issuing him the ticket. He remembers Coulson because he wasn't a regular commuter."

"That's interesting," said Forward. "Apparently Coulson left the Teachers' Centre in Sandleton at about ten past six, and Diane's established that his Astra was seen in the car park at Monks Bay as early as six forty-five."

Wilmott looked surprised. "That means he must have driven straight to Monks Bay from the Teachers' Centre, and then driven back to Sandleton Station to catch the train to Filey."

"No," said Griffiths. "He didn't drive his own car. He left the Astra in the car park. There were several sightings of it there from six forty-five p.m. onwards."

Now Wilmott looked perplexed. "Then how did he get back to Sandleton? It certainly wasn't by cab. I've checked out all the taxi firms in the area and none of them had any fares to or from Monks Bay last night."

"Someone must have given him a lift."

"Someone must have. I spoke to the taxi drivers who hang around Sandleton Station waiting for a fare. One of them is convinced he saw Coulson going into the station at around seven yesterday evening."

"Which fits with him being on the train to Filey at seven fifteen," said Forward. "What about the taxi drivers at Filey? Did any of them recall seeing Coulson?"

"No. No-one at Filey Station saw him get off the train."

"So why did he go to Filey?" mused Griffiths. "And how then did he get back from Filey to Monks Bay? Did he get a train back to Sandleton and then get a lift out here?"

Wilmott shook his head. "Coulson certainly didn't come back from Filey by train. Sygrove, the guard, is sure he never came back on his train. The last one left Filey for Sandleton at eleven thirty-two, and Sygrove was still on shift then."

"Surely there were other trains?" said Griffiths. "Coulson might have come back to Sandleton on one of them."

"No. Only two trains operate that service. Much of it is single track. I've interviewed the other conductor-guard and he's certain Coulson never travelled on his train last night. He must have come back from Filey some other way." Wilmott closed his notebook. "That's all

I've got for you."

"All right, good work," said Forward. He noticed Griffiths' face begin to sour. "Both of you," he added hastily.

At that moment Hoggart came back over. He looked even more peevish than usual. "Isn't it about time we got this press conference over with?" he demanded.

Forward's response was quietly barbed. "Yes. I think I'm ready to begin now."

Amidst a barrage of photographers' flashlights, Forward took up his position in front of the large map of the East Yorkshire coastline. He welcomed the press and media and expressed his deepest sympathy for Mark Coulson's family. He then described the circumstances in which the Headteacher had died. He appealed to anyone who had been in the area of Monks Bay the previous day and had seen Coulson's blue Astra, or anything at all out of the ordinary, to come forward. Photographs of the dead man were made available, and the Chief Inspector informed the journalists that Coulson had almost certainly been on the seven ten p.m. train from Sandleton to Filey, and had been in Filey itself for a period of time, on Monday night. He appealed to anyone who had seen Coulson there to contact the police.

Forward concluded his remarks and invited questions. Immediately, he was besieged by another fusillade of flashes, and a deafening wall of noise as all the press and media people leapt to their feet and shouted questions at him.

Forward raised his hands and called for quiet. "I'm taking one question at a time or none at all!"

The mob fell silent and resumed their seats. Forward pointed to Jack Miller, crime reporter for the *Sandleton Times*. "OK Jack. You first. What's your question?"

Jack stood up and said, with a wry smile, "What was a respectable headmaster doing out at Monks Bay so late at night? Was he up to no good?"

There was a low murmur of assent from the crowd.

"We're still trying to establish Mr Coulson's reasons for travelling to Monks Bay," said Forward. He indicated a red-haired woman who was sitting at the back. She was the TV reporter who'd been speaking to Hoggart. "Right, I'll take the next question from Monica."

The questioning continued for a further twenty minutes. Each question was in essence the same and implied that Coulson had gone to Monks Bay for indecent sexual purposes. The most crudely suggestive of these questions came from those reporters who were stringers for the London based tabloids. Forward neatly side-stepped them all.

The press conference ended, and in response

to requests from local television news teams, Forward left the incident room and went to the Monks Bay car park. There, with the North Sea behind him, and in the presence of white suited officers conducting a fingertip search, he was interviewed on camera.

When the television crews had finished, Hoggart and Wilmott came over to him.

"Congratulations, sir," said Wilmott. "I thought you handled that very well."

Forward, who was a vain man, was deeply gratified. "Thank you, Wilmott."

"Yes. Well done," muttered Hoggart, unconvincingly.

CHAPTER TEN

Forward left the incident centre and drove back to his sea-front home in Sandleton. He fed the cat, and, after much deliberation, changed into a pair of brown corduroy trousers, a green and white checked shirt and a stylish brown leather jacket. When he was officially on duty, Forward's choice of clothes presented no problem to him: he invariably wore a dark suit and a collar and tie. However, choosing the most appropriate off duty clothes always presented him with a dilemma: he had a terror of looking like mutton dressed as lamb.

He inspected himself in the bedroom mirror and was not too displeased with the image that confronted him. True, he had a slight paunch and his dark brown hair was greying progressively at the temples, but his general appearance was still quite vigorous. Satisfied, he went and prepared himself a quick cheese sandwich and a cup of tea.

When he arrived at the High School, he found the whole cast waiting for him in the hall: some were already in costume and make-up. Many of them seemed to be staring at him rather more intently than usual. It was as though he'd suddenly become an object of curiosity or fascination. Coulson's murder had received extensive coverage in the media. Was that the reason?

"I'm surprised to see you here this evening, darling," said Irene Babcock, "with all you've got on your plate."

Forward laughed. "And miss so many great performances? Not a chance."

Several people asked him about the progress of the investigation. He lightly deflected them. "Please, no more questions. I'm off duty," he pleaded. "Now, did you manage to finish the dress, after I left last night?"

"No," said Fred Bright. "Jobsworth wouldn't let us."

Forward gazed at the stage which was set for the opening of the play and considered whether to run the final part of Act Four or trust that it would be all right in performance. His experience told him that nothing in the theatre should be left to chance. He turned to Alice Sims, their stage manager, a bespectacled woman in her thirties, whose day job was teaching business studies at Sandleton High.

"Set up for Act Four please, Alice."

Alice frowned, and went off to organise the stage crew.

Forward stood up and addressed the cast.

"We'll start Act Four where we left it last night. Ranyevskaya's final entrance. There's no need to get into Act Four costume. We'll just run it as you are."

The hall and stage suddenly became full of purposeful activity. The stage crew moved furniture; actors went to take up their positions; and the stage lighting colours were changed to create the plangent, evanescent atmosphere appropriate to the latter part of Act Four.

Forward was glad he'd decided to run through to the end of the Act because a number of problems with entrances and exits were revealed that needed his attention. When these had been resolved, he spent some time rehearsing the curtain call. Afterwards, he brought the whole cast together, produced his director's notebook and gave individual notes on the previous night's dress rehearsal. When 'notes' were finished he said, "Remember, very few people in the audience will have seen the play before, so they won't know what to expect. If things go wrong in performance most of them won't even notice."

Then telling all the cast to 'break a leg' he sent them off to prepare for the performance.

Curtain Up wasn't until seven thirty, and when the cast had departed to their dressing rooms Forward felt rather at a loose end. Not for the first time he reflected on the curious role of the theatre director. Whilst the play was being rehearsed the director was the focal point and intimately connected with every aspect of the production. But once the play was ready to put before the paying public, the director became oddly superfluous. The fate of the play was entirely in the hands of the actors and the stage management. That was why, at that moment, Forward would have preferred to have been one of the actors. He hated being in a position where he was powerless to affect events.

One by one, those members of the Players who weren't directly involved in the production but who'd agreed to serve refreshments and do 'Front of House' duties began to arrive. They didn't appear to need Forward's assistance, so he decided to go back-stage and have a chat with the stage manager and her crew to satisfy himself that everything was in order. However, in their opinion, his decision to run through the end of Act Four, when everything was in place for Curtain Up, had given them unnecessary last-minute work. They were now busily engaged in re-setting the stage for Act One. Although they listened to Forward politely, it was obvious by their determined absorption in their specific tasks that they were greatly miffed with him, and considered him to be very much in the way.

Forward toyed with the idea of going along

to the men's dressing room but decided against it. The actors would be full of nerves, just as he was, and having the director around at such a time would only unnerve them more.

He went and sat on one of the seats in the auditorium, and tried to detach himself from the contending feelings of grave apprehension and delicious anticipation that everyone in the theatre experiences on First Nights. He reflected on past First Nights he'd been involved in: first as a starry-eyed young amateur in his native Hertfordshire; then as a rather more sophisticated drama student at The Central School of Speech and Drama in London; and, of course, there'd been all his First Nights as a professional in repertory at towns not unlike Sandleton-on-Sea. Faces he hadn't recalled for years appeared before him in rapid succession. What happened to them all? Some, he knew, were 'names' now. One or two were international stars. But what had happened to all those others? Had any become police officers, like himself? He doubted it. Surely, they'd have had more sense? The thought made him smile. Yes, it was strange how things turned out. But he wouldn't have changed any of it. He loved being a detective.

His thoughts became preoccupied with the perplexities and contradictions of the Coulson case. Why had a respectable, professional man left a meeting in Sandleton and driven to a remote bay on the coast, when he should have gone home to look after his kids while his wife went out for the evening? Why had he left his car parked at Monks Bay, and then gone back to Sandleton and taken a train on to Filey? And why had he returned from Filey to Monks Bay? What motivation could explain such a bizarre, unexpected and seemingly unnecessary journey? It simply didn't make sense. Yet his experience had taught him that as far as murder was concerned, people often didn't behave logically. That's why it was so important in such cases to eschew logic, and consider the most unobvious forms of cause and effect, including randomness and coincidence.

During these reflections, which resolved nothing, the audience had been steadily entering the hall and taking their seats. It was now more than half full, and he knew that the combined noise of the sociable and expectant chatter would be feeding the butterflies of all the actors listening back-stage.

Forward felt a hand placed on his shoulder from behind. He turned in his seat and found himself looking at Wilmott and his wife, Marjorie. They were both grinning broadly.

"Hello Tony," said Marjorie. "Feeling nervous?"

Forward stood up. "Terrified. I'd sooner be doing night duty in the Met."

"Your TV interview went well."

Wilmott regarded his wife with mock disapproval. "I thought you said we mustn't talk shop tonight."

Marjorie grinned at him. "This isn't shop. I'm talking to a celebrity." She returned her gaze to Forward. "Did you see it?"

"No. I hadn't time."

"It came on about twenty to seven."

"She insisted on watching it," said Wilmott. "It nearly made us late."

Forward chatted to Wilmott and Marjorie for a few more minutes, and then went back-stage to check that everything was ready. Here, he found the usual atmosphere of suppressed hysteria that is always a feature of First Nights; but the anxiety was particularly intense in this case because the actors were amateurs and appeared infrequently before the public.

Satisfied that everything was in order, Forward returned to the auditorium. There were very few empty seats left, yet even now people were still buying tickets. With any luck it would be a full house. Forward took his usual seat at the back of the hall. He always sat at the back during performances of his own productions to keep a check on the actors' projection. Individuals who couldn't be heard were given a sharp note about it at the interval.

Dead on half past seven, the house lights dimmed. The curtains swished back and, simultaneously, the stage lights illuminated the set for the First Act: a room in Madame Ranyevskaya's house which had once been the nursery. It was the early hours of the morning. A door opened stage right and Dunyasha, the maid, entered carrying a candle. She was followed by Lopakhin, holding a book in his hand. Fred Bright spoke Lopakhin's first line confidently, without a trace of nervousness. Then Dunyasha made her reply. Both of them could be heard perfectly. Forward heaved a sigh of relief.

****

First night nerves had given the actors laser-like concentration. This raised the whole level of the play's performance, and Acts One and Two were exceptionally well received by the audience. At the interval, Forward went back-stage to tell everyone how well they were doing and to generally give the cast encouragement. Then he went and joined Wilmott and Marjorie in the refreshment area, which during the daytime was where the pupils of Sandleton High School consumed their school dinners. As he entered, he noticed several people were nudging each other and nodding in his direction. Was it because they were aware he was the show's director or had they seen the interview he'd given to the local TV stations?

"How do you think it's going?" asked

Wilmott.

"I'm quite pleased with it so far," said Forward. He sipped his orange juice and wished something stronger was available.

"It's brilliant," said Marjorie.

Forward was pleased but embarrassed. "Now, you're just saying that."

"You know me better than that."

"I'm finding it a bit difficult to follow," said Wilmott. "It's all those Russian names."

A buzzer went to indicate the end of the interval. Forward began to follow Wilmott and Marjorie into the hall, and immediately felt a touch on his arm.

"Inspector Forward. I wonder if I might have a word."

He turned and found himself facing a woman in early middle-age. She had greying, neatly coiffured hair and was wearing a well-tailored Prince of Wales check suit.

"My name's Dorothy Newbiggin," she said. "I'm sorry to bother you right now, but I saw you on television this evening being interviewed about that poor man's murder. I think I might be able to help you."

They were blocking the entrance to the hall. Forward drew the woman to one side.

"How exactly?"

"On the television you asked for information, no matter how trivial it might seem. I don't know if this will be of any help

159

to you, but yesterday I visited my aunt at Monkhouses. She's bedridden, poor soul, and I always go over on Monday evenings to keep her company."

"Go on," said Forward, his attention riveted.

"Her house is at the end of the village. It's the last one before the car park. As I say, I don't know if this is of any importance, but yesterday evening a car drew up outside the house. I was downstairs in the living room at the time doing a little dusting. At first, I thought my aunt had some visitors, so I went to the window. But the driver didn't get out of the car. He stayed there, staring through the windscreen. Normally, I wouldn't have taken much notice, I'm not the nosey sort, but it seemed strange for him to sit there staring like that. I thought he was looking at the sea, but now I come to think about it he might not have been looking out to sea at all. I think he might have been watching something in the car park, you know, the one on the cliffs."

"You say this happened in the evening?" said Forward. "What time?"

"About half past six."

"Do you remember what the man in the car looked like?"

"He was young. In his twenties or early thirties, I suppose." Her eyes rolled upwards as she tried to recall his image. "He had dark hair and a moustache. Oh, and he was wearing a black, leather jacket."

"Would you recognise him again?"

She pondered for a moment. "I'm not sure. I think so."

"I don't suppose you recognised the make of car?"

"Yes. It was a Sierra. A red Ford Sierra."

Forward was staggered. In his experience ladies of a certain age rarely recognised makes of cars. "You're certain of that?"

"Oh yes. Normally I can't tell one car from another but I knew this was a Sierra because my brother has one, you see." She added lamely, "I didn't get the car's number, I'm afraid."

"No reason why you should," said Forward. "And how long did the man stay there?"

"About ten minutes. A car came out of the car park and the man in the Sierra turned around and went after it."

"He followed it?"

"That's what it seemed like he was doing."

"Can you remember anything about the car that left the car park? It's make or colour, for instance?"

"No, I'm afraid I can't." Her expression was abject. "It was going so fast you see. It took me by surprise."

"So, you didn't get a look at the driver?"

"I'm afraid not."

"Can you remember if it was a man or a woman?"

"No, I couldn't say."

"Was there more than one person in the car?"

"As I said, I simply have no idea. It went by so fast." Now, she began to get vexed. "I'm sorry. I don't think I've been any great help. I didn't want to waste your time, but I thought you ought to know."

Forward saw that she needed reassuring. "On the contrary, every scrap of information is useful. If you give me your address and telephone number, I'll arrange for you to make a photofit or an artist's impression of the man you saw."

Dorothy Newbiggin opened her handbag and produced a small, white card. "This is my business address as well as my home address, Inspector."

Printed in exquisite, silver copperplate on the card were the words. "Miss Dorothy Newbiggin, High Class Fashions, 18, The Strand, Sandleton-on-Sea, East Yorkshire." This was followed by a telephone number.

Miss Newbiggin handed Forward the card and beamed. "*The Cherry Orchard* is my favourite play, you know. I've seen seventeen productions of it, professional and amateur."

Forward was impressed and told Miss Newbiggin so, adding, "I hope you're enjoying this one."

"I certainly am. They're making a very fair stab at it."

Forward escorted Miss Newbiggin into the hall. They were just in time to catch the beginning of the Third Act. He sat down and took out a small notebook and a pencil. There was enough light spilling off the stage for him to make essential notes for the cast. So far, he hadn't needed to write any. The production had flowed without a hitch. After a seamless start to the Third Act, he put the notebook away, settled back, and like the rest of the audience, simply enjoyed himself.

CHAPTER ELEVEN

"We've had a bit of luck," announced DC Griffiths.

It was nine thirty the following morning. Forward and Wilmott were discussing the Coulson case in the Chief Inspector's office at Sandleton when Griffiths burst in on them.

"Oh?" Forward looked up suddenly. At once he raised a hand to massage away the needle-sharp pain in his right temple, the consequence of a whisky too far at the First Night celebration in *The Maypole*.

"A boy and a girl, both sixteen, came into the incident centre at eight o'clock this morning," Griffiths gabbled excitedly. "They said they'd seen two cars in the Monks Bay car park around ten fifteen on the night Coulson was murdered.

"Two cars?" queried Wilmott.

"That's what they said!"

"Why didn't they report this sooner?" asked Forward.

She smiled. "Because they were too

frightened to let on they were out together. The girl's parents can't stand her boyfriend. They warned her never to see him again. But her parents went out on Monday night, so the two youngsters arranged to go for a walk on the cliffs. That's how they came to be passing through the car park at ten fifteen."

Wilmott said, "Obviously one of the cars they saw was Coulson's Astra. But what about the other one, did they get the make of it?"

Griffiths shook her head. "All they could remember was seeing two cars. They couldn't recall anything about them."

"Too busy staring into each other's eyes, I suppose" said Forward. "I don't suppose they saw anyone around?"

"Not a soul."

"That's good information though," said Wilmott. "At least we can be certain now how Coulson got from Filey to Monks Bay."

Forward looked dubious. "Just because Romeo and Juliet saw another car there's no reason to assume it was the one that brought Coulson there from Filey."

"I'd say it's almost certain." Wilmott's expression was obdurate.

"All right, what are you saying? That Coulson met someone in Filey who gave him a lift back to Monks Bay?"

"That's right."

"And murdered him?"

"Presumably."

"But why did Coulson take the train to Filey in the first place? He had his own car. Why didn't he drive there? Instead, he left his car in the car park at Monks Bay. Doesn't that strike you as exceedingly odd?"

"Perhaps he was a railway enthusiast," Griffiths said.

"If he was, I think his wife would have mentioned it," said Forward.

Griffiths looked at him incredulously. "I'm being ironic."

"Ah," said Forward, feeling slightly foolish. "Anyway, I'm sure Coulson left his car in the car park for a reason."

"Like what?" said Wilmott.

Forward sighed and stroked his forehead. "I don't know. So, let's approach the problem inductively from the facts we've been given. First, we know that Coulson left the meeting at Sandleton Teachers' Centre around ten past six. He told his colleagues he wasn't going for a drink with them because he had to take his wife out to dinner. However, Mrs Coulson says she knew nothing about this. On the contrary, she expected him home sometime around seven o'clock. What does that suggest?"

"He was meeting someone and didn't want anyone to know about it," said Griffiths.

"Quite," said Forward, "including his wife."

"He could have intended the meal as a

surprise for her," said Wilmott.

"No way," said Griffiths. "He knew she was cooking the evening meal. Women don't like those sort of surprises just when they've organised dinner."

"I wouldn't object," said Wilmott.

"You're not a woman!"

"No, I think Griffiths is right," said Forward. "Anyway, Mrs Coulson said her husband didn't like surprises because they upset his routine. All of which suggests that whoever it was he was meeting, he didn't expect to be out for very long. He obviously felt sure he'd get home at seven or soon after."

"So why go to Filey?" asked Wilmott.

"Hang on," said Forward, raising his hand. "We're jumping the gun. Let's first establish Coulson's movements from the time he left the Teachers' Centre at Sandleton. According to the Headmaster of Danewold Primary School, Coulson left the Centre at six ten p.m. Let's assume he drove straight from Sandleton to Monks Bay. How long would that have taken him?"

"It would depend on the traffic in Sandleton but I'd say twenty minutes at the most," said Wilmott.

"That puts him in the Monks Bay car park at around six thirty p.m."

"Yes."

"So, between six thirty and six forty-five p.m.

Coulson left his car in the Monks Bay car park and set off back to Sandleton. We can verify that because the earliest sighting of Coulson's Astra in the car park was made by a man called Fergusson who saw it at six forty-five, and Coulson was nowhere around. Now, Sandleton is about four miles from Monks Bay. It's too far to walk back from there to Sandleton. There's no bus service and we've established Coulson didn't take a cab. So, I'm certain Coulson was met by someone at the car park and that 'someone' drove him back to Sandleton and dropped him at the railway station."

Griffiths seemed unconvinced. "How can you be so sure?"

"Because of the information I received last night from a woman who came to see my show." Forward then revealed what Dorothy Newbiggin had told him. Both Wilmott and Griffiths received this in astonished silence. "So, you see," Forward concluded, "it looks as though Coulson was definitely driven back to Sandleton by someone, and the man in the red Sierra followed them."

"But why?" asked Griffiths.

"Let's not pursue that very interesting line of speculation at the moment. Instead, let's concentrate on establishing Coulson's exact movements on Monday night, as far as we can. Now what time's the next confirmed sighting we have of him?"

"Seven p.m. when he was seen by a taxi driver going into Sandleton Station," said Wilmott.

"Yes. And at seven fifteen a ticket was issued to Coulson by a conductor-guard on the Filey train. The train arrived in Filey at … what time Wilmott?"

"Seven twenty-two, sir. The guard said it was dead on time."

"The next time Coulson is seen is by Horace Sissons at Monks Bay around eleven p.m., and he's very, very dead. That leaves over three of his final hours unaccounted for. If most of those hours were spent in Filey, someone must have seen him. There are very few holidaymakers there at this time of year so he will have stood out, particularly as he was wearing a yellow anorak."

"We've already got McIntyre checking out the Filey pubs," said Griffiths.

"Good," said Forward. "And when he's finished with the pubs get him to check the hotels and guest houses. Maybe Coulson met someone in Filey who was staying there overnight."

The telephone rang. Forward lunged towards it. The acute throbbing in his temples instantly caused him to regret the sudden movement.

"Forward," he said, uncharacteristically softly.

"Good morning, Chief Inspector."

Forward immediately recognised the sonorous tones of the Chief Forensic Pathologist.

"Good morning, Sir Andrew."

"I've discovered something about Coulson I think will rather interest you. Would you like to hear it?"

Forward sat back in his chair. "Yes please."

"The contents of Coulson's stomach contained a partially digested meal of fish and chips. He ate them sometime around eight or nine o'clock on Monday night, I'd say."

"That's helpful."

"I thought it would be."

"Right. Thank you. Is that it?"

"More or less. Toxicology reports have so far been negative, so no sign of drugs. Only what you'd expect to find in the bloodstream of a clean-living headmaster. If the rest of the results reveal anything unexpected, I'll let you know."

"Good."

Marston then enquired how the first performance of *The Cherry Orchard* had been received.

"Very well," said Forward.

"Good. I'll have to try and get to one of the performances."

"I'm honoured."

"Guess what?" said Forward, replacing the

receiver. "Marston's been rummaging around in Coulson's stomach. Apparently, he ate fish and chips a couple of hours before he died." His gaze rested on Griffiths. "You'll need to check out all the fish and chip shops and restaurants in Filey that were open on Monday night. Ask if anyone recalls Coulson eating on their premises. Was he alone or was someone with him? And, most importantly, was he wearing a yellow anorak?"

"Why's that so important?" asked Griffiths.

"Because Mrs Coulson says her husband didn't own a yellow anorak." He turned to Wilmott. "Was he wearing the anorak when he was seen by the taxi driver? Or the train guard?"

"No, they both said he was just in a suit."

"Then he wasn't wearing the anorak when he got to Filey. It was pelting down with rain there on Monday night, so someone must have lent it to him. The question is, did they lend it to him before or after he ate the fish and chips?"

Griffiths said, "I'm sorry. You'll think me awfully thick but I don't see the significance of that."

"It provides us with an extra detail that can help us determine his movements with more precision."

"Oh, I see. You mean if he wasn't wearing the anorak when he was eating the fish and chips, then he might have picked it up afterwards from someone's home?"

"Exactly." Forward was glad to discover that the pain in his head had eased. The two paracetamol he'd swallowed an hour before were at last having an effect. "Now before we finish, I'd like you to share with me your speculations on any aspect of the inquiries so far. Feel free to say anything, no matter how absurd or illogical it might seem."

For several seconds neither Wilmott nor Griffiths spoke.

Forward knew he'd have to encourage them. "For example, the young man Miss Newbiggin saw in the red Sierra. Any thoughts about him?"

"He was probably following Coulson," Wilmott suggested tentatively.

"Or perhaps he was following the person who met Coulson in the car park. The one who took him to the station," said Griffiths.

"But why was the man in the Sierra following them?" asked Forward.

"If Coulson was having a bit on the side, the lad in the Sierra could have been her husband," said Wilmott.

Griffiths became suddenly animated. "Try this one for size. Coulson has a mistress who he arranges to see at Monks Bay after his meeting in Sandleton. The mistress has a husband or lover. He gets suspicious and follows her. He parks at the end of Monkhouses' main street so he can get a good view of what she's up to in the car park. Coulson is already waiting for her. He leaves his car and gets into hers."

"Why?" asked Forward.

Forward's opaqueness astounded Griffiths. "So they can go wherever they usually go for a quick one, of course!"

Again, Forward felt foolish. "Go on," he said.

"On the way they realise the husband is following them. So, they panic and drive into Sandleton. She drops Coulson at the station. He jumps on the first train that comes in, and goes off to Filey to save his skin."

"She might even have arranged to pick Coulson up later from Filey," suggested Wilmott.

"It would account for Coulson's inexplicable behaviour, and the single ticket to Filey in his back pocket," said Griffiths, convinced now by her own logic. "You said yourself that Coulson intended only to be away for an hour or so because his meal was waiting for him back home. Unfortunately, things didn't go according to plan and he suddenly finds himself killing time in Filey."

"But why did Coulson have to wait for a lift back to Sandleton?" asked Forward. "Why didn't he just get the next train back? Then he could have got a cab from the station to Monks Bay and picked his car up!"

"Maybe he did do that," said Griffiths, determined not to be put off.

"No," said Wilmott. "He definitely didn't come back to Sandleton by train that night, I've checked. And no taxi firm took anyone near Monks Bay either."

Griffiths' mouth formed into a moué. "Maybe he didn't come back to Monks Bay right away because he was afraid his mistress' husband would be waiting for him in the car park."

"Now, you've definitely got a good point there," said Forward. "The mysterious man in the red Sierra, whoever he was, would have known that Coulson had to come back to Monks Bay to collect his car at some point."

"All he'd have to do was wait in the car park for him," said Wilmott. "And Romeo and Juliet did say they saw two cars in the car park around ten fifteen."

Griffiths looked irritated. "Don't call them Romeo and Juliet," she snapped.

"Why not?" asked Wilmott.

"It just sounds patronising."

"I believe I coined the expression originally," said Forward.

"No, originally Shakespeare did," said Griffiths.

Forward laughed. "So, you're suggesting that when Coulson went to collect his car he was surprised by his mistress' husband or boyfriend, who attacked and murdered him?"

"That's right," said Griffiths.

"Then why wasn't Coulson killed in the car

park?" asked Forward. "How did he end up down in the bay?"

Wilmott and Griffiths were silent.

"And why were virtually all his pockets emptied?"

"To make it look as though the motive was theft," said Wilmott.

"All right. Why hasn't this alleged mistress of Coulson's approached us?"

"That's obvious," said Griffiths. "She's protecting the killer because he's her boyfriend or husband."

"It sounds a bit improbable to me," said Forward. "You see, I asked Mrs Coulson if her husband had a mistress. She was convinced he hadn't."

"The wife's often the last to know," said Griffiths.

Forward gave her a long, hard stare. "So's the husband."

Wilmott looked embarrassed, then quickly said, "You told me Mrs Coulson's sister was convinced Coulson went to Monks Bay to meet a woman."

"That's right. But unfortunately, Miss Newbiggin didn't see who was in the car that was followed by the red Sierra. And if it wasn't a woman in the car with Coulson..."

"My theory collapses," said Griffiths.

"Yes," said Forward. "However, we'd be a lot nearer to substantiating it if those youngsters identified one of the cars they saw around ten fifteen as a Sierra. That would suggest the man Miss Newbiggin saw watching the car park was the same man who was there at the time Coulson died. And that would make him a murder suspect." He looked at Griffiths. "I want you to get those two kids in again and show them pictures of every make of car on the road, especially Ford Sierras. Something might jog their memories."

Forward stood up and started putting on his jacket. Glancing at Wilmott, he said, "Apparently the Education Department at County Hall has a list of everyone who was at the meeting in the Teachers' Centre. Ask them to fax a copy of it over. We'll have to interview everyone on it."

"Right."

"Our only other line of enquiry at this stage is Richard Dangerfield, the teacher's son. But apparently he has an alibi."

"I think it stands up," said Griffiths. "He's got plenty of witnesses."

"We'll check it out anyway."

"Do you want me to do that?" asked Wilmott.

"We'll do it together," said Forward. "Investigating pub alibis can be a rather pleasant activity."

CHAPTER TWELVE

St John's vicarage was in that part of Sandleton known locally as 'The Old Village'. Here, overlooking Church Green, stood the few houses that remained from the period when Sandleton was just another unremarkable fishing village on the Yorkshire coast. All that had changed in the early nineteenth century when the railway lines advanced beyond Hull and York and pincered the village between them. Within a decade, Sandleton had developed into a thriving seaside resort. In the process most of old Sandleton's original houses were demolished, but fortunately the owners of those around the Green had resisted the developers. They had remained unchanged for centuries and had been passed on down the generations. St. John's church, a magnificent example of Norman perpendicular, had endured likewise. It was at the northern end of the Green, and loomed benignly over the timber framed houses and leafy gardens of

Sandleton's only conservation area.

Next to St. John's, down Church Lane, was the vicarage. It was of typical Georgian design and was undistinguished except for an elaborate spider's web fanlight above the front door. The vicarage had been built in 1772, and a succession of clergymen had occupied it until the late nineteen eighties, when St John's Parish had been merged with three other Sandleton parishes and the building had fallen into disuse. A decision was then taken by the diocese to sell it. Unfortunately, it was placed on the market just when the country entered one of its periodic housing slumps, and St John's vicarage remained unsold. However recently, a firm of Leeds property developers with American connections had purchased it with the intention of converting it into flats.

When Forward and Wilmott arrived in Church Lane they were confronted by the usual paraphernalia and signs of activity associated with the building trade. The vicarage was a shell. All the windows and doors had been removed and the exterior was caged in scaffolding. From inside the building came the noise of demolition, which suggested that various connecting walls were being smashed down. Linked sections of plastic tubing, about half a yard in diameter, were attached to the scaffolding for the efficient disposal of the rubble. The bottom end of this tubing was suspended over the gaping mouth of a large metal skip on the ground below.

Forward and Wilmott left the car, passed through a dilapidated wrought iron gate and went up the overgrown path towards the building. In front of the house an elderly, grizzled man in a sleeveless vest was mixing cement with a spade. There were many purple tattoos visible beneath the grey hair on his forearms. On his head was the white, scant ghost of a nineteen fifties 'Teddy Boy' hairstyle.

"Excuse me," said Forward. "I'm looking for Richard Dangerfield. I understand he works here."

The old labourer grinned, revealing a mouthful of nicotine-stained teeth. "Work? Is that what 'e calls it now?"

Forward humoured him with a smile.

"'E's inside," said the man. He plunged his spade into the big mound of cement, where it remained upright. Then he walked towards the building and bawled out, "Richard. The game's up! The father of that girl you've got in the family way's down 'ere!" He chortled and then went back to his spade.

The face of a young man with jet black hair appeared between one of the glassless window frames on the top floor. He looked startled. "You want me?" he said.

"Mr Dangerfield?" demanded Wilmott.

"That's right."

"Police. I'm Sergeant Wilmott. This is Chief Inspector Forward. Can we have a word?"

Dangerfield considered this for a moment, then he said, "Hang on, I'll be right down."

The two policemen stood around waiting.

"Been on this job long?" Forward asked the labourer.

"Aye, about six weeks," the man muttered. He had become very absorbed in his work.

Dangerfield's footsteps echoed inside the gutted house as he pounded down the bare wooden stairs. The pounding stopped suddenly, and a moment later he appeared. Forward observed that he was blinking hard. Was it because he'd emerged suddenly into bright sunshine? Or was there another reason?

Forward pointed to a red Sierra that was parked in Church Lane. "Is that your car, Richard?"

Dangerfield's brown eyes darted a glance at the vehicle, and then came back to rest warily on Forward. "Yes. It is."

"Do you mind if we take a look at it?"

****

"Sergeant Wilmott and I want to clarify certain aspects of the statement you gave to Detective Constable Griffiths, yesterday," said Forward.

Richard Dangerfield shrugged nonchalantly. "OK."

Forward and Wilmott were sitting with Dangerfield in the BMW. Dangerfield was in the front next to Forward and Wilmott was sprawled on the back seat, an open notebook on his lap. Two SOCOs could clearly be seen through the car's side window, scrupulously going over Dangerfield's Sierra. Forward had decided to call them in when he'd noticed Dangerfield's black leather jacket on the back seat.

Forward had been studying Dangerfield's face for some time. He'd already noted the thick, vigorous moustache, the decadently over full mouth, the well-groomed hairstyle and various other features he associated with the preening, narcissistic type known as 'Ladies Man'.

"Before we start, I just want to say one thing," said Dangerfield, who was impressively well spoken. "I didn't murder Mr Coulson. I want to make that clear."

"No-one's suggesting you did," said Forward. "But we need to eliminate you from our enquiries. Our information is that you threatened him in the pub at Melthorpe."

Dangerfield looked aggrieved. "That happened months ago. I apologised to him the next day."

"So your mother told me," said Forward. He consulted Dangerfield's statement. "Now, you say that on Monday night you were at *The*

Drovers Inn in Luffield."

"That's right."

"What time did you arrive there?"

"About eight o'clock."

"So, you didn't go there straight from work?"

"No. I went home first to change and get something to eat. I never drink on an empty stomach."

"What time did you leave work that day? Can you remember?"

"Sometime after six. I can't say exactly."

"And you went straight home?"

"Yes."

"What time did you get there?"

"I don't know. Half past six. Quarter to seven maybe."

"Did you go anywhere on the way home?"

"No."

"You didn't go anywhere near Monks Bay, for example?"

Dangerfield looked exasperated. "I've told you I went straight home!"

"And you arrived there about quarter to seven?"

"Yes."

"Unfortunately, your mother was at a friend's house so she can't confirm that, can she?"

"No."

"Could anyone else confirm you were at home at that time? A neighbour, perhaps?"

"One of the neighbours might have seen my car, I suppose."

"All right," Forward went on, "so you got to the pub in Luffield about eight o'clock and you left about ten?"

"That's right."

"You told DC Griffiths you had witnesses to prove that. Correct?"

"Yes. Dave Sims. He came in just after I arrived. He was sitting at the bar with me all the time I was there."

"Who else?"

"Sandra, the barmaid. I was talking to her on and off all night."

"Now, after you left *The Drovers* at ten you went for a Chinese meal at *The New Friends* in Tumulus Road. Right?"

"Yes."

"Feeling hungry, were you?" asked Wilmott. His tone suggested he hadn't believed a word Dangerfield had said.

Dangerfield twisted round in his seat. He looked at Wilmott hostilely. "Yes!"

"Even though you'd already had your evening meal?"

"I always feel hungry after I've been drinking." A facetious look came over Dangerfield's face. "Anyway, a Chinese helps soak up the beer. You lot wouldn't want me driving over the limit, would you?"

"It's a common misapprehension," said

Forward, "that food reduces your alcohol level. It doesn't. Alcohol remains in the body for hours."

"Well, you learn something every day!"

Dangerfield's impudence greatly irritated Forward. He suppressed the vulgar retort that had instinctively formed in his mind. "Now, what time did you get to the Chinese restaurant?"

"Not long after I left the pub."

"Put a time on it."

"Ten past ten, quarter past ten, something like that."

"And what time did you leave the restaurant?"

"Some time after eleven. Eleven twenty, eleven thirty."

"And the waiters there will remember you, will they?"

"I'm sure they will."

"Why's that?"

"Because I eat there every Monday after the pub. I book a table."

"You go drinking with friends every Monday night, do you?" enquired Wilmott.

"I don't have many friends," said Dangerfield.

"Why's that, Richard?"

"People are a pain in the arse. They always let you down."

"What about girlfriends?" said Forward.

"I don't have a regular one at the moment."

"Playing the field, eh?" said Wilmott.

Dangerfield's look was contemptuous. "It's not a crime, is it?"

Forward said, "I'm sorry, but we're going to have to relieve you of your car for a few days."

Dangerfield looked shocked. "Why?"

"Our forensic department needs to examine it."

Dangerfield raised an arm and pointed through the window at the SOCOs who were dusting his Sierra for fingerprints. "They're doing that now."

"That's just a preliminary check."

"So, I won't be able to drive it home?"

"No, I'm afraid not."

"Great!"

"Don't worry there's a regular bus service to Melthorpe," said Wilmott. "You'll be all right."

"That's about it for now," said Forward. "We'll be in touch with you if necessary."

Dangerfield seemed surprised that the interview had ended.

"Well, what are you waiting for?" asked Forward. "You can go back to work now."

Dangerfield looked relieved. His hand went out to open the car door. Then Forward's voice stopped him.

"Just a moment, Richard. I nearly forgot. Were you wearing your black leather jacket when you left work on Monday evening?"

A faint shadow of anxiety passed over the

young man's handsome features. "Yes. I always wear it. Except when I'm working."

Forward smiled. "Fine. By the way, that'll have to be examined by our forensic department too."

"My jacket?"

"Yes."

For the first time Dangerfield looked completely lost for words.

"You can go now," said Forward. His tone was faintly menacing.

In silence, both policemen watched Dangerfield make his way back up the path to the old vicarage.

Wilmott closed his notebook. "He owns a red Sierra," he said conclusively.

"So do you," said Forward.

"But I'm not a suspect in a murder investigation. Don't you think we should pull him in for an ID check?"

"On what grounds? That he drives a Ford Sierra?"

"He fits the description. He's dark haired, he's got a moustache and he wears a black leather jacket. Miss Newbiggin might recognise him."

"That would only prove he was possibly at Monks Bay around six thirty on Monday evening. No court would convict him on that. Particularly as it seems he's got an alibi for the time of the murder." He turned the key in the ignition. "Come on. Let's check it out. I'm in the mood for a pint."

CHAPTER THIRTEEN

Luffield was a small market town some ten miles inland from Sandleton: to its north rose the steeply undulating hills of the Yorkshire Wolds; to its south lay the vast plain of Holderness and the Humber Estuary. Luffield's geographical position had made it an ideal choice as a centre for trade, particularly wool; and on every Wednesday, for centuries, the hill farmers had brought in wool and livestock to sell at market. In consequence that part of town where trading had occurred became known as 'Wednesday Market'. *The Drovers Inn*, which occupied a prominent position in Wednesday Market, was one of the few reminders that the town had its origins in the wool trade. Until about a year ago it had been Forward's favourite pub in Luffield. Its ancient settles, wooden floors, inglenook fireplace and foaming beer had often provided him with temporary sanctuary from a modern world that daily seemed to grow harsher, and towards which he was less and less sympathetic. He was no Luddite, far from it. It was just that *The Drovers* had always offered him a brief respite from the twentieth century. Alas, no more! A London based hotel chain had acquired the inn and decided it required a certain amount of internal renovation.

Forward pushed open the door to the saloon bar without enthusiasm. He knew what awaited him. The wooden floor was covered now with thick red carpet; the trestle tables and oak settles had been replaced by metal pub furniture; and blazing in the inglenook fireplace was an imitation coal fire with an ersatz flame. A bank of vulgar, light-flashing slot machines which almost completely obscured the seventeenth century oak panelling, completed the desecration of the pub's original ambience. Although these radical alterations to the pub's interior struck Forward as sacrilege, they didn't appear to have affected trade which was its normal level for a market day. Everyone seemed to be quietly enjoying themselves.

Forward strolled over to the bar. Behind it was a young woman with her back turned. She was slicing up lemons. Forward coughed. The woman stopped what she was doing and turned round. She was in her mid to late twenties. She was also outrageously good looking, with long, dark hair and gleaming blue eyes. She smiled at Forward, "Good morning."

"Good morning," said Forward.

"Turned out a bit milder today," she said.

"Much improved," said Forward. By now he was used to these ritual preliminaries concerning the weather and accepted them as a necessary feature of rural Yorkshire life. "Let's hope it keeps like it."

Although the interior had changed beyond all recognition, *The Drovers* had remained a free house - thank God! Forward ordered a pint for himself, and a half for Wilmott, who, at that moment was interviewing Mr Kung, the proprietor of *The New Friends* Chinese restaurant.

Forward sipped his beer. "This place has certainly changed," he said.

The young woman had gone back to cutting up lemons. "Yes. It's a lot nicer now."

Forward decided not to take issue with this, even though he felt strongly inclined to. "Are you Sandra?" he asked.

She spun round surprised. "Yes!"

Forward took out his warrant card from his inside pocket and showed her it. "I'm Detective Chief Inspector Forward of East Yorkshire Police." Seeing the colour had drained from her face, he added quickly, "Don't be alarmed. I only want you to verify something for me."

"What's that?"

"I'm conducting an enquiry and it's my job to eliminate certain people from the investigation. Hopefully you can help me. Do you know a man called Richard Dangerfield?"

She put down the knife she'd been using. "Richard?"

"Good. I see you do know him. Was he in here on Monday night?"

"Monday? Let me see." She thought hard. "Yes, I think so." She seemed to be confirming this to herself. "Yes. Yes, he was."

"What time did he arrive?"

"Sometime just after eight, I think."

"And what time did he leave?"

"Round about ten."

"Was he alone when he left?"

"Yes, as far as I remember."

"Did he make any telephone calls while he was here?"

"No. There's no public phone here."

That's a blessing, thought Forward.

She looked at him anxiously. "What sort of investigation is it? Richard's not in trouble, is he?"

Forward gave her a reassuring smile. "We're just making routine enquiries, that's all." He placed two hands on the bar. "Richard tells me he went for a Chinese meal in *The New Friends* after he left here on Monday night. Did he mention anything about that to you?"

She folded her arms and leaned on the bar.

The movement disconcertingly emphasised the tightness of her white blouse and the ampleness of her breasts. "He says he always goes for a Chinese on Monday nights."

Forward gave a satisfied nod. "Do you know someone called Dave Sims?"

"Dave? Yes. He comes in here most nights." She laughed. "He's part of the furniture, you might say."

"Was he talking to Richard on Monday night?"

"Yes."

"All the time he was here?"

She nodded. "They were both sitting in front of me here at the bar."

"Was Richard in his normal sort of mood?"

"I'd say so. He seemed in good spirits."

"He's normally in good spirits, is he?"

She smiled. "Most people are at their best in a pub, Inspector. They've come out to enjoy themselves."

He decided to try a different tack. "Richard's a very good-looking chap. I expect he's got lots of girlfriends."

"I don't know anything about his private life," she said. "I try not to get too involved with the customers. The pub manager doesn't like it."

Forward thanked Sandra and took the drinks over to a table that was furthest away from the slot machines.

His pint glass was half empty by the time Wilmott returned from the Chinese restaurant. Forward waited until Wilmott had taken a long drink from his half of bitter before he spoke. "Well. What did you get?"

"It seems our friend Dangerfield's not been telling us the complete truth."

"Oh?"

"No. He didn't arrive at the restaurant until at least ten forty-five. Mr Kung's certain of that because Dangerfield's table was occupied by a couple of businessmen who'd got stuck into the wine and were reluctant to leave. Dangerfield had booked the table for ten thirty so Kung was quite glad he didn't appear on time. He didn't manage to get rid of the businessmen until ten forty-five. Dangerfield appeared just as they were leaving."

"Right," said Forward. "We'll get back to him right away and find out what he was doing between ten and ten forty-five."

"If he can't justify where he was then it still leaves him in the frame," said Wilmott. He nodded towards the bar. "Is that the barmaid he mentioned?"

"Yes," said Forward. "She's confirmed he was in here between eight and ten. So I think it's unlikely that Dangerfield is our man."

"No?"

"Of course not. How was he to know the exact time Coulson would turn up at Monks

Bay to collect his car? And even if he did, Monks Bay is fifteen miles from here. We'd have to show how he managed to drive all the way to Monks Bay, kill Coulson and drive back to the restaurant to be in time for his meal."

"It's just possible."

Forward looked at him sceptically.

"But I agree, unlikely."

****

As soon as Forward and Wilmott arrived back at the car a call came in from DC Griffiths.

"I'm on my way back from Filey," she said. "I've found a fish and chip shop owner who's certain he served Coulson on Monday night."

"What time?" Forward asked.

"About eight o'clock. He sat down to a meal of fish and chips in the restaurant at the back of the shop. The owner remembers him because Monday nights at this time of year are usually pretty slack."

"Well done," said Forward. "But that alone doesn't take us very far. It only confirms what Marston told us."

"Yes, but listen to this. There was another man with him!"

"Excellent. Did you get a description?"

"Not a good one, but the chip shop owner has a strong recollection of Coulson though. And here's why. It was a filthy night but Coulson was only wearing a suit."

****

"You're very quiet, sir," said Wilmott.

"I'm doing some lateral thinking," said Forward.

They were driving back to Sandleton. Wilmott was at the wheel.

Unseen by Forward, he rolled his eyes heavenwards. "Ah, yes. That was the thing that was invented by the man with the odd name. Bone? Bonio? Something like that, wasn't it?"

"Edward de Bono. And I'd say he discovered rather than invented it," said Forward pompously.

"Lateral thinking," mused Wilmott. "That's where you think of the most unlikely explanation for something, and it usually turns out to be the correct one."

Forward smiled indulgently. "If by that, you mean looking at familiar situations in a new way, yes. Essentially lateral thinking is a process that eschews conventional logic."

"You've lost me," said Wilmott.

"It's so easy to get locked into a pattern of thinking in this job," said Forward. "We think in the same way as we would climb a ladder: one rung at a time, and then on to the next rung. Dangerfield had a grudge against Coulson: that's one rung. Dangerfield drives a red Sierra: that's another rung. Dangerfield hasn't got a totally tight alibi for the time Coulson died:

that's the next rung. But maybe it isn't really like that at all. Instead of climbing the ladder perhaps we ought to stop, saw it into pieces and place the rungs on the floor."

"Why?"

"Because then we might see a new set of connections. A completely unobvious pattern might emerge that would provide us with different explanations."

"Like what?"

"Explanations involving chance and randomness."

"Coincidence, you mean?"

"Possibly. I don't know. That's why I'm trying to do some lateral thinking. If you'll allow me to."

They drove on to Sandleton in silence.

At St. John's vicarage they were told by the elderly, grey haired labourer that Richard Dangerfield had left the site an hour earlier and hadn't returned.

"It looks like he's bolted," said Forward, as they returned to the car.

"Perhaps he's been doing some lateral thinking too, sir," said Wilmott grinning.

"We'll put out a shout for him," said Forward, unamused.

****

When Forward and Wilmott returned to Sandleton Police Station they found Miss

Newbiggin waiting for them. She'd spent the morning helping an officer produce a photofit impression of the man in the red Sierra who'd been watching the car park at Monks Bay. The result of their collaboration lay on the desk in Forward's office. The moment Forward saw the portrait he became a little more convinced that Dangerfield was the man they were looking for.

"I tried to recall him clearly but that was the best I could do," said Miss Newbiggin.

"You've done an excellent job," said Forward. "It's amazing what you can dredge up when the photofit process starts jogging your memory."

More platitudes were exchanged and then Miss Newbiggin was sent off with WPC Turner to make a formal statement.

"It's him. It's Dangerfield," said Wilmott, as soon as they were on their own.

"It's very like him," Forward admitted.

"As soon as we pull him in, we'll get Miss Newbiggin to come and do an ID."

"Hey, not so fast," said Forward. "We still may not have enough to hold him."

"What. Even with a positive ID?"

"There have been too many cases of mistaken identity," Forward said, sharply.

The telephone on Forward's desk rang. Forward picked it up and found himself speaking to Dr Edwin Painter of the forensic laboratory in Hull.

"Hello, Forward? I've got something I think

will interest you."

Painter told Forward what he'd found, and it did interest him greatly. When the conversation finished, he had several pages of notes in front of him. But before he could break the news to Wilmott, the phone rang again. A message had been received from Griffiths over her car radio. They had found Dangerfield at his home and were bringing him in.

CHAPTER
FOURTEEN

Half an hour later, in Interview Room Three, Forward was confronting Dangerfield across a desk. Wilmott was by the audio equipment recording the preliminaries.

"Case Number 467318. Matter: Mark Coulson deceased. Subject of interview: Richard Dangerfield. Interviewing Officer: Detective Chief Inspector Forward assisted by Detective Sergeant Wilmott. Mr Dangerfield has waived his right to legal assistance. Interview commenced ..." Wilmott paused and consulted his watch, "Three ten p.m. Wednesday 14th April 1993."

Wilmott nodded at Forward to indicate it was OK to start.

Forward formally cautioned Dangerfield and then paused, as though he was unsure how to begin. He was waiting for Dangerfield to meet his eye but the young man seemed reluctant to do so. He continued to stare at the desktop as he'd been doing since the custody sergeant had brought him into the room.

Forward at last plunged in. "Richard, the reason you're here is because we've discovered an inconsistency in the statement you gave us. You told us that on Monday night you were at *The Drovers Inn* between eight and ten p.m., and a witness has verified that. It's what happened after you left the pub that we need to talk to you about.

Dangerfield looked up. "Oh?"

Forward decided he was definitely edgy.

"Yes. After you left the pub, you said you went straight to *The New Friends* and arrived there at around ten-ten or ten-fifteen. Is that right?"

"Now I come to think of it, I don't think it is right."

Forward was surprised. He hadn't expected him to cave in so easily.

"You wish to correct your statement?"

"Yes."

"What time did you arrive there, then?"

"About ten forty-five."

Forward paused. He was considering his next strategy. "I'm pleased you've remembered that, Richard, because Mr Kung has told us you definitely didn't arrive at the restaurant until at least ten forty-five. He's certain, because your table wasn't ready for you and he was glad you were late." He leaned familiarly across the desk. His manner seemed to be inviting a confidence. "So, why did you tell us originally you arrived there at ten fifteen?"

"I was nervous. I forgot it took me so long."

"Half an hour's quite a lot of time to forget, isn't it?" put in Wilmott.

Dangerfield said nothing.

"All right, so you got the time wrong," conceded Forward. "Now, think carefully about this. You left *The Drovers* at ten and you arrived at the restaurant at ten forty-five. What were you doing during those forty-five minutes?"

"Mooching about."

"You were walking around Luffield?"

"Yeah. On my way to the Chinese."

"Come off it," Wilmott broke in. "The restaurant's only five minutes from *The Drovers*."

"I didn't go there right away."

"Where did you go then?" Forward asked.

"I told you. I was just walking around. Why's it so important anyway?"

"It's important Richard because we happen to know the precise time Mr Coulson was killed."

Dangerfield looked guarded. "I told you before, I had nothing to do with that."

"And I believe you, Richard," said Forward. "Now, while you were walking around Luffield did you meet anyone who could confirm your story?"

Dangerfield went very quiet. He stared even

harder at the desktop. Forward's experience told him that the interview had reached a turning point. "You're hiding something from us, aren't you, Richard?"

"No."

"Are you sure?"

Dangerfield nodded.

Forward said, "I know you're hiding something from us, Richard. You went somewhere else before you went to the restaurant, didn't you?"

"It wasn't Monks Bay, if that's what you're thinking."

"It wasn't what I was thinking actually. You wouldn't have had the time. But we know you definitely went somewhere. So, where was it?"

Dangerfield sat back in his chair and stared up at the ceiling. "Oh, all right," he said, "I'll tell you. I didn't go straight to the Chinese. I went to another pub."

"Why was that?" Wilmott asked. "Did you get fed up with the beer at *The Drovers*?"

"I wanted to get some condoms."

Dangerfield's reply stunned Forward and Wilmott into silence.

Smiling, Dangerfield gave them his explanation. "They don't have a machine at *The Drovers*. So, on the way to the Chinese I popped into *The Three Bowmen*."

"And did you make a satisfactory purchase?" enquired Wilmott, with a sneer.

Dangerfield nodded.

"It's commendable that you take your moral responsibilities so seriously," said Forward. "Who was the girl you were hoping to share the condoms with?"

"It was nothing like that. I was buying them on spec. I'm going to a rave on Thursday night. I wanted to be sure I had some on me."

"You don't expect us to believe that, do you?" said Forward, harshly.

"Why not? I get embarrassed buying them in the chemist's."

"I don't believe this!" exclaimed Wilmott.

"We don't find your story convincing, Richard," said Forward. "In fact, we find all these evasions and half-truths highly suspicious."

"I'm telling you the truth. I went in *The Three Bowmen* to get some condoms."

Forward stared at him. He was wearing his most sceptical expression. "Unless you can give us a better story than that we're going to have to arrest you."

"But it's true!" He sighed heavily. "OK. I'll tell you the whole truth. I did get some condoms. But I really went in there to score."

Forward folded his arms and leaned across the desk. Dangerfield's story was at last beginning to sound more plausible, and depressingly familiar.

"So, you're into drugs, Richard?"

"Not in a big way. Just a bit of marihuana sometimes. And a bit of E."

"Ecstasy has killed people. You want to be careful."

"I only use it if I'm going to a rave."

"Like the one on Thursday?"

"Yes."

"And you score in *The Three Bowmen* every Monday? Is that right?"

"Not every Monday."

"How often?"

"It depends. It's not a regular arrangement. Sometimes weeks go by and he doesn't show up."

"Who is this 'he' Richard? What's his name?" asked Wilmott.

For the first time Dangerfield's bravado was absent. He looked genuinely frightened. "No. I'm not naming any names. That's why I didn't want to say anything in the first place. You don't know what these people are like!"

"We certainly do," said Forward. "How did you first make contact with this dealer?"

"He approached me in *The Three Bowmen* one night. Like he approached a lot of people. He told me if I ever wanted anything I should look in on Mondays. He might be in there occasionally."

"And you've 'looked in' every Monday since?"

"Yeah."

"And what did you score last Monday,

Richard?"

"Some pot that's all."

"Not crack?"

Dangerfield looked horrified. "No chance. I wouldn't mess with that shit!"

"What time did you get hold of the cannabis?"

"Around ten fifteen."

"You realise that the only way we can corroborate your story is to find the dealer," said Wilmott.

"I don't want you to find him. If I pointed him out to you, they'd cut my legs off. Or worse."

"Who's 'they'?" Wilmott demanded.

"The people he works for in Manchester."

"Is that why you bolted from work, Richard?" Forward asked suddenly. "Why you left work and went home after we'd questioned you?"

Dangerfield nodded. "I wanted to tell you the truth but I was too frightened. That's why I said I went straight from *The Drovers* to the restaurant. I didn't want you to know about *The Three Bowmen*. After you'd gone, I realised I'd been stupid and I just panicked."

Forward went silent. He was obviously deliberating very hard. Finally, he said, "I'm going to send you home, Richard. But I want you here tomorrow morning for an identity parade. Eleven o'clock sharp."

Dangerfield regarded Forward with a

mixture of amazement and disbelief.

"Identity parade?"

"Yes. You see on Monday evening a witness saw a young man answering to your description sitting outside her aunt's cottage near Monkhouses, in a red Sierra. This was around six thirty in the evening. But as you say you were nowhere near Monkhouses at that time on Monday evening, the simplest way for us to eliminate you from the enquiry is for this witness to have a look at you in an identity parade. Do you understand?"

Dangerfield's face was as white as chalk. "Yes."

"Now before we go to all the trouble of arranging the identity parade is there anything else in your statement you feel the need to change?"

Dangerfield said nothing.

Forward stared at him searchingly. "Is there anything else you think we should know?"

Dangerfield swallowed. "No."

"All right. You can go now," said Forward. "The sergeant will show you out."

****

Forward left Interview Room Three and went straight to his office, stopping only to extract a cup of bitter tasting coffee from the vending machine at the end of the corridor. He went to his desk and picked up the photofit impression of the mystery man Miss Newbiggin had seen at Monkhouses. He studied it carefully. Sure, he decided, it did bear some resemblance to Dangerfield, but was it enough for a positive ID?

When Wilmott came in, Forward was on the phone to Maybury in Drugs, tipping him off about the alleged dealing in *The Three Bowmen*. He finished his call, put the phone down and smiled up at the sergeant. "The drugs boys know all about *The Three Bowmen*. They've had it under observation for weeks."

"Good," said Wilmott. "Maybe they'll be able to corroborate Dangerfield's story."

"I doubt it, but it's worth a try. Send them Miss Newbiggin's photofit."

"I think we were wrong to let him go so soon," Wilmott said stiffly.

"I disagree. Even if Dangerfield was the man Miss Newbiggin saw in the red Sierra, he couldn't have known what time Coulson was going to get back to Monks Bay to collect his car."

"Unless someone tipped him off."

"Like who?"

"Someone who was at Monks Bay already. They could have rung Dangerfield at *The Drovers* and told him that Coulson had arrived back."

"There isn't a public phone in *The Drovers*. I've checked."

Wilmott looked stumped for a moment. Then his face brightened. "There's a private phone there, surely. Somebody could have got a message through to Dangerfield on that."

Forward looked at him astounded. "Wait a minute. Let me get this straight. You're suggesting that Dangerfield had an accomplice waiting at Monks Bay for Coulson to return to pick up his car? And as soon as he did this, the accomplice phoned up *The Drovers* to tell Dangerfield that Coulson had returned?"

"Yes."

"Don't you think the barmaid would have mentioned that? Besides, what was the point of the accomplice notifying Dangerfield that Coulson had returned to Monks Bay? Dangerfield was fifteen miles away. By the time he'd got there Coulson would have picked up his car and gone."

"Not if the accomplice had held Coulson there until Dangerfield arrived."

"But why should Dangerfield have an accomplice? Look, we know Coulson died at around ten twenty-seven. If Dangerfield left *The Drovers* dead on ten and set off for Monks Bay right away, he'd have had just twenty-seven minutes to get there, get down into the bay, kill Coulson and drag his body down to the surf. And he would have had only fifteen minutes to climb out of the bay, drive back to Luffield and arrive at *The New Friends* by ten forty-five. And he'd have been covered in blood. Apart from it being impossible, why should he go to all that trouble just because Coulson had upset his mother months ago?"

Wilmott sat down heavily and sighed. "I just feel it in my bones there's something very fishy about Dangerfield's story. He's not telling us the whole truth. And his description fits the man Miss Newbiggin saw at Monks Bay early on Monday evening."

"All right. If you want to check whether a phone call was made to *The Drovers,* organise a telecoms investigation. But I can tell you now you'll be wasting your time. By the way, have you notified Miss Newbiggin about the ID parade tomorrow?"

Wilmott nodded. He got up and started to circle the carpet. Forward could see that his colleague was preparing himself to be obstructive. He waited.

Wilmott was unable to contain himself any longer. "I'm sorry, sir, but I really think we should run a time test. We need to establish if it was feasible for Dangerfield to get out to Monks Bay, murder Coulson and be back again in Luffield by ten forty-five."

"All right, do it, if it'll make you feel happier," said Forward, ungraciously. "But just answer me this question. If Dangerfield was so keen to bump Coulson off, why did he spend the best part of the evening in *The Drovers* and at the

Chinese restaurant?"

"To establish an alibi."

"An alibi that would leave him only forty-five minutes to get to Monks Bay, do the deed and get back to Luffield?" Forward scoffed.

Wilmott looked uncertain. "I'm just trying to think laterally."

"No, you're not," said Forward, "you're trying to force the facts into a straightjacket of your own theories and prejudices. When we start doing that, we run ourselves and the public into all sorts of dangers. If you want to do some lateral thinking try this." He held up the notes he'd made of his telephone conversation with Dr Painter and waved them at Wilmott. "Painter's come up with some interesting findings. First of all, the anorak that Coulson was wearing is no ordinary one. It's a specialist garment usually worn by deep sea fishermen. It's normally sold by marine suppliers and it costs a packet."

Wilmott whistled, as he resumed his seat. "No wonder Mrs Coulson didn't recognise it."

"Quite," said Forward. "And don't forget we've got a statement from that fish and chip shop owner in Filey who swears Coulson was just wearing a suit at ..." He searched around on his desk for the statement Griffiths had faxed him, "at about eight p.m."

"Bit late for him to have bought it anywhere," suggested Wilmott.

"Oh no, I don't think he got it in a shop," said Forward. "That anorak has seen some service. According to Painter it bore strong traces of sodium chloride."

"Salt?"

"Yes, salt. Salt from the sea. Painter also found specimens of fish scales and fish guts on the anorak."

"Coulson wasn't an angler, was he?"

"No. I've already checked that with Mrs Coulson. He never had any kind of connection with the sea."

Wilmott looked dumbfounded. "Someone must have given it to him."

"There's one more thing. When we found Coulson's body, naturally, there was a lot of blood on the anorak; but according to Dr Painter it wasn't only Coulson's blood. His blood group was O. There was another blood group present. It was AB. And specimens of both blood groups were found on the bottom steps at Monks Bay."

"Sounds as though Coulson got one in before they finished him off."

"Possibly. We know that a knife was in action at some point. Painter's trying to obtain a DNA sample from the AB blood. Then we can tie in any suspects with the scene of the crime."

Wilmott looked wily. "Like Dangerfield, for example?"

Forward smiled. "Sure. Why not? After all,

if he's really innocent he won't object to being eliminated from the enquiry by a scientific test. We'll organise it when he comes in for the ID tomorrow."

"You still haven't told me what the significance of the anorak is," said Wilmott. "Lateral thinking wise that is."

"Earlier I was talking about logic ladders that lead nowhere. Well, this is another one we've been climbing. The first rung: Coulson is a headmaster; second rung: headmasters are respectable; third rung: he must have gone to Monks Bay for sex with someone's wife or lover; fourth rung: his mistress' husband or boyfriend bumped him off. But let's saw the ladder up and arrange the rungs on the ground. Then let's take one rung away, the one that says headmasters are respectable and, in its place, let's put the yellow anorak. Now what do you see?"

Wilmott's brows knitted in intense thought. "Coulson went to Filey to see a fisherman about an anorak?"

Laughing, the Detective Chief Inspector stood up. "Order all available CID to be at Monkhouses by five. I want to hold a case review."

CHAPTER FIFTEEN

"Stop here a moment. I want to check on something."

Forward's finger was indicating Horace Sisson's house in the main street of Monkhouses. The request surprised Wilmott. He braked hard and parked rather wildly. Forward got out of the car and walked up to the small wooden door of the cottage. He raised the ancient knocker and let it fall once. Immediately there was the sound of frenzied barking. The door opened and Horace Sissons appeared with one hand gripped securely around Toby's collar. The dog was growling and baring its teeth in a most alarming display of aggression. Forward exchanged a few words with Sissons and then returned to the car.

"He ought to put a muzzle on that bloody thing," said Wilmott.

"I won't have a word said against darling Toby," said Forward. "If he wasn't so anti-social, Sissons would have walked him at the same time as the other dog owners and Coulson's body wouldn't have been discovered until much later. We have Toby to thank for much valuable information."

"We do?" Wilmott said doubtfully.

"We certainly do."

****

When Forward and Wilmott arrived at the incident centre they found it filled with uniformed police and CID officers. The only members of the public present were the teenage boy and girl who'd reluctantly reported seeing two cars in the clifftop car park around the time of Coulson's murder. They were now referred to as 'Romeo and Juliet' by all the officers much to Griffiths' annoyance. The two teenagers were seated at a desk going through an open volume of Marshall's International Directory of Vehicles. Several other volumes of the directory were lying closed around them. Forward went over to the youngsters and spoke to them. They shook their heads. Forward said something else and they looked at each other and then nodded. Forward talked to them a little longer, and when he'd finished, they closed the big book in front of them, got up and went out of the centre.

Forward caught Wilmott's eye and came over to him. "I've sent those two kids home," he said.

"Have they identified the make of the other car?"

"No. But they've been very helpful in another way."

"Oh? How?"

Forward didn't say anything. Instead, he half raised his hand closing further discussion, and then went and stood in front of the big map of the East Yorkshire coast. The assembled officers went quiet.

"All right, let's make a start," said Forward and then added with a grin, "I've got a show to go to." His weak attempt at a joke was greeted with silence. "I'd like to review our progress so far," he continued, slightly abashed, and started to go over the main developments in the case.

A glazed look came over many faces. They were all too familiar with this. People became more attentive, however, when he mentioned the emergence of Dangerfield as a possible, but not strong, suspect, and announced he was to take part in an ID parade the following morning at Sandleton nick. He gave an account of the various conflicting statements Dangerfield had made and there was laughter when he mentioned his need of the condom machine in *The Three Bowmen*. Forward then moved on to inform the meeting of the main contents of the reports received from the pathologist and the forensic department.

"We've now got several promising leads," he said. "The most significant of these is the anorak that Coulson was wearing when he was murdered. I'll explain why shortly. Mrs Coulson is adamant it didn't belong to her husband. We also know he wasn't wearing it when he was in the fish and chip shop in Filey at around eight on Monday night with another man. So where did he get it? Forensic have told us it had been exposed to marine conditions, so it's unlikely he bought it from a shop, certainly at that time of night. Perhaps he borrowed it from the man he was seen with." He stared directly at DS Drinkwater. "Roger, I'd like you to follow this up. I suggest you get on to the anorak's manufacturers. They might be able to tell us which outlet they originally supplied it to. Take a photo of it around every local shop or business that sells an anorak of that sort. Somebody might remember selling it. Show it to every local fisherman or sailing club member in the area. You can start with those in Filey. It's a specialist garment so they can't be all that common. Now, another lead is the man who was seen in the fish and chip shop with Coulson. It's quite possible he was with Coulson all the time he was in Filey. So, mention that when you show Coulson's photograph to anyone."

"Do we have a description of the man who

was with Coulson?" asked DI Hoggart.

Forward looked questioningly at Griffiths. "Did the chip shop owner come up with a decent description eventually?"

Griffiths shook her head. "A big man about six foot tall, that's all. He didn't take much notice of him."

"Have you organised a photofit?" demanded Hoggart.

Griffiths looked embarrassed. "No."

"Well get him into FR as soon as possible."

Forward frowned. "Yes, it's a shame we haven't got a photofit of the man with Coulson. Someone might have recognised him." He threw Griffiths a questioning look. "Did you have any luck with the A&E Departments?"

"No," said Griffiths, in a subdued voice. "None reported anyone coming in with knife injuries on Monday night or the early hours of Tuesday." She paused and then added, "If you agree, I'd like to widen the search to include hospitals outside our area."

Forward beamed at her. "I certainly do agree. Now that shows initiative."

Griffiths looked pleased.

Forward did not miss the looks that passed between the male officers. He knew very well what they were thinking. Well, they could think what they bloody well liked.

Forward turned his attention to Hoggart. "How's the search going?" he asked.

"No luck yet. We've turned up a few potential murder weapons but all have tested negative so far."

"No sign of a knife or Coulson's wallet or keys?"

"Nothing."

"Well keep at it. Once you've completed the search of the bay and the surrounding cliffs concentrate on the roadside verges around Monkhouses. It's just possible the murder weapon was removed from the bay and discarded inland."

"How far down the road do you want us to search?" asked Hoggart.

"Until you find something," said Forward curtly. "Now, I said earlier that the most significant lead we had was the anorak that Coulson was wearing, and here's why. We've been pursuing this enquiry with our heads stuck in the sand. We've been operating on the assumption that Coulson must have returned overland to Monks Bay from Filey either by road or rail. But the forensic report we've received on the anorak substantiates what I've suspected for some time. That he actually arrived at Monks Bay by boat."

There was a long pause. Everyone become extra attentive.

"Why would Coulson want to do that?" asked Hoggart. "His wife was expecting him home for dinner at seven. Why would he go all the way to

Filey to make a boat trip?"

"That's what we've got to find out. I'm keeping an open mind about motive for the time being. Nevertheless, I'm certain that's how he got to Monks Bay."

"It doesn't make sense!" Hoggart persisted.

"Yes, it does," said Forward, whose patience was being sorely tested. "It explains why Coulson was found down in the bay. It also explains why he was wearing an anorak that his wife had never seen before. He wouldn't have needed a protective garment like that if he was coming back from Filey by train or car. Only by sea."

Forward looked at his watch. Then he addressed DS Harper, who had recently returned to duty following an assault by a drunken woman he'd arrested. "I want you to take a team down to Filey right away. It's only ten past five, so plenty of fishermen should still be around on the Coble Landing. See if any of them recall seeing any unusual boats in or around the bay on Monday night. Show them Coulson's photograph and see if they recognise it. I want every fisherman questioned. I've already checked with Horace Sissons, and he swears he saw a boat's lights off Monks Bay around the time he found the body. That would have been around eleven o'clock."

"Why didn't he mention that before?" Wilmott demanded.

"Because we never thought to ask him about boats," said Forward. "I've also checked with the teenage couple who saw the two cars in the car park around ten fifteen. They tell me that during their walk along the cliffs they saw the lights of at least two boats."

"Well, they would, wouldn't they? There are always fishermen out at night," said Hoggart, obviously unconvinced.

"But they saw the lights just before ten thirty. The time we're sure Coulson was murdered," said Forward.

"Why didn't Romeo and Juliet see what was going on in the bay, then?"

Griffiths glared at Hoggart. "Because being Romeo and Juliet, they had other things on their minds!"

Everyone laughed.

Still smiling, Forward said, "It wasn't just that. They were walking in the opposite direction to Monks Bay when they saw the lights."

"So, you think that the people who brought Coulson by boat were the ones who murdered him?" said Hoggart, who'd refused to see the joke.

"I don't know, but it's got to be a strong possibility. The big question is where did the boat go after leaving Coulson in the bay? Wilmott and I are going back to Sandleton now. We'll have a word with the Harbourmaster there. He should have a record of all boats that were in the vicinity of Monks Bay and Flamborough Head on Monday night. He should also know if any strange craft berthed in Sandleton Harbour after the time Coulson was murdered. Well, I've finished," he said. "Sorry to load you with all these new leads and then leave you to it."

"Don't you worry about that, sir. You just run along to your play," said Hoggart.

CHAPTER SIXTEEN

"You shouldn't allow him to talk to you that way, sir. You shouldn't really. What you do with your own time is your affair. Me, I like to go home to the wife and kids. You haven't got a family. So, if you choose to spend your time producing plays for the local amateurs, what's it got to do with Hoggart?"

"We're not having this conversation, Sergeant," said Forward.

They were in Wilmott's Sierra following the coast road into Sandleton.

"I know I'm speaking out of turn, him being a senior officer, but his attitude really annoys me. He always seems to be implying that we don't accomplish very much and can't wait to get off duty, whereas, in fact, every major break on this case has been down to us."

This was a familiar theme of Wilmott's and Forward was growing tired of it. He was also annoyed that Wilmott had chosen to ignore his signal that he'd no wish to pursue the discussion.

"That's hardly fair, you cloth head," said Forward. "He's been tied down searching for the murder weapon. Now let's talk about something else."

Wilmott had no wish to talk about anything else, and so they drove on in silence. The coast road started to run downhill into Sandleton's North Bay. Ahead, and below them, Forward could see the immense curving jetties of Sandleton's artificial harbour. They were like the two huge claws of a crab protectively encircling the many seagoing craft sheltering between them. Beyond the harbour, Forward could see the road start to climb up again into the resort's South Bay. This was where the largest and poshest hotels were to be found.

The Harbourmaster's office was located at the end of the North Jetty. Inside, they found Dan Thwaites, the Harbourmaster, seated at his desk and holding a huge mug of tea. He was a man in his early fifties but he looked about ten years older. A few remaining white hairs just prevented him from being totally bald, and decades of exposure to sun and spray had turned his complexion unnaturally ruddy. An unkempt, white beard enhanced the premature ageing effect and gave him an unmistakably nautical appearance. "Oh no," he said, good humouredly. "What's dredged you up?"

"We need some information about some

craft movements, Dan," said Forward.

Thwaites eyes twinkled merrily. "Aye. What is it this time? Drugs, guns or illegal immigrants?"

Forward smiled. At one time or another Thwaites had assisted Sandleton police with enquiries into all three of these offences. The Yorkshire coast had seen its fair share of smuggling. "It's murder, actually, Dan."

Thwaites nodded gravely. "I've got you. That poor bugger they found out at Monks Bay."

"That's the one. It's just possible he got there by boat from Filey. Obviously, the boat had to go somewhere after it left Monks Bay, and I was wondering if it put in here."

"When would that be, now?"

"Monday night. Late. Sometime after ten thirty."

"We did have a foreigner in on Monday night as I recall. But it was early."

"A foreign boat?" said Wilmott.

"No. British. It's just my way of talking. Any boat that isn't a Sandleton boat is a foreigner as far as I'm concerned."

"I'll have the details on it anyway," said Forward.

Thwaites stood up and led the way through to an adjoining office. The room contained several filing cabinets, a computer terminal and a desk. A young man, wearing a navy-blue sweater, was seated at the desk.

"Give me the details of that foreigner we had in on Monday night, Jimmy," said Thwaites.

Jimmy went over to the computer and deftly operated the keyboard. Columns of information appeared on the visual display unit. "That was the *Phaeton*," he said. "An eight-berth cruiser. Arrived five forty p.m."

"Five forty?" said Wilmott, and gave Forward a disappointed look.

"Make a note, anyway," Forward told him.

Wilmott took out his notebook and went over and stood behind Jimmy at the visual display unit.

"No need for that," said Jimmy. "I can give you a print-out later." He pressed the keyboard again and a different information set appeared. "Last port of call was Leyden in Holland. Registered in London. Owned by a company: Pulverisation International Limited."

"A lot of them are owned by companies nowadays," commented Thwaites. "Use 'em to impress their clients."

"Crew of five," Jimmy went on. "Three men and two women. Want to see their details?"

"Yes, please." Various names and addresses appeared on the screen. They meant nothing to Forward.

"All their details will be on the print-out," said Jimmy. "Let's see, what else is there? Cleared customs check. Departed for Lowestoft five a.m. Tuesday morning."

"Early?" said Forward.

"Aye. Caught the ebb tide," said Thwaites.

Jimmy once again applied himself to the keyboard and the computer's printer whined into action.

"Thanks very much, Dan," said Forward. He turned to Jimmy. "And, of course, you too."

Thwaites noticed Forward's downcast look. "The *Phaeton* came in too early to be of any use, eh?"

"I'm afraid so," said Forward. "I was banking on it coming in here after ten thirty."

"Only the usual stuff's recorded for that time," said Jimmy.

"He's talking about the in-shore fishing cobles, lobstermen, that kind of thing," Thwaites explained. "It's the wrong time of year for pleasure craft." He rubbed his nose thoughtfully. "Your boat could have put in further down the coast, of course, at Hull or Grimsby. Or it could have gone back up the coast to Scarborough or Whitby."

"Can you check that out for me?" asked Forward.

"Certainly can," said Jimmy.

Thwaites pointed at the computer. "That wonderful machine over there is plugged into the Trinity House Main Computer System. It can tell you what colour underpants are being worn by the crew of any bark in the kingdom."

Forward and Wilmott both laughed. "There

are some details we don't need, Dan," said Forward.

The printer stopped. Jimmy went over to it and tore off the print-out and handed it to Forward. "Give me a little time and I'll have all the information you need about craft movements within a two-hundred-kilometre sweep of here. Continental ports too, if you want them."

"How long?" asked Forward.

"Couple of hours. I'll ring when it's ready."

"That would be most helpful," said Forward. "We'll arrange for it to be collected."

Forward studied the information on the *Phaeton's* crew during the short drive back to the station. There were five names: David Nathan, Vincent Soule, Mark Evans, Francesca Beaton and Sylvia Imrie. None of the names were known to him. Nevertheless, there'd be nothing to lose in running them through the national police computer.

****

The cast of *The Cherry Orchard* were already in the school hall when Forward arrived three quarters of an hour before Curtain Up. As he made his way down the aisle to the seats at the front, he was dismayed to find the intense concentration of the previous evening had been replaced by a mood of careless light-heartedness. People were sitting about in small groups laughing and giggling. Up on the stage, Wayne Peart, an affected Sandleton teenager, cast as Yasha, Madame Ranyevskaya's servant, was playing a tune on his guitar. Meanwhile, at stage left, Alastair Sidebottom, a thin and gangly twenty-three-year-old who was cast as the revolutionary student Trofimov, was performing his favourite party piece: a three-minute Hamlet. Shrieks of laughter indicated that this was being hugely enjoyed by his large band of female admirers.

As an experienced director of amateurs, Forward knew that first night nerves gave way to second night over confidence and this inevitably disadvantaged the show. It was particularly significant that, although Curtain Up was only three quarters of an hour off, none of the cast had any costume or make-up on. Forward decided it was time to give them all a bollocking.

After exchanging greetings with various individuals, he called loudly and bad-temperedly for quiet, and then started to give every actor ultra-critical notes on the previous night's performance. When he'd finished, they were all rather subdued.

"Remember, no matter how wonderful you may think you are, you are not professionals and so have no real technique," he warned them. "Lack of technique and massive over confidence is a fatal combination on-stage.

Now your first night nerves are over, there's every chance you'll lose your grip on the production. There's only one way to avoid that. You must concentrate even harder than you did last night. If you don't, you'll end up embarrassing yourselves and embarrassing the audience. Finally, if I arrive at this time tomorrow night, I'll expect everyone to be in costume and fully made-up. You'd better go and do that now."

As one, the cast trooped off to their dressing rooms to get ready. Forward was pleased to see they all left in silence and there was generally what is known as 'an atmosphere'. Hopefully it would focus their minds and help them to concentrate on their roles.

The First Act, as Forward had feared, got off to a terrible start. Curtain Up, for some reason, was five minutes late. Fred Bright forgot one of his lines and he and the actress playing Dunyasha frantically improvised dialogue for the next minute until they both dried and had to be rescued by the prompter. Things deteriorated even further when the actor playing Yepikhodov missed his entrance and came on late. Something then went wrong with his normally hilarious exit, and he failed to get his laugh. Worse disasters followed: the actor playing Pishchik didn't look where he was going and trod rather hard on Charlotta Ivanovna's dog, which immediately howled and took a bite out of Pishchik's leg before running off the stage and ruining the scene. When Trofimov made his entrance, the false moustache he was wearing started to slide down his face, sending all those on-stage into fits of giggles: this led to more forgotten lines and even more loud and obvious prompting. Forward found himself scribbling furiously on his notepad all the way through to the end of the Act.

Fortunately, the Second Act was a great improvement. Forward assumed this was because the cast had been shaken rigid by the previous on-stage disasters. He was relieved to hear the audience laughing in all the right places for a change. When the interval came, he went straight round to the men's dressing room. As he entered all the actors gazed at him warily.

Fred Bright, who was changing into the trousers of his Act Three costume, said, "You don't have to say anything, Tony. We all know we made a right pig's arse of that First Act."

Forward smiled. "Well, it certainly has gone better. I made hundreds of notes but I'm not going to bother you with them now. You all recovered in the Second Act and it went fine. I'll just put the First Act disaster down to a general lapse of concentration." He turned to Clive Roberts, the elderly actor playing Simeonov-Pishchik, who had been bitten by Charlotta

Ivanovna's dog. "How's the leg? You weren't bitten too badly, were you?"

Clive placed his right foot on a chair, rolled up his trouser leg and offered Forward his bare flesh for inspection.

"Where?" said Forward. "I can't see anything."

"There!" said Clive, indignantly pointing to an almost imperceptible scratch above his ankle.

"You're lucky," said Forward, "it hasn't broken the skin."

"Fortunately, I've had a tetanus."

"You'll need more than a tetanus," said Alastair Sidebottom, who loved winding Clive up. "An anti-rabies shot at least."

Everyone laughed.

"Bloody thing needs muzzling," said Clive.

Forward remained chatting and joking in the men's dressing room for several minutes. He was just about to leave when he was approached by Jason Holtby, who asked if he could have a word.

"Of course," said Forward. "What is it?"

"I mean in private."

This usually meant trouble. Forward nodded and led Jason out of the dressing room and into the corridor.

"Well?"

Jason looked uncomfortable. "It's about my first exit. Doreen keeps mucking it up and spoiling it."

Jason played Yepikhodov, an unlucky, accident-prone man who was madly in love with Dunyasha, the chambermaid. At the beginning of Act One he had a comic exit during which he collided with various items of furniture. Jason was an excellent comedy actor and his exit normally brought the house down.

"Yes, I noticed something was wrong with it. It looked as though Doreen came in too quickly with her line."

"She did. She's supposed to hold her line until well after I've exited. She knows that. It's not the first time, either."

"Have you spoken to her about it?"

"I've tried, but you know what she's like."

Forward did indeed know what Doreen Foster was like. Despite being an exceptionally attractive and feisty young woman, her attitude towards her fellow actors made her unpopular and even actively disliked by some of the Players. She was one of those selfish actors who believe that their character is the only important one in the play, and who tries constantly to upstage the others and steal their scenes. In Forward's opinion, she was a good actress but a poor artist: she had no temperament for ensemble playing and always wanted to be remembered as the best thing in the play, even when she was performing a tiny part. Her inability to subordinate herself to the demands of the production as a whole unbalanced any scene in which she appeared because she over-milked her role with too much business and exaggerated straining for effects. Forward found it frustrating to rehearse with her because she frequently resisted his direction; and when asked to modify or tone down her performance she often became a complete prima donna, sometimes throwing the most spectacular tantrums. He still bore the scars from several past confrontations with her massive ego.

"When you spoke to her, what did she say?" Forward asked.

"She said you'd told us to get a move on and come in with our lines quickly, not hold everything up with loads of long pauses, so she was only doing what you'd asked."

Chekhov plays were famous for having a significant number of dramatic pauses. Towards the end of rehearsals, the cast had fallen into the amateur trap of 'Chekhovian playing' and were inserting a pause after almost every line. To counter this, Forward had asked the actors to speed things up by speaking bang on their cues except at those places where there was supposed to be a dramatic pause. Now it was obvious Doreen was using this as a justification for ruining Jason's exit, which normally got him a huge laugh: something, of course, she would have bitterly resented. She really was a most unpleasant piece of work.

"All right, I'll have a word with her," said Forward.

Jason immediately looked anxious. "You won't tell her that I..."

Recalling how aggressive Doreen could be, Forward quickly reassured Jason that his name wouldn't be mentioned.

Forward left Jason and went along the corridor to the women's dressing room. Irene Babcock opened the door in response to his knock. "You can come in, darling," she said. "We're all decent." She opened the door wide, ushering Forward inside.

The other four members of the cast were sitting in front of their mirrors. Like Irene, they were all in their Third Act costume and wearing long skirts and blouses buttoned right up to the neck. They all turned to him expectantly.

"I'll bet you've come to give us a rap over the knuckles for that wonderful First Act," said Nina Spillers.

"That would be true if the Second Act had gone just as badly," said Forward. He turned to Irene who was playing Charlotta Ivanovna. "By the way, have they given Whiskey the antidote yet?"

Whiskey was the dog that had taken a nip at Clive Roberts' ankle.

Irene looked at him blankly, as did the

others. Finally, the penny dropped and they all laughed.

"You dreadful man," said Irene, giving him a playful tap on the shoulder. "I'll tell Clive exactly what you said."

"Careful, that's assaulting a policeman," said Audrey Ticehurst. "He'll run you in."

Irene regarded Forward with a salacious grin. "That's all right. I wouldn't mind being alone in a cell with him."

There was a lot of ribald laughter.

"The audience are a bit quiet tonight," said Linda Chapman, a serious-minded woman who was playing Varya.

"That's because they're intelligent and are concentrating on the play," said Forward. "Don't worry, most of the audience reactions are coming in the right place." He turned to Doreen Foster and said, lightly, "Which reminds me, Doreen. You ruined Yepikhodov's laugh tonight by coming in too quickly with your line. Wait until Jason's right off-stage, will you, before you tell Lopakhin that Yepikhodov's proposed to you."

"He was off-stage."

"No, I mean right off-stage. He'd only just gone out of the door when you delivered your line. I've given you notes about this before. After the door closes you must take a beat and then you and Lopakhin should exchange a look. Hold the look for another beat. That will give time for the audience's laughter to continue and build. If you come in straight away, you'll tread on Jason's laugh. Which is a shame because it's an incredibly funny exit and should get the biggest laugh in the show."

Doreen's head went back and her jaw set. "I'm only doing what you said. You said we had to speed it up and come in quickly on the cues."

"Generally, yes. But there are a number of exceptions and this is one of them."

"Has Jason been complaining about me?"

"No."

"Yes, he has. Well, if you don't like the way I'm doing it I can always leave!"

Doreen's hands flew to her throat and she started unbuttoning the front of her blouse. Everyone stared.

"What are you doing?" Forward demanded.

"What does it look like?"

"You can't walk out now, it's the interval," cried Irene Babcock. "You'll ruin the show!"

Doreen said nothing. The front of her bra was now clearly visible. She finished unbuttoning her blouse, pulled it off and flung it into the corner. She stood up, thrusting out her prominent breasts. Next her hands moved to the buttons fastening her long, black skirt.

Forward felt his gaze being drawn irresistibly to her breasts, as though pulled there by gravity. He forced himself to keep his eyes level with hers.

"Just a minute, Doreen," he said calmly. "Before you embarrass yourself and everyone else let me tell you that if you walk out now, I'll have no choice but to put Ellie on in your place with the book."

Ellie Simpson was an excellent actress with a superb temperament. She was currently working back-stage on *The Cherry Orchard* because each actor in the Players was required to help stage manage at least one production a year. Doreen and Ellie were rivals: they were both black-haired, blue-eyed beauties, and always competed for the same parts. "If Ellie replaces you now the part is hers and she keeps it for all the other performances," Forward warned.

Doreen's hands stopped fumbling with the buttons of her skirt and slowly dropped to her sides. Her insecure look told Forward she wasn't sure if he was bluffing or not. So that she could be in no doubt, he said, "And if you walk out now halfway through the performance, that will obviously influence me when I consider you for any future roles."

Doreen gave a huge cry of frustration. Then she stomped over to the corner of the dressing room where she'd thrown her blouse, retrieved it and started putting it back on.

"Good," said Forward. "I'm glad you've seen sense." He moved towards the door. When he'd opened it halfway, he turned back to address her. "And please remember, Doreen, not to tread on Jason's laugh."

When he reached the corridor outside the dressing room Forward was surprised to find Audrey Ticehurst following him. He stopped, and she rolled her eyes and pulled a face. "It's all right. We'll see she calms down. There's more to it than you think. Jason's not taking enough notice of her. You know what she's like."

Forward was glad to get to the refreshment area and leave behind the febrile atmosphere back-stage. After acquiring an orange juice, he stood around observing the people who were taking advantage of the interval for a smoke or a chance to stretch their legs. Fortunately, he didn't recognise anyone, which was a blessing. The First Act had caused him to squirm with embarrassment. Still, if there were going to be disasters, it was better they happened on a night when none of his friends or acquaintances were in.

A tall, distinguished looking woman in her early forties appeared to be trying to catch his eye. Forward was sure he knew her but for the life of him couldn't remember who she was. She began to glide elegantly towards him. An older, equally distinguished looking man followed in her wake. As she drew closer, Forward solved the little mystery of her identity. It was Lady Fernshawe.

"Inspector, Good Evening. I am enjoying

this."

"Glad you could come," said Forward.

"I hadn't expected the play to be quite so funny."

Forward at once became defensive. "Unintentionally, I'm afraid. There've been some technical problems with the First Act tonight. But, you're quite right, it is supposed to be a tragi-comedy."

"It's brilliant," said Lady Fernshawe. She turned to her male companion. "Darling, this is Chief Inspector Forward. The policeman who's investigating poor Mr Coulson's murder." She turned back to Forward. "This is Paul Cartwright, my husband."

Forward extended his hand. "How do you do?" he said, wondering why Lady Fernshawe's husband didn't have a title, and bore a totally different name to Lady Fernshawe.

"A terrible business," said Cartwright. "He was a good man too. An excellent headmaster."

"Did you know him well?"

"Only by reputation." Cartwright looked at his wife. "Isabella speaks very highly of him."

"Paul only met him on one occasion. He's abroad much of the time."

"Really?"

"I'm an industrialist," explained Cartwright. "My work involves me in extensive travelling."

"He returned home just today," said Lady Fernshawe.

"Are you in a position to charge anyone yet, Inspector?" asked Cartwright.

Forward, like most police officers, became uneasy in social contexts when inquisitive members of the public began asking questions about individual cases. He treated Cartwright to his stock answer. "The investigation's at an early stage. Fortunately, the public are being very co-operative."

Cartwright smiled. "I suppose that means no."

Lady Fernshawe looked shocked. "Paul!"

"Sorry," said Cartwright. "I didn't mean to sound rude."

"You'll have to forgive him," said Lady Fernshawe. "It's just his manner. Businessmen are notoriously direct." She gave Forward a dazzling smile. "Now Inspector, you will be coming to our musical evening at the Hall next Monday, won't you?"

"I wouldn't miss it for anything," Forward said.

CHAPTER SEVENTEEN

The following morning Forward arrived at his office at seven a.m. to work on the Attridge file. This was a case of Grievous Bodily Harm. Attridge had been remanded in custody and was due to appear at Sandleton Magistrates' Court that morning for committal proceedings. The Crown Prosecution Service had already notified Forward he'd be required to give evidence in court and he wanted to be completely prepared.

He got down to work straight away, familiarising himself with the details of the case and ensuring that the paperwork was complete.

Wilmott arrived just before eight. He came in holding a plastic cup and drawing heavily on a cigarette. He looked dog tired.

Forward was surprised. Wilmott had successfully given up smoking for the past three months.

"I know, I know," said Wilmott. "I'm smoking

again."

"What started that?"

"We've been up all night with Linda. She screamed the house down. Her teeth, I suppose."

Forward nodded understandingly. Linda was Wilmott's eight-month-old daughter.

"Well, you can have a good sleep this morning," said Forward, attempting to cheer his sergeant up. "I'm in court and there's only the ID parade. Mitchell's handling that, isn't he?"

Wilmott nodded. A neutral officer who was unconnected with the Coulson enquiry had to supervise the identity parade in order to ensure impartiality. "Mitchell's not happy. He wants to use Dangerfield's own Sierra for the ID."

"Well, he can't. It's with forensic. He knows that."

"He says it'll be prejudicial, otherwise."

"Sod him!"

"I volunteered my own Sierra. Mitchell said he'd think about it."

"DI Mitchell is not famous for his thought processes," said Forward. "Oh, well. Do your best."

****

By eleven thirty a.m. the Sandleton magistrate had ordered Attridge to be remanded in custody pending his trial at York

Crown Court. As Forward left the courtroom with Parsons, a senior Crown Prosecutor, a uniformed PC touched his sleeve.

"Telephone call for you, sir. In the office."

It was Wilmott. He sounded vexed. "Dangerfield's done a runner, sir. He failed to attend the ID parade and his mother says he didn't come home last night."

"Shit! That's all we need. Didn't anyone do a house check on him?"

"I'm afraid not, sir."

"Why the bloody hell not?"

"No-one was asked to."

"No-one was asked to? Do I have to think of everything?"

Wilmott didn't respond.

"Does his mother have any idea where he might be?"

"None at all."

"Have you put out a shout?"

"Of course."

"Good. That's all we can do. Let's hope he turns up."

"The Superintendent was looking for you. I told him you were tied up in court."

Forward was silent. He knew what that meant. "Any other developments?"

"Yes. You'll like this. A fisherman says he saw a motor dinghy in Filey Bay on Monday night round about eight thirty p.m."

"Excellent. You see, Wilmott, when you ask

the right questions, you eventually get some useful answers."

"I hope so, sir. Everybody's pretty browned off here about having to call off the line-up. The Superintendent looks as though he's about to commit a murder. He's been complaining about the waste of public money and the damage to public relations."

Forward deliberately ignored Wilmott's remarks. "Meet me at Monkhouses in fifteen minutes. From there we'll go on to Filey. It's time we did a bit of fishing."

****

The officers involved in the search of the surrounding area had just returned for their break when Forward arrived at the incident centre. They were all lolling around drinking tea and eating sandwiches.

Forward went over to one of them, a PC called Barker. "Any joy?"

Barker gulped down his tea. "Not a thing."

"How far up the road have you got?"

"Barely five hundred yards out of Monkhouses. It's all verge, and the grass hasn't had its Spring cut yet. That's what's slowing us up."

"Well keep at it. We must find the lump of chalk that killed Coulson."

Forward left Barker to his lunch. He went and got himself a cup of tea, found a spare desk and sat down to read the statement of Arnold Kimber, fisherman of Filey. He was re-reading it for the third time, when DC Griffiths arrived. She came straight over to him.

"I hear our prime suspect bottled out of the line-up, sir."

"Dangerfield was never a prime suspect, Constable," said Forward coldly. "The ID parade was organised simply to eliminate him."

"Did he realise that, sir?"

"Of course, he did."

"Why d'you think he did a runner, then?"

Forward turned his attention back to the statement in front of him. "When he turns up again, we'll ask him," he muttered.

Griffiths waved a piece of paper under his nose. "You might be interested in this, then, sir."

Forward grasped the paper. It gave details of average speeds, mileages and times.

"So, they timed it," said Forward, trying to make sense of the figures.

"Yes. It took them fifteen minutes from *The Drovers* to Monks Bay."

"That proves I was right. Dangerfield couldn't have got to Monks Bay, murdered Coulson and got back to Luffield in the time available. He'd have had only a few minutes to do the murder and clean himself up."

"Ah, but look at the average speed they did, sir."

Forward glanced at the piece of paper. "Fifty-nine point seven mph. So what?" He was beginning to get irritated.

"The point is they timed it inside the speed limit." She pointed to a further set of figures on the sheet. "But look at these other projections. If Dangerfield really put his foot down, did eighty or ninety most of the way, he could have got from Luffield to Monks Bay in eleven minutes or even ten. That would have given him nearly half an hour to do the murder and get back to Luffield in time for his prawn crackers."

"You're not thinking straight," said Forward, finally exasperated. "Coulson was found in the bay, remember? It would take even a fit young man several minutes to go up and down those cliff steps.

"Nevertheless, it is feasible, sir."

"Feasible!" Forward snorted. "His clothes would have been covered in blood. Now, when we interviewed Mr Kung at the Chinese restaurant, he omitted to mention that. I think he might have commented on it, don't you?"

"If Dangerfield planned Coulson's murder, he could have organised a change of clothes. Had them in the back of his car."

"And how would he have got the time to do that? By driving to Monks Bay at a hundred miles an hour?"

Everyone in the incident room was staring at

Forward. He realised he'd been shouting.

At that moment Wilmott arrived. Forward picked up the statement from his desk, got up and walked towards him.

"Don't take your coat off, Sergeant," he said. "We're not stopping."

CHAPTER EIGHTEEN

The vast, curving arc of Yorkshire coastline that is Filey Bay has its furthermost southern point at Flamborough Head. However, at the bay's northern end is a curious promontory known as Filey Brigg, which is close to the unspoilt town of Filey. Once, when man's violence was not the dominant force on earth, Filey Brigg was a long headland extending straight out into the North Sea, standing as high as the coastline that surrounded it. Geologically, this coastline was a sandwich of clay, sandstone and limestone. Over millennia, the action of vicious cross-currents swirling over the Brigg eroded the soft clay, and later, the relatively harder sandstone, until all that remained was the adamantine limestone. Now, each day when the tide recedes, this limestone reef reappears: standing several feet above the surrounding sea and extending many hundreds of yards out into the water.

With Flamborough Head on one side, and

the Brigg on the other, the bay offers excellent natural shelter for Filey's fishermen. At low tide they can launch their boats from the beach; and if the tide is still low when they return, they can land them directly back onto the beach. Once landed the fishing boats, called cobles, are then hauled over the sand by ancient, rusting tractors to their places on the Coble Landing. This is a long, cobble-stoned jetty, which runs parallel with the cliffs and shelves gently down onto the beach. Some maintain the Coble Landing is so called because of the cobbles from which it was originally made; others say it's to do with the fishing cobles that use it. Whatever the reason for its name, even at high tide boats can be launched from it. Therefore, whatever the state of the waves, the fishermen of Filey always have access to the sea.

Some twenty minutes or so after leaving the incident centre, Forward and Wilmott could be found walking slowly down this Coble Landing. Leisurely they strolled past boats, discarded lobster pots, yards of green and orange nets and men busying themselves with all kinds of tackle.

Forward stopped suddenly. The midday sun was pleasantly warm on his back, and the breeze was no more than the merest soughing on his cheek. He looked from left to right, taking in the whole scene. "I love this place," he said. "Whenever I come here, it reminds me of my childhood."

"Came here for your holidays, did you?"

"Of course not. What I mean is, it reminds me of all those perfect seaside holidays you thought you had when you were a child."

"We always went to Spain," said Wilmott.

"You're an unsentimental sod," said Forward. "Come on, let's see if we can find this Mr Kimber."

Wilmott crossed over to the other side of the Landing, and went to speak to a small group of fishermen gathered round an aged and weathered looking coble. He returned a few moments later, pointing seawards.

"He's down there, sir. Just coming in."

Forward's eyes followed the direction of Wilmott's outstretched arm. The tide was far out, and as it wasn't the holiday season the smooth, marmalade coloured beach was relatively deserted. Just a few people out walking their dogs down by the water's edge, and some men attempting to manhandle a fishing boat into position over a half-submerged bogie. Nearby, a tractor waited.

Forward and Wilmott set off down the Landing towards the beach at a rather more urgent pace than before. They crossed a great expanse of sand, and when they reached the scene of activity around the boat, stood for a moment watching. Forward noted the coble's name, painted somewhat inexpertly on its bow: *Octopus*. The fishermen took no notice of them. They were obviously quite used to sightseers.

"Which one of you is Mr Kimber?" Forward called out.

The men stopped what they were doing, straightened up and stood where they were, watching Forward and Wilmott with suspicion.

Then the oldest and burliest of them jumped down from the boat. He remained where he'd landed in the shallow water, which was halfway up his wellington boots.

"That's me."

Forward produced his warrant card. "Chief Inspector Forward, East Yorkshire Police. This is Sergeant Wilmott."

Kimber waded through the surf to join the two policemen on the sand. He was tall and broad shouldered and looked to be in his mid-forties. His olive skin, hooked nose and long, dark hair combed straight back off his forehead, gave him a faintly piratical appearance.

"Tell your men to leave off landing the boat for the moment," said Forward.

Kimber carried out Forward's instruction. Then he said, nervously, in a strong East Yorkshire accent, "I've already given t'other lad a statement, Inspector."

"Don't be alarmed. There's just one or two points I need to clarify." Forward took out the copy of Kimber's statement from his inside pocket and scanned it briefly. "You say you were on the Coble Landing on Monday night when you saw a small dinghy heading out to sea. This was just after eight thirty p.m. How can you be so sure of the time?"

"I checked it before I came out. It said eight twenty-five. If it were any later, I wouldn't have bothered. The weather were that crap."

"I see. How far is your home from the Landing?"

"Five minutes, no more."

"What made you come down to the Landing?"

"I were going to do some work on me son's bike and I found I'd left some tools be'ind in the boat."

"Right. Now, this dinghy you saw, was it far out at sea?"

"No, not far. An 'undred yards mebbe."

"And there were three people in it. Is that right?"

"Aye."

"Were they all men?"

"I dunno. It were pitch dark and I only saw their backs. They looked like men. I didn't take that much notice. It were a filthy night."

"But you're sure the dinghy was heading out to sea?"

"That's what it looked like."

"What kind of a dinghy was it?"

"One of them inflatable jobs. Y'know, with an outboard motor."

"It's not unusual to see a dinghy here at that time of night, is it?"

"Not unusual, no. There's all sorts of craft out in this bay at night. Even in bad weather."

"Were there any other boats around?"

"Aye, one or two."

"Near the dinghy?"

"No, much further out. But they weren't dinghies. They were proper boats. Fishing vessels."

"Like yours?"

"Aye."

"And you didn't see this dinghy return to the beach, is that right?"

"To tell you the truth I only glanced at it a second or two. As soon as I got me tools out of the boat, I was straight off 'ome. Like I said, it were a filthy night."

"So, presumably the Coble Landing was deserted? No-one was around but you?"

"Aye, that's right."

Forward showed Kimber a photograph of Mark Coulson. "Ever seen this man before?"

Kimber shook his head. "The other copper showed me that. No, I don't know him. Never seen him."

"Thank you very much for your information,

Mr Kimber," said Forward. "There's just one other thing. I'd like to hire your boat. And your crew too, of course."

Kimber's eyes grew dark and wary. "What for?"

"I'd like you to take us to Monks Bay."

"What? Up at Flamborough?"

"Yes, please."

"What? Now?"

"If you don't mind, Mr Kimber."

****

Arnold Kimber was unable to persuade any of his crew to accompany them on the trip to Monks Bay. They were far more interested in getting their midday meal. However, they did agree to lend the policemen their waders and to help get the *Octopus* underway. A metal bogie with four wheels had been pushed into the water and wedged bow first underneath the boat. This was done by the crew when landing, in order to transport the fishing coble easily over the beach. Now, Forward and Wilmott stood watching as Kimber's men put their shoulders to the bow of the boat and forced it slowly off the bogie and back into the sea, where it became perkily buoyant again.

Arnold Kimber had taken up a position in the wheelhouse. "Get aboard!" he ordered. He appeared much more confident now he'd assumed command of his vessel.

Forward splashed through the water towards the *Octopus*. He gripped the side of the boat up by the bow and tried to hoist himself aboard. But he had no experience of boats, and it took three attempts before he could even get his leg over the side. Laughter came from the men on the beach who were watching his pitiful attempts to climb aboard with great amusement. His pathetic struggle continued for several more seconds. Then he saw Arnold Kimber coming out of the wheelhouse. Kimber gripped him under both arms, hauled him inelegantly over the side and landed him on the smelly deck as if he'd been nothing more than a big cod.

Forward had just got to his feet, when Wilmott swung himself into the boat. He collapsed and lay spread-eagled with his back to the deck, panting.

"Not as easy as it looks," said Forward.

"I never thought it looked easy!"

Kimber invited Forward and Wilmott to squeeze in beside him in the boat's cramped little wheelhouse. Ahead of them, through the windows, was the long, chalk coastline of Flamborough Head, looking as unintimidating as a museum model. Forward started giving Kimber his instructions. He told him he wanted the boat to stay as close to the cliffs as possible all the way down to Monks Bay. At Monks Bay they would hove-to for a while off the bay, and then continue on until they rounded the headland. From there, they would head for Sandleton Harbour.

Kimber turned a switch and the engine started. He put the boat into gear, and then reversed a short distance to get away from the shore and into deeper water. Then he changed to forward gear, spun the wheel to port and set off, keeping the long sweep of Flamborough Head to starboard.

Forward glanced at his watch, then took out his notebook and made a note of their departure time in it.

Soon the boat had left the resort of Filey, and Arnold Kimber was steering it ever closer to the long headland which lay to starboard. When seen from the Coble Landing, the cliffs of Flamborough Head had seemed just a low, white wall on the horizon. Now, as the *Octopus* laboured towards them, they gradually grew larger by the minute, until they became immense, looming precipices three hundred feet high: accessible only to the multitude of seabirds that wheeled and soared, wings outstretched, around them.

"Can you take the boat any closer to the cliffs?" Forward asked.

"Bloody 'ell," said Kimber. "We're only fifty yards off 'em now. What do you want to go closer for?"

"You don't want to go any closer?"

"No, I don't. It's too dangerous."

"What's the problem?" said Forward. "Don't you know where the reefs are?"

"My family have fished out of Filey for generations," Kimber retorted. "I know the sea-bed like the back of my 'and. That's why you won't catch me going any closer in-shore than this."

The boat continued slowly but relentlessly on its course, and Forward found himself contemplating with wonderment the erosive power of the elements. Years of weathering had caused parts of the cliffs to collapse, forming miniature islands called stacks. These lone chimneys of rock towered out of the sea, some of them isolated from the land by quite large stretches of water. In the cliffs themselves were many V shaped inlets that the sea had cut deep into the chalk. And all this was formed, Forward reflected, before men and women walked the earth. He was reminded of his father's observation on his deathbed. 'Minerals mock us,' he'd said. 'Minerals mock us.' They did indeed.

"Plenty of places to land," said Wilmott.

"Only a fool 'ud land there," said Kimber. "Besides, the only way up out of those coves is to climb the cliffs."

Kimber suddenly took one hand off the wheel, raised his arm and waved. Several hundred yards out to sea on their port side, a small fishing boat was anchored, its nets trailing at right angles to it. "That's Pete Stone," Kimber explained.

"Do you know all the fishermen on this coast?" asked Forward.

"Not all, no. A good many though."

"Would any of them have been around this spot on Monday night?"

"One or two, I daresay."

Forward noticed that the motion of the boat had changed. It was pitching and rocking more noticeably.

"It's cutting up a bit rough," said Forward.

"Aye. It'll get worse. It always gets rougher as we near the end of the headland."

Kimber turned the wheel to port and the boat began to draw away from the shore. "There's a nasty spot coming up. We don't want to get tangled up with that."

Wilmott's face had gone grey. "How much longer before we make Monks Bay?" he asked.

"Another twenty minutes or so," said Kimber. "We're going against the flood y'see. We'd also get there much quicker if we weren't so close into the shoreline."

"What's your speed?" asked Forward.

"Around eleven knots. It's no speedboat."

"That dinghy you saw the other night," said Forward. "How many knots do you think that could do at top speed?"

"I wouldn't like to say. Twenty mebbe. Mebbe

more."

****

"There you are gentlemen, Monks Bay," announced Kimber.

Forward and Wilmott peered ahead through the wheelhouse window.

"Where?" asked Wilmott. "I can't see it."

"You will in a minute."

A huge stack was sticking out of the water ahead of them, filling their vision. Kimber steered the boat carefully around it, and at once a picturesque cove appeared, far wider and cut more deeply into the cliffs than any they had seen so far. Forward took out his notebook, checked his watch and made a note of the time.

"How long's it taken?" asked Wilmott.

"Forty-two minutes."

Kimber cut the engine and the boat began to drift with its bow at right angles to the shore.

"I don't want to go in any closer," said Kimber. "This bay's treacherous."

"Would that dinghy you saw have been able to land here?" asked Forward.

"More easily than this could. It'd 'ave 'ad only a fraction of the draught."

They stared at the scene before them for some time in silence. Although the tide had turned and was strongly on the flood, the water in the bay was still low enough for a substantial area of the beach to remain exposed. On it,

Forward could see officers in white suits, down on their knees conducting fingertip searches. Other officers from the dog unit stood and watched as a Springer Spaniel and a German Shepherd sniffed their way punctiliously across the chalk littered strand. How small and insignificant they seemed.

As Forward watched the sea powering into the bay, appropriating more and more of the exposed shore with every curling wave, he reflected on how different the bay looked when observed from the perspective of a boat off-shore: how sheer the cliffs were; and how numerous the steps leading out of the bay, to where the police vehicles could be clearly seen parked on the clifftop. For some reason, the sight made him more confident than ever that Dangerfield could never have murdered Coulson. He kept checking his watch until he'd established that ten minutes had elapsed. Then he said, "OK, Mr Kimber. Take us on to the entrance to Sandleton Harbour."

"You still want me to keep 'er close in to the shore?"

"As close in as you dare."

***

The next leg of the trip was so alarming that even the normally macho Wilmott expressed anxiety. After leaving Monks Bay, the wind beat up and gusted with sufficient force to keep the windows of the wheelhouse constantly obscured with a fine film of spray. The boat ploughed on through pounding six-foot waves as Kimber wrenched the wheel from side to side and struggled to hold the bow straight on against the incoming tide; all the time keeping an anxious eye on the treacherous coastline that lay so close to starboard.

As they drew near the gleaming white tower of Flamborough lighthouse that beckoned to them from the very end of the Head, the boat began to behave like a startled stallion. In the cramped wheelhouse, the three men clung to anything that was at hand to keep themselves upright. Even so, they still couldn't stop their bodies colliding and banging into each other as the boat pitched and tossed in the turbulent swell.

"I'll say one thing," Kimber shouted. "You've got bloody good sea legs. And my God, you'll need 'em for this next bit."

They began to round the Head.

Now, not only did the boat buck and toss, it was tilted from side to side. As he was flung from right to left across the wheelhouse, and back again, it seemed to Forward that the craft's angle was at a constant forty-five degrees.

"It's the cross-currents and the cross-winds," exclaimed Kimber. "That's what's making it so rough. This place 'as 'ad more wrecks than any other part of the coast."

"Let's hope we're not one of them," Forward yelled back.

"It wouldn't be so bad if we weren't 'uggin' the shore!"

After what seemed an age, the nightmare eventually passed. To Forward's immense relief the wind died, the waves subsided, and the familiar and comforting sight of Sandleton and its harbour appeared off the starboard bow. The boat had cleared the maelstrom around the Head and entered the comparative calmness of Sandleton Bay.

When they were within reasonable distance of the entrance to Sandleton Harbour, Forward again took out his notebook and made another careful record of the time.

"How long?" Wilmott enquired.

"An hour and twenty minutes in all, and that includes the stop-over at Monks Bay." Forward turned to Arnold Kimber. "Presumably, we'd have made much quicker time if the tide hadn't been against us?"

"That's right. We've had the flood tide against us all the way from Filey. It's slowed us down."

"What was the condition of the tide on Monday night?"

Kimber thought for a moment.

"It changed from ebb to flood about seven o'clock."

"So, the tide would have been against any boat going from Filey to Monks Bay, from seven onwards?"

"Nay, not right away. Tide takes about an hour to turn. You don't feel much while it's turnin'."

"But from eight o'clock onwards?"

"Oh aye. It would have been strongly against them from eight onwards."

"So, on Monday night it would have taken someone as long to get from Filey to Monks Bay as it's taken us?"

"Aye. If they were in a boat with the same size engine that did the same rate of knots."

Forward was silent. He was thinking.

Kimber nodded in the direction of Sandleton Harbour. "Do you want me to take her in?"

"No thanks. We're not getting off here," said Forward. "Tell me, Mr Kimber, could we have made this trip in that little dinghy you saw? And at night?"

Kimber roared with laughter. "If we 'ad rocks in our 'eads we could 'ave done."

"You're saying it's not possible, is that right?"

"You saw 'ow it was coming round the 'eadland. If we'd been in a dinghy that close to those cliffs, we'd 'ave been tipped straight into the drink."

"But could someone have got as far as Monks Bay in the dinghy?"

"Aye, if you were a local and you 'ad eyes like

a cat."

"So, only a fisherman could have done it?"

"No, I'm not saying that. There are a few experienced club sailors 'oo might 'ave done it."

"In a dinghy?"

"Aye. But no further than Monks Bay. Not on round Flamborough 'ead. Even I wouldn't do that in a dinghy tight on those cliffs at night, lad." Kimber looked at Forward quizzically. "Can I go 'ome for me dinner now?"

Forward nodded. "You can. I think we're all a bit hungry."

Kimber turned the wheel slowly to port.

"Do you still want me to keep close into the shore on the way back?"

"Er, that won't be necessary, sir, will it?" Wilmott said quickly.

"No, not this time," said Forward, enjoying the look of utter relief on his sergeant's face.

****

The return trip was relatively pleasant. At Filey, Kimber's crew came out to meet them with the tractor. Forward thanked Kimber for all his help and handed him two ten-pound notes. Then he and Wilmott managed to scramble over the side of the boat without getting too badly soaked.

As they walked across the beach towards the Coble Landing, Forward said, "What made a respectable headmaster take a trip like that on such a filthy night?"

Wilmott was silent for a moment; then, tentatively, he said, "If he did take such a trip, sir."

"You don't think he did?"

"It seems completely unbelievable to me."

"Does it?" Forward looked put out. He sighed. "Oh well, I'll have to find some way of convincing you."

They walked on in silence. Wilmott began to regret he'd dismissed his Chief Inspector's pet theory so conclusively. "Of course, the timing fits," he said, trying hard to make amends. "If Coulson had left Filey shortly after eight thirty, he would certainly have arrived at Monks Bay well before ten twenty-seven, the time he was killed."

Forward remained silent. Wilmott was accustomed now to his guvnor's intense brooding moods that were both disturbing and oppressive. "He's more moody than a woman," he'd complained to Marjorie on one occasion. Her instant retort of "Sexist!" had stopped him from making any further comments in a similar vein.

They reached the Coble Landing. "How did your play go last night, sir?" Wilmott enquired in an attempt to lighten things up.

Forward snorted, and launched into an account of some of the disastrous incidents that had occurred in the First Act. Wilmott's laughter encouraged him, and he went on to provide several more anecdotes. When he'd run out of these, he described his meeting with Lady Fernshawe and her husband.

They left the Coble Landing and strolled down Filey's Promenade.

"I can't understand why Lady Fernshawe's husband doesn't have the same name as she has," mused Forward. "And why hasn't he got a title?"

"I can tell you the reason for that," said Wilmott. "Lady Fernshawe is a Viscountess in her own right. Her family inherits through the female line."

"Really?" Forward tried to sound unimpressed. "I didn't realise they could do that."

"I believe it's quite rare, sir. Originally the Fernshawe family used to inherit through the male line, but way back in the seventeenth century there were three sons who were such utter scumbags their father disinherited them in favour of his daughter. He made it a condition in his will or something, that, from then onwards, the eldest daughter would take the title. If there was no female child, then the nearest female relative in line got it."

"I see. That explains why her husband has a different name." He regarded Wilmott satirically. "I had no idea you read Debrett."

Wilmott laughed. "I don't, sir."

"How did you find all this out, then?"

"At a darts match."

Forward was incredulous. "At a darts match?"

"Aye, last year in *The Blue Boar* at Melthorpe. Some of the locals were talking about her - y'know how they do. They're always gossiping about the Lord of the Manor in these village pubs. Anyway, I fell into conversation with them and they told me what I've just told you. They didn't agree with it, y'see. They thought the title should pass through the males."

"Did they tell you anything else about her?"

Wilmott thought for a moment. "They said she was a handsome woman."

"She is," said Forward.

"Apparently, she inherited the title only a couple of years ago. The word is she was something of a poor relation. Well-bred though, naturally. Used to be a market gardener near York. Then one day, she woke up and found herself a Lady. The previous Viscountess died without leaving any children, y'see."

"Lucky for some," said Forward.

"Aye."

"You've missed your way, Wilmott."

"How's that?"

"You're in the wrong profession. You should have been a Court correspondent!"

They neared the point on the Promenade

where Forward's car was parked. As they approached the vehicle, they heard a voice calling Forward on the RT.

"What now, I wonder?" said Forward, quickly unlocking the BMW. He got in and immediately reached for the radio. "Yes. Forward here."

"It's Hoggart, Chief Inspector. We've been calling you for over an hour."

Forward and Wilmott exchanged a quick grin in response to Hoggart's reproachful Birmingham twang.

"We've been on a boat ride," Forward said with relish.

There was outraged silence at Hoggart's end.

"Are you still there, Inspector?" asked Forward.

"They've found Dangerfield," said Hoggart.

"Good."

"He's at Viking's Chine. He's hanged himself."

CHAPTER NINETEEN

Viking's Chine was a beauty spot on the southern side of Flamborough Head. It was a deep, narrow ravine, which began a quarter of a mile inland and ended at the sea as a wide chasm in the cliffs. Through the bottom of the Chine flowed an innocuous little stream. Unbelievably, this small stream's relentless downhill questing for the sea had over time chiselled the deep gash of Viking's Chine into the landscape. The stream was also partly responsible for the presence of the ash and maple trees that overhung the Chine, and the lush, verdant woodland surrounding it. The source of the stream was a spring which emerged from high ground just above the Chine. The constant supply of fresh water and the shelter afforded by the steep walls of the ravine were the main reason Norsemen had established a settlement here, over a thousand years ago.

As it was on an isolated part of the headland,

the Chine could only be approached by a single-track road with passing places. Eventually, the road petered out in a clearing amongst the trees where there were toilets and a small parking area. When Forward and Wilmott arrived here, they found, in addition to the usual police vehicles, a white Ford Fiesta. Next to it stood DC Griffiths, talking to a young man in a tweed suit. Forward parked the BMW, and as he and Wilmott got out, Griffiths detached herself from the young man and came up to them.

Forward nodded in the direction of the stranger. "Who's that?"

"Alan Rawson. He's the nature warden here."

"Did he discover the body?"

"No. A couple out walking did."

"Where are they now?"

"I took their statements and sent them home," said Griffiths.

"Never do that," said Wilmott. "You should always keep anyone who finds a body isolated, until they are interviewed by a senior officer."

"They were very shocked."

"That's not the point."

Griffiths appealed to Forward. "They had nothing of any significance to add to their discovery of the body. I got their address if you want to speak to them."

"Didn't DI Hoggart interview them?"

"No, sir. He went straight over to Melthorpe

to break the news to Dangerfield's mother."

"It definitely is Dangerfield, then?"

"Oh yes." She pointed to the white Fiesta. "That's his mother's car."

"Right," said Forward. "Let's take a look at him."

Griffiths led her two colleagues to the Chine's entrance, which was a stile set within a hawthorn hedge. On the other side of the stile was a path, which went between lofty trees and then ran along one side of the ravine, shadowing it down to the sea. As Forward and Wilmott approached the stile, they saw the body of Richard Dangerfield. It was hanging by the neck from a thick branch of an ash tree which overhung the path, just a couple of yards beyond the stile. The weight of the body had curved the branch over in a tight arc. On the ground, just by Dangerfield's suspended feet, was a large metal litter bin lying on its side. Presumably this was what Dangerfield had stepped off into the unknown.

A number of SOCOs wearing face masks were engaged in various routine tasks connected with the ghoulish spectacle: Skipsea was dusting the litter bin for prints; Randall was placing a polythene bag on one of Dangerfield's limp and waxen hands; Grice was taking photographs of the corpse; Atkins had her tape measure out and was measuring the distance between the corpse's feet and the ground. Sir Andrew Marston was there too, also in a face mask. They all looked up as the detectives approached.

Any corpse commands attention, and despite themselves, Forward and Wilmott felt compelled to stare over the stile at the hanging man. Even though the face and neck were congested with dark red blood, and the features had been twisted by rigor mortis into an unnatural grimace, the face was undeniably that of the handsome ladies' man, Richard Dangerfield.

Wilmott took a small, involuntary step towards the corpse. Instantly he retreated with his hand over his mouth. "Christ! It stinks!"

"They usually do," said Sir Andrew Marston, from the other side of the stile. "Hence the face masks. Hanging invariably produces a bladder or bowel collapse. Sometimes both. If suicides knew beforehand the indignities associated with hanging, they might choose some less humiliating form of despatch."

"It's definitely suicide?" Forward enquired.

"A simple case, Chief Inspector," said Marston. "If suicide can ever, of course, be described as simple. Cause of death was self-inflicted asphyxia. Note the staring eyes, the blood red face, the protruding tongue, the bruises on the neck."

"I already have," said Forward.

"No other injuries," Marston went on, "and

no sign of a struggle. As you've probably guessed he took his last walk off that litter bin."

"What about a note?"

"No sign of a note," said Griffiths.

"Ah!" exclaimed Forward.

"In my experience," said Marston, "those who are serious about doing away with themselves rarely leave a note. They allow the deed to speak for itself."

"What time was the body found?" Forward asked Griffiths.

"Just after noon."

"By a couple who were taking their usual morning walk," explained the nature warden, who had joined them at the stile.

"That'll teach them to take exercise," quipped Marston and laughed.

"Do you live around here, Mr Rawson?" asked Forward.

The warden shook his head. "No. I live in Sandleton."

"Did you see any unusual people about the place yesterday? Anyone acting suspiciously?"

"Sorry, I can't say I did. But I can only speak for the afternoon. I don't start work until one. I'm employed part-time. The cuts, you see."

"Does anybody live out here? Anyone who might have seen anything?"

Rawson smiled wryly. "Only the squirrels and the badgers."

Forward asked Rawson some further routine

questions and then informed him that his presence was no longer required. When the warden had gone, Forward turned to Marston and said, "What time did Dangerfield do this?"

"Judging by the body temperature, the extent of rigor and the lividity, I'd say it was in the very early hours of this morning. Between one and two a.m. something like that." He prodded Dangerfield's upper leg with his gloved finger. "He's quite stiff."

"Yes. Now we know why he didn't make the bloody ID," said Wilmott grimly.

Randall came over to speak to Forward. "Excuse me, sir, but do you want Grice and me to go over Dangerfield's car for dabs?"

"Of course! Why not?"

Randall looked uncertain. "I just thought ..."

"As far as I'm concerned, we're still conducting a murder enquiry," Forward rasped.

"Yes, sir," said Randall, embarrassed. "Sorry, sir." He went back to join the other SOCOs.

Marston took a step back, looked up and regarded Dangerfield's body. "I understand this chap was one of your main suspects in the Monks Bay business."

"No, he wasn't actually," said Forward. "But he will be now, of course. It's too convenient!"

****

Forward left Wilmott to supervise the

lowering of the body for removal to the mortuary, and drove back to Sandleton Police Station. There were many pressing reasons why he needed to return to his office but principal among them was his desire to get away from the scene of Dangerfield's death. Richard's suicide, for suicide it undoubtedly was, had devastated him. He felt responsible for it. Other officers might have salved their consciences with the justification that Dangerfield had brought his own death upon himself. Not Forward. He was convinced it was his misguided belief in the young man's innocence that had contributed to his death. That was the top and bottom of it. If only he'd banged Dangerfield up until more evidence had become available, he'd still be breathing. In a cell, but breathing. All the way back to the police station Forward castigated himself. If only he'd listened to Wilmott. If only he'd held the identity parade yesterday. If only he'd never let the lad go.

"If only life weren't so bloody full of 'if onlys'," he muttered, as he drove into the police station's car park.

Forward realised his mistake as soon as he entered the station's reception area. Dangerfield's mother was sitting next to the duty sergeant's desk. A handkerchief was clenched in her fist and the skin around her eyes was raw from crying. Why hadn't he gone in by the back way as he usually did?

Mrs Dangerfield rushed straight over to him. "Inspector! Have you any idea what you've done? My son - my son is dead. Do you know that?"

"Mrs Dangerfield, I'm very sorry ..."

"Dead because you hounded him. Why didn't you leave him alone?"

Forward was aware that everyone in the reception area was watching him. It wasn't pleasant.

The vicar of Melthorpe, who had been sitting next to Mrs Dangerfield, came up and enclosed her wrist supportively between both his hands. "Maureen, dear," he said gently, "please calm yourself."

Mrs Dangerfield wrenched her arm away. "Leave me alone!" she screeched.

Out of the corner of his eye, Forward saw the duty sergeant coming round from behind his desk. "Mrs Dangerfield," said Forward, "I assure you, I never hounded your son."

"Then why has he hanged himself?"

Forward was unable to answer her. This was no time for the brutal truth.

"You think he did it because he murdered that man Coulson, don't you? That's what you think, isn't it?"

"Let's go to my office," said Forward quietly. "We can talk there."

"No!" Mrs Dangerfield screamed. "I have only

one thing to say to you. My son was no murderer! I know that. He was my son. I know he could never have killed anyone!"

She could control herself no longer. First the tears came, sudden watery rills slithering down her cheeks, and then great, shuddering sobs wrenched straight out of her heart.

The vicar's expression was one of enormous sympathy. He placed his arm around her shoulders for comfort and walked her slowly back to her seat. Forward could only look on impotently.

The duty sergeant came up to him. "She's taking it very badly, sir," he said in a voice just above a whisper.

"What do you expect?" said Forward. "It's her only son."

The sergeant took a step back. "Superintendent Jones wants you in his office, sir."

Forward breathed out heavily. "OK."

"He wants you right away, sir. As soon as the Chief Inspector comes in, that's what he said."

"Thank you, Sergeant. Oh, and when Mrs Dangerfield calms down tell her I'd still like a word with her."

****

Detective Chief Superintendent Jones was a high flyer who had entered the force after obtaining an honours degree in law at Leeds

University. He had made Sergeant at twenty-three; Inspector at twenty-eight; and Chief Inspector by thirty-one. Therefore, by his standards, making Chief Superintendent had been a bit of a slog: he'd had to wait another eight years before achieving his latest exalted position. Now, at the age of thirty-nine he coveted elevation to Assistant Chief Constable, and nothing was going to be allowed to interfere with his career plan.

Forward, of course, knew nothing of his superior's ultimate ambitions, but was aware, as were all the other officers, of the Welshman's lust for promotion. There'd been several occasions when Jones, sensing his promotion prospects threatened by Forward's original and unorthodox approach to detection, had responded by making his chief inspector's life as difficult as possible. This was the reason Forward now entered the superintendent's office in a state of apprehension. The sight of the Coulson file on Jones' desk only increased his anxieties.

"Sit down, Tony," Jones said briskly. He opened the file and picked up the first document. "This is the transcript of the interview you had with Dangerfield yesterday. Have you seen it?"

"No, sir."

"Well, I have. How, after an interview like that, could you have let the man go?"

"I believed his story, sir," Forward said calmly.

"Which story, man? He changed it so many times!"

"That's because he was frightened, sir."

Jones laughed derisively. "Of course, he was frightened. He was on suspicion of murder. A murder it now appears he committed."

"Why do you say that, sir?"

Jones looked astonished. "My God man! Haven't you heard? He's topped himself!"

"I know that, sir," said Forward patiently. "I've just come from the scene." He gave Jones a sharp stare. "But his death hasn't been confirmed as suicide yet."

"From what I hear it's only a formality." Jones returned Dangerfield's statement to the file. "By the way, where were you all morning? Hoggart said something about a boat."

"I was pursuing a line of enquiry, sir. I have a theory that Coulson arrived at Monks Bay by boat. I wanted to check it out."

Jones smiled patronisingly. "In the light of what's happened, Tony, I'd suggest that Coulson's means of conveyance to Monks Bay is now only of academic interest."

"That depends, sir."

"Depends on what?"

"On whether or not you think Dangerfield murdered Coulson."

The Superintendent sat back in his chair. He

was clearly bewildered. "Why else did he hang himself? Do you know something I don't?"

"No, sir. But there could be other reasons for it." Why was he saying this, he asked himself. To avoid the guilt?

"Such as?" demanded Jones.

"I don't know, sir."

"Well, I'll give you a reason," said Jones, bombastically. "The best possible reason. He was facing an ID parade and he knew he was going to be picked out!"

"That is a possibility, sir."

"In view of all the other evidence I'd say it was a certainty. Why did you let him go? You could have held him for thirty-six hours before applying for an extension. You know that. It would have given you plenty of time to set up the ID parade. He could have walked straight from his cell to the line-up. Now all this has happened. I've had a most distressing interview with his mother. I'm expecting her to lodge an official complaint."

"She has no grounds for that. I let him go because I thought he was innocent. Unwisely, I admit. But what did she expect me to do? We can't lock up everyone who falls under suspicion."

"She's claiming you hounded Dangerfield."

"She can't have it both ways, sir. I regret very much that I released Dangerfield. If I hadn't done so, he'd be alive now. But at the time it seemed the right decision."

Jones' mask of civility dropped. He flexed his wrist and thumped the flat of his hand down on the desk. "You've acted most irresponsibly. You should have stuck to established procedures. If you were so keen to establish his innocence, why didn't you expedite the ID parade?"

Forward sighed. "Because I believed his alibi witnesses, sir. There were gaps in his story but they weren't so big they'd have given him time to get all the way out to Monks Bay, murder Coulson and then get back to Luffield."

Jones' grey eyes had the look of a foxhound that has cornered the fox. "Well, you were wrong, weren't you? The time projections we obtained for that journey proved it was technically possible. More evidence, you couldn't wait for!"

"I still don't accept it was possible for Dangerfield to have done the murder in the time available," Forward said, wearily. Suddenly he found himself fighting back. "And even if it had been, how was Dangerfield to know Coulson was going to be at the bay at that particular time? A windswept bay on Flamborough Head is not the place you'd expect to find a respectable headmaster late at night in early April."

"What about Wilmott's theory that he was tipped off by phone from someone waiting in the car park at Monks Bay?"

"We've done a telecoms check on that. There were no calls between Monks Bay and Luffield that night. And why would Dangerfield want to murder Coulson anyway? Because sometime last year, Coulson upset his mother? It just doesn't stand up."

"All right. So why didn't you hold him until you were able to eliminate him?"

"I wish I had now." Forward's gesture showed his frustration. "It would have saved all this."

"It would have saved his life!"

Jones hesitated. Forward guessed he was about to say something insensitive. "Could it be, Tony, that you fell down on this because your attention was elsewhere?"

"I don't know what you mean."

"This show you're producing. It's taking up a lot of your time."

"It's my hobby, sir."

Jones looked smugly self-righteous. "I don't have a hobby. My job doesn't give me time for one. And that's how it is for most officers on this station."

"With respect, sir, I live alone and I have a good deal of time on my hands. Are you suggesting I should devote it exclusively to police duties?"

"Of course not, but Hoggart said you were very keen to get off early last night. You had to get to your show."

Forward stood up angrily. "I did not let Dangerfield go, sir, because having him in custody would interfere with my show."

"No. Of course you didn't. I wasn't implying that."

Forward struggled to control his temper. "Can I go now, sir? I have an appointment with Mrs Dangerfield."

"Is that wise?"

"I think so. I hope to convince her I haven't been hounding her son."

Jones considered this. "All right. It's worth a try. You might be able to persuade her not to take the matter further."

"Do I assume you want me to continue with the Coulson enquiry, sir?"

"Yes," said Jones. He handed Forward the file. "But only until Dangerfield's inquest."

****

Forward had to wait until he returned to his office before giving proper vent to his feelings. His office door bore the brunt of them. He slammed it rather harder than he intended, and a long crack appeared in the glass panel. This made him angrier than ever. Swearing, he flung himself into the chair behind his desk and reached for the phone. Then he had second thoughts. Should he ask for Mrs Dangerfield to be sent to his office or would it be more considerate if he went down to collect her? She might resent being brought up to his room like a wrongdoer. On the other hand, if he went down to collect her, she might create another scene in the reception area. That wouldn't go down well with Jones and his obsession with public relations.

He reached again for the phone. "Hello. Forward here. Get someone to bring Mrs Dangerfield up, will you? I'm in my office."

"I'm sorry, sir," said the duty sergeant. "Mrs Dangerfield's gone. Inspector Hoggart's taken her to formally identify her son's body. I told him you wanted to see her but he said it couldn't wait."

Forward thanked the sergeant and slammed the phone down. Who the bloody hell did Hoggart think was in charge of this enquiry?

A thought suddenly occurred to him. He immediately picked up the phone again and pressed for an outdoor line.

CHAPTER TWENTY

The 'CLOSED' sign was in place on the door of Miss Newbiggin's shop. Forward knocked and the door opened almost instantly. Miss Newbiggin already had her coat on and she looked very nervous. Forward waited for her to lock up and then escorted her to the BMW, where in the front passenger seat Wilmott was waiting for them. Forward introduced Miss Newbiggin to the sergeant and then started the engine.

"I've never seen a dead person before, Chief Inspector," said Miss Newbiggin, as they travelled the short distance to the hospital. "Not in the flesh, anyway."

"We're sorry to put you through this," said Forward, "but this young man may have been the one you saw watching the car park at Monks Bay. It's vital that you see him."

The hospital car park was some distance from the Pathology Department. As they approached it on foot, Forward's stomach turned over. DI Hoggart and Mrs Dangerfield were coming out of Pathology followed by the vicar. Forward stopped and said to Wilmott, "Take Miss Newbiggin through and get yourselves gowned up. I want a word with Mrs Dangerfield."

Forward stood waiting for the subdued trio to draw near him. Mrs Dangerfield was wracked with grief. Her handkerchief was clenched in her hand and she was constantly dabbing at her eyes. There was no need to ask whether she'd made a positive identification of the wretched young man they'd found hanging at Viking's Chine.

Forward acknowledged Hoggart and the vicar with a nod, then stared directly into the moist, tormented eyes of Richard Dangerfield's mother. "Mrs Dangerfield, I want you to know how upset I am about your son's death."

He was relieved to see that the look she returned him wasn't overtly hostile. "Thank you, Chief Inspector," she said in a voice that was barely audible.

"I'd still like to talk to you at the station if you feel up to it."

She nodded slowly, like someone in a trance.

"I'll see you later then. Hopefully I shan't be too long."

He left them and walked on quickly, thankful that Mrs Dangerfield hadn't asked him who Miss Newbiggin was and what she was doing there.

****

Forward entered the Pathology Department, smiled at the receptionist and then went down a corridor to the gowning-up area. He pulled on a green gown and then passed on through the labs and into the mortuary. At the far end of the room the drawer of one of the bottom cabinets had been pulled out. Sir Andrew Marston and Wilmott were standing on one side of the drawer, Miss Newbiggin on the other. They were all staring at Dangerfield's body. Forward moved towards them.

Only Dangerfield's head was visible. The rest of him was covered by a green sheet that went all the way up to his chin, concealing the shocking bruises on his neck. Marston had not yet commenced his autopsy so Dangerfield's skull was unshaved, and his thick, youthful hair gave his ghastly appearance at least some recognisable vestige of humanity. His face, still unnaturally engorged with blood, was now stippled with tones of purple and blue. The eyelids were only half closed, and the eyes behind them were rolled ghoulishly upwards so that only the whites showed. He looked as though someone had told him a particularly corny joke.

As Forward came up to them, Wilmott immediately shook his head at him and pulled a doubtful face. Sensing this, Miss Newbiggin looked up. The deep furrow of a frown appeared on her forehead and her facial expression was a mixture of fear and regret. "It's difficult because his face is so red," she said. "The man in the car didn't have a red face like that."

Forward silently exalted. He'd been hoping desperately she wouldn't be able to identify Dangerfield as the same person she'd seen sitting in the red Sierra. Nevertheless, he quickly reminded himself that as a detective his duty was to establish the truth, regardless of his own personal interests.

Marston gave Miss Newbiggin a superior smile. "That's what happens when you hang yourself. The face becomes congested with blood." He pointed to what appeared to be a series of fine cuts on Dangerfield's eyelids and lips. "Do you see these? Hanging compresses the veins, but the arterial blood continues to flow. That's why you get these tiny bleeding sites. You see them inside the mouth too."

Miss Newbiggin's expression became one of total compassion. "Poor creature," she whispered.

Forward decided that in the circumstances Marston's explanation had been unnecessarily anatomical. The last thing he wanted was for Miss Newbiggin to become morbid and sentimental. "Have another look and try to forget about the redness," he said.

Miss Newbiggin took in Dangerfield's horrific countenance again. She studied it for several seconds before saying, "I think it's him, Inspector. He's got the same hair and moustache." She gave an exasperated sigh, hunched her shoulders and turned her head from left to right in a vexed manner. "I don't know. I just don't know. Oh dear, I so want to get this right."

"Take your time," said Forward softly. "There's plenty of time."

"Yes, he's not going anywhere," said Marston tilting his head in the direction of the body.

Miss Newbiggin gave Marston a faint smile and then returned to her contemplation of the corpse. "He was sitting in the car all the time, you see. I only saw him in profile."

"Bend down until your eyes are level with the side of his head," Wilmott suggested.

"Wait a minute. She's on the wrong side," said Forward. "You saw his left profile, didn't you?"

Miss Newbiggin nodded. She walked round to the other side of the body, bent her knees and dropped down until she could see Dangerfield in profile.

"Yes, that's him," she said. "That's definitely him."

Forward was experiencing the acute emptiness that accompanies the abandonment of hope. "I think you'd better have a look at his clothes just to be absolutely sure."

"You've missed them," said Marston. "They were collected by forensic just before you arrived. If you'd let me know you were coming over, I'd have hung on to them." He brought his mouth close to Forward's ear and in a confidential tone said, "By the way, there was something of interest there."

He was about to continue but Forward held up a hand to stop him. "Sergeant, take Miss Newbiggin through to get changed, will you? Then contact forensic and tell them you'll be bringing a witness over to take a look at Dangerfield's clothing, particularly his leather jacket."

Marston looked perplexed. "He wasn't wearing a leather jacket."

"Forensic already have it."

"Ah."

Forward watched Miss Newbiggin and Wilmott leave, and then said, "Sorry, Sir Andrew, you were saying?"

Marston went over to the body, lifted the green sheet and pulled it back. He pointed to the knuckles of Dangerfield's right hand. They were stained with a rust-coloured substance that looked like dye. The stain extended in a faint streak along his hand and ended at the wrist.

"I found this stuff on the cuffs of his shirt

and jacket as well," said Marston.

"What is it?"

"Dunno. Possibly vegetable in origin. Forensic are checking it out."

"Looks like he brushed against something," said Forward, "up at the Chine maybe."

"I'm sure it's of no consequence; he undoubtedly committed suicide."

Forward stared down at the naked torso. Now that the sheet had been pulled back it was possible to see the full horror of the violence Dangerfield had inflicted on himself. The noose had cut deeply into his neck leaving behind an ugly brownish yellow groove in the shape of an inverted 'V'.

"When will you do the post-mortem?" asked Forward.

"Funnily enough, I was preparing to open him up when your sergeant and that good lady appeared. Want to stay and watch?"

"No thanks, but I'd like you to telephone me as soon as you get the results."

"Will do. How's *The Cherry Orchard* going?"

"Better than this case," said Forward. "And that's saying something." He started to walk away and was stopped by a sudden thought. "Were you here when Mrs Dangerfield identified her son?"

"I was," said Marston grimly. "She took it extremely badly."

"Did Hoggart show her the rope?"

"Yes."

"Did she recognise it?"

"No. She told Hoggart she'd never seen it before in her life."

CHAPTER TWENTY ONE

Forward drove Wilmott and Miss Newbiggin back to Sandleton Police Station, and there, Miss Newbiggin was transferred to Wilmott's car. While the Chief Inspector and his sergeant stood a short distance off chatting, Miss Newbiggin sat in the front passenger seat waiting patiently to be driven to forensic.

Wilmott nodded in the direction of Miss Newbiggin. "I was hoping to get away early tonight. Now I've got to take her all the bloody way to Hull."

Forward followed Wilmott's gaze and laughed. Miss Newbiggin's expression suggested she was anticipating the long drive with even less enthusiasm than Wilmott.

"No more early nights, Superintendent's orders," said Forward. "From now on we're all career policemen."

Wilmott gave him an understanding grin. He'd already been given an account of Forward's interview with Jones.

Forward watched them drive off, and then entered the building by the back entrance. He went straight along to his office. A pile of newly arrived documents and reports lay on his desk awaiting attention. He ignored them and picked up the phone.

"It's Forward. Is Mrs Dangerfield there? Good. Get someone to show her up to my office, will you? Oh, and tell her she can bring the vicar too, if he's still there."

Forward put the phone down. He picked up a paper knife and started to slit open a large buff coloured envelope. Inside was a bundle of computer print-outs: the record of craft movements that Jimmy, the Harbourmaster's assistant, had promised him. Forward turned over the pages, scanning them quickly. One page, however, engaged his attention much longer than the others. He picked up a pen and made some calculations on a notepad.

There was a knock, and then the door immediately opened. Mrs Dangerfield stood in the doorway. Behind her was WPC Turner.

"Mrs Dangerfield, sir," announced Turner. She waited until Mrs Dangerfield entered the room and then left, closing the door behind her.

Forward stood up behind his desk. He was relieved to see that Mrs Dangerfield was maintaining her composure. Her eyes still told the story of her grief, but she seemed to have regained possession of herself. He waited until she'd sat down and then told her how glad he was she'd been able to come and see him. She nodded, and for a few seconds they stared at each other awkwardly.

"I told them at the desk you could bring the vicar with you. Did you get the message?"

"Yes, I did, but I prefer to talk to you privately."

"That's fine," said Forward. "Just as you wish." He paused, then plunged in. "I want you to know you have my deepest sympathy at this difficult time."

"Thank you."

"I also want you to know that I never deliberately hounded your son. Quite the contrary. I was trying to do everything I could to establish his innocence."

Mrs Dangerfield's expression was uncompromising. "You think I'm going to make an official complaint, don't you?"

"That's entirely a matter for you. If you feel you have the grounds for one."

"I'm not sure that I do."

"Good, because I assure you my officers and I have acted with complete professionalism throughout this investigation. As I've already said, I believed Richard was innocent of Coulson's murder. I felt he had a very strong alibi for the time of Coulson's death."

"Then why did you force him to take part in

an identity parade?"

"Because I was certain he wouldn't be picked out. Then I could eliminate him from the enquiry."

"I still don't understand. Why did he have to be in the identity parade in the first place?"

"He didn't explain the reason to you?"

"Of course not. Why else would I be asking?"

"I'm sorry. A witness came forward who said they saw someone who looked like your son sitting in a red Sierra parked at Monks Bay early on Monday evening."

"I see."

"Naturally, we had to investigate that."

"Of course. But you said Richard had an alibi."

"That's right. At the exact time Mr Coulson was killed, Richard was fifteen miles away in Luffield. And he had several witnesses to prove it."

"Then, if you thought he was innocent and he had a strong alibi, why did he hang himself?"

"I don't know. That's what I'm trying to find out. So, if you're up to it, I'd like to ask you some questions about your son's movements yesterday."

"Very well."

"After my interview with him yesterday, your son was returned home by police car. The driver's time sheet shows he arrived at your house at four thirty-five. Were you in when he arrived?"

"No, I was still at school. The public don't believe this, but teachers work on long after the children have been sent home."

"I know they do," said Forward. "I knew someone who was a teacher." He was thinking of his ex-wife. "Was your son at home when you got in?"

"Yes."

"What time was that?"

"About six o'clock."

"What was his mood?"

The muscles around her mouth tightened. "He was very upset. He said you'd spoken to him that morning at work and you'd taken away his car and his jacket. Then in the afternoon he'd felt ill and got a taxi home. He'd only been in the house for half an hour when the police appeared and carted him off like a criminal."

"I'm sorry we had to do that," said Forward. "But we discovered he hadn't been completely honest with us. When we went back to question him again at his place of work, we found he'd disappeared."

Mrs Dangerfield said nothing, but Forward knew his explanation hadn't satisfied her. "When you last saw him would you say Richard was very depressed?" he said.

"Anxious rather than depressed. He was

worried about the identity parade."

"But he didn't say why?"

"No." Mrs Dangerfield shrugged her shoulders unhappily. "He wouldn't discuss it. But I could tell he was nervous about it. He'd never been involved in anything like that before."

"All right. What did he do for the rest of the evening?"

"He went up to his room. I wanted to cook him some dinner but he said he didn't have any appetite. Then, about an hour later, he went out and … and I never saw him again." She closed her eyes. Her chin went down on her chest and she sobbed quietly. Forward waited. It was always best to say nothing and wait until they became more composed. Eventually she ceased sobbing.

"So, he left the house at around seven?" he prompted her gently.

"Something like that."

"Did he give you any idea where he was going?"

"No. He seldom told me anything like that."

"Did he have a girlfriend?"

She looked aggrieved. "I wouldn't know. Like I said, he seldom told me anything. He knew I'd disapprove. His way of life was so alien to me you see. He was a very bright boy. At one time I expected great things of him, university and all that. I never dreamed he'd end up working on a building site and squandering his money on drink."

"Did he drink a lot?"

"Far more than was good for him. He often had terrible hangovers."

"Were you aware that he was taking drugs?"

Mrs Dangerfield stared at Forward as though he was psychic.

"Yes, I was," she said. "How did you know that?"

"He admitted it to us. How did you find out he was using drugs?"

"I found them in his pockets from time to time when I was getting his clothes ready for the wash. He was very careless, and I'm a teacher, don't forget. I know what to look for. Mr Coulson was a great anti-drugs campaigner. Every year he'd invite your colleagues to bring a film into school on the dangers of drug abuse."

"Did you ever tell Richard you'd found drugs in his pockets?"

"No." She gestured helplessly. "It would only have caused another scene."

"Did Richard ever mention a pub called *The Three Bowmen*?"

"I don't think so. It's in Luffield, isn't it?"

"Yes." Forward considered his next question. He decided that however he put it, it was going to sound brutal. "Can you think of any reason why your son should commit suicide?"

She looked mystified. "No. None. None at all. He enjoyed his dissolute life too much. I can't think of any reason why he should have wanted to end it."

"Then why do you think he did end it?"

She thoughtfully shook her head. "I don't think he did. I'm sure it was done against his will. It wasn't in his nature."

"You think he was coerced into it?"

"It's the only explanation."

"The pathologist told me you didn't recognise the rope that Richard used."

"No, I didn't. There was nothing like that in the house."

"You're suggesting he was murdered?"

Mrs Dangerfield's chin lifted defiantly. "Yes. I am."

"I'm sorry to tell you the pathologist disagrees with you. He's convinced it was suicide."

She stared at him levelly. "And you? What do you think?"

Forward did not answer. He folded his arms across his chest. "I'm going to be completely frank with you, Mrs Dangerfield. Yesterday I believed your son was innocent of Mr Coulson's murder. That's why I let him go. But there's new evidence now that indicates very strongly he may have done it. I'm sorry."

"What new evidence?"

"I'm afraid I can't go into that at this stage."

Mrs Dangerfield was obviously trying very hard to take in the implications of what Forward had said. "So, you're saying Richard murdered Mr Coulson and then became overwhelmed with guilt and killed himself?"

"That's a possible explanation."

She shook her head vehemently. "I find that totally incredible. Why should he kill Mr Coulson? The difference of opinion I had with him blew over months ago. What could Richard have possibly hoped to gain by Coulson's death?"

What indeed, Forward wondered. But he kept his doubts to himself. "It does seem an odd motive for killing someone, but I have come across even more bizarre motives in my career," he said. "Perhaps he cared about you more than you realised."

Her look implied he was insulting her intelligence. "That's sentimental nonsense, Inspector, and you know it."

"Could Coulson have become an obsession for Richard? For example, did he constantly keep mentioning his name or making threats about him?"

"No, nothing like that. Ever. I told you that when I spoke to you before."

"Let me get this absolutely clear. You're saying your son never bore Coulson a grudge. Is that right?"

"That's right."

"So, when he threatened Coulson in the pub it was done simply because he knew Coulson had rowed with you earlier, and made you upset?"

"Yes."

"But Richard had something of a bad temper, didn't he?"

"When he'd had a lot to drink, yes. But he was never physically violent."

Forward decided to focus on her relationship with the headmaster. "You said you and Mr Coulson didn't always see eye to eye professionally. Does that mean you had a lot of rows?"

"Yes. Several, I'm afraid. You see, during the past six months his behaviour began to get very strange." She paused. Forward suspected she was not the sort of woman who talked ill of the dead, and this was not easy for her. "I often thought he was on the verge of a nervous breakdown," she continued. "In fact, when I learned he was dead, my first thought was that he'd committed suicide. I suppose I ought to have told you this before, when you first interviewed me, but the shock of his death put it completely out of my mind."

"You say his behaviour was very strange. In what way?"

"There were hundreds of tiny little examples, I can't remember them all."

"All right. Tell me why you rowed with him

the day Richard came home and found you crying."

She nodded in recollection. "It was over the stock cupboard. I've been a teacher at the school for nearly twenty years, and during all that time the school stock, you know, pencils, exercise books, that sort of thing, was kept in a cupboard in my room. Then, one day, about five months ago, Mr Coulson said he was concerned about the amount of stock that was being wasted. He said he was going to put it all in a cupboard in his own classroom and keep it locked. If anyone wanted any stock, they'd have to let him know and he'd get it for them. After a couple of weeks of this, I went and told him that the part-time teacher in the school and I found this arrangement very inconvenient. I asked him if he would at least keep the cupboard unlocked so that we could have access to the stock. He refused. I told him that he was being very unreasonable and he got incredibly angry. We had a terrible row. That's why I came home in tears."

"Were there any other incidents like that?"

"Yes, there were." She smiled sadly. "It's odd, isn't it? Once you start talking about these things, everything comes flooding back."

"Go on."

"I had another set-to with him over the school fund. Just before the Christmas holidays Mr Coulson and the school governors organised several fund-raising events. They were to help buy an extra computer for my classroom. Three hundred pounds in cash was raised. Yet towards the end of January, I still hadn't received the computer. I asked Mr Coulson when it was going to come and he said he didn't know but it was on order. Another couple of weeks went by and the computer still hadn't arrived, so I decided to give the company that was supplying it a ring. I was looking for the phone number in the secretary's office when I came across a folder with all the school fund's bank statements in it. The latest statement was for January, but the three hundred pounds hadn't been credited to the account. There was no sign of it on the December statement either."

"He hadn't paid it in?"

"Well, what else was I to think?"

"What did you do about it?"

"At first, nothing. As you can appreciate, it put me in a very difficult position. I couldn't approach him directly about it because it would look as though I was accusing him of keeping the money for himself. In the end I told him that if the computer didn't arrive that week, I was going to ask one of the school governors to complain to the company. I thought it might force him to pay the money into the account, you see."

"And how did he react to that?"

"Very badly. He blew his top. Told me I was trying to teach him how to do his job and that I had no right to approach anybody about the computer but him."

"Did the computer ever arrive?"

"Yes, four days later. He went and collected it himself."

"So, everything turned out all right?"

"Yes." Her eyes grew wide. "But this is the most extraordinary thing. By then I'd become quite suspicious of him, so I decided to keep a check on the monthly bank statements. When I looked at the statement for February, the three hundred pounds still hadn't been paid in, but the sum of twenty thousand pounds had."

"Is that unusual?"

"Of course. The school fund usually has only a few hundred pounds in it. It's money raised by the governors and parents. Our school could never have got hold of that kind of money."

"Where do you think it came from?"

"I've no idea. I never said anything about it. I didn't want anyone to know I'd been snooping around, you see."

Forward wrote something down on his notepad. "Which bank deals with the school fund?"

"The Great Northern in Luffield. The same one I use. Mr Coulson has his own personal account there too."

"Did anything else happen that you thought

was unusual?"

"Not that I can think of. Most of Mr Coulson's temper outbursts were caused by very trivial things." She had a sudden thought. "Wait a minute though, he did have an argument with a parent a few days before he was killed. But I don't suppose that's significant."

"Tell me about it anyway."

She frowned as she tried to recall the incident. "It would have been last Wednesday, I think. I was at home when I realised I'd left some marking in my classroom. So, I went back to get it."

"What time was this?"

"About five thirty. As I entered the school, I heard raised voices in Mr Coulson's room. Mr Gibbard, the parent, was asking Mr Coulson to do something. I don't know what it was but Mr Coulson was refusing. I heard Mr Gibbard say something like 'You must do it, you've got no choice,' and Mr Coulson shouted back, 'I don't respond to this kind of pressure, you should know that.' They were getting quite heated. I didn't hang around; I went straight to my room and collected my work. They were still going at it hammer and tongs as I left."

Forward made some more notes. "Thank you for telling me this, Mrs Dangerfield," he said. "When you get home, I'd like you to write down what you've just told me and anything else that comes to mind. I may require you to sign a formal statement in due course."

Mrs Dangerfield looked affronted. "I'm not speaking ill of Mr Coulson because I'm trying to clear my son's name."

"No, I'm sure you're not." His tone became supportive. "But even if you were, it would be a perfectly understandable reaction."

She seemed slightly mollified. "Will there be an inquest?"

"For Richard? Yes."

"And will the inquest decide whether he was guilty of Mr Coulson's murder?"

"The coroner will want to enquire into all the possible reasons for your son's death, but he won't be in a position to decide if Richard murdered Mr Coulson." Forward stared into her vulnerable blue eyes and hoped he looked reassuring. "If Richard really was innocent of Coulson's murder, I will do everything in my power to prove it. I promise you that."

CHAPTER TWENTY TWO

As soon as Mrs Dangerfield had left, Forward began to selectively wade through the mountain of papers that had accumulated on his desk. The first report he studied was the national police computer response to his request for a previous convictions search relating to the crew of the *Phaeton*. The large, blank spaces under each crew member's name told him at once that none of them had any major 'form' to speak of. Only one had a previous conviction and that was for a petty motoring offence. Forward turned his attention to the other items on his desk. Those connected with the Coulson case consisted mainly of copies of statements made in the course of enquiries. He filed these away carefully, then rang for a messenger. He had just replaced the receiver when the phone rang. It was Sir Andrew Marston.

"I didn't expect you to be there at this time," barked the familiar, imperious tones.

"We're on a productivity drive. Well, what have you got?"

Marston laughed wickedly. "As his own hangman this chap Dangerfield was not an overwhelming success. What makes hanging the suicide's preferred choice is that if done properly it severs the spinal cord in one clean break and the lights go out immediately. This fellow botched it and strangled himself to death. Judging by his elevated carbon dioxide levels, he must have been dancing on the end of the rope for several seconds. Result: death by asphyxiation and cerebral ischemia."

"Anything else?"

"Nothing much. No external wounds or marks apart from those made by the rope and that funny stain on his wrist. The labs are doing an analysis of that by the way. Bit of a heavy drinker, I would say. Some very slight damage to the liver and a touch of irritated bowel syndrome. Otherwise, he was a perfectly healthy young man. If his mind had been in the same condition as his body, he'd have lived for years."

"What about the time of death?"

"We've pinpointed that to after midnight, probably between one and two a.m. His stomach was empty, hadn't eaten anything since around lunchtime. He'd had a drink though, about one and a half pints, four or five hours before he died. We're running the usual toxicology tests for poisons and so on, but I'd be surprised if they yielded anything."

"So, in your view he definitely committed suicide?"

"That's what the evidence suggests."

Forward said, "Is it possible he could have been strangled elsewhere and then strung up at the Chine to make it look like suicide?"

Marston was adamant. "No. The injuries to his neck are not consistent with manual strangulation. Besides, there were no marks on the ground to suggest that his body had been dragged across it to the tree where it was suspended."

"He could have been carried there," Forward suggested.

"Possibly," said Marston. "But when a corpse is suspended after death, the rope is tied around the neck first and the body hauled up. That would have left distinctive marks on the branch of the tree, showing that the rope had been moved upwards from below. This was definitely suicide because the marks on the branch show that the rope travelled downwards under Dangerfield's weight. Fibres from the rope were also found on Dangerfield's hands. They wouldn't have been there if someone had suspended him after death. He definitely put the noose around his own neck."

"I see," said Forward. "If anything comes up on the blood tests, I'd like the results at once."

He was clutching at straws and he knew it.

"You won't get it from me, I'm afraid. I'm off to see *The Cherry Orchard*. Aren't you going to be there?"

Forward's heart sank. "I'll be dropping in at some point."

"Good. Perhaps you'll join me for a drink afterwards. I'll entreat you to my skills as a drama critic."

"I can't wait."

Sir Andrew rang off just as Hudson, one of the civilian assistants, appeared. Forward picked up the report detailing the previous convictions of those who'd been on board the *Phaeton*, hastily scribbled a note on it and handed it to Hudson. "Photocopy this and fax it off to NCIS," he instructed. NCIS (pronounced 'encis') were the initials of the National Crime Intelligence Service, a central police agency that collated details of various crimes from all over the country. If any of the *Phaeton's* crew had had the remotest connection with anything illegal, their details would be on the NCIS central database.

After Hudson left the room, Forward picked up the phone and dialled the number of the incident centre at Monkhouses. It was Hoggart who answered. Forward enquired if there'd been any developments.

"None at all. There's no sign of the murder weapon or the knife. No-one's recognised the anorak either. One thing though, Sergeant Fellows of York CID has been on. He interviewed Helen Coulson, Coulson's ex-wife today. They're faxing her statement over to you."

"Oh? What's in it?"

"Helen Coulson said she hasn't spoken to her ex-husband for a couple of years. And she has a cast iron alibi. She's a music teacher at some comprehensive in York. On Monday night she was conducting the school orchestra in a concert. Her daughter, Rachel, was in the concert too, playing the cello. It didn't finish until ten p.m. and there was a reception afterwards. Neither of them got home until after eleven. The last time the daughter saw her dad was a couple of months ago, and she didn't notice anything unusual about him."

"What about the boy? Philip. Where was he on Monday night?"

"Ah, now he left home months ago. Drove off on his motor bike and wasn't seen again."

"He's a missing person?"

"Yes."

"And he drives a motor bike? So, he could have driven it to Monks Bay on Monday night?"

"No. Fellows has been on to the DVLA. Philip sold his motor bike in Leeds to a second-hand bike dealer just a few days after he left home. Must have needed money. DVLA say he's no longer registered as owning any kind of

312

vehicle."

"Still, we'd better put out a shout."

"I have done but it's all pretty academic now."

'Academic'. That was the word Superintendent Jones had used. Had those two been talking? Forward had always suspected them of being very thick. Like Jones, Hoggart lusted after power.

Forward became disingenuous. "Why do you say it's all academic?"

"Stands to reason. Dangerfield killed Coulson. That's why he topped himself."

Forward knew he was obliged to inform Hoggart that Miss Newbiggin had been to the mortuary and formally identified Dangerfield as the man she'd seen in the red Sierra. But he couldn't bring himself to do it. "We must be very careful about making assumptions," he said. "And Superintendent Jones agrees with me about that. He's authorised me to continue with the Coulson enquiry at least until Dangerfield's inquest."

"Oh." Hoggart sounded disappointed.

Forward said, "Now, Thwaites mentioned that on Monday night between ten p.m. and midnight, three fishing boats returned to Sandleton Harbour. Get someone over to the Harbourmaster's office to find out who owns them and have them checked out."

"You think one of these fishing boats took Coulson from Filey to Monks Bay?"

"I doubt it, but they need investigating because they were the only craft to enter Sandleton Harbour around the time that Coulson was murdered. Will you get someone onto it?"

"Very well. Are you doing a case review later?"

Forward looked at his watch. It was twenty past five. "I think I'll let you supervise the review this evening. I've a lot on my plate at the moment and I have to make one or two further enquiries."

There was silence at Hoggart's end. Eventually he said, "You'll be missing your play tonight, then?"

"Oh, I expect I'll find time for that," Forward said provocatively, and hung up.

The phone rang again immediately. It was Chief Superintendent Jones.

"Hello Forward, did you have a word with Mrs Dangerfield?"

"Eventually, yes."

"Is she going to make a complaint?"

Forward smiled to himself mischievously. It would be fun to keep Jones on the hook. "I don't know," he said. "She never actually said."

****

Half an hour later Wilmott appeared in Forward's office. The news he brought did nothing to lift the Chief Inspector's spirits.

"Miss Newbiggin recognised Dangerfield's leather jacket, sir. She's completely convinced now it was him she saw sitting in the Sierra."

"That's a shame," said Forward.

"A shame, sir?"

"Yes. I was rather hoping she wouldn't."

"But surely it means Dangerfield must have had something to do with Coulson's death?"

"Logically, yes."

"But not laterally?"

Forward smiled and said, "Come on, let's go for a drink."

Wilmott looked uncomfortable. "No thanks. I'm late as it is: I promised Marjorie I'd be home before six. She's had Linda on her hands all day. She resents it if I don't give her an hour or two off in the evenings."

"I'm not inviting you for a social drink, Sergeant, we're still on duty. Marston says that Dangerfield went for a pint about four or five hours before he died. He died between one and two a.m. in the early hours of this morning. So that means he was drinking after seven p.m. last night. We need to check that out. It's possible he was drinking in Luffield, so we'll make a start in his favourite watering hole, *The Drovers*."

"Right you are, sir," said Wilmott. "Can we go in our own cars? At least then I'll be able to drive straight home when we've finished."

"Now that's interesting."

"What is, sir?"

"Nothing, Sergeant. Just thinking laterally again."

****

The Drovers was crowded. Forward and Wilmott had to squeeze past several bodies to get to the bar. Sandra, the barmaid, had her hands full, but as soon as she saw Forward she left the customer she was serving and came down the bar towards them. She looked apprehensive.

"Yes? Is anything wrong?"

"We need to ask you a few more questions," said Forward. "But serve your other customers first."

Sandra smiled nervously and went back to the pumps.

A young, formidable looking man perched on a bar stool next to Forward was staring at him curiously. Forward turned his back on the man and asked Wilmott what he wanted to drink.

"Just a half please. What time do you think we'll be finished? I need to phone Marjorie and tell her when I'll be home."

"If we get the right answers here you could be on your way in ten minutes. If not, we'll have to work our way round all the pubs in Luffield."

"I'll give her a ring anyway."

"Not from here you won't. There's no public

phone, remember."

A middle-aged man in a grey suit came down some stairs behind the bar directly opposite where they were standing.

"Can I get you gentlemen a drink?" he enquired.

Forward gave him their order. Afterwards he handed Wilmott a five-pound note. "Pay for the drinks with this," he said. "I need to go to the gents."

Forward's visit to the toilet was not just from biological necessity. He wanted to establish that there was no condom machine in there. There wasn't. He returned to the bar and gave Wilmott this information.

Wilmott took a sip from his half pint glass. "You still think Dangerfield was telling the truth, don't you?"

"If you thought that as a result of your decision a man had died, wouldn't you be trying to justify it?"

"I expect I would."

At that moment Sandra came back. She glanced quickly at the man sitting on Forward's left. "Well. What else do you want to know?"

"Was Richard Dangerfield in here again, last night?"

She seemed surprised. "I think so. Yes, he was."

"What time was that?"

"Let's see. About half past seven."

"Weren't you surprised to see him?"

She looked uneasy. "No. Why?"

"I thought you said he only came in on Mondays."

"He came in regularly on Mondays, but he sometimes dropped in during the week as well."

Forward took a mouthful of beer. "What sort of mood was he in last night?"

"I don't know. I hardly spoke to him. It was very crowded."

"Did he seem his normal self?"

"How could I tell? I don't know him that well. He didn't seem strange, if that's what you mean."

"Did he meet anyone here?"

"I don't think so. I didn't take much notice. Like I said, it was very crowded."

"What time did he leave?"

"He didn't stay long. Left just after eight I'd say."

"And he didn't give you any idea where he was going?"

"No. I barely spoke to him."

"Who are these people, Sandra?"

The interruption came from the young man sitting next to Forward.

"They're the policemen I was telling you about." She made a sudden, nervous gesture in Forward's direction. "This is Inspector Forward." She stared at Wilmott. "I'm sorry, I don't know your name."

"Wilmott, Sergeant Wilmott."

"This is Terry, my husband," said Sandra.

Sandra's husband nodded.

"We're enquiring about a man called Richard Dangerfield," said Forward. "Do you know him?"

"No, I don't. I don't get in here much. Sandra says he comes in on Monday nights."

"Not any more, I'm afraid," said Forward. "He's dead. He was found hanged this morning."

The glass that Sandra was holding slipped from her grasp and smashed into fragments on the floor behind the bar. For a split second all conversation ceased and the pub went silent. Then there was a drunken cheer followed by a ripple of amusement that went all round the room and after that talking resumed.

Sandra's outspread palm was pressed flat to her chest just below her throat. "Oh, what a shock. What a terrible shock."

"Yes, it was rather," said Forward, "for all concerned."

****

Forward and Wilmott left *The Drovers* and walked down Luffield's main street.

"While we're here I think we'll call into *The Three Bowmen* and see if anyone remembers seeing Dangerfield in there on Monday night.

We should have done that yesterday. I slipped up there."

"It wouldn't have made much difference though, would it, sir?"

"I'd have felt better."

Forward left Wilmott in a telephone box and went into *The Three Bowmen* alone. It was even more packed than *The Drovers*. Two barmen were serving. Forward showed them Dangerfield's photograph. Both young men had been working behind the bar on Monday night but neither of them could recall serving Dangerfield.

Disappointed, Forward left his drink unfinished and made for the door. On his way out he had to pass the gents. He took a quick look inside to see if there was a condom machine on the wall. There was.

Forward left *The Three Bowmen* and walked back down the street to the telephone box. Wilmott was still in there talking to Marjorie. When he saw Forward was waiting for him he quickly ended his call.

"Any luck, sir?"

"No. No-one remembered him being there. Hardly surprising. The place was packed to the gills. I don't suppose the bar staff even look at their customers when they're serving. They're just a blur. A sea of anonymous faces."

"Marjorie sends her regards."

"Thank you," said Forward. He looked

pleased. "How's the little terror?"

Wilmott smiled. "Driving her up the wall. She was very glad I'll be home in half an hour."

They retraced their steps back up the main street to where their cars were parked.

"I wonder why Coulson never phoned his wife?" Forward asked suddenly.

"On Monday night, you mean?"

"Yes. Like you just did. You knew you were going to be late and your wife didn't. So you rang her up and told her what time you'd be home. I expect you told her not to worry, something like that, didn't you?"

"I did actually."

"Yes. So why didn't Coulson do that?"

"Perhaps there wasn't a phone available."

"There are plenty of phone boxes in Filey. And there's one in the car park at Monks Bay."

"I'm sorry. I don't understand what you're getting at, sir."

Forward stopped suddenly, halted by the power of his own insight. "Look, you phoned your wife because you thought you were going to be late."

Wilmott looked at him uncertainly. "Yes?"

"But Coulson didn't phone his wife even when he got to Filey. He didn't want her to know he was going to be late. Even though he knew she'd be anxious." Forward became animated. His eyes were gleaming. "Don't you see? Despite all the anxiety he knew his lateness would cause her, he still didn't ring her."

Wilmott considered this. "I'm sorry I don't quite understand. Are you saying he didn't want her to know where he was?"

"When you rang your wife just now, did she want to know how late you were going to be?"

"Yes."

"Did she ask what time she could expect to see you?"

"Yes."

"I thought as much. It's perfectly natural."

Wilmott looked perplexed. "So, Coulson didn't ring his wife from Filey because he couldn't tell her what time he'd be home?"

"Almost certainly."

"I see. But how does that help us?"

Forward didn't answer. They walked on and arrived at their parked cars. Wilmott bade Forward a grateful good night and got into his vehicle. As Forward watched his sergeant drive off down the main street, a small but sudden revelation came to him. For the first time that day he experienced a trickle of optimism.

****

The Sandleton Players were well into the Second Act of *The Cherry Orchard* as Forward entered the darkened school hall. Attendance at that evening's performance was lower than on previous nights and he had no difficulty in finding an unoccupied seat. He settled down and tried to apply himself to the technical aspects of the actors' performances, but was annoyed to find that the events of the day kept impinging on his thoughts. He was relieved when the interval came.

He was standing in the refreshment area, chatting to some ex-members of the Players, when he noticed Sir Andrew Marston. He was by the serving hatch getting a glass of orange juice. Forward excused himself and strolled over.

"Ah, Forward," said Sir Andrew, raising his glass as though he were about to propose a toast. "Excellent production. Almost as good as the one I saw at York two years ago. You've done wonders with these amateurs."

"A director's only as good as the talent he works with," said Forward.

"Come, come, Inspector. No false modesty please. I've seen this lot in many, many productions. It was all they could do to find their way around the stage and be heard!"

Even at a quiet, conversational level Marston's resonant and perfectly enunciated tones were audible to those standing at the other end of the room. A number of disapproving glances from friends and relatives of the cast were being shot in his direction. Forward decided it was time to quickly change the subject. "Isn't Lady Marston with you this evening?"

"No. It's not in my wife's nature to be a social animal, Forward. She made her annual attendance at the golf club dinner and as far as she's concerned that's enough for this year. I sometimes wonder if it isn't something to do with me."

I can't imagine why, Forward thought.

"Did you get my message?"

"Message?"

"Phillips, my assistant, was going to ring you with some information on the Dangerfield boy."

Forward glanced around uncomfortably. He took Marston by the arm. "Let's go into the foyer."

"What on earth for? It's freezing out there."

"I'm not happy about discussing this in front of half of Sandleton."

Marston laughed. "You exaggerate your attendance figures, surely. But I take your point."

They strolled into the foyer. Sir Andrew lit a cigarette. "Shouldn't be using these damn things. I see what they do to people's lungs every day."

"What do you have to tell me about Dangerfield?" asked Forward, patiently.

"A trivial thing really. We discovered small traces of cannabis in Dangerfield's blood and urine. Probably the residue of a much larger amount he'd consumed earlier on in the week."

"When?"

"Oh, I couldn't possibly tell you that with any precise accuracy. Sunday or Monday I should say. Probably Monday."

CHAPTER
TWENTY THREE

At ten o'clock the next morning, Forward obtained a warrant from the Sandleton Magistrates' Court authorising him to search Mark Coulson's personal bank account; also, the school fund account of Melthorpe Primary School. An hour later Forward and Wilmott were sitting in the office of Andrew Wilson, the manager of the Great Northern Bank in Luffield. On the desk in front of him were computer print-outs of the various accounts they'd asked to see.

"The school fund is kept in two accounts," said Wilson, a surprisingly young man. "One deposit and one current." He handed Forward a computer print-out. "That's the deposit account."

Forward examined the print-out carefully. It revealed that on the third of February, twenty thousand pounds had been credited to the account; and on the eleventh February, eight thousand, four hundred pounds withdrawn.

"Weren't you surprised that such a large amount was placed in this account?" Forward asked.

"Not really. Schools often sell off their playing fields and recreation areas to builders these days."

Forward looked incredulous. "Didn't you ask where the money came from?"

Wilson smiled complacently. "It's not our policy, Inspector, to enquire where the money comes from. If we did that every time a deposit was made, we'd never get any work done."

"Was the money paid in by cheque?"

"Let me have a look," said Wilson. He held his hand out for the computer print-out. Forward passed it to him.

"No," he said glancing at it. "Cash."

"The twenty thousand was deposited in cash?"

"Yes."

"Isn't that unusual?"

"Not as unusual as you'd think. We often receive cash deposits for large amounts."

"I see that eight thousand, four hundred pounds was withdrawn on the eleventh of February. Was that taken out in cash?"

Wilson scanned the account record again. "Yes, it was."

"We'll need to know who paid the twenty thousand in, and who withdrew the eight thousand, four hundred. Can you find out for us?"

"Certainly, just hold on a minute." Wilson picked up his phone, applied himself to the account record again and then phoned through the details.

It took Wilson several minutes to obtain the information requested. "The twenty thousand in cash was paid in by Mr Coulson personally. He also personally withdrew the eight thousand, four hundred in cash." He handed the print-out back to Forward.

"Thank you," said Forward. "We'll have a look at the other two accounts now."

The school fund current account revealed nothing of interest. It had a balance of four hundred and sixteen pounds and during the past year only small sums had passed through it. But no sign of the three hundred pounds raised for Mrs Dangerfield's classroom computer. Mr and Mrs Coulson's joint account was, however, much more interesting. For the past six months it had been consistently overdrawn.

"It seems Mr Coulson wasn't very proficient at organising his personal finances," commented Forward.

"Yes," said Wilson distastefully. "He made an agreement with us to reduce the overdraft at the rate of a hundred pounds a month. As you can see, he rarely kept to it."

Forward passed all the account records into

Wilmott's safekeeping and then stood up. "Thank you for your assistance, Mr Wilson."

"Glad to help," said Wilson rising to his feet. "I hope what you've found has been useful to you."

Forward gave him a sudden, unexpected smile. "It certainly has!"

****

"Who would want eight thousand, four hundred pounds in cash, Wilmott?"

They were in the BMW now on their way over to Melthorpe.

"Dunno. People who want to avoid VAT?"

"Builders you mean? People like that?"

"Aye."

"It's possible, I suppose, that Coulson paid cash for some repairs to the school or something. But is it likely that someone would even suggest a bent trick like that to a respectable headmaster? A pillar of the community?"

"Not very likely, no," said Wilmott. "Perhaps Coulson wanted the money for himself?"

"We're talking fraud, then."

"Not if the twenty thousand was his own money."

"But if it was his own money, why put it in the school fund account? Particularly as his own account had a huge overdraft. He could have paid it off."

"It must be the school's money then," said Wilmott. "But where did it come from?"

"We'll ask Lady Fernshawe. She ought to know. She is Chair of the School Governors."

****

"This place was on the market a year or so ago," Wilmott whispered to Forward. They were following Wending up the broad, oak staircase at Melthorpe Hall. "Marjorie and I were thinking of buying it but we decided it was a bit too small for our needs!"

Forward smiled. Wending arrived at the first landing and they followed him down a corridor for a short distance. He stopped at the set of doors leading to the library, opened them and then stood aside to allow the two policemen to enter.

"Please take a seat," said Wending. "Lady Fernshawe will attend to you shortly." He left, closing the big, double doors behind him with ceremonial dignity.

"Is he for real?" Wilmott asked.

"I think so. No-one's reported any waxworks escaping from Madame Tussaud's."

"I could fit my house into this room," said Wilmott, looking around. His expression changed to astonishment and awe as he contemplated the gilded stucco ceiling.

"Yes. It's a wonderful size," said Forward. He began moving towards the bookshelves. "Some very interesting books too."

"This carpet alone must be worth a fortune," said Wilmott, propelling his stocky body gingerly over the Axminster, as though eggshells were concealed beneath it. He was drawn to the windows through which he could see the great park of Melthorpe Hall. "What a view!"

Forward removed a book from the case in front of him and began turning over the pages.

At that moment Lady Fernshawe entered the library. Forward immediately replaced the book. "Good morning, Lady Fernshawe," he said.

"Good morning, Chief Inspector."

"This is Sergeant Wilmott."

"Good morning, your Ladyship," said Wilmott. He looked a little awed.

"I'm so pleased to see you again, Chief Inspector," said Lady Fernshawe. "Paul and I had to hurry away the other evening and I wasn't able to tell you how much I'd enjoyed the rest of the play. Such a moving production. I really felt great sympathy for those characters."

"Yes, it did get rather better towards the end," said Forward, unable to hide his gratification. "I'm very glad you enjoyed it."

"Do have a seat." Lady Fernshawe indicated one of the sofas at right angles to the fireplace. Once Forward and Wilmott were seated, she took her place on the sofa opposite so that she was directly facing them. "I was just about to go and visit Mrs Dangerfield to offer her my condolences. Richard's death was a terrible shock to me. I've been feeling so guilty ever since I heard about it."

"Guilty?" said Forward.

She crossed and re-crossed her long, elegant legs.

"Why yes. After all, I was the one who told you about the threats he'd made to Mr Coulson. I never dreamed it would lead to his suicide."

"Who said anything about suicide?" said Forward.

"But he hanged himself, didn't he?"

"He was found hanging, yes."

"I'm sorry. I assumed he'd committed suicide. Are you saying, he didn't?"

"Only the coroner can make a decision about that."

"I see. Will it be necessary for me to attend the inquest?"

"Possibly."

"Is that why you've come to see me?"

"No. I've come about another matter entirely."

"Oh?"

"I understand Mr Coulson deposited twenty thousand pounds in the Melthorpe School fund back in February this year. Were you aware of that?"

Lady Fernshawe looked surprised. "Yes, of

course I was aware of it."

"Oh?" Forward had not expected this. "Would you mind telling us where the money came from?"

"Not at all. It was a legacy from one of his maiden aunts. When she died her house was sold and a portion of the money came to him."

"So it was his own money?"

"Yes."

"But why did he put it in the school's deposit account?"

"He said he didn't need the money for a couple of months and the school fund might as well benefit from the interest on it."

"I see."

"It was very generous of him. Two months interest at eight per cent on a sum that size amounts to over two hundred and fifty pounds. A very welcome amount for a small school such as ours."

"I'm sure it must be," said Forward. "I also understand that Mr Coulson failed to pay into the school fund three hundred pounds raised by the governors and parents. Do you know anything about that?"

Lady Fernshawe smiled. "Who have you been talking to, Inspector?"

"I'm afraid I can't tell you that."

Lady Fernshawe's smile became more knowing. "Mrs Dangerfield, I'll be bound."

"Do you know anything about the three

hundred pounds?"

"I certainly do. Mr Coulson and I made an arrangement. His legacy hadn't arrived and he needed some money rather urgently, so we agreed he could keep the three hundred pounds raised by the school and he would leave three hundred pounds behind in the account when he eventually withdrew all his own money. So, you see, he did pay the three hundred pounds into the school fund as part of the twenty thousand. It was to simplify things, that's all."

"I see," said Forward. "Well, thank you for clarifying that for us, Lady Fernshawe."

"My pleasure," said Lady Fernshawe, standing up. "I'd hate poor Mr Coulson to go to his grave with any suspicion of financial misconduct hanging over him. Particularly, as you can see, it would be completely unfounded."

****

"Well, we've got our explanation for the twenty thousand," said Wilmott, as soon as they were inside the car.

"No, we haven't," said Forward.

Wilmott's eyebrows crinkled in surprise. "We haven't?"

"What we've got is the explanation that Coulson gave Lady Fernshawe. And it's a pretty thin one at that."

"It seems plausible to me," said Wilmott. "He

was just being generous, that's all. He wanted to help the school."

"For God's sake, Sergeant, just try thinking a little, will you? Coulson had a massive overdraft he'd been trying to pay off for months. Yet, when he receives a legacy for twenty thousand pounds, he makes no attempt to get his current account out of the red and instead becomes Mr Philanthropist. Doesn't that seem odd to you?"

Wilmott looked sheepish. "I hadn't thought of it that way."

"Quite. And there's another thing," Forward continued. "A few years ago, my ex-wife received a small legacy from an aunt. It came in the form of a cheque from her aunt's solicitor." He paused and looked at Wilmott shrewdly. "But Coulson's bank manager told us that the twenty thousand was deposited in cash. Have you ever known a solicitor part with twenty thousand in cash?"

Wilmott shook his head.

Forward turned the key in the ignition. "I think we need to have another word with Mrs Coulson," he said.

CHAPTER TWENTY FOUR

Mrs Coulson was not at home. Her father-in-law explained that she was in the village hall organising the flower arranging exhibition.

When Forward and Wilmott eventually located the village hall, they found Mrs Coulson standing in the middle of it. She was alone and deep in thought. Surrounding her on all sides were long, trestle tables on which stood a number of attractive examples of the flower arranger's art. At the sound of Forward and Wilmott's heavy footsteps she spun round, startled.

"Oh, it's you," she said, quite obviously relieved. "Sorry I jumped. I thought I was all alone here."

"That's all right," said Forward. "You remember my sergeant, don't you? Sergeant Wilmott."

"Yes, of course."

"Your father-in-law told us you were here," said Wilmott. He began to walk slowly down the line of trestle tables. "What a lovely display."

"Oh, it's nothing like ready yet. In fact, when you came in, I was wondering what to do next." Her tone became personal, more confidential. "I'm trying to get my life back to normal, you see. I volunteered to organise this exhibition before Mark..." She swallowed. "Before Mark died. I hadn't the heart to go on with it at first, but everyone convinced me it would take my mind off things." She gave them a weak smile. "So, here I am."

"I'm sure you made the right decision," said Forward. "Is your own flower arrangement here?"

"No. I'm still working on mine. I haven't been able to give it much attention recently." She seemed about to be overwhelmed by her feelings and making a conscious effort to master them. "We've been set quite a difficult theme this year. Enchantment. That's why so many people have chosen Enchantment Lilies, as you can see."

"Oh? Which ones are they?" asked Forward. "I know nothing about flowers."

"Those orange ones."

"Ah yes. Quite beautiful." He pointed to some other flowers that were similar in shape but a delicate yellow colour. "And these? Are they lilies too?"

"Yes, that variety is called Connecticut King."

"There are many varieties, then?"

"Yes, several." Her manner became business-like. "Now, I'm sure you haven't come here to talk about flower arranging, Inspector. Why did you want to see me?"

"We need to ask you some personal questions about Mark's finances," said Forward. "Perhaps the house might be a more appropriate place."

"There's no-one else here apart from us, as you can see; and I'm not expecting anyone to come and help me for at least half an hour, so we can talk freely. Besides, I'd rather not be in the house at the moment. This is the first time I've been outside it."

"Of course, I understand," said Forward. "We're hoping you might clear up one or two matters that are puzzling us."

"Yes?"

"Mark came into a legacy recently. Is that right?"

Mrs Coulson looked bewildered. "A legacy?"

"Yes. Twenty thousand pounds."

"Twenty thousand pounds?" She laughed. "You must be joking!"

"No, we're not joking, Mrs Coulson," said Forward quietly.

Her lips pressed together into a thin, hard line. "No, I can see you're not joking." She took a deep breath. "I think there must be some mistake. Who told you this?"

"Lady Fernshawe."

"Lady Fernshawe? What's she got to do with it?"

"Your husband told her he'd received a legacy for twenty thousand pounds and he wanted to put it into the school deposit account so that the school could benefit from the interest. He needed her permission to do this."

"But he hadn't got twenty thousand pounds!"

"Yes he had. That's the amount he paid into the school deposit account. We've checked."

Mrs Coulson placed a hand upon her head. She seemed genuinely perplexed. "I can't believe this. He put twenty thousand pounds in the school fund account?"

"Yes."

"But what on earth for?"

"Because he said he wanted the school to benefit from the interest on it." Forward's tone became more insinuating. "Unless you can think of another reason."

She threw up her hands in bewilderment. "I'm sorry, I'm as much in the dark as you are."

"You've no idea where the twenty thousand came from?"

"None. None at all. There's no way Mark could have got hold of that kind of money." She gave a hollow laugh. "God knows we needed it though."

"Mark's always been short of money?"

"All the time! I told you he even had to sell his

car. That's why he was driving mine."

"Did you ever see him bring home large amounts of cash?"

"Never, I told you, he was broke. We couldn't even manage on his salary."

"Did he owe anybody any large amounts of money, say about eight thousand pounds?"

"Eight thousand pounds?" She looked away. Was she being evasive or merely thinking? Forward couldn't be sure. "He did owe some money to someone once, but that was a while ago and it was nothing like eight thousand pounds. The man rang up about it a few times. He was very aggressive. Most unpleasant."

"Do you know this man's name?"

"No."

"Can you remember what he said, exactly?"

She thought for a moment. "Tell your husband I want my money and if he doesn't give it to me, he'll regret it. Something like that."

"Did you tell your husband about these calls?"

"Of course. He told me not to worry. It was only a small amount and he'd pay it. The man stopped ringing after that so I assumed Mark had paid it."

"When was this?"

"When did I get the calls, you mean?"

"Yes."

"During November and December of last

year. Quite often then. And once or twice in January and February of this year."

"And they stopped in February?"

"Yes."

"Your husband didn't tell you why he owed the money or who to?"

Her tone went hard. "He didn't have to. I knew."

"You knew?"

Mrs Coulson looked away again. When she looked back at them there was a different expression on her face. It was a mixture of bitterness and resignation.

"My husband was a gambler, Inspector. That's why we were always broke. That's why we had to leave our lovely house in Chester and move here. We needed to sell the house to pay off Mark's gambling debts. He was lucky to get the Headship of the school here in Melthorpe because a house came with it. We got it for a tiny rent. Otherwise we wouldn't even have had a roof over our heads. And now he's dead I haven't even got that. I'll be kicked out as soon as they appoint a new Head."

"I want to be sure I've got this right," said Forward. "You sold your house in Chester to pay off all your husband's gambling debts?"

"Yes. That's what made me so bitter. I'd lost my beautiful home and we hadn't anything to show for it. I never forgave Mark for that."

"Did he give up gambling when you moved

here?"

"For a time, yes." She sighed heavily. "But I knew it wouldn't last. I knew he was up to his old tricks again when that man started ringing up demanding his money. That's how it was in Chester. People were ringing up all the time. It was a nightmare."

"So, it's possible Mark could have won the twenty thousand pounds gambling?"

"No. He would have told me."

"Not if he knew you disapproved of how he got it, surely?"

"You don't understand. He wanted to get back in my good books. He was always promising me a new house that would be better than the one we'd lost. Twenty thousand pounds would have cleared our overdraft and given us a really good deposit. He wouldn't have kept that from me."

"Perhaps he was hanging on to the money," said Wilmott, "hoping he'd win some more and give you a really big surprise."

Mrs Coulson shook her head. "If he'd won twenty thousand pounds, I'm sure he would have told me about it. Have you ever seen gamblers when they've won? They can't keep it to themselves. They love to boast about it!"

"So why do you think he kept the twenty thousand from you?"

"I haven't a clue."

"What did he mainly bet on? Horses?" asked

Forward.

"Anything! Horses. Cards. Slot machines. Even the winner of the Eurovision Song Contest, one year. He was a gambler! It was cards he enjoyed most though. Poker and Bridge were his favourite games. Bridge was his downfall when we were in Chester. If you play Bridge, you sometimes play for very high stakes. As much as ten or twenty pounds a point. That's why he got into such a huge amount of debt."

"Was he playing Bridge with anyone after you moved to Melthorpe?"

"No, I'm fairly certain he wasn't. You see, he lost his Bridge partner when we left Chester."

"Who was that?"

"Someone called Harry Vaughan. Our solicitor. Without him Mark couldn't have played another game."

"You're sure of that?" said Forward sharply.

"Oh, yes. Nobody around here played Bridge. Mark was always complaining about that. You can imagine how relieved I was about it."

"So he turned his attention to horses?"

"I expect so. Horses or dogs."

"Do you know if he used any particular bookmaker?"

"Do you really think he would have told me, Inspector?"

"No. I suppose not. Thank you, Mrs Coulson. I think that's all we need to know at the moment."

Mrs Coulson covered her face with her hands. "Is there really any point going into all this?"

"Don't you want to find out who murdered your husband?" asked Forward severely.

She took her hands away from her face and looked at him, confused. "I thought you knew that already. Everyone's saying Richard Dangerfield did it."

"I'm not," said Forward. "Not yet, anyway."

She looked relieved. "I'm glad. Richard Dangerfield was a really nice guy. I was devastated when I heard he'd hanged himself. I can never believe he was responsible for Mark's death."

****

After leaving Mrs Coulson at the village hall, Forward and Wilmott drove the short distance to Melthorpe Primary School and parked outside it. Wilmott was instructed to go in and find out the address of Mr Gibbard, the parent whom Mrs Dangerfield had said was involved in an argument with Coulson a few days before he'd died.

Number Fourteen, Woldgate Drive was one of several nineteen fifties council houses located just off Melthorpe's main street. Forward knocked several times but there was no reply.

"They're probably at work," said Wilmott.

"Never mind," said Forward. "I only wanted to find out what his argument with Coulson was about." He smiled at Wilmott. "You can try again this evening and call in on your way home."

Wilmott looked disgruntled. "Melthorpe isn't on my way home, sir."

****

As they approached the outskirts of Sandleton a radio message came through from control for Forward. Inspector Hoggart wanted to speak to him car to car.

"Go ahead," said Forward.

"Hoggart here. We're on our way to the incident centre. We've picked up a young tearaway in Sandleton called Bobby Smith. He was caught trying to buy a camcorder on Mark Coulson's credit card."

"What?"

"Do you want me to repeat the message?" asked Hoggart.

"I was merely expressing surprise."

"Bobby's father is already waiting for us at the incident centre. Do you want the lad taken there or to Sandleton nick?"

"No. Better take him to Monkhouses. We'll meet you there."

CHAPTER
TWENTY FIVE

Bobby Smith was fifteen years old. He was blue eyed, thin faced and had long, lank hair that peppered the shoulders of his shell suit with dandruff. He was sitting alongside his father in the incident room at Monkhouses when Forward and Wilmott arrived.

"He's been in and out of trouble since he was thirteen, Inspector," said Mr Smith, a grey haired, well-groomed man in his late forties. "Doesn't take any notice of me whatsoever. What he needs is a spell in the army. That'd soon change his ways."

Forward was examining a transparent evidence bag containing Mark Coulson's credit card wallet. The wallet was open and two credit cards with Coulson's name on them were clearly visible.

"Where did you find this wallet, Bobby?" Forward asked.

Bobby looked down. "On Flamborough Head. At South Landing."

South Landing was a picturesque inlet on the Sandleton Bay side of Flamborough Head.

"When was that?"

"On Tuesday."

"What were you doing there?"

"Me and me mates were just messing about, that's all."

"What are their names?"

"Billy Sexton and Shane Boyse."

"We'll be getting in touch with them. So, if you want to change your story, you'd better do it now."

Bobby looked up, his eyes flashing indignantly. "I don't need to change it. It's the truth."

"Good. Now, I want to know exactly where you found the wallet."

"I told you. South Landing."

"No. I mean did you find it up on the cliffs or down on the beach?"

"Near the sea. It were in a rock pool."

"And you thought you'd use Mr Coulson's credit cards to get a camcorder. Is that it?"

"He were dead. I didn't think he'd need them."

Forward was staggered. "Mr Coulson was murdered. Did you know that?"

The youth nodded.

"Didn't it occur to you that the police might need them?"

"I didn't think."

"You never think!" shouted Mr Smith. "That's why you're always in trouble."

"Have you used this credit card anywhere else?" Forward asked.

"No."

"Where were you on Monday night, Bobby?"

"This Monday? Just gone?"

"Yes."

"I were at karate."

"That's right, Inspector," said Mr Smith. "I was with him. I'm a member of the Sandleton Karate Club. I enrolled him in it a few months back. Thought it might teach him a bit of discipline."

"How long were you both at the karate club?"

"From eight 'til half past ten," said Mr Smith.

"And you both left the club together?"

"Yes. We came home and had a cup of tea and a sandwich. I watched television and he went up to his room to play all his mad music."

Bobby looked at his father as though he were mouse droppings. "It's not mad music!"

"It's a bloody racket."

"Where's Mrs Smith?" asked Forward.

"She ran off years ago." Mr Smith jerked his thumb at his son. "He takes after her."

Forward left the father and son with Wilmott and went over to speak to Hoggart.

"It appears that Coulson had a gambling problem," said Forward. "I want you to contact every bookmaker in the area and find out if he had a credit account with any of them."

"Right," said Hoggart. "I'll get Phipps and McIntyre onto it." He nodded at Bobby Smith. "What about him?"

"Bobby's clean as far as Coulson's concerned. Have him show you the exact spot at South Landing where he found the wallet and ask the SOCOs to give it the once over. Then get him over to the juvenile branch. They can charge him."

"Has he admitted the fraud?"

"What else could he do? He was caught red-handed!" Forward handed Hoggart the evidence bag. "After this wallet has been checked for dabs get it over to forensic by special courier."

"Is it going to be of any use?" asked Hoggart.

"I don't know," said Forward. "We'll have to ask Thwaites."

****

On their way back to Sandleton Police Station Forward and Wilmott called in on Thwaites at the Harbourmaster's office.

"One of your constables was here earlier," said Thwaites. "He was asking about fishing boats."

"That's right," said Forward. "Three fishing boats put in here on Monday night after ten o'clock. I wanted the names of their owners and crew."

"Jimmy's already given him the information. Do you want a print-out too?"

"Yes please. But there are also one or two other things I need to ask you about."

Thwaites nodded towards the adjacent office. "Will we need the computer?"

"That depends. Would you be able to tell us from your records if the crew of the *Phaeton* went ashore on Monday night?"

"No, once a craft's been given the all clear by customs, we don't record the crew's comings and goings."

Forward looked surprised.

"We keep our eyes open naturally," Thwaites assured him. "But we don't see everything, of course."

"I need to know if any of the *Phaeton's* crew went ashore on Monday night, and if so, what time they came back on board."

"I can't tell you that because I don't work after six p.m. But Charlie, my deputy, might have seen something. He does nights."

"Would you find out for me?"

"Course I will. I won't ring him now though. He's probably tucked up in his bunk. But he comes on just before six. I'll ask him then and let you know."

"Fine," said Forward. "There's just one other thing."

Thwaites leaned back in his chair, stretched his arms out and gave a massive yawn. "What's that?"

"A wallet belonging to the man who was murdered in Monks Bay has been found at South Landing. It might have been thrown into the sea from a boat on Monday night. What I want to know is this: was it thrown overboard north of Flamborough Head or south of it? In other words, in Filey Bay or Sandleton Bay?"

On Thwaites' desk lay a half-eaten sandwich. He popped it into his mouth, brushed the crumbs out of his beard and went over to a map of the East Yorkshire coast that was on the wall of his office.

"How far out to sea would this boat have been?"

"It was very close in-shore I would say."

"That's easy. If the wallet was found at South Landing it was most likely thrown in Sandleton Bay."

Forward looked at Wilmott. "So, they definitely carried on round the Head from Monks Bay then!"

****

"I don't understand why you're so interested in the crew of the *Phaeton*, sir," said Wilmott. "It berthed in Sandleton Harbour around five forty p.m. on Monday evening. Coulson was still alive and at his meeting then, so no-one on the *Phaeton* could have taken his credit cards and thrown them into the water. He still had them on him."

"Quite right, Wilmott." Forward was only half listening to his sergeant. His main attention was focussed on the list of fishing boats that had returned to Sandleton Harbour after ten p.m. on Monday evening. It told him very little, so he put it down and selected a different piece of paper from amongst the untidy pile of documents and messages that had accumulated on his desktop. This one's contents greatly aroused his interest.

"Listen Wilmott!" His voice rose in excitement. "This is a message from NCIS. I asked them to check out the *Phaeton's* crew. Two of the names, David Nathan and Francesca Beaton, are on their computer. They've interviewed these two about their association with known drugs dealers, but it's never been possible to pin anything on them. NCIS want to know what our interest in them is."

"But what's it got to do with Coulson, sir? He wouldn't be involved in drug dealing, surely?"

"Why not? He needed the money. And it would explain where the twenty thousand came from."

"But he's a headmaster!"

"The prisons hold a fair number of headmasters," Forward said, shooting him a sagacious look. "Could be just a coincidence but it's worth following up." He handed the message to Wilmott. "Get on to NCIS and tell them everything we know about the *Phaeton*. How we became interested in it and so on. The *Phaeton's* probably been abroad during the past year. Ask them to find out where and get us dates." Forward stared down at his desk. "Meanwhile, I'll try and shift some more of this bloody paper."

****

Forward's mountain of paper had been reduced to a small hill by the time Wilmott returned.

"NCIS were very interested in the *Phaeton*, sir. They're going to check on it right away."

"Good."

The telephone rang.

"Yes? Forward!" He listened attentively for a long time to the voice on the other end. Finally, he said, "OK. Thanks very much. Yes, it is. Extraordinary!"

Forward replaced the receiver and looked up at Wilmott, beaming. "That was Edwin Painter over at forensic. Do you remember that funny orange stain that was on Dangerfield's hand and his sleeves?"

"Yes?"

"It was pollen."

"Pollen?"

"Yes. Painter and his team got that far and then they were stumped. They couldn't work out which flower the pollen was from, so they sent a sample to the Institute of Botany at Hull University. They identified the flower immediately."

Forward deliberately paused.

"Well?" urged Wilmott. "Don't keep me in suspense."

"You're going to love this! It came from the lily!"

Now Wilmott was excited. "Lilies! They were in the village hall at Melthorpe. Tons of them! In the flower arrangements we saw."

"Quite," said Forward. "I want you to get over to Viking's Chine right away and contact the warden there."

Wilmott looked astonished. "Surely we ought to be going over to Melthorpe?"

"Why?"

"That's where all the lilies are."

"And what are we going to do when we get there?" Forward asked with a sneer. "Contact everyone who used lilies in their flower arrangements and ask them if Dangerfield brushed against it?"

"We could, couldn't we?"

"Don't be dense," Forward snapped. "If someone did murder Dangerfield, do you think they're going to admit to that?"

"What do you want me to ask the warden at the Chine, then?" Wilmott demanded. He was clearly struggling to control his temper.

"Before I can make proper use of this new

evidence, I need to be absolutely sure that Dangerfield didn't come into contact with lilies in the Chine. The warden will be able to tell you if any are growing there."

Without a word, Wilmott turned and stomped out of the room.

Forward stared at the door that Wilmott had slammed behind him. "Moody bastard!"

He turned his attention to the paperwork remaining in front of him. He'd spent less than a minute on it when the telephone rang. Swearing, he grabbed at the receiver.

It was Collins, the desk sergeant. "There's a woman on the line, sir. She refuses to give her name and she says she wants to speak to you."

Forward sighed heavily. "OK. Put her through."

There was a click, and then an eerie sound like someone whistling far off in a tunnel.

"Is that Inspector Forward?"

"It is." Forward recognised the voice but couldn't put a name to it.

"It's Sandra Turnbull."

"Who?"

"Sandra Turnbull. The barmaid at *The Drovers* in Luffield. Do you remember?"

"Yes, of course. What can I do for you?"

"I need to speak to you, urgently."

"What is it?"

"No, I don't want to say anything on the phone."

"All right. You'd better come over. I'll be here for most of the afternoon."

"No, I don't want to go near police stations. Can't you meet me somewhere?"

"Where are you now?"

"I'm in a phone box in Luffield but I don't want you to meet me here."

Forward was getting exasperated. "Where then?"

"Do you know Sledmere Monument?"

"Yes."

"There's a small parking space next to it. I'll be parked up there in about half an hour. I'll be in a blue Fiesta."

"I'll see you in half an hour then."

"You won't be driving a police car, will you?"

"I'll be in my own car, a BMW," said Forward. "Do you want me to wear a beard and a false moustache as well?"

"It's no joking matter, Inspector!" she cried, and put the phone down.

CHAPTER
TWENTY SIX

The monument to Sir Tatton Sykes, Baronet, lies on the B1252 between the villages of Garton-on-the-Wolds and Sledmere and is known locally as the Sledmere Monument. It is a huge Gothic tower, over a hundred feet high, which tapers to a fine point and stands imperiously on the summit of Garton Hill. It was erected two years after Sir Tatton's death in 1865 by the people of the Wolds to commemorate the Baronet's achievements as a sportsman and farmer. Any tourist to the Wolds who wishes to visit this magnificent example of Victorian architecture does not have to search hard. It dominates even this hilly landscape, and can be seen from almost every part of it, thrusting at the sky like a medieval lance.

Few tourists, however, visit the Wolds in April, and only Sandra Turnbull's Fiesta was parked in the small parking area next to the Monument when Forward arrived. She got out of the Fiesta and walked urgently towards the BMW. Forward opened his front passenger door for her and she slid in beside him.

Previously, he'd only seen her behind the bar at *The Drovers,* and there she'd appeared quite confident and mature. Now, removed from that context, she seemed much younger, far less sure of herself, more like a vulnerable teenager. Perhaps it was her clothes that emphasised her youth: she was wearing a powder blue tracksuit and big white trainers. The light blue of the suit emphasised the darker blue of her eyes; and her blue-black moussed hair gleamed with the kind of health that was so youthfully authentic it looked artificial. Forward knew that if he'd been twenty years younger, he would have fallen for her heavily: as it was, she merely reminded him he was middle-aged and that was the last thing he needed.

She fixed him with frank and serious eyes. "I'm sorry I was a bit rude on the phone," she said, "but I've been beside myself ever since I heard... Richard had died."

She gave an involuntary sob before she spoke the last three unbearable words, and then began to cry quite freely. He guessed, correctly, that this was the first time she'd allowed herself the catharsis of open grief, and he waited patiently for it to stop. In his job he saw many people cry.

She dabbed at her eyes with a handkerchief.

"I'm sorry, it's just that I'm behind the bar every night and I hear people talking about him, saying things I know aren't true."

"What sort of things?"

"They say Richard hanged himself because he killed that Coulson man. He didn't kill him! I know he didn't!" She pressed the tight ball of handkerchief hard against her mouth as though somehow she thought it would staunch her pain.

He stared at her expectantly. Maybe this wasn't going to be just a tedious waste of time after all. "You know he didn't kill him? How do you know that?"

"He couldn't have. He was with me!"

Forward felt immediate disappointment. "Yes, on Monday night in the pub. You told me."

Her look signalled that he wasn't comprehending. "No. After the pub closed. He stayed with me on Monday night."

Forward felt all his senses become alert. "Just a minute. Are you saying he slept with you on Monday night?"

"Yes. Just like he always did. He stayed with me at the pub every Monday night." She stared out of the car window at the Monument. "We've been having an affair for months. My husband works on the oil rigs and he's away for weeks at a time. He's very violent, so I never took Richard back to my place because I was frightened the neighbours would see him.

Obviously, we couldn't go to Richard's place because he lived with his mother. So every Monday night Richard slept at the pub with me."

"Did the manager know about this?"

"No, of course not. He'd give me the sack if he found out."

"How did you arrange to do it, then?"

"Monday is the manager's day off. He's divorced you see, but he's got some woman in Barnsley. He goes to see her every Monday and comes back on Tuesday mornings."

Forward was confused. "Wait a minute. You said Richard left the pub at ten o'clock and went to a Chinese restaurant."

"That's right. That's what he did every Monday so no-one would suspect anything. He'd stay in the Chinese until he was sure the pub was empty, and then he'd come back and I'd let him in by the back door."

"And that's what he did this Monday night?"

"Yes. So you see, he couldn't have killed Mr Coulson."

Forward suddenly saw a way of confirming this. "Sandra, Mr Coulson died just before ten thirty. Where do you suppose Richard was at that time?"

"In the Chinese restaurant, I should think."

"No. He didn't arrive there until ten forty-five. So, where else could he have been?"

"He must have been in *The Three Bowmen*."

Forward felt elated. "Doing what?"

"Having a drink. He liked to go there before he went to the restaurant."

"Why?"

She was silent.

"Sandra, listen. I need you to tell me why he went there. If you give me the right answer then I'll know he was definitely in *The Three Bowmen* on Monday night around the time Coulson died and so had nothing to do with his murder." He touched her arm reassuringly. "Don't be afraid, tell me. I'm not interested in your social habits. I'm conducting a murder enquiry. Now, why did he go to *The Bowmen*?"

Her voice was a whisper. "For drugs."

"And did he score any?"

She nodded. "Some pot." She looked at him anxiously. "Is that the right answer?"

"Ten out of ten," he said. He shifted awkwardly in his seat. "Do you mind if I ask you something personal?"

"No. Go ahead."

"Was he embarrassed about buying condoms?"

Her immediate response was an intrigued smile. "How do you know that?"

"Is it true?"

"Yes, it is," she said and giggled. "He hated going into chemists for them." She raised her eyebrows and looked at him quizzically. "A lot of men do, don't they?"

"So I understand," said Forward. "Where did Richard get them, then?"

"Usually, *The Three Bowmen,* I think. I know he got in a terrible state one night because the machine in there was empty." She smiled sadly. "I often used to tease him about that."

"All right," said Forward. "Let's talk about what happened later on Monday night when Richard joined you back at the pub. What time did he get there?"

"About a quarter to midnight."

"I assume you both smoked the pot. Is that right?"

She nodded.

"What sort of a mood was Richard in?"

She shrugged. "The pot was good stuff. It put us on a big high so I couldn't really say."

"Before he took the pot!" said Forward, unaccountably irritated. "What was he like before he smoked it?"

"He was just his normal self."

"Had he changed his clothes?"

"Changed his clothes?" She looked bemused.

"Yes. Was he still wearing the same clothes he'd worn in the pub earlier?"

"Yes. Of course, he was."

"What did you talk about?"

She raised her eyes salaciously. "We didn't do much talking if you understand what I mean."

Forward smiled. "Surely you didn't spend the whole night with him without exchanging a word?"

"We just talked about the usual things, that's all."

"Oh? What were they?"

"Richard's work, my husband, what we were going to do."

"Did he ever talk about Mr Coulson?"

"Sometimes." Her expression darkened. "He talked about Sheila more than him though."

"Sheila?"

"Sheila Coulson."

"Mrs Coulson? Why?"

Sandra looked uncertain. Forward sensed she was in the grip of some inner ethical struggle. "I swore I'd never tell anybody this," she said finally. "But Richard had an affair with her some time last year. Her husband found out about it and made her finish it. That's why Richard hated him so much."

Forward felt his brain flip over. "Richard was having an affair with Coulson's wife?"

"Yes. No-one else knew about it, except me."

"Richard's mother didn't know?"

"No. I'm certain she didn't. It was all kept very quiet."

Forward was at sea. He'd just convinced himself that Dangerfield couldn't have murdered Coulson and now he'd been presented with one of the strongest motives in the book.

"Tell me, did Richard ever give you the

impression that he'd like to harm Mr Coulson?" he asked.

"No, never."

"But you just said Richard hated him."

"That's right, but he never said anything about killing him!"

"All right, what did Richard have to say about Sheila Coulson?"

Sandra's eyes took on a hurt look. "He didn't speak about her much except when he was drunk or depressed. Then he'd tell me how much he still loved her and that one day he'd get her to leave Mr Coulson for good."

"He said this in front of you?"

"Yes."

"But I thought you and he were having an affair?"

Sandra angrily sprang to her dead lover's defence. "He only ever said it when he was depressed!" She turned away again to look out of the window. "Besides," she said, reflecting aloud in her attractive but self-consciously refined voice, "I don't kid myself. We weren't in love or anything. We were just having sex. We fancied each other and we liked each other but it was Sheila he really wanted. She could talk about books and art and all that. Richard was interested in those sorts of things too. He might have worked on a building site but he was a very clever lad. He came from quite a good background, you know. I'm just an ordinary Luffield girl. I wasn't in his league."

"You're saying he used you?"

"We used each other." She looked at him defiantly. "I'm not complaining. We had a bloody good time." Tears began seeping into her eyes again and she wiped them away with the back of her hand. "While it lasted."

Forward fell silent. His thoughts were in disarray. He wasn't sure how to proceed. Finally, he managed to form a coherent question. "You told us that Richard was in *The Drovers* on Wednesday evening and you hardly had time to speak to him. Was that the truth or was it just for your husband's benefit?"

She suddenly looked fearful. "My husband mustn't find out about me and Richard. He's got a terrible temper. I'm terrified of what he'll do to me." She gripped Forward's arm frantically. "He won't have to know, will he?"

"Not necessarily. I'll keep you out of it. I promise."

Her relief was evident. "Thank you." She released his arm. "It was only the thought of what my husband might do that stopped me telling you all this before."

Forward was aware that he'd given her an unfulfillable promise, but he needed her to tell him everything she knew. "Now, tell me what Richard actually said to you the last time you saw him on Wednesday night," he requested softly.

"Not much. It really was busy, so we didn't have a chance to talk properly. But he did say something I thought was strange. He said that by the end of the week he'd have a lot of money and he was going to leave Luffield and start a new life somewhere. I was amazed."

"He'd never mentioned anything like this before?"

"No. Never."

"Did he give you any idea where this big sum of money was coming from?"

"No." Her expression had changed. She looked downcast and angry with herself as though she was already beginning to regret what she'd divulged. She reached for the door handle. "Look I've got to get home and get ready."

"Just a moment. When was the last time Richard saw Mrs Coulson, do you know?"

She paused with her hand on the door handle. "I don't know. He always said he hadn't seen her since she gave him the big heave ho."

"When was that exactly?"

"Last year. Last back-end."

As a Southerner Forward always liked to demonstrate his knowledge of the East Yorkshire dialect. "Last autumn?"

"Yes."

She stared at him unhappily. The mixture of confused and anguished emotions that emanated from her dark blue eyes raked through his own feelings and elicited his immediate sympathy. "You'd better go now, Sandra," he said.

She kept her hand on the door handle but made no attempt to open the door. Instead, she looked down, as though she was considering some difficult problem and forcing herself to come to a decision. Then she removed her hand from the door, and, placing it on her lap, turned back to Forward and said, "No. Not yet. There's something else you need to know."

CHAPTER TWENTY SEVEN

After leaving Sledmere Monument, Forward drove on over the Wolds to Melthorpe. When he arrived, he went straight to the village hall expecting to find Mrs Coulson there. But the door was closed and locked so he drove round the corner to the schoolhouse.

Mrs Coulson was obviously surprised to see Forward again. When she answered his knock and found him standing on the doorstep, she developed an anxious, probing expression.

"Inspector?"

"I need to speak to you urgently."

She tensed and her face grew grave. "Certainly. Come in."

She led Forward towards the sitting room where Coulson's father was sitting in an armchair reading a copy of *The Times*. He looked up. "Good afternoon, Inspector."

Forward returned his greetings and responded as honestly as he could to Norman Coulson's concerns about the progress of the case. Eventually, Forward turned to Mrs Coulson and said, "I'd like to speak to you privately, if you don't mind."

Her finely chiselled features became pinched with anxiety now. "We'd better go to the study, then."

As he followed her up the stairs his eyes were drawn to the shapely legs that flexed and un-flexed beneath her taut, black skirt. He completely understood the physical effect she must have had on Richard Dangerfield. But had it been strong enough for him to kill her husband?

"When did you last speak to Richard Dangerfield?" Forward asked as soon as the study door was closed.

Slowly, she turned her back on him and, head down, walked over to the window. When at last she turned to face him, he knew Sandra Turnbull had told him the truth.

"On Wednesday. He rang me."

"May I ask why?"

"He said the police suspected him of murdering Mark. He wanted me to know he had nothing whatsoever to do with his death."

"Did he mention anything else?"

Mrs Coulson went silent.

"Did he, for example, suggest you should resume your affair?"

She reacted by bursting into tears. This time Forward did not wait for her to stop but kept up the pressure.

"You did have an affair with him once? That's true, isn't it?"

She nodded.

"Why didn't you tell us about it?"

"I didn't think it had any bearing on Mark's death."

"But you knew Richard was a suspect. I told you myself he was under suspicion because of the threats he'd made to your husband."

She jolted her tearful, anguished face towards him. "And I told you Richard wasn't the sort of person to kill anyone."

"You knew all the time the real reason why Richard Dangerfield had threatened your husband," Forward continued harshly. "It wasn't because Mark insulted Richard's mother. That was just the pretext. It was because Mark wouldn't give you up and let you go and live with Richard. That's what it was really all about, wasn't it?"

She nodded her head slowly. "Yes."

"So, why didn't you tell us the real reason Richard threatened your husband?"

Mrs Coulson said nothing.

"I'll tell you why, shall I? Because if we'd known you and Richard Dangerfield had once had an affair, we'd have realised he had an excellent motive for murdering Mark. And that was the last thing you wanted us to think, wasn't it?"

Slowly she was re-gaining control. She wiped away her tears with the back of her hand. "No. Not entirely. I wanted to protect Richard certainly. But there was another reason too. Shame. I didn't want all the narrow little minds in this place to start wagging their evil tongues."

Forward nodded understandingly. "When did your affair start?"

"Last summer."

"Tell me about it."

"Do you want all the salacious facts, Inspector? Where we did it and at what time?"

"All I'd like is a brief history, please."

"All right. As I said, it was in the summer. Richard wasn't working and so Mark arranged for him to do some gardening for us. My husband was at school all day; so were the children. It was a very hot summer. Surely you can imagine the rest?"

"Was it a casual affair as far as you were concerned?"

"At first, yes, but as it developed it became very serious. That was the problem. I told you that Mark was a good deal older than me. Over the years we'd drifted apart. His only interests were his job and his gambling. We weren't even friends any longer. If it hadn't been for the children, I'd have left him long ago."

"Did you and Richard plan to live together?"

"Yes, we were going to run off one night

and take my girls with us. But before we could get everything arranged, Mark came home unexpectedly one afternoon and found us in bed." She gave him a sudden, searching look. "Who's been telling you all this, Inspector? I was sure only the three of us knew."

"One of Richard's friends."

She scoffed loudly. "Richard didn't have any friends when I knew him."

"This was a woman."

"Oh, I see." She looked crushed for a moment and Forward felt almost sorry for her. She shrugged philosophically. "Well, I can't blame Richard. After all I was the one who got rid of him."

"Why was that?"

"Mark was a Catholic. He said he'd never give me a divorce and would get the courts to take the children off me if I set up home with Richard. I couldn't bear the thought of that. So I finished it."

"Last year, in the autumn?"

"So, you know that too. What else do you know?"

"Nothing really, except Richard's friend told me, if it's any consolation, he quite often spoke about you in his more depressed moments."

"Really?" She visibly brightened. "What did he say?"

"That he loved you and was determined to get you away from Mr Coulson."

"He loved me? He said that?"

"So I understand." Forward was embarrassed by her rapturous response to her dead lover's declaration. "Now, tell me, before the telephone call on Wednesday, when was the last time you spoke to Richard?"

"When I last saw him, which was back in late September. September the twenty seventh to be precise. At nine thirty. That's when I told him, in front of my husband, that it was all over."

"How did he take it?"

"Very badly."

"Did he threaten your husband?"

"No. He left the house without a word. That's how I knew he'd taken it badly."

"Are you sure that was the last time you saw him?"

"Absolutely. You don't forget things like that. Not when you love someone as I loved Richard."

"If you both loved each other so much, why didn't he come round to see you when he found out your husband was killed? After all, to put it bluntly, your husband was no longer an obstacle to your happiness, was he?"

Her face became fierce. "You didn't give him much of a chance, did you? When he rang me on Wednesday, he said it would be better if we didn't see each other for a while until he'd proved to the police he'd nothing to do with Mark's death."

"He was depressed, was he?" said Forward.

"Not depressed enough to hang himself, Inspector. And why would he do that? He had everything to look forward to. We had a great future together. So why hang himself?"

Forward privately had to concede it was a good question. If they'd murdered Coulson for his insurance money and to gain their freedom, it was hardly likely Dangerfield would have hanged himself at the last moment in a sudden fit of remorse. On the other hand, Dangerfield had told Sandra Turnbull he was expecting to come into a lot of money and intended to start a new life somewhere. It was all very curious.

His reflections were interrupted by a sudden knock on the study door. It was Coulson's father.

"Excuse me," he said. "I was trying to read my paper but I couldn't concentrate because of all the noise going on up here." He stared with great concern at his daughter-in-law. "Is everything all right?"

How noisy had they been, Forward wondered. Loud enough for the old boy to learn of his daughter-in-law's adultery? He hoped not. Mrs Coulson had trouble enough.

"Everything's fine," he said. "I'm afraid I had to ask some rather difficult questions." He turned to Mrs Coulson. "When we were in the village hall you told me you were using lilies for your flower arrangement. I wonder if I could have a look at them?"

She looked puzzled.

"I have my reasons," he persisted. "May I?"

"Certainly, yes."

Forward and Coulson's father followed her downstairs. The old man went back to his newspaper and Mrs Coulson took Forward into the dining room. On the dining table were two large flower arrangements, although Forward thought the term 'flower sculptures' more appropriate to describe these beautiful constructions. One was a simple arch composed of delicate yellow lilies. The other was even more exquisite: a grotto had been created using coloured stones and gleaming crystals, and clinging to its exterior were many small alpine plants. A mixture of sand and seashells had been strewn in front of the grotto to suggest a beach; and at the grotto's mouth a rock pool had been created with larger stones into which had been placed starfish, sea urchins and fronds of seaweed. Discreetly attached to the arrangement was a label bearing the title: *The Enchanted Grotto*. Forward stared at it approvingly. "This is very fine," he said. "Congratulations."

Mrs Coulson blushed. "That's not mine, it's Lady Fernshawe's. She dropped it in earlier on her way to London."

"She's gone to London today?"

"Yes."

The news that Lady Fernshawe had gone away upset Forward. He had one or two important questions to ask her. He said, "Did you tell Lady Fernshawe that the twenty thousand pounds your husband put into the school account wasn't a legacy?"

"Yes, I did. I wanted her to know I intended to claim the money in the school account as my own, even though I'd known nothing about it. Why? Shouldn't I have done that?"

"It doesn't matter. What did she say?"

"She said there was nearly twelve thousand left and she'd see I got all of it."

"I'm not talking about that. Wasn't Lady Fernshawe shocked that you didn't know where the twenty thousand had come from? It meant your husband had lied to her!"

Forward's exasperated tone seemed to unnerve Mrs Coulson. "I don't think it really registered. She had a lot on her mind. She'd heard today that one of her relatives was very ill. That's why she was going to London."

Forward decided he wasn't going to make much more progress on this tack. "You said you were organising the flower arranging exhibition. Do you know the names of all those who are using lilies in their arrangements?"

"Yes. I put in a bulk order for everyone with the florist in Sandleton. I've got a list somewhere."

She went to a drawer and took out a sheet of paper.

Forward glanced at the names on the list. "Do you need this at the moment?"

"I do actually. I need it to collect the money for the flowers."

"I'll get it copied and returned to you," he said. "I'd hate you to be out of pocket."

Forward deliberated whether or not to ask Mrs Coulson to accompany him to Sandleton Police Station for further questioning. The fact that she had deliberately withheld information concerning her relationship with Dangerfield worried him, for it raised doubts about the truth of other statements she'd made. Was she, for example, as unaware of her husband's so-called legacy, as she insisted she was? He was fearful of making another wrong decision. He'd made enough cockups in this case as it was. Yet, reluctantly, he was forced to conclude that generally her answers had been truthful; and although she'd withheld information, it had been done, quite understandably, to protect her former lover. Nevertheless, to be on the safe side, he determined to place her under surveillance for the next few days.

CHAPTER TWENTY EIGHT

Forward decided that as he was already in Melthorpe he would save Wilmott an unnecessary trip and call in on Mr Gibbard himself. He was therefore surprised when he turned into Woldgate Drive to find Wilmott's car parked outside number fourteen. His knock was answered by a plump woman in her thirties with dyed blonde hair. She was wearing a black shell suit which bulged in so many unflattering places it looked at least two sizes too small for her.

"Yes?"

"Detective Chief Inspector Forward, East Yorkshire CID. I believe my sergeant's with you?"

"Yes, he is. Come in. He's talking to my husband."

Forward followed her down a narrow passage and into the lounge. Wilmott was sitting on the sofa. A large white cup and saucer was on the coffee table in front of him.

His open notebook was in one hand and a pen in the other.

"Hello, sir," said Wilmott. He leant towards Gibbard who was sitting opposite him in an armchair. "This is my guv'nor. Chief Inspector Forward."

"'Allo,'" said Gibbard. He was a blonde, round-faced man with big, light blue eyes that bulged slightly. The sleeves of his grubby yellow shirt were rolled up. Forward noticed a blue anchor was tattooed just under the crook of his right elbow. A purple chain trailed from the anchor looping its way down to Gibbard's wrist. Forward placed him at around thirty-five or six.

"Mr Gibbard?"

"That's right." Gibbard began to play with some of the straggling hairs at the end of his thick, untrimmed moustache.

"Has the sergeant told you why we wanted to see you?"

"Yes 'e 'as. I were just telling 'im I didn't really 'ave an argument with Mr Coulson."

"You didn't?"

"No. It were just a difference of opinion, that's all. Y'see, our Cheryl was in Mrs Dangerfield's class, but I thought she ought to 'ave been in Mr Coulson's class because she's very bright and most of the children of 'er age are in there. So, I went along to see if I could 'ave 'er transferred to 'is class, but 'e would 'ave none of it."

"So, you lost your temper?"

Gibbard folded his arms. "Well, I did get a bit aerated, it's true, but Mr Coulson explained why it were necessary for Cheryl to be in Mrs Dangerfield's class, so in the end, I 'ad to accept it." He laughed. "It wasn't worth murdering 'im for, if that's what you're suggestin'."

"Would you like a cup of tea, Chief Inspector?" asked Mrs Gibbard.

Forward politely declined her offer and turned back to Gibbard. "Nobody's suggesting anything, Mr Gibbard." He looked at Wilmott. "Have you asked Mr Gibbard where he was on Monday night, Sergeant?"

"No, sir. We didn't get that far."

"Would you mind telling us, Mr Gibbard?"

Gibbard sat up straight in his armchair. "Not at all. I got 'ome from work about 'alf past five. I 'ad me tea, read the paper and then Cheryl and Emma read their reading books to me and then I spent the rest of the evenin' watchin' telly."

"Were you in all evening too, Mrs Gibbard?"

Gibbard looked at his wife. "You went to the flower arranging class till ten, didn't you?"

"Aye, I were at the flower arranging class until about ten, and then I came 'ome and watched the telly with 'im till about eleven. Then we went to bed."

"Thank you," said Forward. "There's a lot of interest in flower arranging in this village. It must be very popular."

"Oh, it is," said Mrs Gibbard. "But anything that goes on at the village 'all is always well attended."

"Have you entered the flower arranging exhibition?" asked Forward.

"Yes, I 'ave. I'm 'opin' I'll win it too!"

"A lot of people are using lilies," said Forward. "Are you?"

"Aye. Enchantment Lilies. Mrs Coulson ordered them for us, poor soul. Would you like to see what I've made with them?"

"The Inspector doesn't want to see all that rubbish," said Gibbard.

"No, really, I'd like to see it," said Forward. "I'm thinking of taking it up as a hobby when I retire."

"It's a woman's 'obby," said Gibbard.

"No it's not," shrieked Mrs Gibbard indignantly. "Some of the best flower arrangers are men. I'll get it for you, Inspector."

Mrs Gibbard left the room. Her husband looked at Wilmott and gave him a grin. "It keeps 'er 'appy," he said. Wilmott nodded and grinned back at him, knowingly.

"It's nice to see a bit of male bonding," Forward muttered. Gibbard stared at him. He looked puzzled.

At that moment Mrs Gibbard returned with her creation. She displayed it to Forward proudly. "It's taken me days to get it right," she said.

Forward examined the lilies in it closely. He couldn't work out what Mrs Gibbard's flower arrangement was supposed to represent but he kept this to himself. "It's lovely. I wish you lots of luck with it." He stood up. "And now I think we'd better go." He looked towards Gibbard. "We may need you to sign a formal statement later. We'll call you if necessary. What's your work telephone number?"

Gibbard reeled off a series of digits. "You won't be able to speak to me there cos I'm outside most of the time, but you'll be able to leave a message."

"Where do you work as a matter of interest?"

"Melthorpe Hall," said Gibbard. "Three days a week. I'm a sort of general handyman there."

****

"What did the warden say?" Forward asked Wilmott as they left the Gibbards'.

"There aren't any lilies at Viking's Chine. Never have been."

"Then Dangerfield must have picked up that stain somewhere else."

They stood by Wilmott's car. Wilmott nodded back in the direction of number fourteen and dropped his voice. "What about in there, sir? Was there anything unusual about Mrs Gibbard's lilies?

"It was impossible to tell. Some of the

stamens were heavy with pollen, others weren't, but they all had some pollen on them. It was the same at Mrs Coulson's."

"You've been to Mrs Coulson's?"

"Yes. She's given me a list of all the people who ordered lilies for the show."

"I could have picked that up for you, sir. Why didn't you ask me? You knew I was coming over."

"I didn't visit Mrs Coulson just to pick up that list."

"Why did you go then, sir?"

"I'll tell you about it when we get back to Sandleton," said Forward. He grinned wryly. "It'll reinforce all your stereotypes about married women."

CHAPTER
TWENTY NINE

Forward was in his office at Sandleton writing up the notes of his interview with Sandra Turnbull when he received a phone call from DI Hoggart. McIntyre had traced Coulson's bookmaker. His name was Tommy Eden and his betting shop was in Sandleton.

Forward went along to the canteen to collect Wilmott. He sat around impatiently while the sergeant bolted down a belated lunch of sausage and chips.

"I'll end up with indigestion," Wilmott complained between mouthfuls.

"And worse," said Forward, who was virtually a vegetarian. "You should only eat white meat and never anything fried."

"I like fried food," said Wilmott. "Most of that stuff you eat is rabbit food."

"I'll bet rabbits don't get indigestion, though."

Wilmott cleared his plate and placed his knife and fork down. "Have I got time for a sweet?"

"No. I want to get over and see that old rogue Tommy Eden before he does a bunk with the day's takings."

"What do you need me for?"

"He's fly," said Forward. "I want some corroboration."

****

Tommy Eden's betting shop was in Sandleton High Street. Forward and Wilmott entered it just as the four fifteen steeplechase at Sandown Park was being broadcast. They weaved their way through punters oblivious to everything but the equine images on the television screen, and Forward's lungs went into spasm as he inhaled a foul mixture of stale air and cigarette smoke. With Wilmott following him, Forward coughed and spluttered his way over to the betting office clerk and held his warrant card up to the security glass.

"Detective Chief Inspector Forward, East Yorkshire Police. I'd like to speak to Mr Eden."

The clerk immediately reached for the phone. A minute later a tiny man in a blue, mohair suit and a garish floral tie appeared behind the clerk. He opened the metal door next to the security window, and furtively ushered the two detectives within.

"Hello, Tommy, how's tricks?" Forward asked

jovially.

Tommy Eden shrugged. "Terrible. This recession's killing me."

"You're breaking my heart!" said Forward.

They followed Eden through a door in the back, and then up a flight of dingy wooden stairs to his office on the first floor. This was surprisingly luxurious. There was wall to wall carpet, brown leather armchairs and an impressive looking desk. Two huge television screens were set side by side in a wall unit at the far end of the room. They were broadcasting race meetings without the sound.

The detectives took a leather armchair each. Eden slipped on to the swivel chair behind his massive desk and instantly seemed more diminutive than ever.

Forward said, "You have a client called Mark Coulson."

"The headmaster who got his head bashed in?"

"That's the one. We'd like to ask you a few questions about his account."

"Our clients' accounts are strictly confidential," said Eden, smiling like a crocodile with imperfect teeth.

"You know as well as I do, Tommy, that I can leave Sergeant Wilmott here and be back in an hour with a court order empowering me to scrutinise every account you've got. Now, I'm sure you wouldn't want that, would you? Who knows what we might turn up, eh?"

Eden shrugged, and darted his head from point to point in frustration. "All right. All right." He got up and went over to a row of beige filing cabinets, opened one of the drawers and took out a buff-coloured file.

"There it is," he said, shoving it rudely into Forward's hands.

Forward surveyed the file's contents with distaste. He got up, went over and placed the file in front of Eden on his desk. "I've never had a good head for figures, Tommy, so it might be easier if I asked you a few questions about it."

"Fire away."

Forward returned to his seat. "When did Mr Coulson open the account?"

Eden glanced down at the file cover. "Back in June of last year."

"Did he bet regularly?"

"Depends what you mean by regularly. How often do you bet, Inspector?"

"I occasionally have a flutter on the Grand National."

"If I had to depend on punters like you, I'd have gone bankrupt years ago." He checked through the file. "This man was a good client. Placed a bet four times a week. Every day sometimes. Went through the card. Usually, a pony on an each-way-double. Occasionally a monkey to win."

"Speak English," said Forward.

"I think he means he bet fifty pounds on two races each time, sir," explained Wilmott.

"That's right," said Eden. "A pony, that's twenty-five pounds, each way, on a double. That makes fifty pounds."

"So he spent fifty pounds a day?" queried Forward.

"No. Much more than that," said Eden. "More like a hundred and fifty a day."

"He went through the card, sir," said Wilmott. "That means he bet on every race at a particular meeting. And sometimes he bet a monkey, that's five hundred pounds, on one horse that he thought would win."

"I thought people always bet on a horse they thought would win!" exclaimed Forward.

"No," said Eden. "If you bet a horse each way, that means you can still get some winnings even if it comes in second or third."

"This is very confusing," said Forward. He looked at Wilmott quizzically. "I never realised you were a betting man, Sergeant!"

"I'm not, sir. My dad was, though."

"How interesting." He turned back to Eden. "So, Coulson was betting a hundred and fifty pounds a day, four days a week. That's six hundred pounds. And sometimes, in addition, he bet an extra five hundred pounds. So, in some weeks he was betting eleven hundred pounds?"

"That's right," said Eden. "Like I said, he was a

very good client."

"But he was only on a headmaster's salary. It's a wonder he didn't go bankrupt within a month."

"Ah, but he won from time to time, don't forget," said Eden.

"A lot of money? Say, twenty thousand pounds?"

Eden laughed. "Twenty thousand pounds? No chance. He always picked first and second favourites. You can't win that sort of money putting a pony on first and second favourites."

"But he did win?"

"Yes. Quite often he broke even. Sometimes he even made a profit."

"Would you say he was a clever gambler, then?"

Eden smiled slyly. "I wouldn't say he was clever, because he didn't know when to stop. But he knew what he was doing. First and second favourites give you security, you see, because they usually come in well placed. The downside is that they have such small prices they don't pay out very much."

"Did Mr Coulson pay you a large sum in February of this year in cash?"

"Yes, he did. Over eight grand. It was to clear his account."

"His account for last year?"

"That's right."

"Why did you allow him to run up such a

large debt?"

"Because he promised me he'd pay it off after Christmas. He said he had a legacy coming. One of his old aunts had died. He was a respectable man, a headmaster, so I took his word. Mind you, I had me doubts."

"Is that why you kept ringing up his wife and pressuring her?"

Eden looked cagey. "I have no need to resort to those practices."

"I'm not interested in your business ethics," said Forward. "I just want to find out if you were the person who was ringing her up and threatening her husband. It's important."

"I did ring her once or twice."

"Threatening her husband?"

"It was eight grand, Inspector. That's a lot of money. And you know as well as I do gambling debts aren't recoverable at law."

"Is there any money owing on the account now?"

"Yeah. He's run up nearly three grand since he last paid it off. I suppose I can kiss that good-bye. Got any idea who topped him?"

Forward ignored the question. "Where were you on Monday night?"

"What, this Monday just gone?"

"Yes."

"I was at Sandleton Golf Club. My wife and I went to the annual club dinner. We were invited by the president."

"What time did you leave?"

"About two in the morning."

"Sir Andrew Marston was there. Did you speak to him?"

"I didn't actually."

"Pity. I'm sure you and he could have had a most diverting conversation."

Forward stood up. "Right. Thank you, Tommy." He scooped up Coulson's account from Eden's desk. "We'll take this with us and study it."

"Eh, you don't think it was me who did Coulson in, do you?"

Forward couldn't resist a little wind up. "He still owed you three grand, Tommy. You said so yourself."

Eden saw through it. "Come off it, Inspector," he said, smiling. "If I topped everybody who owed me three grand, I wouldn't have a business!"

CHAPTER THIRTY

At five p.m. Forward and Wilmott arrived at the incident centre at Monkhouses for the case review. Everyone from Sandleton CID was there, except Griffiths, who was still doing a company search on Pulverisation International Limited, the owners of the *Phaeton*. She knew she was going to be late and had already phoned in her apologies.

Forward went straight over to the pinboard and spent some time creating a series of visual aids to illustrate the key developments in the case. These were mainly labels bearing the names of people and places, or short descriptions of important incidents. He attached each of them to the pinboard and then used lengths of green tape to demonstrate any connections between them. Soon a network of criss-crossing green appeared on the pinboard, visually representing the investigation's growing complexity.

When he'd completed his task, Forward

turned to the rows of seated officers who were waiting for him to begin. Being an ex-actor, he was acutely sensitive to vibrations and was instantly struck by the sense of malaise and irritation that seemed to be emanating from his audience. It was as though they resented being there. He was used to them exhibiting stress from the pressure of over-work, but this was different: their critical, occasionally hostile glances, and frequent guarded asides, were contributing to the creation of an atmosphere of increasing resentment that seemed to be directed specifically towards him.

Forward raised himself to his full height and cleared his throat. "All right. I don't want to keep you any longer than necessary, so we'll begin. Let's start with Inspector Hoggart's report on the progress of the fingertip search." Forward nodded at Hoggart. "If you don't mind, Reg?"

Hoggart got to his feet. "The search of the bay - and of the cliffs five hundred yards either side of the bay - is now complete. So is the search of the Monks Bay car park. The search of roadside verges has now been extended a quarter of a mile west of Monkhouses. SOCOs, and a small number of assigned officers and the dog unit, are currently searching the shore at South Landing where Mr Coulson's credit cards were found. So far, the murder weapon has not been recovered. Nor the knife. All that has been recovered are five hundred plus items of litter." Hoggart looked around balefully. A long-suffering tone entered his voice. "I am presently coming under a lot of pressure from commanders whose forces have been depleted because of the search, and have requested me to stand down as many uniformed men..." Here he paused and, somewhat unwillingly, corrected himself. "...Er, to stand down as many uniformed *officers* as possible, and return them to their stations. That's the end of my report, sir." An arch expression appeared on Hoggart's plump features. "However, sir, I would appreciate it if you could tell me as soon as possible how many officers you intend to remove from search duties."

Nice one to chuck at me right at the end without a word of consultation, thought Forward. "Thank you, Reg, for that very full report. It's not your fault nothing's been found, I'm sure." He reflected for a moment and then asked Hoggart directly, "What percentage of officers do you think we could lose without compromising our capabilities?"

Forward was being disingenuous. He knew that Hoggart's grasp of mathematics was shaky to say the least. He looked into Hoggart's panic-stricken eyes and said, smiling, "Just a rough estimate will do. It doesn't have to be a precise percentage."

"A third, I think. Yes, a third would do it."

"Right. Thirty-three per cent can go back to normal duties. In actual numbers that would be, how many?"

Hoggart said nothing.

"Reg?"

"I can't say exactly. There've been several replacements, you see. I'll have to work it out."

"OK. You do that. And then you make the arrangements, will you?"

"Yes, sir."

Forward moved closer to the pinboard and, occasionally with reference to his visual aids, gave an account of the major developments to date.

"I'll start with the Coulson case. Sergeant Wilmott and I have established that Coulson was a gambler and had big money troubles. His wife didn't know it, but he'd run up a huge debt of over eight thousand pounds with Tommy Eden, a Sandleton bookie. However, by February of this year, Coulson had managed to get hold of twenty thousand in cash from somewhere. He didn't want his wife to know about this either, so he secreted it away in his school's deposit account before paying Eden off. That twenty thousand pounds provides us with a possible reason for his trip to Filey. My feeling is he went there to earn it."

"How?" demanded Hoggart. "Doing what?"

"That's the million-dollar question. You don't get that kind of money teaching evening classes. So I'd like all your thoughts on it."

Several reasons were suggested for Coulson's trip to Filey. They included attending dog fights, smuggling and illegal gaming.

"We've run pre-cons checks on Coulson and Dangerfield, and they're both as clean as a whistle," said Forward. "But there certainly wouldn't be any harm in pulling in a few ex-cons. Put some pressure on them to find out if they've come across Coulson - or even Dangerfield - in the course of their nefarious activities." Forward looked in Hoggart's direction. "I can leave that to you, Reg, can I?"

Hoggart nodded so slowly it bordered on insolence.

"Now, let's focus on a different aspect of the case. One which suggests a potential smuggling dimension. The *Phaeton* is an eight-berth motor cruiser that arrived in Sandleton Harbour at five forty p.m. on Monday afternoon. The National Crime Intelligence Service have told me that two of the crew of the *Phaeton*, David Nathan and Francesca Beaton, are suspected of various drugs offences. However, they've got no form to speak of and NCIS have never been able to pin anything on them. It seems to me to be too much of a coincidence that a foreign craft, the *Phaeton*, berthed in Sandleton Harbour just a few hours before Coulson was murdered. Particularly now we've found Coulson's credit cards which washed up at South Landing. Thwaites is certain that if they were thrown into the sea from a boat, it must have been done when it was in Sandleton Bay. So, it rather looks like whoever killed Coulson in Monks Bay, continued on from there round Flamborough Head and either put their boat in at Sandleton Harbour or travelled further on down the coast."

"Excuse me," said Hoggart, "you said that the *Phaeton* put into Sandleton Harbour at five forty p.m. on Monday evening. That was too early for any of the crew to have murdered Coulson."

"I agree. That's why I asked you to check on those three fishing boats that entered Sandleton Harbour after the time Coulson died."

"We didn't have much luck with them, sir," said DC Phipps, opening his notebook. "They were all small fishing cobles each with a two-man crew. The one that berthed at ten forty p.m. belonged to a Fred Williams. The next one to come in belonged to a Percy Sygrove. That was at eleven fifteen. The last one belonged to a Peter Stone. That berthed at eleven forty. They'd all been out since the early afternoon on Monday and none of them reported anything unusual."

"Well, of course they bloody well wouldn't!" exclaimed Forward. "Didn't you impound the boats and ask SOCOs to go over them?"

"You only asked us to interview them, sir."

"I said check them out. And I meant check them out!"

"Hang on a minute, sir," said Hoggart. "We can't search every fishing boat along the coast because it's just possible Coulson was brought to Monks Bay by sea."

Forward looked exasperated. "But I'm not asking you to do that, Inspector. I asked you to check out those three boats specifically, because they came into Sandleton Harbour soon after Coulson was murdered."

"I'm sorry," said Hoggart, adding pointedly, "we all make mistakes, sir."

The criticism was not lost on Forward.

"I'll get it done right away, sir," said Phipps.

"You'll be lucky," said Forward. "They're fishing boats. They'll be out fishing now. You'll have to wait till midnight. Right. Have you got anything else for me?"

"We've not had much joy with that special waterproof Coulson was wearing, sir," said DS Drinkwater.

"Oh?"

"We couldn't find out who'd bought it. Very few of the shops round here stock them, and those that do, don't keep records of purchases. They only have till rolls. One chap said those sort of anoraks were mostly used by deep sea trawler men and we ought to try in Grimsby or

Hull."

"And did you?"

"Not yet, sir."

"Then I suggest you get on with it! Is that all? Nothing else? Where's that company search I asked for?"

"DC Griffiths is still working on that, sir," said Phipps. "It should be here shortly."

Forward looked round at the assembled officers in amazement. "What's wrong with you all? I thought you'd have generated at least one or two new leads by now! Instead of which you haven't even followed up the current ones properly."

Hoggart cleared his throat. "I think the problem is we all think it's rather a waste of our time. In view of Dangerfield's suicide, sir."

"I shall be coming to that in a moment," said Forward.

"The other problem is that none of the officers now have sufficient time to complete their investigations," Hoggart continued. "Sandleton has started assigning every officer here to additional duties."

"They've no right," said Forward. "Not without Chief Superintendent Jones' authority."

"Yes, I've checked on that and it appears they've got it, sir."

"You mean Superintendent Jones is winding down this investigation?"

"It appears so."

"I'll have to have a word with him," said Forward grimly. "But first let me tell you what I've found out about Dangerfield."

Forward spent the next fifteen minutes describing in detail his interviews with Sandra Turnbull and Sheila Coulson, in which they'd both admitted having had affairs with Richard Dangerfield. As he got towards the end, DC Griffiths entered the incident centre and tried, unobtrusively, to find herself a seat.

Forward concluded his account of the interviews. "Well, I can see you all enjoyed that," he said, grinning.

"Dangerfield had it coming to him, I reckon," said DS Harper. "Dirty little bugger."

"Let him without sin cast the first stone is what I say," said Forward, staring at Harper, whose extra marital affairs were the talk of the station. Harper became unusually thoughtful.

Forward then grudgingly announced that Dorothy Newbiggin had identified Richard Dangerfield's corpse, and was convinced he was the man she'd seen in the red Sierra at Monkhouses.

Hoggart immediately pounced. "Just a moment, sir. You say Miss Newbiggin identified Richard Dangerfield as the man she saw at Monkhouses. And you've just told us Dangerfield had a sexual relationship with Mrs Coulson. Surely that gave him a strong motive for murdering her husband? It's extremely suspicious that Mrs Coulson withheld from us the existence of her relationship with Dangerfield."

"That's true. And I've taken the precaution of having her placed under surveillance. But I still don't believe Dangerfield had the opportunity to murder Coulson. If you're going to go along that road you have to explain how Dangerfield engineered it so he could travel the fifteen miles from Luffield to Monks Bay; get down into the bay at exactly the moment Coulson appeared; murder him; clean himself up; drive another fifteen miles back to Luffield; score some pot and arrive at the Chinese restaurant - all in the space of forty-five minutes. You also have to explain why, when he joined Sandra Turnbull after the pub was closed, he was wearing the same clothes he'd had on earlier in the evening and they weren't blood-stained. And finally, you'd have to explain how anyone, after all that, could behave perfectly normally; because that's how Sandra Turnbull said he was behaving when she saw him later on that night."

The officers were all sitting up in their seats now, all attention. Forward's arguments in support of Dangerfield's innocence seemed to have galvanised them.

"Don't forget the condoms, sir. He had to get the condoms too," Harper called out coarsely.

Everyone except Griffiths roared.

"Trust you to remember that little detail, Harper," Forward said, feigning a straight face amidst the laughter.

Hoggart's nasal Birmingham tones cut through the room, flushing the laughter out of it. "But suppose Sandra Turnbull is lying?"

Forward paused, collected himself and said, "She isn't."

"But how do you know?"

"Because of something she told me this afternoon which I don't intend to reveal until the appropriate time." Forward turned his attention to the whole gathering. "Right. We have all the reasons why Dangerfield didn't kill Coulson. What we don't have is the evidence to prove whether Dangerfield himself was murdered. Now, what about the rope? I understand Dangerfield's mother didn't recognise it."

"That's right, sir," said Hoggart. "She said she'd never seen anything like it."

"Have there been any developments on it?"

"It's still with forensic, sir."

"Well hurry them up." He looked straight at DC Phipps. "The rope must have come from somewhere. When you search those boats in Sandleton Harbour make sure the SOCOs impound every stray length of rope and get it over to forensic."

Phipps looked embarrassed. "The fishermen

use the ropes, sir, for their trade like. They might object."

Forward looked annoyed. "Object? This is a murder enquiry!"

"Dangerfield's death isn't being treated as murder, sir."

It was Hoggart who had spoken. Forward stopped and looked around. He could see they all thought he was clutching at straws because he felt responsible for Dangerfield's suicide. "Yes, you're right, Reg, but Coulson's death was murder. And I think the two deaths are connected." He returned his gaze to Phipps. "If any of the owners of those boats object to you searching them, remind them it could be construed as an admission of guilt. If that doesn't work, get a warrant. No matter what time it is. Get the magistrate out of bed if necessary."

Forward pointed to his drawing of a flower on the pinboard. "Now, this terrible drawing of mine is supposed to represent a lily. I've been finding out a lot about lilies recently. They're delightful flowers but if you get their pollen on your skin or clothes it's almost impossible to remove. That's a good thing for us, because Marston found lily pollen on Dangerfield's body and his clothing. Of course, all that tells us is that before Dangerfield died, he went somewhere where there were lilies and brushed or fell against them. There's no evidence he picked up the pollen stain in the murderer's home. Nevertheless, it's a strong possibility." Forward took out of his pocket a piece of paper and waved it at his audience. "This is a list of all the people in Melthorpe who ordered lilies for their flower arranging exhibition. Dangerfield's mother is on the list, so it's more than possible he picked up the stain at home. But there are thirty other names here, and it's equally possible that Dangerfield was in a house belonging to one of these people before he died."

Forward addressed DI Hoggart. "That's why, Reg, Superintendent Jones permitting, I'd like you to select a small team to go over to Melthorpe and interview all the people on the list and their families. Find out what they were doing between six p.m. Wednesday night and the early hours of Thursday morning, when Dangerfield is supposed to have hanged himself. Find out where they were at the time Coulson was murdered on Monday night, as well. It's possible that whoever murdered Coulson also murdered Dangerfield. I want the names of anyone who hasn't got a cast iron alibi. And I want them by this time tomorrow."

"Do you want the lilies examined, sir?" asked Hoggart.

"Yes. I looked at some lilies today but I couldn't see anything unusual. SOCOs might though. The stamens definitely made contact with Dangerfield's shirt cuff and jacket sleeve. So you're looking for stamens that have had their pollen disturbed. One or two minute fibres might also have stuck to the stamens. If they're there, SOCOs will find them. The exhibition is being held tomorrow, so all the entries will be in the Melthorpe village hall."

"Shall we get a warrant for those as well," Hoggart asked slyly.

I know what your game is, thought Forward. "Let's not get ahead of ourselves," he said.

"What makes you so sure Dangerfield didn't string himself up?" asked DS Harper.

"A priori reasoning," said Forward. Everyone looked at him blankly. "If we accept that Dangerfield didn't murder Coulson, then what possible reason could he have had for hanging himself? With Coulson gone, Dangerfield could look forward to renewing his relationship with Mrs Coulson, who was the love of his life and who was going to get her husband's insurance money. What's more, according to Sandra Turnbull, who saw Dangerfield just hours before he died, he wasn't in the least depressed. He told her he was coming into a considerable amount of money and was planning to move off somewhere and make a new start. With all this to look forward to, is it likely that five or six hours later he'd go and hang himself?" Forward turned to Griffiths. "Now, have you got that company search I asked for?"

Griffiths got up from her seat and walked over to Forward, holding the record of the search she'd requested from the Registrar of Companies. Today she was dressed in a navy-blue business suit with a very tight skirt. The eyes of many of the male officers followed her progress across the room with more than a casual interest.

Forward scanned quickly through the search while Griffiths returned to her seat. "You'd better fill everyone in on the details," Forward told her.

"Right." Griffiths consulted her notes. "Pulverisation International Limited, which owns the *Phaeton*, is a private limited company. It was incorporated in 1986. The registered office is in London, in Wapping. Its main business is demolition but it also does some building. Its nominal share capital is a hundred pounds. The most recent set of accounts were filed in 1992. They show it made an operating loss of thirty-seven thousand pounds. That was the year in which the company acquired the *Phaeton*, second hand. That was in..." She searched through the notes on her lap, "... in May last year. The boat cost sixty-three thousand. The company's in hock to the bank for a hundred and fifty thousand, and so far it's never made a profit."

"Who are the shareholders?" Forward asked impatiently.

Griffiths smiled graciously back at him. "I was just coming to that, sir. There are only three. Pauline and Ivan Walters are a married couple who live in Surrey, and they're the minority shareholders. The principal shareholder is another company, Finesse Holdings and Investment Associates Limited. It owns eighty-one per cent of the share capital and its registered office is in Wapping too."

"Have you done a search on this other company, Finesse Holdings?" asked Forward.

"I've applied for one but I haven't got it yet. The Registrar of Companies was just closing."

"What time did you do this search, for God's sake?" Forward demanded.

"Four o'clock, sir."

"Four o'clock? I asked you to do it first thing this morning!"

"I know, sir. I'm sorry but Sandleton switched me to other duties. I've been on a sexual assault and a hit and run till four o'clock."

Forward exploded. "Christ! I'll have to have a word with Jones. This is supposed to be a murder enquiry!"

All around the room looks were exchanged.

Forward quickly regained control of himself. "All right. Thank you. Make sure I get that search on Finesse Holdings first thing tomorrow morning. Any comments?"

"It doesn't seem to be a very big or successful

company. What did they want a boat for?" said Wilmott.

"Quite. I think we all know what the answer to that is. A few trips across to Holland to pick up a hefty consignment of drugs would boost their profits no end. We'll pass these details onto NCIS. Although they probably know a lot more about the *Phaeton* than we do by now."

"Have we got a photofit of the man who was in the fish and chip shop with Coulson, yet?" asked Hoggart. The question was directed at Griffiths.

"Mr Follett, the chip shop owner, is in Facial Recognition now. It's not going very well, I believe."

"Anything else?" asked Forward. Nobody said anything. "Right. Get to it. I want some results. And if Sandleton start switching you to other duties refuse and refer them to me."

CHAPTER
THIRTY ONE

Forward was in a filthy mood all the way back to Sandleton. His face was set in an angry rictus as he sat clenching the wheel, staring straight ahead through the windscreen at the oncoming traffic. Wilmott tried to draw him out of it, but all his efforts were met with silence. After the third attempt he gave up.

Within minutes of his return to Sandleton Police Station, Forward had sent Wilmott down to Facial Recognition to see if Mr Follett had completed his photofit. He'd also arranged an interview with the Chief Superintendent.

Ten minutes later, he flung open the door of Jones' office.

"I've just come back from Monkhouses and do you know what they're saying over there? They're saying you've stood down the investigation. Is that right?"

Jones, who was working at his desk, was taken aback at the sight of Forward standing before him, glowering with anger.

"You'd better sit down, Tony. You don't look very well."

Forward stubbornly remained standing. "Just answer my question!"

"Not until you sit down. And calm down!"

Truculently, Forward sank into the chair in front of Jones' desk. There was nothing on the desk except a leather-bound blotter and two metal baskets, both of which looked self-righteously empty. He thought of the shambles of paper, pens, books and discarded coffee cups that usually covered his own desk. The comparison was unfortunate, because it served only to emphasise the immense personality gulf which lay between Jones and himself. It did nothing to dispel his anger.

Jones got up, went over to the door, shut it and resumed his seat. "That's better," he said. "You must try to control these adolescent rages of yours."

"I feel I have something to be enraged about."

Jones' eyes were slits. "Now look here, Tony. The last time I spoke to you, I promised you'd remain in charge of the Coulson investigation until Dangerfield's inquest. What I didn't promise you was unlimited manpower."

"No sir, you didn't, but you did promise I'd keep my existing officers."

"Efficiency and cost-effectiveness. Those are the criteria for running a modern police force. I can't have vast numbers of officers engaged on unproductive duties." He raised his hand to silence Forward, who was about to interrupt. "Yes, I'm sure that's not how you see it, but do you realise what I'm in the middle of right now? A Home Office audit. I've got civil servants on my neck demanding I justify every single administrative decision in terms of its productivity and value for money. You don't have to justify the huge sums in overtime payments generated by the Coulson case. I do!"

"I appreciate that, but I'm in charge of a murder investigation. Two murder investigations. I need to keep all the CID I've got. And I need them full time."

"Two murder investigations?"

Forward's expression became apologetic. "It's my fault. I haven't been keeping you in the picture. There've been significant developments in both the Coulson and the Dangerfield cases."

"Really?"

Forward could tell he didn't believe him.

Jones looked at his watch. "Well, I've got ten minutes before my next meeting. You'd better tell me what these significant developments, as you call them, are."

Forward described the main areas of progress that had been made in both cases; all the time aware of Jones' sceptical expression. However, when he mentioned the valuable contribution made to the investigation by

NCIS, the Chief Superintendent perked up. He leaned intently across the desk and his expression became one of genuine interest. Forward had anticipated this, and so he slightly exaggerated the extent of the NCIS involvement. It was a deliberately cynical attempt to appeal to Jones' vanity and lust for promotion. He knew the Chief Superintendent would be impressed by the involvement of NCIS, for it guaranteed his name would be mentioned in important circles in London, and, of course, that would do wonders for his career prospects.

"So, if nothing else, we've at least assisted NCIS," Jones mused, in a gratified tone. "They might even make several arrests for drugs offences."

"That's right."

"How near are you to making an arrest?"

"I'm not that close, yet. There's still a lot of leg work to be done. That's why I need those officers. But I'm sure that with the help of NCIS I'll be able to put a name in the frame very shortly."

Jones stood up looking at his watch. "I'm late for my meeting."

"Please, sir, keep my officers off other duties," Forward pleaded.

"All right," said Jones. "But only for forty-eight hours."

Forward went back to his office and

immediately got on the phone to Hoggart.

****

"I've not had much joy with that photofit," said Wilmott as he entered Forward's office. "Mr Follett's gone back to Filey to open his fish and chip shop."

Forward looked up from his paperwork and groaned. "It's not ready, then?"

"No, his memory's gone blank. Lucas has been showing him photos for the past two hours without much success. All he's got so far is a head shape."

"I hope Lucas isn't giving up."

"No. Follett's coming back first thing tomorrow morning."

"You might as well get off home then," said Forward. "There's not much more you can do here tonight."

"I've still got several statements to type up."

"Why don't you do them at home?"

"No thanks, I like to work in peace and quiet."

Forward smiled wryly. "Yes. I'd forgotten what family life is like."

"That's why I envy you sometimes, sir."

Something in Forward's expression made Wilmott realise he'd said the wrong thing. He'd forgotten how sensitive Forward could be about the subject of his divorce.

"I'm sorry, sir," said Wilmott awkwardly. "I didn't mean... I wasn't..."

"That's all right. It's quite true. I don't have a wife or family any more. The theatre's my only family now. Those people in the Sandleton Players. Sad, eh? But you know what? I prefer it that way. At least I can keep them at arm's length when I need to." He looked at his watch. "In fact, it's time I paid them a visit."

Forward was just leaving when the phone on his desk rang. He turned and stood in the doorway, shaking his head at Wilmott to indicate he'd already left and wasn't going to take any more calls. The sergeant lifted the receiver, and Forward lingered out of curiosity, listening to Wilmott's responses. When Wilmott said into the phone, "So you've no idea why he wanted to speak to you?" Forward mouthed at him, "Who is it?" Wilmott placed his hand over the mouthpiece. "It's someone called Alex Armstrong, sir. Says he's the editor of the *Fundleton Gazette*. You called him earlier but he was out."

"I'll take it," said Forward, putting his hand out for the phone.

CHAPTER
THIRTY TWO

Forward ought to have been enjoying himself. The hall of Sandleton High School was filled to capacity and the performance of *The Cherry Orchard* was going brilliantly. Yet he still felt restless and strangely dissatisfied. The cause was plain: anxieties about the progress of the investigation were worrying away at his mind. He was sure both the Coulson and Dangerfield deaths were connected, and that the investigation had thrown up enough pointers and clues for him to have identified who'd killed them. Yet one vital piece of information was missing, and its absence was preventing him from gaining an overarching perspective of the whole case. He was certain that if he could only grasp what the missing element was, all the disparate pieces of the puzzle would fuse together to form a complete picture of causes and effects that would lead him to an arrest. The answer was probably quite simple and was staring him directly in the face. Why the hell couldn't he see it?

In this troubled mood, the first three acts of the play passed before him. And that was another thing! He had the discomforting conviction the play itself somehow contained the vital information he sought. With every performance he'd sensed this more and more strongly. Yet, he couldn't, for the life of him, interpret what it was that this old masterpiece was obliquely conveying to him; or how it could possibly be relevant.

When the performance finished, the cast took nine curtain calls: the largest number they'd achieved so far. The audience, mainly composed of friends, relations and sixth-form students, refused to let them leave the stage. In the end, the exasperated stage manager refused to raise the curtain anymore and the cast trooped off happily to their dressing rooms. Straightaway, Forward went back-stage and congratulated them all. They begged him to join them for a drink in *The Maypole* but he politely declined. He still had a lot of thinking to do and he wanted to keep his head clear. He drove homewards with the intention of having a relatively early night for a change.

Forward's route back to his sea-front flat took him past Sandleton Harbour. By the North Jetty, two fishing boats and the water around them gleamed refulgently in the beams of police arc lights. The sight made Forward feel immensely relieved. He was a scrupulous detective who demanded nothing less than perfection from himself and others. The failure to organise a thorough forensic examination of the boats had horrified him. Although his officers had been responsible for the oversight, Forward couldn't help thinking it had been caused fundamentally by some deficiency in his own communication skills. Still, at least it was underway now.

He stopped his car by the amusement arcade, got out and strolled down the jetty towards the activity around the boats. It was well past eleven now but a large crowd of sightseers had gathered. Their loud and uninhibited voices suggested that many of them had been on the way home from their Friday night pub crawls, when their attention had been arrested by the unusual scene. Fortunately, someone had erected waist high metal barriers around the investigation.

Forward passed through the crowd and pressed up to the barrier. Standing on the other side of it was DS Harper. Forward caught his attention and was allowed through.

"Is Inspector Hoggart around?" Forward asked.

"No sir. He's gone off home. He said he was feeling done in."

"He has had rather a long day," said Forward. "Well, have we found anything?"

"Nothing yet. We're still waiting for Pete Stone's boat to come in. Something might turn up there."

Forward stood around chatting to Harper for a few more minutes and then left the scene.

When he arrived home he went straight into the kitchen and took a well-chilled bottle of Pouilly Fumé from the fridge. He'd decided he could use a drink after all. It might induce some originality into his thought processes. He carried the bottle and a glass through to the sitting room and selected from his collection of recordings of classical plays, John Gielgud's interpretation of King Lear. He shoved the audio tape into the cassette player, filled his wine glass to the brim and sat back, preparing to be transported by Sir John's mellifluous tones.

He remained there for nearly an hour drinking and meditating on all aspects of the case. By a quarter to one his spirits were as empty as the bottle. He had made no progress. The great leap of the imagination he'd hoped would synthesise all the disparate and unconnected facts of the investigation into one complete picture hadn't occurred. All he could see was a series of unrelated and contradictory events. Yet he was still unwilling to go to bed. When the flash of insight came, the last thing he wanted was to be asleep.

He managed to stay awake for another

half hour, but then alcohol and fatigue overwhelmed him and he stumbled off to bed.

Two hours later, an excruciating headache and a bladder that demanded to be emptied dragged him unwillingly back to consciousness. He got up, and after he'd visited the bathroom, went into the kitchen and washed down a couple of paracetamol with a welcome glass of water. He was on his way back to bed when something made him change his mind. He went into the sitting room and picked up from the coffee table his dog-eared copy of Chekhov's collected plays. Wearily, he sat on the sofa, turned to *The Cherry Orchard* and scanned several pages until he came to the speech in Act One, where Gayev, the elderly landowner, waxes sentimentally over an old bookcase. Tired and hung-over as he was, Forward found himself sitting bolt upright and rigid with attention. He muttered ecstatically, and immediately re-read the speech. Then, in a growing fever of excitement, he found Lopakhin's speech in Act Three, where the businessman announces he has bought the estate and gives an elated account of the bidding at the auction.

"Of course," Forward mumbled, closing the book. "That's it."

CHAPTER
THIRTY THREE

By four in the morning Forward had given up trying to sleep. He took a shower, dressed and left his home while it was still dark. At five thirty a.m. he was in his office clearing his desk. By six thirty he'd dealt with everything that required his immediate attention and had filed the rest of the bumph away. After that he got out the Coulson and Dangerfield files and went through every document line by line, frequently pausing to make notes in his illegible, spidery writing. By seven forty-five he had a complete grasp of all the available details and had supplied some of those that were missing from his own imagination. He was sure now why Coulson had taken the train to Filey, what had happened when he'd arrived there and how he'd died. He could also see where Dangerfield fitted into the picture, and why he too had had to die. Forward was certain now who was responsible for both deaths. But how soon should he move in on them? Right away? No. He needed more evidence and there were still too many missing details. He would have to be patient and wait.

Wilmott appeared in Forward's office at nine thirty a.m. He was holding a cup of coffee in one hand and a rolled-up copy of *The East Yorkshire Messenger* in the other. He placed both on Forward's desk and sat down. "You look as though you've been here all night," he said.

"That's what it feels like. I'm warning you I've had a terrible night's sleep. I've got an obstinate hangover and I'm on a very short fuse."

Wilmott stood up. "I'll keep out of your way then."

"No, you can do better than that. Go down to Facial Recognition and hurry them along with that photofit. After we've seen it, we'll go over to Melthorpe."

When Wilmott had gone, Forward rang up a firm of estate agents in Sandleton. They couldn't provide him with the information he required but suggested a firm in Luffield who'd almost certainly be able to assist him. This proved correct, and after speaking to them, Forward made another call, this time to Chester.

Ten minutes after his call to Chester, the telephone in Forward's office rang. It was Wilmott. The photofit was ready.

"This is a real break, sir," said Wilmott. "I

think I've recognised who it is but I'm not saying until you've seen it. I don't want to influence your judgement."

"I'll be right down."

****

The Collation of Evidence Department at Sandleton Police Station was the engine room of criminal investigations. Here, fingerprints, photographs and other physical evidence were recorded, catalogued and examined. As befitted its vital function the department occupied a whole floor and was equipped with all the latest technology, including automatic fingerprinting facilities. Designed on the open plan model, the department was Chief Superintendent Jones' pride and joy and reflected his zeal for integrated organisation methods.

The lift doors opened straight onto the department. Forward stepped out of the lift, turned left and passed through the futuristic equipment of the fingerprint section, and then on past the banks of computer terminals until he arrived at the Facial Recognition Unit. Here he found Wilmott chatting to Sam Lucas, a thickset, balding officer who was the head of the section. Lucas was at his desk and Wilmott was sitting on the desk opposite, swinging his long legs. They were heatedly discussing the reasons for Hull City's failure in the FA Cup. At right angles to Lucas' desk was a large, free-standing Perspex screen. Displayed on it was the photofit image of a man wearing a tight-fitting woolly hat.

Sitting close to the Perspex screen were a man and woman Forward did not recognise. The man, who was in his fifties, was plump and grey haired and possessed a pair of shrewd blue eyes that seemed forever alert. The woman was considerably younger: she was large and big boned, with heavy intimidating features and hennaed hair. Forward assumed that the man was Follett, the Filey fish and chip shop owner. But who was the woman?

At Forward's appearance, Wilmott and Lucas brought their conversation to an abrupt end. They knew very well that Forward, unlike some other senior officers, did not share their passion for football.

Wilmott stood up, and, nodding towards the man and woman, said, "This is Mr Follett and Mrs MacDonald, sir. Mrs MacDonald is a waitress. She was working in the fish and chip shop on Monday night."

Forward surveyed Mrs MacDonald with interest. "Really?"

"Actually," said Mrs MacDonald, in a strong Scots accent and sounding slightly affronted, "it's the fish *restaurant* I work in."

"I beg your pardon," said Wilmott.

"Tina came along to jog my memory," said

Follett.

"He told me what a terrible time he was having making the photofit: and I said I was the one who should be doing it because I got a better look at Mr Coulson and the other fella than he did."

"You waited on their table?" said Forward.

"Yes."

Forward pointed at the photofit. "And this is a good likeness of the man you saw with Mr Coulson?"

"It's him to the life."

"Are you sure he was wearing a woolly hat?"

"Oh yes. I remember thinking at the time it's hot in here. Why don't you take your hat off?"

"Do you remember anything they said to each other?"

"No. They clammed up as soon as I came to the table. Just the usual 'Please' and 'Thank you' and 'Can I have the bill, please?'"

"The man who was with Mr Coulson. What sort of accent did he have? Was it local?"

"I think so."

"Who paid the bill?"

"The man in the woolly hat."

"In cash?"

"Yes. Gave me a nice little tip. I always remember those who give me a tip."

Forward thanked Mrs MacDonald warmly for her assistance. Then turning to Mr Follett, he said, "Did you tell Detective Constable

Griffiths that Mrs MacDonald was working in the restaurant on Monday night?"

"Aye, I did."

"Didn't DC Griffiths ask to speak to her?"

"No, she only seemed interested in what I saw."

Forward nodded grimly. "But surely you told Mrs MacDonald about DC Griffiths' visit?"

Mrs MacDonald cut in. "He couldn't because I only work on Mondays and Fridays. I found out about his problems with the photofit only last night."

"I see," said Forward, and sighed heavily. Once again, he thanked Follett and Mrs MacDonald for their efforts and told them they could both go.

As soon as the pair had gone Forward went over to the screen and examined the photofit image carefully.

Wilmott said, "Do you recognise him, sir?"

Forward stroked his chin and continued to study the image. "I can't say I do. I've never seen him before."

"Yes you have, sir. Try to imagine him without the hat."

Forward stared intently at the photofit for several more seconds. Then, shrugging his shoulders, he turned to Wilmott. "My mind's a blank."

"It's Gibbard, sir," said Wilmott.

"Gibbard?"

"The parent at Melthorpe who had a row with Mr Coulson. Lady Fernshawe's handyman."

"Gibbard!" Forward concentrated even harder on the photofit before him.

Although the man's head was almost totally covered by his woolly hat, tell-tale wisps of blonde hair straggled out from beneath it. His unkempt, blonde moustache provided another clue, but it was the round, moonlike face and the big, light blue protruding eyes that put his identity beyond any doubt.

"Well, I'll be damned!" Forward exclaimed. "Our friend Gibbard. The greatest illusionist in the North. The only man who can be home watching telly and eating fish and chips in Filey at the same time!" He turned and beamed at Wilmott. "You're a genius, Sergeant!"

Wilmott smiled modestly. "I did spend a little bit longer with him than you did, sir."

"Nevertheless, a stunning piece of observation."

"It gets better, sir. He's got form." Wilmott reached out and picked up some sheets off Lucas' desk. "ABH and GBH; three convictions for burglary; two convictions for receiving stolen goods. That was in his late teens or early twenties. Spent a grand total of four years inside. There's been nothing since he last came out. Went straight. Probably got back into his legitimate trade which was - listen to this -

working the trawlers out of Hull!"

Forward beamed. "Oh, we're so close to it now, Sergeant. Can't you feel how close we are?"

Wilmott nodded. "Shall we pick him up right away?"

"No, not immediately. There's just one more missing detail I need." Forward pointed to the photofit. "Get me a copy of this, will you Sam?"

"Sure," said Lucas.

"I want Thwaites to have a look at this face," said Forward. "It might ring one or two bells."

****

Forward parked his BMW at Sandleton Harbour and then he and Wilmott began walking along the North Jetty towards the Harbourmaster's office. Near to it they could see Hoggart. He was standing by a lone fishing coble that was tied to the jetty. DS Harper was standing in the bow of the coble. McIntyre and Skipsea were bending down examining something by the wheelhouse.

As Forward and Wilmott came up to him, Hoggart pointed at the boat and said, "This was the last one to come in."

"Find anything?" asked Forward.

"Skipsea has sent a couple of items away to forensic, including a length of rope. He's not very hopeful though. Have you ever searched a fishing boat for evidence?"

"Not a pleasant task, I should imagine," said

Forward. He stared at the boat's bow which bore, in faded paint, the name *Gannet*. "Isn't this the one that came in last on Monday night too?"

"That's right. Berthed at twenty to twelve. Belongs to a man called Stone. Pete Stone."

"Where is he now?"

"Gone home in a huff. Said he wasn't going to stand around and watch while his boat was taken to pieces. He's threatening to put a claim in for loss of earnings. And he's not the only one."

"You'd better come with us," said Forward. "We're off to see Thwaites."

"What for?"

Forward turned to Wilmott. "Show him."

Wilmott took Gibbard's photofit out of the briefcase he was carrying.

"Who's this?" asked Hoggart.

"His name's Charles Gibbard. On Monday night he was supposed to be at home with his family watching TV. At least that's what he told us, but he was actually eating fish and chips with Coulson in Filey. He's got form too. And, guess what, in another life he was a deep-sea trawler man."

Hoggart gave a low whistle.

At that moment Thwaites emerged from his office. He came straight over.

"Morning, Inspector," he said. "When are you going to release these boats so their owners can earn an honest living?"

"When we've proved they've not been earning a dishonest one," said Forward. He took Gibbard's photofit out of Hoggart's hand and showed it to Thwaites. "Ever seen him before?"

Thwaites reached inside his jacket and brought out a pair of spectacles. He put them on and scrutinised the photograph for some time. "Yes, I know him. Used to work the deep-sea trawlers out of Hull. Came up here and set up as a lobsterman." He stroked the top of his head. "What was his name now?"

"Gibbard?" prompted Forward.

"Gibbard! That's him."

"Was he based in this harbour?"

"Oh yes. Jacked it in about a year ago. Couldn't make a go of it."

Forward's face fell. "He doesn't have a boat any more, then?"

"No. He sold his share in it to his partner." Thwaites pointed at the *Gannet*. "That's the boat there."

"This one? Stone's boat?"

"That's right. Stone was his partner. They both came up from Hull together."

"Does Gibbard still use this boat?"

"He goes out with Stone from time to time."

"Did he go out with him on Monday night?"

"Now that I couldn't tell you."

"I'll have to find out myself then," said

Forward. "Thanks very much Mr Thwaites. Remind me to buy you a drink."

Thwaites chortled. "That's what you said last time I helped you out. I'm still waiting for it!"

"If this case achieves a result, you'll be drinking off me all night," said Forward. "Now, would you excuse us?"

Forward walked Hoggart and Wilmott some distance down the jetty. Then he stopped and addressed Hoggart. "Wilmott and I will pick up Stone. I want you to go for Gibbard. Wilmott will give you his address, but you might find him at Melthorpe Hall. He works there. Gibbard and Stone must both be kept well away from each other back at the nick. We don't want them comparing notes."

****

Pete Stone lived in Mead Lane, one of the many long streets that radiated out from Sandleton Harbour. Number twenty-nine was indistinguishable from any of the other houses in this drab thoroughfare. Like the others, it was a two up, two down, narrow terraced house with a black slate roof and net curtains at all the windows. As Forward got out of the BMW he glanced towards the upstairs window. Behind the curtains an indistinct figure was observing him, obviously under the illusion that the nets made his or her presence undetectable from the street. Forward stopped and stared hard at the amorphous shape behind the curtains. A few seconds later it had vanished.

With Wilmott at his side, Forward banged on the front door several times with the coarse and pitted knocker. Eventually, the door was opened by an adolescent boy aged about fifteen.

"I'm looking for Mr Stone," said Forward. "Is he your father?"

"That's right."

Forward showed the youth his warrant card. "Is he in?"

"He's upstairs, asleep."

"That's all right," said Forward, forcing his way past the boy and stepping into the narrow, dimly lit passage. "We don't mind waiting for him."

The teenager looked uncertain and apprehensive. He set off down the passage and ran up the stairs. Forward and Wilmott heard him knock on a door after which there was a low, murmured conversation. Immediately afterwards Stone appeared on the landing with his son behind him. He was fully dressed and Forward wondered if the man always slept in his clothes. He came down the stairs followed by his son.

"Yes?"

"Pete Stone?"

"Yes."

"Detective Chief Inspector Forward, East Yorkshire Police. The man standing on the doorstep, because he's got better manners than I have, is Detective Sergeant Wilmott."

"What's it all about? The boat? 'Ave you finished going over it?"

Forward deliberately ignored the question. A sixth sense told him that brusqueness would produce the best results from Stone. He was a short, middle-aged man with an open face, kind eyes and a solicitous expression. The kind of man who looks inherently decent. There was nothing shady or shifty about him, yet he looked decidedly nervous. "We're investigating the murder of Mark Coulson..." Forward was about to continue when he noticed the almost imperceptible look that passed between Stone and his son at the mention of the word 'murder'. It was a look Forward had seen pass many times between those who shared secrets that were best kept hidden. An ambiguous look: part conspiratorial, part supportive, part warning. But for that look, Forward would have pulled only the father in for questioning. As it was, he insisted the son came along too.

CHAPTER
THIRTY FOUR

At Sandleton Police Station Charles Gibbard, Pete Stone and his son, Daniel, were all placed in separate cells. Meanwhile Forward discussed with Hoggart and Wilmott how the interviews with the suspects would be structured.

"I think we should all go for Stone's son first," said Hoggart. "He's young and he's obviously quite frightened. He'll open up first."

"I'm not so sure," said Forward. "He looks a stubborn little sod to me. If he knows his dad's neck is on the line, he may refuse to say anything."

"I think we should start with Gibbard," said Wilmott. "We've got him dead to rights. How's he going to account for being in Filey and in his own home at the same time?"

"No, Gibbard's an experienced criminal," said Forward. "He'll front it out. Invoke his right to silence, all that sort of thing. Stone, on the other hand, is a different sort of character altogether. As far as we know, he's never been given so much as a parking ticket. Besides, we can use his son as a lever. Stone will probably agree to anything to keep him out of gaol."

"There's nothing to suggest his son is mixed up in anything," said Hoggart.

The telephone rang. Forward picked it up and gave his name gruffly. He suddenly became much more alert and listened with great absorption. Several times he said, "I see". Then he told the person on the other end that he'd detained three people and was about to question them in connection with the Coulson murder and drugs offences. He continued to listen in silence for some while, and then he said, "Right, I'll let you know."

"Was that Superintendent Jones on your back again?" asked Wilmott. At once disapproval registered on Hoggart's face at this familiarity.

"Not this time," said Forward. "But no doubt he will be before the day's out. No, that was Inspector Arden of NCIS. He wanted us to know he's interviewed all the crew of the *Phaeton,* except one, who's unfortunately died. They all told the same story. All the men worked for Pulverisation International Limited. They had some leave owing to them, so they took the *Phaeton* over to Holland for a long weekend. Took along a couple of girls they knew, as well. NCIS are holding on to them and checking the boat over now. They've found out from the

Dutch authorities that the *Phaeton* has been back and forth to Leyden six times since it was purchased by Pulverisation International."

"You said that one of the crew died. Who was that?" asked Wilmott.

"One of the young women, Sylvia Imrie. NCIS couldn't trace her. Then, last night, a private clinic in West London contacted the local police station. Apparently, Sylvia Imrie had been brought in yesterday morning in a coma. They'd diagnosed a drugs overdose and proceeded to treat her. But she was too far gone. She died an hour or so later. NCIS are sure that if she'd recovered, the overdose would never have been reported, it's that sort of clinic. As it was, the clinic had to notify the police."

"Who brought her to the clinic?" asked Hoggart.

"A friend found her. Apparently, Imrie had attended the clinic's detoxification unit sometime in the past. The friend knew this, that's why he took her there instead of the local hospital."

"Well, that definitely shows there was a drugs connection to the *Phaeton*," said Wilmott.

"It's only the slimmest of connections and it doesn't prove anything," said Forward. "All it proves is that one of the women who was on board the *Phaeton* had a drugs habit. Relevant, I know, but hardly evidence. Now, let's go and question Stone. That might produce a real connection."

****

At twelve thirty Pete Stone was brought into Interview Room Three by the custody sergeant and told to sit down at a desk opposite Forward and Hoggart. Wilmott was over by the tape recorder dictating into it the date, the case reference number and the names of all present.

"Before we begin, Mr Stone," said Forward, "I understand from the custody sergeant that you've been informed of your rights to legal representation but you've waived them. Is that correct?"

Stone avoided Forward's eye. "I don't need no expensive lawyers. I've done no wrong."

"As you wish," said Forward. "I must inform you that you do not have to say anything unless you wish to do so, but what you say may be given in evidence. Do you understand?"

"What am I charged with?" Stone demanded.

"Nothing yet," said Forward. "You are being detained because of our suspicion of your involvement in certain criminal offences. All you have to do is answer a few questions to our satisfaction and you'll be able to go."

"And if I don't?"

"Don't what?"

"Answer them to your satisfaction?"

"Then I'm afraid you will stay here until you

do." Forward's face had a stubborn, determined look.

Stone said nothing.

"Now then, Mr Stone," Forward continued, "I understand you know a Charles Gibbard of Melthorpe. Is that right?"

Stone nodded.

"I wonder if you would mind affirming that out loud Mr Stone. Unfortunately, our tape recorder doesn't record nods of the head."

"Yes, I know Charlie Gibbard."

Forward detected a certain bitterness in the tone. "And at one time you and Mr Gibbard were both part owners of a fishing coble called the *Gannet*? Is that so?"

"Yes."

"When did you and Mr Gibbard cease to be partners?"

"About nine months ago. The fishin' were so poor two people couldn't make a livin' out of it. Charlie got a job at Melthorpe 'All and I bought his share in the boat." As he finished Stone looked at Forward for the first time. In his eyes was the desperation of those who spend most of their time trying to get enough money to eat and pay the rent.

"He still used to go out with you in the boat quite a bit though, didn't he?" asked Forward.

"Aye, from time to time."

"Was he out with you on Monday night?"

"No!"

"Come on, we know he was. So, Mr Stone, apart from Gibbard was anyone else out with you on Monday night?"

Stone shifted uncomfortably. He looked from side to side and then started nibbling gently on one of the knuckles of his right hand.

Forward pressed him harder. "I said, did anyone else go out with you and Gibbard?"

Stone brought his hand down suddenly on the table. "I heard you!" He stared at Forward defensively. "I'm not saying. You told me I didn't have to say anything and I'm not."

"The other person who was in the boat with you and Gibbard on Monday night was your son, Daniel. That's the truth, isn't it?"

Stone shook his head vehemently. Too vehemently, Forward decided.

For the benefit of the tape recorder, Forward said, "Mr Stone has shaken his head in response to that question." He returned his attention to Stone. "All right, Mr Stone, let's get back to you and Mr Gibbard. Where exactly did you go on Monday in that little boat of yours when you were supposed to be fishing?"

Stone remained silent. He stared impassively ahead.

"Mr Stone. Do you intend to answer any more of my questions?" asked Forward.

Stone shook his head.

"Mr Stone has shaken his head again in response to my question," said Forward. He sighed. "Very well. As Mr Stone refuses to answer any more questions, I am therefore terminating this interview. The time is now twelve thirty-five p.m."

Wilmott turned off the tape recorder.

Stone looked from Forward to Hoggart and back again uncertainly. "What 'appens now?" he asked.

"We shall detain you in custody while we interview your son and Mr Gibbard. Your wife is also being collected from her place of work and she too, in due course, will be questioned."

"You can't keep me 'ere," protested Stone. "I've got a livin' to earn."

"We can detain you if we suspect you're withholding vital evidence," Hoggart said.

Stone's chubby features became downcast. "Right then, I want a lawyer."

"You'll get one, Mr Stone. I shall see to that," said Forward.

"And for my son. I want a lawyer for my son and all."

"I'll ensure your son gets one too."

Forward made no move to get up. He remained sitting and staring calmly into Stone's moist, spaniel eyes. "Look Pete," he said, in a surprisingly familiar tone. "Not only do we know Gibbard and Daniel were in your boat on Monday night, we know all about the *Phaeton* too."

Stone looked amazed.

"If your son wasn't involved in the murder, we needn't bear down too hard on him."

Stone returned Forward's stare. "Daniel wasn't involved. Neither of us were involved."

"Good. You can tell me all about it then."

Stone said nothing.

"All right," said Forward getting up. "I'll get it from him."

Stone was immediately on his feet. "You leave 'im be," he yelled. "'E's seen enough. Just you leave 'im be!"

Wilmott had moved quickly to subdue Stone but his fast reaction was unnecessary. Stone sank back into his chair. The expression on his face slowly became one of resignation. Meekly he asked, "Could you really keep Daniel out of all this crap?"

"Provided he hasn't committed a serious offence, yes," Forward assured him. "And if you co-operate with us, the court is bound to deal more leniently with you."

"All right," said Stone. "I'll tell you all you want to know. But first you must promise me something..."

"What's that?"

"Police protection. I want police protection for me and my family."

"If you really think it's necessary, we can arrange it," said Forward.

"It is necessary. It's bloody necessary. And I don't just mean for now, I mean for ever. Can you do that?"

Stone's anxious, frightened face evoked Forward's pity. "You'd be surprised at what we can do," he said. "Now, are you going to answer my questions this time?"

Stone nodded. Forward signalled Wilmott to turn the tape recorder back on.

"Right, tell us exactly what happened," said Forward, after Wilmott had again dictated the formalities. "And don't leave anything out!"

Stone cleared his throat. "You're right, Daniel and Gibbard were with me in the boat on Monday. We left Sandleton 'arbour in the afternoon about two o'clock. We were on course to meet up with the *Phaeton* about ten miles off Filey Bay."

"Did you know where the *Phaeton* was coming from?" asked Forward.

"Gibbard said it was coming from 'olland."

"Go on."

"The people on the *Phaeton* transferred some stuff to my boat, and then the *Phaeton* carried on to Sandleton. It were going to moor up in Sandleton 'arbour, all innocent like. Meanwhile we lay off Filey Bay pretending to fish. We were waiting until it was dark enough to bring the stuff ashore at Monks Bay."

"Did you know what this stuff was?"

Stone again shifted uncomfortably in his seat. "Cocaine."

"OK. So what time did you rendezvous with

the *Phaeton*?"

"Just before four."

"And everything was unloaded as planned, is that right?"

"Yes."

"What were the drugs packed in?"

"Big 'oldalls. You know, weekend bags."

"And how many of these holdalls were there?"

"Three."

"What happened next?"

"We fished on until about six thirty, and then we were supposed to pick up Mr Coulson from Filey at seven thirty. Gibbard had to pick 'im up at the Coble Landing."

"Why?"

"He were going to come with us in the boat to Monks Bay. His car was already parked there. That's what 'appened the last time."

"So, you'd done it before?"

"Yes, just the once."

"When?"

"In February."

"Was Daniel with you then too?"

"No. Only me and Charlie and Mr Coulson."

"I see. Go on."

"Well, we started to make towards Filey but before we got there the engine cut out. The oil pump 'ad gone. Fortunately, I always carry a spare. Gibbard started getting edgy. He asked me 'ow long I thought it would take to fix the engine. I told him it would take about two hours. In that case, he said, I'd better let my people know we'll be late."

"Who did he mean by 'my people'?" demanded Hoggart.

"I dunno. He never said."

"Come on. You know very well who they are!" Hoggart insisted.

"I don't. I swear I don't. Charlie kept me in the dark about all that."

"You didn't even know who was paying you?"

"No, it were all done through Charlie. He said the less I knew the better."

"How much were you being paid, as a matter of interest?" asked Forward.

"Eight 'undred pounds."

Hoggart looked astounded. "Eight hundred! You poor chump. Do you know how much that cocaine was worth? Millions!"

Stone looked miserable.

"What time were you supposed to be at Monks Bay to make the drop?" Forward asked.

"Just after eight," said Stone. "But we 'adn't a hope of getting there on time, not with the engine gone. I suggested to Charlie that we should unload it on Filey beach, but he would 'ave none of it. He said it were too dangerous. Someone were bound to see us. Anyway, it would wreck all the plans. So, Daniel took Gibbard into Filey in the outboard dinghy. He arranged to pick him and Coulson up at eight thirty. Then Daniel left them and came back and 'elped me with the engine."

"Why didn't Gibbard and Coulson come straight back to the boat?"

"Gibbard told Daniel he wanted to get summat to eat."

"The fish and chips, sir," said Wilmott.

"That's right, they did have fish and chips as it happens," said Stone.

"Go on," said Forward, with a touch of impatience.

"Well, it got to nearly 'alf past eight and I still 'adn't fixed the pump, but I sent Daniel off to Filey to collect Charlie and Coulson anyway. When they got on board and found out I still 'adn't fixed the engine they got in a right state. Gibbard said 'e'd phoned and told 'is people to meet 'im and Coulson at Monks Bay at nine thirty and he wasn't goin' to let 'em down. He wanted to put the stuff in the little outboard dinghy and go all the way to Monks Bay in it. I told 'im 'e must be mad. Mr Coulson didn't like the sound of that either, I could tell."

"What sort of state was Mr Coulson in?"

"He were terrified. He didn't want to be there."

"Why was he there?"

"'To carry the drugs ashore, of course."

"There were three of you. Enough to bring the drugs ashore without Coulson."

"Wait a minute. My son Daniel wasn't

supposed to be there. I only brought him along at the last minute at Charlie Gibbard's suggestion. He said it would make the boat look more innocent with a young lad on board."

"Ingenious," said Forward. "Who would suspect a couple of in-shore fishermen and a teenage kid of drugs running? All right. Go on."

"In the end, I managed to fix the engine and we set off for Monks Bay."

"What time was this?"

"About twenty past nine."

"Keeping close in-shore to avoid the Coastguard's radar? Yes?"

Stone seemed impressed by Forward's knowledge. "Aye, we kept in-shore all the way. The tide 'ad turned against us by then so we didn't get there until ten. There were a couple of cars parked up on the cliff above the bay. One of them flashed their 'eadlights when they saw us. I lay the boat just off the bay and then Charlie and Mr Coulson loaded the stuff in the dinghy and took it ashore. There were some people waiting there for them.

"Did you see who they were?"

"No. Not clearly. It were too dark and our boat were laid too far off the bay."

"Tell us what you saw," said Hoggart.

"Just figures, that's all. One of them were a woman though. I know that because one of the figures were quite small and when Gibbard got back to the boat 'e kept sayin': 'The stupid bitch.

The stupid fuckin' bitch', and he were covered in blood."

"Are you saying Gibbard killed Coulson?" Hoggart demanded.

Stone shook his head emphatically. "No. No. Gibbard didn't kill 'im. It were the woman."

"You're going too fast," said Forward. "Tell us exactly what you saw on the beach from the moment Gibbard and Coulson landed there in the dinghy."

Stone paused, screwing up his eyes as he cast his mind back. "They got out of the dinghy and walked up the beach towards the steps."

"Carrying the holdalls?"

"Yes."

"The people they were going to meet. How many were there?"

"Two."

"A man and a woman? Is that right?"

"I think so. I think the taller one was a man; I can't be sure. One was small and one was quite tall. That's all I know. They were both wearing anoraks with 'oods. I couldn't see their faces."

"And were they already on the beach?"

"No, they were coming down the steps as Gibbard and Coulson got ashore.

"All right. What happened then?"

"They all met up at the bottom of the steps. They exchanged a few words and then suddenly the man lashed out at Coulson."

"Hit him?"

"Yes."

"Go on."

"Well, Coulson threw a punch at 'im and 'e fell down. Then the woman starts lashing out at Coulson too."

"Stabbing him?"

"Aye, could 'ave been. Coulson and 'er started strugglin' and she fell down on the steps. Then Gibbard and the other bloke 'eld Coulson by the arms. To restrain 'im, I suppose. Then, the woman who'd fallen down got up, and she picked up a rock or somethin' and started 'ittin' Coulson over the 'ead with it. Coulson fell down but she still went on 'ittin' 'im."

"Did anyone attempt to stop her?" Forward asked.

"Aye. Gibbard and the other bloke did. They were both struggling with 'er but she were in a real frenzy. Eventually, she stopped 'ittin' 'im and they all stood around lookin' at Coulson's body. Then Charlie and the other bloke dragged the body down to the water and left it there. After that, all three of 'em carried the bags of drugs up the steps. When Charlie came back 'e did a quick bit of clearin' up."

"What do you mean, 'clearing up'?" asked Forward.

"He scuffed all the footprints and marks they'd left in the sand. Then 'e got in the dinghy and came straight back to the *Gannet*."

"Presumably, your son saw all this as well?"

447

"Yes, I'm ashamed to say he did," said Stone. He looked as though he was about to cry.

"What sort of state was Gibbard in when he got back to the boat?" asked Forward.

Stone swallowed hard. "'E were goin' frantic. Rantin' and ravin' all the time."

"Can you remember anything he said?"

Stone thought hard. "He said Coulson 'ad bottled out and the stupid bitch 'ad killed 'im. First, she tried to stab 'im and then she'd bashed 'is 'ead in."

"What did he mean, 'Coulson had bottled out'?" asked Hoggart.

"I dunno. He wouldn't say any more. It didn't make sense. I mean, why should 'e want out?"

"I think I know why," said Forward.

Hoggart and Wilmott looked at the Chief Inspector for an explanation but he simply smiled back at them enigmatically. "What else did Gibbard say, Mr Stone?"

"Nothin' much. He just told us to carry on back to Sandleton 'arbour which we did."

"Did he say what the name of the woman was who'd killed Coulson?" Hoggart asked.

"No."

"Are you saying that having just witnessed a murder, you didn't even ask him who'd done it?"

Stone became indignant. "Of course, I did. Of course, I asked 'im! But 'e said it would be best if we didn't know. The least we knew the better. He told us to forget everything we'd seen if we valued our lives. The people he were dealin' with were very nasty. Then he went and cleaned himself up. Cleaned the blood off."

"So, you left Monks Bay and went straight on to Sandleton Harbour?" said Forward.

"Aye. We set off to go there, but we 'adn't got very far when we 'ad a panic. You see we'd given Coulson an anorak to wear." An enlightened look passed between all three police officers. "It were an old anorak Gibbard wore when he worked the deep-sea trawlers. He always kept it on my boat. Well, it were still on Coulson's body. I wanted to forget about it but Gibbard insisted we went back to get it. So we turned the boat round and went back to Monks Bay. As we approached the bay, we could see someone was sittin' 'alfway up the steps and there were a dog runnin' around on the beach, so we forgot about the anorak, turned round and carried on back to Sandleton 'arbour."

"On the way did you see Gibbard throw anything into the sea?"

Stone looked upset. "Aye, I did."

"What was it?"

"Some things of Mr Coulson's."

"What things?"

"A couple of wallets."

"His car keys?"

"No. I never saw them. But there were a knife."

"How do you know?"

"Charlie showed it me before 'e chucked it in. 'E said 'e'd been told to get rid of it."

"Was there blood on it?"

"I don't know. I didn't look too closely. It fair turned me stomach."

"And Gibbard threw this knife in too, did he?"

"Yes."

"Where?"

"In Sandleton Bay."

There was a long pause.

"Do you have any idea where the drugs went after they'd been landed?" asked Forward.

Stone shook his head. "No. Charlie never told me anything about that side of it."

"Just tell me this," said Hoggart. "Do you know how the cocaine you brought into this country is used?"

Stone looked at him blankly. "It's injected, isn't it?"

Hoggart's voice took on a hard edge. "No, Mr Stone, it's not injected. First of all, the dealers turn it into something called crack. Individual pieces of crack are called 'rocks'. The drug user takes one of these rocks and heats it over a direct flame. This turns the cocaine in the 'rock' into a vapour which is inhaled. Because it's a powerful stimulant it gives you an overwhelming feeling of euphoria. It makes you feel on top of the world. But the feeling doesn't last long and when the crack wears off you feel depressed; paranoid; suicidal. You feel so bad you can't wait to get hold of another 'rock' and start all over again. You see, you only have to take crack once and you're an instant addict."

Hoggart stood up and towered threateningly over Stone. "But crack's expensive, it can cost four hundred pounds a day. That's why kids of fifteen, the same age as your son, are mugging old ladies and robbing building societies to finance their habit." He looked at Stone with disgust. "That's what you've just brought into the country, Mr Stone. For eight hundred pounds!"

Stone looked thoroughly miserable. He placed his elbows on the desk and cradled his face in his hands.

Forward stood up. "Right, Mr Stone. I'm going to charge you with being an accessory to murder. You will also be charged with various drugs offences. We'll need to interview you again in the presence of your solicitor."

"Will my son be charged too?"

"If he's committed an offence," said Forward.

Stone's eyes became angry. "But you said you'd go easy on 'im."

"We'll put in a good word for him at court," promised Forward.

"Anyway, he was with you, wasn't he?" Hoggart said harshly. "You can't expect us to ignore that."

"But 'e didn't know anything," Stone pleaded. "He didn't even know it were drugs we were carryin'."

"Don't give me that," said Hoggart. "What did he think was in those holdalls? Toys?"

"He didn't know it were drugs. I wouldn't tell him."

"Then you should have done," said Forward. "If he'd known what was going on, he might have chosen not to be there."

CHAPTER
THIRTY FIVE

DC Griffiths was waiting in Forward's office. She jumped up excitedly as he entered and waved some sheets of paper under his nose.

"Here's your search into Finesse Holdings Ltd. I think you'll find it very interesting, sir."

Forward took the sheets and glanced at them. "I can't read this scrawl," he complained.

Griffiths' features darkened. "Sorry, sir. I haven't had time to type it yet. You did say you wanted it right away."

Forward handed the sheets of paper back to her. "Just give me the salient details."

"Right. Well, if you remember, Finesse Holdings and Investments Associates Ltd are the principal shareholders in Pulverisation International. That's the company that owns the *Phaeton...*"

"Yes, yes, we know all that. Get on with it."

Griffiths threw a look at Wilmott who'd just entered the room followed by Hoggart. "Just re-iterating the context, sir," she said coolly. "Now, what's most interesting about Finesse Holdings are the shareholders. There's a married couple, Mr Paul Cartwright and his wife, Isabella."

"Ah!" All of Forward's senses were suddenly alert.

"They have a West London address." She noticed his changed expression. "Do you know them, sir?"

But Forward was too overwhelmed by his own insight even to be aware of her question. "Of course! A Bridge technique. How could I have missed it?"

"A Bridge technique?" queried Wilmott. He received no answer from Forward who was staring into space, eyes glazed in thought. "I'm sorry, sir, but you've lost me there."

Forward snapped out of his reverie. "You mentioned other shareholders," he cried, turning on Griffiths so forcefully even her confidant poise was shaken.

"There's only one other shareholder," she said quickly recovering. "Sylvia Imrie."

"Well, well!" exclaimed Hoggart.

"What's her address?" Forward demanded.

"234, Beta Road, London W.1. The same as the Cartwrights. Now, isn't that a cherry?"

"I don't understand," said Wilmott. "Is she their lodger?"

Forward didn't answer. Instead, he opened the Coulson file which was lying on his desk.

He checked the address given for the Sylvia Imrie who had been crewing on the *Phaeton*. It was the same: 234, Beta Road, London W.1. He put her details away, pulled his notepad towards him, reached for the phone and dialled.

The number Forward was calling rang several times before someone answered.

"Hello. Melthorpe Hall? Is Lady Fernshawe there, please?" Forward listened while an explanation of Lady Fernshawe's whereabouts was given. "I see," he said at length. "Just tell me this. What is the name of Lady Fernshawe's daughter?" Wilmott and Griffiths strained their ears to hear it, but Wending's low, discreet tones made it impossible. "I see. That was the name of her first husband, was it?" He then asked Wending if Monday was usually his day off. Again, Wending's reply was inaudible to Wilmott and Griffiths.

Forward put the receiver down and stared at them. "Well, that's cleared that little matter up." He looked enormously gratified, and also, not a little relieved. "Lady Fernshawe, or, as she is otherwise known, Mrs Isabella Cartwright, is Sylvia Imrie's mother. Imrie was the surname of Lady Fernshawe's first husband, Raymond Imrie. Sylvia Imrie is also, of course, Paul Cartwright's stepdaughter."

"Was, sir," Wilmott reminded him.

"Quite, Wilmott." He looked at Griffiths.

"Was."

"Sylvia Imrie's dead," Wilmott explained to Griffiths. "Died of a drugs overdose."

"She was one of the crew on the *Phaeton*," said Forward. "The boat you've now discovered is owned by Lady Fernshawe and her husband. And we've established that the *Phaeton* was running drugs into this country from Leyden, assisted by a couple of local fishermen."

"Lady Fernshawe a drugs runner!" exclaimed Griffiths. "It's unbelievable!"

"Not only a drugs runner," said Forward. "A murderer too."

Wilmott looked very surprised. "You think she murdered Coulson?"

Forward ignored the question, not through rudeness but because he was experiencing the most extraordinary leap of insight. "Griffiths, go straight to Melthorpe village hall," he commanded. "They're holding a flower arrangement competition there. One of the entries is from Lady Fernshawe. It's entitled *The Enchanted Grotto*. I want you to impound it and take it straight over to Dr Edwin Painter at the forensic laboratory."

Griffiths was obviously puzzled. "But why...?" she began.

"Don't worry, I shall be ringing up Dr Painter. I'll tell him you're coming over. He'll know exactly what to look for. Now, get on your way. Remember it's *The Enchanted Grotto*."

Stiff with resentment, Griffiths set about her errand.

"She doesn't like being treated like a servant, you know," complained Hoggart. "She's an intelligent woman. She likes to be given reasons for things. Likes to be kept in the picture." Then he added pointedly, "Like we all do."

Forward ignored the criticism. It was a bit rich to be accused by Hoggart of treating Griffiths badly.

"Has Daniel Stone's mother arrived yet?" he asked.

"She's waiting downstairs."

"Right. Let's interview Daniel. I'd like both of you to do that next. Get his story and then we'll compare it with his father's for discrepancies. If he shows a reluctance to talk, make sure he knows the full extent of what his father's already told us."

"What about Gibbard?" asked Wilmott.

"We'll leave him until last. Let him stew for a bit. It'll be good for his soul."

"Apparently he's accepted the offer of a lawyer."

"Good. He'll need one. After we've finished with him, we'll turn him over to the drugs boys."

"Aren't we going to arrest Lady Fernshawe or at least haul her in for questioning?" asked Wilmott.

"Later. First, I have a lot of telephoning to do," said Forward. He picked up the phone. "Now, if you'll excuse me..."

****

It seemed to Forward that he spent the next hour on the phone. His first call was to Inspector Arden of NCIS. He gave him a full account of his recent interview with Stone, and asked Arden if he would arrest the *Phaeton's* crew. Forward then explained the connection between Lady Fernshawe, Cartwright, Sylvia Imrie and the *Phaeton,* and requested Arden to arrest Lady Fernshawe and Paul Cartwright at their West London address. But Arden had bad news for him. That day officers from the Met had gone to Beta Road to search Sylvia Imrie's home following her death. They'd been told by the next-door neighbour that Sylvia's parents had been there for a short period the day before, and had left early that morning. Forward was disappointed. He told Arden he wanted to tie up some forensic evidence, and asked for the name of the Home Office forensic pathologist who was dealing with the Sylvia Imrie case. He spent another five minutes discussing various aspects of the joint investigation and then rang off.

Forward's next call was to Dr Painter. He told him that DC Griffiths would shortly be bringing him *The Enchanted Grotto,* and explained the nature of the tests he'd like conducted on it. Then he gave Painter the name of the forensic pathologist in London who was investigating the Sylvia Imrie death, and asked Painter to liaise with him without delay. Painter agreed to this and then provided Forward with details of further forensic evidence he'd obtained. When Forward finished the call to Dr Painter, he was in a state of euphoria. He immediately contacted Jones on the internal phone.

The phone was answered at once, and Forward heard the self-consciously pompous tones that were mimicked all over the station. "Chief Superintendent Jones."

"Forward here. Re: the Coulson matter. I want to put in a request for a firearms issue."

"How many?"

"Sufficient for half a dozen officers."

"You must be very close to an arrest," said Jones.

"I am."

"What's your reason for the firearms issue?"

Forward appraised him of all the latest developments. "NCIS think we're doing a wonderful job," he concluded.

"Excellent," purred Jones.

****

"Chief Inspector Forward entered the room at two fifteen p.m." It was Wilmott who spoke this into the tape recorder as Forward came into Interview Room Three.

Stone's son, Daniel, was sitting hunched at the big table opposite DI Hoggart. His cheeks were still red from crying and he looked distraught. Next to him sat his mother and a WPC. Forward raised an eyebrow questioningly at Hoggart.

"He's provided us with the necessary corroboration," said Hoggart. "Even admitted he knew what substance the *Phaeton* was carrying."

"Good," said Forward. He looked at Daniel Stone benignly. "I'm glad you've decided to tell us the truth, Daniel. It saves a lot of messing about."

Daniel nodded.

"What happens now?" Daniel's mother asked nervously. She was a tiny, bird-like woman with big staring eyes and was understandably distressed.

"Has he been formally charged?" Forward asked.

"Not yet," said Wilmott.

Forward pointed to the WPC. "WPC Skelton will take him downstairs for now. Later, in your presence, we shall formally charge him with assisting in the importing of a controlled drug. We shall then consider whether to prefer other charges against him. After that we may either release him on bail, or place him in the care and custody of the Local Authority until the proceedings against him are heard."

Mrs Stone nodded and immediately burst into tears.

"What about Dad?" asked Daniel.

"We're going to have to keep your father here a lot longer," said Forward. "His involvement in the offence is much more serious and it's unlikely he'll receive bail." Forward nodded to the WPC. "Take him down."

When Daniel and his mother had been taken out, Hoggart said, "He gave virtually the same account as his father, except in one respect."

"What was that?" asked Forward.

"He had more opportunity to observe Coulson on the trip from Filey to Monks Bay. He said Coulson was in a right state, swearing to himself and crying. He was really worked up about something. Daniel was sure that, as they neared Monks Bay, Coulson threw something into the sea, but he didn't see what it was."

Forward's eyes took on a glazed look again as he assimilated Hoggart's information. As he registered its implications, he nodded very slowly to himself several times, astonished and delighted at his insights. "How very interesting," he said.

"What shall we do now?" asked Hoggart. "Put the pressure on Gibbard?"

"Don't worry about him for the moment. I've got another job for you. I want you to go over to Melthorpe Hall and arrest Lady Fernshawe and her husband. I've had clearance from Jones for you to take half a dozen armed officers with you."

"Is that necessary?"

"Indeed, it is. Cartwright could be armed. NCIS have been targeting him for months without success. They say he's a very nasty customer."

"What charges do you want me to arrest them on?"

"Importing a controlled drug," said Forward. "That should be enough to hold them. Make a thorough search of the premises and of their vehicles." Forward looked impatient. "Go on then, get over there. Her Ladyship won't be hanging around. You can bet on that."

As Hoggart was leaving the room, the custody sergeant came in. "Gibbard's brief is here," he said. "He's demanding to see his client."

"You'd better let Gibbard see him then," said Forward. "Who's his solicitor?"

"Whittaker."

Wilmott shot Forward a look and raised his eyebrows.

"Himself?" asked Forward.

"In person."

"He's right out of Gibbard's league. Did Gibbard specifically ask for him?"

"Yes, sir," said the custody sergeant.

"Gibbard must have some very powerful people behind him," said Wilmott.

"Come on," said Forward. "I want to get over to Melthorpe."

"What about Gibbard?"

"Oh, we'll ignore him for the moment."

"But shouldn't he be questioned?"

"When we're ready."

Forward picked up the phone and dialled. It was answered almost immediately. "Hello, is that Mrs Howard? Oh good, I'm glad I found you in. It's Detective Chief Inspector Forward here. Look, I know it's Saturday but I need you to open up the school for me."

****

The main doors of Melthorpe Primary School were wide open when Forward and Wilmott arrived there just before three p.m. Mrs Howard, the schoolkeeper, appeared in the entrance to welcome the two detectives. After thanking her for turning out so promptly Forward said, "I want to have a look in Mr Coulson's classroom. Would you open it for me, please?"

Mrs Howard led them through the school until they came to the room. She produced a bunch of keys, selected one and unlocked the door. Once inside, Forward strode straight over to the stock cupboard. "Has the lock been changed on this?"

"It has now," said Mrs Howard. "Council came and changed it yesterday afternoon. About time too. I've been on the phone to them since Tuesday."

"I want to look inside."

Still grumbling, the schoolkeeper clicked through her prodigious bunch of keys and selected the only one that had not been dulled by time. She inserted it into the stock cupboard's gleaming new lock and opened the door inwards.

Forward followed Mrs Howard into the cupboard. It was the size of a small room. There were wooden shelves all round from floor to ceiling. They were loaded with school equipment.

"Where are the props and things to do with Lady Fernshawe's concert?" Forward demanded.

"She's already collected them," said Mrs Howard. "You've just missed her."

"How long ago?"

"About ten minutes, that's all."

Forward's anger was almost choking him. "Why didn't you tell me this before?"

Mrs Howard looked cowed. "I never thought. Why? Is it important?"

"Never mind. These things she collected. Were they in holdalls?"

"Yes. But there was only one." The schoolkeeper looked confused. "I helped her carry it out to her car. It was very heavy."

"Was there a man in the car?"

"There was, yes."

Forward set off at a run. "Come on, Wilmott," he cried.

****

The BMW's speedometer was showing ninety as Forward overtook the oil tanker. He was relieved to see that the road beyond was clear, and he could keep the accelerator pedal pressed down to the floor.

The voice of the controller at Sandleton suddenly came on the radio.

"One Nine. Calling One Nine."

Wilmott reached for the handset. "One Nine. Sergeant Wilmott here."

"Inspector Hoggart for you, Sergeant. Car to car."

There was a faint crackle followed by a metallic ping in the ether, as though a guitar string had suddenly broken. Then Hoggart's voice came on.

"We've just arrested Lady Fernshawe and her husband," Hoggart crowed. "And guess what? They were in possession of about half a million pounds worth of cocaine."

Forward grabbed the handset out of Wilmott's hand.

"Congratulations, Hoggart. Where did you pick them up?"

"In the grounds of Melthorpe Hall."

"Did they give you any trouble?"

"Not a bit. Cartwright had a gun but when he saw we were tooled up he thought twice about using it."

"OK," said Forward. "Where are you now?"

"On the way back to Sandleton with the prisoners."

"Fine. We'll meet you there. And make sure you keep them apart."

Forward passed the handset back to Wilmott, who tut-tutted his tongue against his teeth, "Trust Hoggart to get all the bloody glory!"

Forward shook his head. "It's Superintendent Jones who gets the glory, Sergeant. The rest of us get the team prize." He took the pressure off the accelerator and the car slowed to a respectable fifty miles per hour. There was no need to rush now.

****

As soon as Forward got back to his office he made a long telephone call to forensic in Hull. Then, along with Hoggart and Wilmott, he questioned Charles Gibbard for over an hour in the presence of his solicitor. Gibbard was obstructive at first, but when he realised the game was up, he was gripped by a very strong sense of self-preservation and made a full statement. Gibbard was taken back to his cell and Stone was interviewed again. Several points which had arisen from Gibbard's statement needed clarification and only Stone could clear them up. He again proved most co-operative.

After Stone had been removed from the interview room by the custody sergeant, the three detectives relaxed back in their chairs. "Right," said Forward. "This has been a most productive afternoon. I think we're sufficiently in possession of the overall picture. All we need are the final forensic reports and we'll be in a strong position to question Lady Fernshawe and her husband."

"Who shall we take first?" asked Hoggart.

"Lady Fernshawe, I think," said Forward. "She's just lost her daughter. She'll be the most vulnerable."

He hated himself for saying it, but there it was.

****

"We only got Gibbard's photofit because of Mrs MacDonald," Forward thundered. "Follett was no good. He hadn't a clue what Gibbard looked like. You should have asked Mrs MacDonald to do the photofit, not Follett!"

Griffiths was sitting on the other side of Forward's desk looking completely astonished. When she'd appeared minutes earlier in his office with her marvellous news, a dressing down was the last thing she'd expected.

She immediately sprang to her own defence. "As Follett was the owner, I thought he was the one who got the best look at the man who was with Coulson."

"But he told you Mrs MacDonald waited on Coulson's table. Why didn't you arrange to speak to her? If you'd spoken to her, you'd have realised she was the one to construct the photofit not Follett."

"It must have slipped my mind."

"That's not good enough."

"I had so much to do. So much to remember."

"That's how it is in this job. If you want to make a career with us, you'd better get used to it. You've got to learn to think on your feet and ask the right questions. For example, how many customers in Follet's restaurant on Monday night were known to him?"

"I don't know."

"You didn't think to ask?"

"No."

"That's a pity. If you'd got some of the customers' names you could have contacted them. They too might have helped with the photofit."

Griffiths stared down at her lap.

"Did you ask to see any cheques received by Follett on Monday night? Or any credit card receipts?"

Griffiths looked thoroughly miserable. "No."

"Well, you should have. They would have provided signatures. Names. That's the kind of thing you have to be thinking about when you're looking for witnesses."

"I'm sorry."

"Don't be sorry. Get it right. The photofit was crucial to solving this case. If Wilmott hadn't recognised Gibbard we'd still be floundering around in the dark. And we'd never have had the photofit without Mrs MacDonald. It was just a chance conversation between Follett and her that enabled us to get it. And if we hadn't had the photofit, that would have been entirely your fault!"

She nodded vigorously. "I know."

"It's very disappointing, especially as you've done such an excellent job otherwise."

"No-one can be perfect all the time, sir." She paused, and added pointedly, "As you very well know."

She'd passed over the line. Forward was about to tell her he had every justification for putting her on a disciplinary, when he experienced a sudden detachment from the situation. What the hell was he doing shouting and bawling at an inexperienced young woman who was a conscientious copper and a bloody good one? She was only doing her best, for God's sake, like they all were. He suddenly felt very ashamed of himself. "If you're alluding to Dangerfield's death, there've been some developments you're not aware of," he said quietly.

The telephone on Forward's desk rang. He picked it up and listened. Then he said, "OK. I'll be down."

Forward replaced the receiver and looked into Griffiths' resentful eyes. "Mrs Coulson is downstairs. Apparently, she's desperate to see me." He stood up. "You'd better come along."

Forward and Griffiths descended the stairs in silence. There was no sign of Mrs Coulson amongst those seated in the waiting area. Forward went over to the desk sergeant and said, "Where's Mrs Coulson?" The desk sergeant nodded at a dark-haired woman in her forties who was sitting next to a teenage girl. The woman immediately stood up. "Are you Chief Inspector Forward?" she asked.

"That's right."

"I'm Helen Coulson, Mark Coulson's first wife." She gestured towards the youngster, who had now also stood up and was at her side. "And this is my daughter, Rachel." There was a tremor in her voice as she continued, "I haven't had a moment's rest ever since I spoke to the police in York. They said if I had anything further to say, I should contact you. Is there somewhere we can talk?"

CHAPTER THIRTY SIX

At six thirty p.m. Forward began questioning Lady Fernshawe in Interview Room Two. He was assisted by Hoggart and Wilmott and had given them strict instructions to remain silent throughout.

Lady Fernshawe was accompanied by her solicitor, David Greville. Greville was one of the most accomplished and expensive criminal lawyers in the North. He was in his late forties and always wore Savile Row suits, striped shirts and ties with large spots. He and Forward had crossed swords on many occasions; and, from experience, the Chief Inspector had learned to hold him in the same regard a rabbit holds a snake.

After the preliminaries were recorded and Lady Fernshawe had been formally cautioned, Greville said, "I want to make it clear, Chief Inspector, that my client denies any knowledge of the matters under your investigation and reserves her right to silence."

Forward fixed Lady Fernshawe with an incredulous stare. "You deny that when arrested you and your husband were found to have a bag in the boot of your car containing twenty-five kilogrammes of cocaine?"

She said nothing, but returned his stare with an assurance that was impressive.

"And do you deny that earlier today you previously removed the same bag from the stock cupboard in Mark Coulson's classroom?"

Again, she said nothing. She merely humoured him with a condescending smile.

"And do you also deny that when we searched your home, we found three other bags containing seventy-five kilogrammes of cocaine?"

"My husband and I hadn't the faintest idea what was in those bags," said Lady Fernshawe. "We were looking after them for some friends."

"Then why did you tell Mrs Howard, the Melthorpe schoolkeeper, that the bag in the stock room contained items connected with your concert?"

"You're under caution," Greville suavely told Lady Fernshawe. "You don't have to answer any of these questions."

She nodded, and staring hard at Forward said, "No comment."

"All right. Who were these friends you were looking after the bags for? What are their names?"

Lady Fernshawe smiled graciously. "No comment."

"Where can we contact them?"

"No comment."

"You're wasting your time," said Greville. "My client is not going to answer any of your questions."

"That's a pity," said Forward. He indicated to Wilmott that he wanted the tape recorder switched off. "You see she has everything to gain from co-operating with us. Not only do we know about the drugs offences, we also know Lady Fernshawe was both an accessory to murder and personally committed a murder."

Lady Fernshawe gave an incredulous laugh. "Don't be absurd!"

"If you're so sure my client committed these offences, why don't you just charge her?" asked Greville.

As always, Forward was finding Greville's superior public-school drawl intensely irritating. "Oh, I certainly intend to do that," he said. "I have more than enough evidence." He looked at Lady Fernshawe coldly. "Would you like to hear the evidence I have against you?" He stood up. "Or would you rather we simply charged you and returned you to your cell?"

Lady Fernshawe raised one hand. "Wait," she commanded. "I'd be very interested to hear what this so called 'evidence' is."

"Good," said Forward, resuming his seat. "I

shall be delighted to tell you. I hope it will persuade you to co-operate with us."

The Chief Inspector now willed himself to concentrate harder than he'd done at any time in his career. In court, Lady Fernshawe was going to make an excellent witness for her own defence. She was a most plausible liar and gave the impression she was the unlikeliest person in the world to commit an illegal act. Obtaining an admission of guilt from her was going to be very difficult.

He raised his eyes thoughtfully to the ceiling like a university don preparing to deliver a tutorial. "Where to begin?" he mused. His eyes rested on Lady Fernshawe. "I suppose the most appropriate place to start would be with the cause of all your misfortunes: your inheritance. When you inherited the Melthorpe Estate you didn't have any great personal wealth, and you were married to a failed businessman whose companies were losing money hand over fist. At first the inheritance must have seemed like a godsend. But then you discovered, just as I have, that the estate was in debt for nearly a million pounds and you weren't in a position to pay off the annual interest on the loans. This was a disturbing problem for you and your husband, but not an insoluble one. You had a great asset, Melthorpe Hall and its estate. So, you placed it on the market for sale by auction.

Unfortunately, the economy was entering a recession. The supply of eager buyers in the shape of London currency dealers, self-made millionaires and other examples of new money had dried up. The estate didn't even achieve its reserve price and you were forced to take it off the market. That was in April of last year. It was about then, I would guess, that you decided to adopt an illegal solution to your problems. Isn't that the case?"

Lady Fernshawe's expression remained impassive.

"I don't know who first had the idea, whether it was you, your husband, or your daughter, Sylvia Imrie. Not that it's important. I suspect it was probably the brainchild of all three of you. Sylvia was a drug addict, wasn't she? We know she spent a long period in detoxification at a private clinic in London. She had many contacts on the drugs scene. She knew who the dealers were and was easily able to put you and your husband in touch with them.

"Your approaches to these dealers couldn't have been made at a more fortuitous time. An enormous market for crack cocaine was opening up in London and all the major cities. The dealers couldn't get their hands on enough of the stuff, so you entered into a simple contract with them. They would arrange with their associates on the continent for the movement of cocaine into Holland. You would collect a supply of it and smuggle it into this country. You'd deliver the drugs, and in return would get a hefty cut of the profits. All you had to do was purchase a boat: which you were able to do quite legitimately, if somewhat secretly, through the various companies you were involved in. The *Phaeton* was purchased in May of last year. Just one month after Melthorpe Hall was taken off the market."

Forward paused. He wanted to gauge the effect of his words on her. So far, she appeared merely disinterested and a little irritated. Other than that, her expression told him nothing.

"At first your scheme went exceedingly well. We know the *Phaeton* made six trips from Holland to England between June and November last year, and highly profitable they must have been. But then things began to go wrong, didn't they? Two of your associates, David Nathan and Francesca Beaton, who often served as crew on the *Phaeton*, came to the attention of the National Criminal Intelligence Service, who were making enquiries into other drugs offences. So, you all decided to lie low for a while. It was at this time that your relationship with Mark Coulson intensified."

Lady Fernshawe sat up indignantly. "I've never had a relationship with Mark Coulson!"

Forward smiled. "No, I'm not suggesting a sexual relationship. I'm talking about a Bridge relationship. You and your husband are top flight Bridge players and Mark Coulson was an inveterate gambler and Bridge fanatic. Bridge was the common interest between you. Now, I know something about Bridge because my in-laws were great enthusiasts. It's a game for four players. When I realised that Coulson played Bridge with both of you regularly, I began to speculate as to who his Bridge partner could be. Mrs Coulson told us that no-one of their acquaintance in Melthorpe had any knowledge of the game, but that her husband did have a Bridge partner of long standing. His name was Harry Vaughan, a Chester solicitor. Surely it couldn't be him, I thought. But I rang him anyway, and found that although his practice is based in Chester, he also has an office in York. Which was very convenient, wasn't it? On the days Vaughan attended his York office, he could arrange to join you, your husband and Mark Coulson after work for some very expensive Bridge games. When I spoke to him, he told me the four of you met for Bridge on at least a dozen occasions. He admitted to losing very heavily. Ten thousand was the sum he mentioned, but he's a rich man and could afford it. Mark couldn't. That's why he kept those games a secret from his wife. She'd have been horrified if she'd known. She strongly disapproved of his gambling because it once cost them their lovely house in Chester.

Naturally, she disapproved of Harry Vaughan too. So Coulson told her the reason for his frequent visits to Melthorpe Hall was to discuss school matters, which as Chairman - I'm sorry, Chair - of the School Governors, you were very much involved in."

Lady Fernshawe began to tap the beautifully manicured fingernails of one hand slowly against her cheek.

"I imagine it was very embarrassing for all concerned that Mark owed you and your husband so much money and couldn't pay you," continued Forward. "But you saw a way to turn the situation very much to your advantage, didn't you?"

Lady Fernshawe's stare suddenly became vindictive. Forward was encouraged.

"One of your problems was finding a safe place to hide the drugs you'd landed. Originally, you'd brought the drugs into the country via the isolated North Lincolnshire coast, and then stored them in your London home. But with all the police interest in Nathan and Beaton, you decided the best plan was to keep the supply as far away from London as possible. But where could you store the stuff up here until it was safe to make the transfer? Certainly not at Melthorpe Hall. There was always the possibility that one of your operations could go wrong and you'd be caught in possession. That's when you had an inspiration. It was a stroke of genius. Who would ever think of looking for drugs in the stock cupboard of the local village school?"

Lady Fernshawe's eyes widened. She licked her lips, and then pursed them.

"At first, I would imagine that Coulson wasn't very keen on the idea. But when you promised him that in return for the use of his stock cupboard, you'd be willing to write off his gambling debt and in addition give him a large sum of money, he agreed. He desperately needed the money for a deposit on a new dream home for his wife. That was in December of last year. How do I know? Because it was in December that Coulson changed the location of the school stock cupboard from Mrs Dangerfield's room to his own, and insisted it should be kept locked and access to it should be restricted solely to him."

Lady Fernshawe gave Greville an incredulous look, and then returned her gaze to Forward. "You can't be serious?"

Forward's look was unflinching. "You now had a safe place to store the cocaine. But you and your husband still had a problem. How were you to get the drugs ashore without being detected? East Yorkshire has one of the most dangerous coastlines in Britain. Yet, it's ideal for smugglers because there are so many isolated coves and inlets. The *Phaeton* was too large a craft to enter one of these safely, and there was always the danger that the presence of the *Phaeton* so close in-shore would arouse the suspicion of Customs. What you ideally needed was a local sailor or fisherman who would rendezvous with the *Phaeton* far out at sea and bring the drugs ashore at an isolated point along the coast. Finding this person was easy because he was already working for you as a handyman. His name was Charles Gibbard and he'd once been a Hull trawler man. But what really made him the perfect candidate was that his ex-partner, Pete Stone, still worked an in-shore fishing boat called the *Gannet* out of Sandleton Harbour. And Stone knew every inch of the local coastline like the back of his hand."

Lady Fernshawe shrugged her shoulders at Greville. "I have never heard of this person!"

Forward had anticipated this. He ignored her and went on, "Gibbard, like Stone, was very hard up, so they both readily agreed to smuggle the drugs ashore for you. Gibbard's asking price was three thousand pounds per trip, which, given the size of your profits, I suppose you considered quite reasonable."

Lady Fernshawe laughed. "I've never heard such nonsense."

"You and your husband put your new plan into operation for the first time in January of this year, and everything went perfectly. Sometime in the afternoon of Wednesday the thirteenth of January, Gibbard and Stone sailed out of Sandleton Harbour in the *Gannet* and rendezvoused with the *Phaeton* ten miles off Filey Bay. The drugs were transferred from the *Phaeton* to Stone's boat. The vessels then split up and the *Phaeton* continued on to Sandleton Harbour where it berthed shortly after five thirty p.m. Stone then sailed the *Gannet* to within a couple of miles of Filey, anchored and put his nets out. His intention was to fish until it was time for Gibbard to go to Filey in the outboard dinghy and collect Coulson from the Coble Landing. Meanwhile, at six thirty p.m. that evening, you and Coulson travelled from Melthorpe to Monks Bay in separate cars. Coulson left his car in the clifftop car park and you drove him on to Filey, where he was collected by Gibbard and taken out to Stone's fishing boat.

"Why was it necessary for Coulson to accompany Gibbard and Stone in the boat from Filey to Monks Bay? Why didn't he just sit in the car park along with you at Monks Bay and wait for the boat to arrive? I must say this aspect of Coulson's behaviour puzzled me greatly. However, Gibbard has explained that it was necessary for Coulson to be with them because Stone didn't want his boat to linger at Monks Bay for too long. He wanted the drugs put ashore quickly, and two men were better for that than one. Perfectly understandable.

But there was also a more invidious reason, wasn't there? Gibbard says you wanted Coulson to travel from Filey to Monks Bay in the boat because you were afraid that if the operation went wrong Coulson would deny all knowledge of it. He would simply say he'd been duped by you into putting the holdalls into his stock cupboard because you'd told him they contained props and costumes for your concert. You were also frightened Coulson might lose his nerve and betray you to us. So, to ensure Coulson's complete loyalty, it was vital to make him an accomplice to your crime. And Gibbard swears those are the real reasons you made Coulson travel in the boat from Filey to Monks Bay."

Lady Fernshawe shook her head incredulously.

"But let's return to your drugs run in January. After you left Coulson at Filey, you drove to Sandleton Harbour and collected your daughter from the *Phaeton,* which had already berthed there. You took her to Monks Bay and you both sat in your Jaguar waiting for Coulson and Gibbard to arrive in the *Gannet* with the drugs. At about eight p.m. you and your daughter went down into Monks Bay and met Gibbard and Coulson, who by now had brought the drugs ashore in the dinghy. The drugs were unloaded and Gibbard went back alone to join Stone on the *Gannet.* Then he and Stone took the fishing boat off-shore and continued down the coast. Eventually they returned to Sandleton Harbour with their catch, having to all appearances completed a perfectly normal day's work. Meanwhile, you, Sylvia and Coulson had carried the three holdalls containing the drugs up the steps at Monks Bay and into the car park. The holdalls were all placed in Coulson's car. While you returned Sylvia to the *Phaeton*, Coulson drove to Melthorpe, where he placed the three holdalls in his school stock cupboard. Sometime later, towards the end of January, he removed two of the holdalls from the cupboard and passed them on to you. You released the drugs into the hands of the dealers in London and received your handsome cut. In return for his assistance, you rewarded Coulson by writing off his Bridge debt, which didn't cost you anything anyway, and you also gave him twenty thousand pounds on the understanding that your arrangement would continue. Such a large sum presented Coulson with something of a problem because he didn't want to draw attention to it. So, you and he conspired to put it into the school fund account. If anyone asked questions about it, you both had an elaborate lie ready. You were going to say the money was a legacy from one of Coulson's dead aunts."

Lady Fernshawe poured herself a glass of water from the plastic jug on the desk in front of her. Forward watched and waited while she took a long drink from the glass.

"Things didn't go so smoothly the next time you carried out the operation though, did they? Coulson wasn't very enthusiastic about taking part a second time. Do you know why?"

Lady Fernshawe emitted a long, theatrical sigh suggesting that she was infinitely bored.

Forward persisted regardless. "Do you know why?"

"I've already made it clear my client denies all knowledge of these matters," said Greville.

Forward's gaze remained fixed on Lady Fernshawe. "I'll tell you why. Because he developed a conscience. You see, ironically, Mr Coulson was passionate about health education and frequently gave his Year Six pupils lessons on the dangers of alcohol, cigarettes, solvent abuse and illegal drugs. I understand that in the week before the *Phaeton's* second drugs run, at Mr Coulson's invitation, one of our officers from the drugs squad visited the school to warn the older children about taking cannabis, cocaine and heroin. Imagine the scene in Mr Coulson's classroom: our officer was spelling out to those little kids the perils of drug taking, and all the time Coulson was sitting there knowing that just yards away from him his stock cupboard was stuffed full of cocaine. Cocaine which he'd helped to import illegally into the country.

How do you think that made a so-called respectable headmaster feel, eh?"

Lady Fernshawe shrugged. "How the hell should I know?"

Greville inclined his head towards his client. "You don't have to say anything."

Lady Fernshawe nodded and took another drink of water.

"It wasn't just the drugs squad officer's visit that made Coulson decide he wanted no more to do with your drug running operation. It was Helen, his ex-wife. She came to see me to-day to tell me that several days ago she'd phoned Coulson to discuss their eighteen-year-old son. For reasons which need not concern you, Coulson and the young man had been estranged for some years. A couple of months ago, he'd gone missing from home. Helen's phone call to Coulson was to tell him she'd concealed from him the fact that his son had a drugs habit. He'd recently been seen by an old school friend in Manchester, and was now living there as a junkie. Helen had wanted to tell Coulson this herself before he heard it from their daughter. Naturally, this was a terrible shock for Coulson, and coming on the day after the visit to his school by our drugs officer, I imagine it compounded the immense guilt he was already feeling. I believe it's what made him decide to tell you he wanted nothing more to do with your drugs smuggling. He was sickened by what he'd got into. But Coulson's co-operation was vital for the success of your plan. That's why you sent Gibbard round to the school last week to intimidate him, wasn't it?"

Lady Fernshawe sat up straight-backed. "You've really gone too far now, Chief Inspector! Why on earth would I send a man like Gibbard to threaten the Headmaster? I'm his Chair of Governors, for God's sake! Not some sort of Mafia boss!"

Forward was aware that Hoggart was casting an uneasy, sidelong glance at him. He ignored it and continued. "Nevertheless, the threats worked, and last Monday the plan was executed again. This time with disastrous consequences.

"Unfortunately, an unexpected meeting had been called that afternoon at Sandleton Teachers' Centre, which both you and Coulson had to attend. You also had a further complication: there was a flower arranging class in Melthorpe village hall on Monday evening, beginning around seven, at which you were expected. Your intention was to go to the class early, give an excuse and leave.

"The meeting at the Teachers' Centre ended just after six p.m. You and Coulson left the centre at the same time in your separate vehicles. We know this because one of the people at the meeting recalled seeing you drive off. Coulson's Astra set off first and you followed him in your Jaguar. You both drove to Monks Bay and parked in the car park on the cliffs just as you'd done in January. Coulson again left his Astra there and joined you in the Jaguar. But time was getting short, wasn't it? And you had to be at the flower arranging class at seven. So, instead of driving Coulson straight to Filey, as you'd done last time, you told him to take the train there. You dropped him off near Sandleton Station about seven p.m. We have a witness who will testify that he saw Coulson enter the station at around that time. Another witness has confirmed that Coulson was on the train which arrived in Filey at seven twenty-two p.m.

"After leaving Coulson near Sandleton Station you then drove straight to the flower arranging class at Melthorpe village hall. According to Mrs Dangerfield, a fellow instructor, you arrived there after seven and left early, giving as an excuse a migraine attack. This headache was to be an excellent alibi for you."

Lady Fernshawe scoffed. "It was a genuine headache."

Undaunted, the Chief Inspector continued. "However, when you arrived back at Melthorpe Hall you found a disturbing message from Gibbard waiting for you on your answering machine." Forward paused to consult a notebook that was in front of him on the desk and read from it aloud. "'Hello, Charlie here. We made the switch OK but bad news. The engine's packed up. Pete reckons it'll take a good while to fix it. I don't think we'll be at the bay until after nine. Maybe much later. You'll just have to play it by ear. I've got Mr Coulson with me, so that's good. We're going for something to eat now. I'll call you again before we set off.'"

Forward stopped reading and looked up at Lady Fernshawe. He was gratified to see she was considerably paler now than when he'd last looked at her moments before. "You didn't know we had that, did you? Of course, we've also got your answering machine with the original recording on it. Fortunately, someone forgot to wipe the tape. Other things on your mind, I suppose."

For the first time Greville looked discomforted. He gave Lady Fernshawe a long, sideways look.

"Naturally, you understood what Gibbard's message meant," Forward went on. "The cocaine had been transferred safely from the *Phaeton* to the *Gannet,* but the engine on Stone's boat had packed up and they probably wouldn't be able to land the drugs at Monks Bay until nine, or possibly ten, p.m."

Forward paused. He was gratified to see that Lady Fernshawe was listening intently.

"This was a huge set-back, but you decided to stick to your original plan as closely as possible.

You went straight to Sandleton Harbour and collected Sylvia from the *Phaeton,* which was now berthed there. We know this because the assistant Harbourmaster recalls seeing her leave the *Phaeton* on Monday night along with a woman answering your description."

"How could I have been in two places at once? I was at home in bed with a migraine attack. Why don't you believe me?"

Forward pointedly disregarded her objection. "That's when the really alarming thing happened. After collecting Sylvia, it took you just a few minutes to realise that on the way over from Holland she'd succumbed to temptation and helped herself quite liberally to some of the cargo. She was high on cocaine. You decided to get her out of the way as soon as possible, so you took her back to Melthorpe Hall. There you could stay with her until it was time to drive to Monks Bay. This was perfectly safe. There was no chance of her being seen by the staff because none of them lived in. And Wending was at the theatre in York because you'd changed his day off from Wednesday to Monday to make your alibi stick. You wanted everyone to believe you'd come home with a migraine attack on Monday night and gone straight to bed.

"But taking Sylvia back home with you in her high state was a terrible mistake, wasn't it? Because it was in your kitchen that Sylvia was able to get her hands on a knife. Who knows why? But we do know crack can make you paranoid and easily violent. Perhaps the knife made her feel secure. Wending has confirmed to us that on Tuesday morning, as he was about to make your breakfast, he noticed that an extremely sharp kitchen knife was missing. The same knife that Sylvia attacked Coulson with."

"That's purely circumstantial," said Greville. "Have you got the knife?"

"No. But Gibbard has described it clearly and it was just like the one Wending says disappeared. An extraordinary coincidence, don't you think?"

Forward observed Lady Fernshawe closely. Her confident attitude was diminished and her face had lost even more of its colour. Greatly heartened, he ploughed on. "Gibbard was as good as his word. He phoned you again from Filey, just before he and Coulson were picked up by Daniel in the dinghy and taken back to the *Gannet*. That would have been around eight thirty p.m. During the phone call Gibbard told you to be at Monks Bay for nine thirty. He also told you that Coulson was again losing his bottle."

"I could not possibly have had that conversation. I was fast asleep with a headache."

You have to admire her sangfroid, Forward

thought. He said, "And I suppose you didn't meet Sylvia, either?"

Lady Fernshawe did not answer.

"I find it extraordinarily difficult to believe your daughter came all the way from Holland, stayed overnight in Sandleton Harbour, and made no attempt to see you when you lived just a few miles down the road. I think a jury will find that as incredible as I do."

Lady Fernshawe smiled acidly. "Some families aren't particularly close."

"Later, you drove Sylvia to Monks Bay and parked the car in the clifftop car park, facing seaward. When the *Gannet* appeared in the bay about ten p.m. you flashed your headlights at it, and then you and Sylvia descended the steps into the bay. You didn't go down to the sea but waited with Sylvia at the bottom of the steps. It was a wild night; the flood tide was coming in and half the bay was already under water.

"Gibbard and Coulson left Stone and his son, Daniel, on board the *Gannet,* and brought the drugs ashore in the outboard dinghy. They placed the three holdalls at the bottom of the steps. Sylvia was still quite high. Gibbard has told me that when he met you and her in the bay, he realised she was drugged out of her mind. Coulson was in something of a state too, wasn't he? There, at the bottom of the steps in Monks Bay, just as you were all about to carry the drugs up to the cars, he told you he didn't want anything more to do with it. He wasn't going to put the drugs in his car and he wasn't going to keep them in his school. At first you didn't believe him. You only became convinced when he told you he'd thrown his car keys and the key to the stock cupboard overboard between Filey and Monks Bay. At that point you lost it and lashed out at him. Coulson struck back with his fist. This sent you reeling. Probably thinking you were in danger, Sylvia panicked. She pulled out the kitchen knife and lunged at Coulson. Coulson put his hand up to protect himself. That's how he received a deep cut on his left palm. Coulson grappled with Sylvia and cut her quite badly on the wrist. Then she lost control. While you and Gibbard were trying to restrain Coulson, she picked up a large piece of chalk and crashed it down on his head. Coulson fell to the floor but by now Sylvia was in a drug induced frenzy. She went on raining blows on his head, smashing his skull to pieces. You and Gibbard panicked. You dragged Coulson's body down to the sea, hoping the incoming tide would carry it away. You both went through Coulson's pockets in case he'd been lying about the keys and they were still on him. They weren't. He really had thrown them into the sea. We know this because Stone's son, Daniel, saw him do it. This was a terrible blow for you. You knew there was nearly two hundred thousand pounds worth of cocaine in the holdall that was still in Coulson's cupboard, and you had to get to it before anyone found it. You told Gibbard to take anything that could identify Coulson and throw it overboard into the deep water of Sandleton Bay. You also gave him the blood-stained kitchen knife and told him to do the same thing with that. Then you and Sylvia and Gibbard carried the drugs up to the car park. You didn't have Coulson's car keys, so all three bags had to go in the boot of your Jag. When this was done, Gibbard returned to the bay and obliterated any marks that had been made in the sand, before returning in the dinghy to the *Gannet*. When the *Gannet* rounded Flamborough Head and entered Sandleton Bay, Gibbard did as he was told and threw the kitchen knife and Coulson's wallet and credit cards overboard. At eleven forty p.m. the *Gannet* berthed in Sandleton Harbour. Gibbard, Stone and Stone's son were all seen disembarking by the assistant Harbourmaster. He recalled this clearly because of the presence of the teenager. Meanwhile, Sylvia had been badly cut on her wrist, hadn't she? After cleaning her up at Melthorpe Hall, you drove her to a hospital to have the wound stitched. Afterwards, you took her to Sandleton Harbour and put her back on the *Phaeton* shortly after four a.m. We know this because the assistant Harbourmaster recalls you returning with her at that time. You probably gave the *Phaeton's* crew instructions to set sail at the earliest opportunity, because they slipped out of Sandleton Harbour at five that morning. When the boat arrived in Hull, Sylvia left it and caught a train for London. Meanwhile, you had taken the three bags of drugs back to Melthorpe Hall. You had no choice now, but to unload and store them there. And that's why we found them in your possession."

"This is preposterous. Pure fantasy!" Lady Fernshawe was still dismissive but her tone had lost some of its conviction. "I told you we were looking after the bags for friends."

Forward twisted his mouth in contempt. "Don't insult our intelligence!"

"You haven't presented us with any evidence for these assertions, Chief Inspector," said Greville, whose composure remained intact. "You've got no forensics and you seem to be basing all these allegations against my client on the word of Gibbard. It'll never stand up in court."

"Not quite," said Forward. "Certainly, the events I've described to you are based on a statement made by Charles Gibbard, who was a key witness to the murder of Mark Coulson. But his statement has been corroborated by his accomplice, Pete Stone; and Stone's teenage son, Daniel. They both witnessed the murder of Coulson from their position aboard the

Gannet which was hove-to just off Monks Bay." Forward turned from Greville to Lady Fernshawe, who was staring at him warily. "Because of your height and build Stone wasn't sure whether you were a man or a woman."

"Ah!" cried Greville, gimlet eyed.

"But Stone and his son saw everything that happened. And Charles Gibbard, who was with you on the beach, has confirmed that you and your daughter were the two involved. And that it was Sylvia who gave Coulson the head injuries which killed him. All three key witnesses were interviewed independently and tape recorded in the presence of three police officers. But we also have a statement from another vital witness." Forward paused for effect and then addressed Lady Fernshawe directly. "Sylvia was in a bad way, wasn't she? She was losing blood. It was essential to get her to hospital to have her wound stitched. So, where did you take her?"

Lady Fernshawe did not reply. She looked suddenly demoralized.

"You couldn't take her to a local hospital, could you? Far too dangerous. At first, we couldn't trace any casualty department in the local area that had recorded anyone being admitted with knife wounds late on Monday night or early on Tuesday morning. But having tried the hospitals at Scarborough, Hull and York, one of my resourceful detective constables decided on her own initiative to enquire further afield. This was most fortunate because a junior doctor in Middlesbrough recalled stitching up a knife wound on the arm of a young woman in the early hours of Tuesday morning. The hospital record shows the young woman's name was given as Sylvia Cartwright, and she was accompanied by her mother and next of kin, Mrs Isabella Cartwright. Your married name is Cartwright, isn't it?"

Lady Fernshawe said nothing.

Forward locked eyes with Lady Fernshawe and tilted his head back inquisitorially. "Surely you can answer that question? Is your married name Cartwright?"

"Yes!"

Forward felt gratified. "So, rather than risk going to a local hospital, you drove your daughter all the way across the moors to Middlesbrough in the early hours of the morning. We know that because of the statement the junior doctor has given us. You gave him your London address and told him you'd been staying with friends in the borders. You said Sylvia had cut herself when she'd tried to open a tin of orange drink with a penknife as you'd been driving back to London. The doctor was immediately suspicious, but he was harassed and over-worked and you have such an imperious, intimidating presence he was rather frightened of challenging you.

"But even without those statements, we would still have enough evidence to indict you and your husband. You were caught in possession of four holdalls containing cocaine, one of which we can prove you retrieved from the school stock cupboard. We can also prove that cocaine from the drugs run in January had been placed in the boot of Coulson's Astra."

Lady Fernshawe looked taken aback.

"You seem surprised. Our sniffer dogs have excellent noses and can detect drugs long after they've been removed from a location. Even when they've been masked by other odours."

"That implicates Coulson, not my client," said Greville.

Forward kept his eyes on Lady Fernshawe. "You were also in possession of the murder weapon: the chalk boulder which your daughter used to batter Coulson to death."

Lady Fernshawe recoiled as though she'd suddenly been slapped. She recovered quickly and said, "I think you are very much mistaken!"

"Our inability to find the murder weapon bothered me greatly. I was sure that our exhaustive searches would have found it somewhere on the beach, even if it had been thrown into the sea, because the tide goes out a fair way at Monks Bay. But there was no trace of it. It wasn't found by any of the huge number of officers searching for it or by our sniffer dogs. I was forced to conclude that whoever had been involved in the murder had taken it away with them. A couple of days ago I actually came across it quite by accident. It was right under my nose but I didn't realise."

Forward leaned across the desk and brought his face closer to Lady Fernshawe. "It was only this morning when I'd received other information that I appreciated the full significance of your extraordinary flower arrangement, *The Enchanted Grotto*."

Lady Fernshawe glanced quickly towards Hoggart who was sitting over by the window. She then switched her gaze to Wilmott, who was on the other side of the room drumming his fingers silently on the tape recorder. When her eyes returned to rest once more on Forward, he savoured the amazement in them.

"The original flower arrangement you intended to submit was damaged beyond repair on Wednesday night, wasn't it? But you had a number of spare plants and materials available and you improvised brilliantly. Rather too brilliantly, as it turned out. What macabre impulse, I wonder, made you clean the blood off the large piece of chalk that had murdered Coulson, break it up into a few smaller lumps and use them to create the rock pool in your grotto? Was it the thrill of audaciously parading your guilt in a manner you were sure would be completely undetectable? Did you do it because you thought it was a novel way of getting rid of the evidence that linked you directly to this terrible crime? Or did you do it from a more practical impulse understood only by artists? Because it was the only material suitable for creating your overall artistic effect? Unfortunately, your artifice wasn't sufficient to conceal the fact that it had been used as a murder weapon. Of course, you made strenuous efforts to clean it up, but our forensic team found minute traces of Coulson's blood on nearly every one of the pieces of chalk in your *Enchanted Grotto*. Blood, like the pollen from the stamens of the lily, is notoriously difficult to remove completely. Trained police sniffer dogs can detect the presence of blood even when it's been scrubbed off surfaces. They can also find microscopic blood specks invisible to the naked eye. We can reveal these invisible amounts of blood with chemicals and ultra violet light. Did you know that?"

He continued staring at her impassive face as he waited for her reply. None came. "Was it just instinct that made you remove the murder weapon from the bay after Sylvia had battered Coulson to death? Or did you arrogantly think no-one would ever dream of looking for it at Melthorpe Hall, the home of Lady Fernshawe? Why didn't you give it to Gibbard to throw overboard with the knife? Perhaps you simply forgot. But it was a terrible mistake on your part, for it enables us to connect you directly with Coulson's murder."

Lady Fernshawe's expression was now sullen and conflicted. Forward inwardly rejoiced. Obviously, the discovery of the murder weapon had been a direct hit.

"Would you care to explain to us how pieces of the murder weapon came to be included in your flower arrangement?"

Lady Fernshawe said nothing. She stared down at her lap.

Not so cocky now, are you, My Lady? Forward thought. He directed his attention to Lady Fernshawe's solicitor. "You asked for forensic evidence, Mr Greville, and there it is. You'll also be pleased to hear we have even more forensics to support Gibbard's account of what happened on Monday night." He returned his gaze to Lady Fernshawe. "We know that while Coulson and Sylvia were struggling over the knife, she received a bad cut on her wrist. That's why two different blood groups were found on the steps at the bottom of Monks Bay. There was Coulson's, of course, which was Group O; but there was also another blood group, AB. There were a lot of traces of this AB blood on the handrail of the stairs leading out of the bay too. This naturally led me to the conclusion the AB blood was that of Coulson's murderer. In the old days, it was difficult for us to prove that somebody was at the scene of a crime just because their blood group happened to be found there. The blood group alone might have belonged to anyone. But now we have the DNA test. Are you familiar with it?"

Lady Fernshawe shook her head distastefully.

"The DNA test enables us to obtain, from a blood sample, the biological equivalent of a fingerprint, because every person's DNA is unique. Our forensic scientists in Hull extracted the DNA from the AB blood sample found on the Monks Bay steps. This DNA will be compared with another sample of DNA taken from Sylvia Imrie's body in London. We are confident they will match, and confirm that Sylvia was there in Monks Bay and murdered Coulson."

"So, she was there," Lady Fernshawe exclaimed contemptuously. "That doesn't prove she murdered him."

"You're not obliged to say anything," warned Greville. He looked rather glum.

"Yes, but traces of your daughter's blood group have also been found on some of the pieces of chalk in amongst your *Enchanted Grotto*. Obviously, while she was striking Coulson with the chalk boulder, some of the blood from the cut on her wrist got on to it. If the DNA found on those lumps of chalk is the same as that taken from your daughter's body, it will prove she used the chalk boulder as the murder weapon!

"Now, let's turn to the other charge I intend bringing against you. That you murdered Richard Dangerfield."

Lady Fernshawe gasped.

"When you arrived home in the early hours of Tuesday morning you were shaken up, but you thought you were safe, didn't you? You were sure no-one had seen you in the bay and so no-one could possibly connect you with Coulson's murder. But you were wrong. Someone had seen you. Not at the time of the murder, but earlier on in the evening when you and Coulson had driven separately from Sandleton to Monks Bay. That person was Richard Dangerfield. It was the merest coincidence and awfully bad luck for you. Richard had left work in Sandleton sometime after six on Monday evening. He came to a crossroads and the traffic lights were against him. He saw a Vauxhall Astra go across the junction and recognized it because it belonged to his ex-lover, Sheila Coulson. But she wasn't driving it; her husband was. Dangerfield was very surprised to see your car following Coulson's. He recognised your car too because it's very distinctive: a Jaguar XJS, and he could see you in the driving seat. When the lights changed, on an impulse, he followed both of you. Now, why should Richard do that? Well, he was still in love with Sheila and he hated Coulson's guts for forcing her to end their affair. Perhaps he hoped that you and Coulson were having an affair, and thought if he could dig up some dirt on Coulson it might persuade Sheila to leave him. We shall probably never know what his reasons were, but he certainly did follow you to Monks Bay. There he parked up and watched Coulson leave his own car and get into yours. He then followed your car back to Sandleton and saw you drop Coulson off in the main road by the station. How do we know this? Because Dangerfield told his latest girlfriend what he'd seen and she told me."

Forward paused to observe Lady Fernshawe's reaction. She was sinking slowly back into her chair, like a boxer reeling from a decisive blow.

You didn't expect that one, did you? Forward thought. Hugely encouraged now, he went on, "Richard must have thought your behaviour and Coulson's most strange. But everything became clear to him the following day when he learned of Coulson's murder. Sometime on Tuesday evening, Richard Dangerfield came to see you; and told you he knew you were in some way connected with Coulson's death because he'd seen you both at Monks Bay on Monday and then followed you back to Sandleton. He also told you the police had been questioning him about his own whereabouts on Monday night. This presented you with a terrible difficulty. For earlier on Tuesday, unaware of what Dangerfield had seen, you attempted to put us completely off the scent by arousing our suspicions about him. You tried to convince us Dangerfield had a motive for murdering Coulson because he'd had an argument with him in the pub a few months earlier. And now here was Dangerfield telling you he knew how deeply implicated you were in Coulson's murder. Dangerfield assured you he hadn't yet told the police he'd seen you and Coulson at Monks Bay, but he made it clear that if you wanted him to go on keeping his mouth shut it was going to cost you an awful lot of money. How much exactly? Gibbard tells us Dangerfield asked you for a hundred thousand pounds in cash."

Lady Fernshawe looked at Greville appealingly and shook her head. But the solicitor stayed silent.

"You told Dangerfield you couldn't lay your hands on that kind of money at short notice, and he was to come back the following evening for it. As soon as Dangerfield had gone, you alerted your husband, who was in London, and asked him to come up to Melthorpe at once. The next day, Wednesday, you and Paul Cartwright devised a plan to get rid of Dangerfield."

"I didn't!" cried out Lady Fernshawe. She shook her head vigorously. "This is getting more and more unbelievable!"

"You don't have to listen," Greville urged.

"No. I want to hear this man's outrageous story to the end."

She was clearly shaken now. Forward left her dangling on the hook for a few more moments. He knew he was closer now to breaking her than he'd ever been. "You told Gibbard that Dangerfield was a blackmailer and was planning to blackmail all of you. You ordered Gibbard to be at the Hall by nine p.m. with a length of rope to tie Dangerfield up. You told him that you and Paul intended to give Dangerfield a huge fright. When Dangerfield arrived at Melthorpe Hall on Wednesday evening he was surprised to find the door opened by Gibbard. Gibbard took Richard through to the library, and told him that you and Paul had both gone to see my production of *The Cherry Orchard*. This was not what Dangerfield had expected and he wanted to leave straight away, but Gibbard pulled a gun on him. Not his own gun, but one provided by your husband. Gibbard's job was to keep Dangerfield there while you and Paul were establishing a pretty good alibi. How could I, as the investigating officer, suspect either of you of being involved in Dangerfield's death when for most of the evening we'd been watching the same play together? That's why you made a particular point of singling me out during the interval to introduce me to your husband."

"Nonsense! I was merely being polite."

Forward noted that her confident façade was now only a pale imitation of what it had been previously.

"When you both returned to Melthorpe Hall it was about half past eleven. You and Paul went to the library, where Gibbard and his captive were waiting for you. Paul told Dangerfield he was just a nobody who'd stumbled into a game for very big players and was going to be taught a lesson he'd never forget. Dangerfield panicked. He knocked the gun out of Gibbard's hand and tried to get away. Gibbard grabbed him, and in the struggle that followed they both crashed into your flower arrangement, the one you'd intended to enter for the competition in the village hall. It was completely ruined. Unlikely as it may seem, this flower arrangement was one of the main keys to the case."

Lady Fernshawe blinked and regarded Forward quizzically. He could see she was wondering what other devastating ammunition he had at his disposal.

"Eventually your husband got hold of the gun and threatened Dangerfield with it. When everything had calmed down, Paul and Gibbard forced Dangerfield into your Jaguar. Your husband got into the driving seat and Gibbard, still threatening Dangerfield with the gun, forced him into the back. You, meanwhile, took

Dangerfield's car keys and got into the car he'd borrowed from his mother, a Ford Fiesta. Both cars set off for Viking's Chine. When you got to the car park at the Chine, you held a flashlight while Gibbard and Paul forced Dangerfield to pick up the metal litter bin in the car park. He was then made to carry it through the stile and a short distance down the path that runs by the side of the Chine. At this stage, Gibbard says he was convinced the plan was merely to teach Dangerfield a lesson and give him a fright. But Gibbard reckoned without you and your husband's ruthlessness. In the light of the flashlight, Gibbard coiled the length of rope over a thick branch of a tree by the path. He formed the other end of the rope into a noose. Paul then ordered Dangerfield to stand on the upturned litter bin and told him to put the noose round his neck. Dangerfield obeyed. Then Paul ordered Dangerfield to tighten the noose. Again, Dangerfield obeyed. Why, I wonder, did he always obey? Well, for a start, Paul was holding a gun on him. I think if someone was holding a gun on me, I'd do anything they said. After all, better to do that than risk them pulling the trigger. Besides, as Gibbard tells it, your husband kept reassuring the young man the whole time, telling him he was only going to give him a fright. Imagine Gibbard's feelings then, when you suddenly ran up to the litter bin that Dangerfield was standing on and kicked it away from him!"

"That's outrageous!" cried Lady Fernshawe. She turned to Greville. "It's a lie!"

Forward shook his head. "That's Gibbard's story, Lady Fernshawe. Just an hour ago he described to us how all three of you stood and watched Richard Dangerfield jerk and twitch on the end of that rope. When Dangerfield was dead, you coolly wiped your fingerprints off his car keys with a handkerchief and put them in his back pocket. You used the same handkerchief to remove your fingerprints from the interior of the Fiesta. Afterwards, you left the Fiesta in the Chine, and all three of you drove back to Melthorpe Hall, where, Gibbard assures me, you gave him several glasses of Champagne."

Lady Fernshawe looked truly horrified. "This is the most ludicrous thing I ever heard!"

"You thought we'd all assume Richard hanged himself because he couldn't live with the guilt of being Coulson's murderer. And some of us were fooled. But not Richard's mother; not his girlfriend; and most definitely not me!"

Lady Fernshawe threw up her hands in disbelief. "The whole thing's a complete lie. I was nowhere near the Chine that night, nor was my husband. Neither of us had anything to do with Richard Dangerfield's death."

Greville was looking quite worried now. In

a dispirited voice he said, "Again, you only appear to have Gibbard's word for this."

"No. I have rather more than that," said Forward. "I have the rope that Richard Dangerfield was hanged with." He returned his gaze to Lady Fernshawe. "The rope you asked Gibbard to bring to Melthorpe Hall on Wednesday night. Our forensic people have matched it to a much longer length of rope that was found on Stone's boat. Under the microscope the fibres from both ends match perfectly."

Greville became slightly more cocksure. "That incriminates Gibbard and Stone, not my clients."

"I also have the evidence of the pollen from the lilies," said Forward. He turned his concentration back on Lady Fernshawe. "You see, our pathologist found a very strange rust-coloured stain on Dangerfield's arm, and also on his clothing. This stain was later identified as pollen from the lily. It's a stubborn stain and is difficult to remove from fabrics of any kind. Dangerfield picked up this stain from the lilies in your original flower arrangement when he crashed into it during his struggle with Gibbard in your library on Wednesday night."

"He could have picked up that stain anywhere. Lots of people have lilies in the village," said Lady Fernshawe quietly.

"Ah yes, they do. You're quite right." Forward

produced a folded piece of paper from his pocket. "But only you had the variety known as Stardust Lilies." Forward unfolded the paper. "This is a list of all those who ordered lilies for the flower arranging exhibition. It was given by Mrs Coulson to the florist in Sandleton." He leaned across the desk fixing her in a gaze as intense as a laser. "You were the only one who ordered Stardust Lilies. And it was pollen from Stardust Lilies that was found on Dangerfield's hands and clothing. Those pollen stains could only have been found on him if he'd been in the library at Melthorpe Hall shortly before he died. Forensic have also confirmed that extensive specimens of pollen from the Stardust Lily were recovered by our Scenes of Crime Officers from the carpet in the library at Melthorpe Hall."

"You couldn't possibly get a conviction on that. It's only a tenuous connection," said Greville.

Forward's expression was scornful. "Tenuous? How can it be tenuous in the light of all the other evidence?" Forward smiled triumphantly at Lady Fernshawe. "For example, there's Dangerfield's thumbprint that was discovered in the back of your Jaguar."

Lady Fernshawe's imperious confidence suddenly returned. "That's no surprise. I've often given him a lift."

My God, thought Forward, I've thrown all

this at you and you're still sitting there calmly batting it back. For the first time it occurred to him that despite all the evidence against her, he was never going to get her to confess. He summoned up all his determination and said, "We also found one of your fingerprints under the metal clasp of the safety belt in Dangerfield's Fiesta. Your handkerchief missed that, didn't it? And then, of course, there are the tyre casts that were found next to Coulson's Astra in the Monks Bay car park; and also, in the car park at Viking's Chine. They make a perfect match with the tyres on your Jaguar."

There was a long silence. Lady Fernshawe placed her elbow on the desk and leaned forward massaging her forehead pensively with her long, elegant fingers.

Forward was aware that both Hoggart and Wilmot were staring at him. They were obviously wondering if he had anything left in the locker. Well, he did. One last trump.

Concentrating every iota of his attention on Lady Fernshawe, he said, "We know Sylvia was admitted to a private clinic on Friday morning suffering from a massive overdose. We also know you went down to London yesterday to see her. But you were too late, weren't you? When you arrived, she was already dead."

He waited.

Subtly, almost imperceptibly, Lady Fernshawe's chest jerked in a series of sudden heaves, as though something was catching at her breath. Greville inclined towards her solicitously. Forward continued to watch and wait. As her distressing movements continued, they became more pronounced and more violent. Soon she was snatching for air, but otherwise she made no sound. It was obvious she was trying to stop herself from sobbing. Forward was deeply impressed by her efforts to retain command of herself. To the end she was determined to bend her emotions to her will and subdue them. He admired her for that. But it was essential that she be broken; and this, he knew, was the perfect moment to apply the pressure.

"It wasn't supposed to end like that, was it?" he said. "You thought Sylvia had come off drugs. That she was clean. And that's how she would have stayed if it hadn't been for chance; coincidence; fate; bad luck. Call it what you will. The cruel and unexpected combinations of cause and effect that make the best laid plans go astray, and put you in the land of 'if only'. For example, if only you hadn't smuggled the drugs into the country, Sylvia wouldn't have been tempted to start using again and she wouldn't have killed Coulson in a fit of psychotic rage. If only the traffic lights in Sandleton had been at green when Dangerfield came to them on Monday evening, he'd have driven straight over the junction and never seen Coulson's Astra or your Jaguar. And, of course, then he'd never have followed you, hoping you and Coulson were having an affair. And if he hadn't followed you to Monks Bay, he'd never have connected you with Coulson's death and attempted to blackmail you. And then you would never have taken him to Viking's Chine and murdered him. And if only he hadn't fallen on your flower arrangement whilst he was struggling with Gibbard, we might never have connected you to his death"

Lady Fernshawe gave a short, pathetic whimper.

"Again, all down to coincidence and chance. Or we can look at it another way. If only Coulson hadn't lost so much money through gambling, he wouldn't have been forced to sell his house in Chester and relocate to Melthorpe. His wife wouldn't have felt humiliated because they didn't own their own home. Coulson wouldn't have been desperate for money to provide a new one for her, so he wouldn't have started gambling again in order to get it. And you wouldn't have been able to force him to smuggle drugs. And then again, if only the police hadn't come to speak to the children in Coulson's class about the dangers of drugs while he had a bag full of cocaine in the stock cupboard, he might not have felt such intense guilt. And if only the next day his ex-wife hadn't phoned him, he might not have bottled out of your drugs operation. And then, of course, Sylvia might not have killed him. But worst of all, if only you and your husband hadn't turned to crime in the first place, Sylvia would still be alive today."

Forward waited, and was soon rewarded for his patience. A deep, visceral sob wrenched itself out of Lady Fernshawe; followed by another; and then another. Tears spilled out of her eyes and streamed down her face.

The effect was moving, but Forward knew he mustn't stop. He had to go on crowbarring her open with her own guilt. "But perhaps the chain of coincidence, chance and bad luck goes even further back in your case. Everything might have been so different if your father hadn't lost your entire estate in a game of poker."

She looked up: at first astonished, then immediately mortified. The memory was obviously traumatic. She gave a long, pitiful cry, placed her arms in front of her on the desk, laid her head on them and now sobbed freely without any attempt at restraint.

"Oh yes, I know all about that. You see I've been doing a little research into your background. Alex Armstrong, the editor of the *Fundleton Gazette*, has been particularly helpful. He was a senior reporter when you became Lady Fernshawe and inherited Melthorpe Hall. It was a big story locally.

The headline, I believe, was 'Florist's Assistant Elevated to the Peerage'. Armstrong told me you were born into a situation of immense wealth and position in Lincolnshire. You spent your childhood at Fiddlingfoot House, a magnificent stately home set amidst the beautiful Lincolnshire Wolds. Until you were thirteen, you lived a life of privilege and splendour. But your father was a waster, an inveterate gambler. And one night, on the turn of a card, he staked your entire house and its estate - and lost. Until that night you and your mother had lived an idyllic existence. And then your dad went and threw it all away in a poker game. You hated him for that, didn't you? And that's why you now have no sympathy for losers. Particularly those who lose heavily gambling on cards. Poor old Coulson didn't stand a chance, did he?"

Lady Fernshawe raised her head. She sat up and turned to Greville as though she was about to deny this as well, but suddenly seemed to change her mind. Her head fell back onto her arms and she continued to sob.

"What a come down it must have been for you when your father lost everything. It can't have been easy when you were forced to leave your prestigious girls' private school and go to the comprehensive in Fundleton. They bullied you unmercifully there, didn't they? Because of your upper-class accent. And it must have been very hard adjusting to life in a cramped, little flat when you'd known nothing but the spacious interiors of Fiddlingfoot House. And on top of all that, at sixteen you had to go to work because your mother needed the money. She couldn't work herself because she'd had a nervous breakdown. That was after your father hanged himself, wasn't it? And his family were no help either. They wouldn't give you a penny. They resented you and your mother anyway, because she'd been your father's servant before he married her. But you enjoyed working in the florist's, didn't you? It was the reason you were able to acquire the skills of flower arranging so quickly from Richard Dangerfield's mother when you came to Melthorpe Hall. The woman you repaid by murdering her son!"

Lady Fernshawe responded with an unbearable keening noise. The depth of emotional agony this revealed made Forward wonder, for a moment, if enough was enough. But he forced himself to go on.

"Of course, you didn't want anyone in Melthorpe to know you'd worked in a florist's, so you told everyone, including me, that you'd owned a market garden. But that's not true, is it? It's a story you made up because you were deeply ashamed of your past. But that's understandable. It must have been very demeaning for you to work in that florist's, knowing your family had once owned

Fiddlingfoot House and its grand estate. You thought all that was going to change, though, when you met your first husband, Raymond Imrie. He wasn't at all rich; but he had prospects as an up-and-coming estate agent. Shame he had such a love of speed and fast cars. When he was killed in that terrible road accident, just months after Sylvia's birth, you were left virtually penniless, weren't you? Your world had again collapsed. Fortunately, after years of living hand to mouth you eventually met and married a businessman, Paul Cartwright. He wasn't very rich either, but he was comfortable, and at least you were able to stop working in the florist's and give Sylvia a private education. Things were starting to look up. And then came a really marvellous stroke of luck. You learnt that a remote cousin on your father's side had died. You were to become Viscountess Melthorpe and inherit Melthorpe Hall and its entire estate. You were ecstatic, I imagine. But not for long. You and Paul soon discovered the extent of the debt the Melthorpe Estate was in. What a cruel reversal of fortune that was! The only solution was to sell it. And so you put it on the market. But it didn't even fetch its reserve price. You and Paul were facing bankruptcy. After your terrible experiences you couldn't face going back to the gutter again. You were determined to hang on to Melthorpe Hall and its estate, whatever it cost. That's why you turned to crime. And you might have succeeded if your daughter hadn't murdered Coulson.

"Coulson's death put you in a real fix though, didn't it? You had three holdalls full of cocaine in the boot of your Jaguar, and there was another bag full of the stuff from the previous run in Coulson's classroom. The only problem was you couldn't retrieve it because Coulson had thrown the stock cupboard key into the sea. And it was the only one. You knew you had to get to the drugs before anyone else, otherwise your whole plan would be rumbled. So, you decided to hold your nerve, didn't you? And wait until the stock cupboard lock was changed.

"But again, poor Sylvia ruined your plans. When she returned to London she overdosed on cocaine and had to be taken to a private clinic by a friend. And then yesterday she died there. Alone. You and Paul panicked, didn't you? You decided to flee. Possibly abroad. But first you had to get hold of your drugs stash and sell it. You and your husband drove back here. On the way to Melthorpe Hall you stopped off and pestered Mrs Howard to open the stock cupboard with the new key. You were about to flee back to London with the four bags of drugs when we arrested you."

Forward pushed his chair back and stood up. "Now, whether you speak to me or not I intend to charge you with being an accessory to the murder of Mark Coulson. I am also going to charge you with the murder of Richard Dangerfield. Your actions have brought about the death of one man, you've murdered another and you've killed your own daughter. How the hell can you live with yourself?"

"I can't!"

Lady Fernshawe's cry was so anguished, so full of torment it shocked even Forward into silence.

"That's enough. You're overstepping the mark here, Forward!" Greville shouted. He turned to Lady Fernshawe and attempted to comfort her. Then, as she continued to sob, he said, "I need to confer with my clients."

"Certainly," said Forward. "We'll leave you to talk alone with Lady Fernshawe in here. When you've finished, we'll inform the custody sergeant and you'll be able to talk to Mr Cartwright."

Forward and his two colleagues left the room and went into the corridor. Forward ensured that the door of the interviewing room was closed behind them before he said, "You'd better wait here just by the door. I don't think they'll be very long." He smiled, gave Hoggart and Wilmott a triumphant thumbs up, and then walked off jubilantly down the corridor.

****

Twenty minutes later Forward was sitting at his desk nursing two fingers of Scotch poured from a bottle he kept locked away in his desk drawer. Normally, he never drank on duty, but the interrogation of Lady Fernshawe had been a brutalising experience and had left him feeling empty and dehumanized. On top of that he'd failed to extract from her the confession that would have made it all worthwhile.

As he sipped the harsh but analgesic liquid, he reflected yet again on the many shocking manifestations of human behaviour he'd witnessed in the interview rooms on the floor below. In his time, he'd listened to the most appalling accounts of human selfishness and cruelty. Yet, paradoxically, Lady Fernshawe had revealed the least, and she was the one who'd upset him the most. She was implicated in the death of one man and had killed another, yet had shown no remorse for the deaths of either. Only when he'd reminded her of her loss of wealth and status had she cracked and revealed any natural human emotion. There was something incredibly sad about that, and he pitied her more, in a way, than all those other suspects he'd had to question, who'd been driven by naked lust or greed or jealousy to do the terrible things they had. He recalled his old drama teacher telling him that the essence of tragedy was a great fall. Well Lady

Fernshawe had had a great fall all right. Twice.

The telephone on Forward's desk rang. It was the custody sergeant on the internal line. David Greville wanted to see him. "Send him up," said Forward. He knocked back what was left in the glass and replaced the bottle of Scotch in the drawer.

When Greville appeared, he came straight to the point. "My clients have come to the conclusion that you have an overwhelming case against them," he said. "They're prepared to admit everything."

CHAPTER
THIRTY SEVEN

"You still haven't told us how you knew Lady Fernshawe and her husband were Bridge players," said Wilmott.

Forward was sitting with Wilmott and Marjorie in a private room upstairs at *The Maypole*. They'd just enjoyed a wonderful cold buffet meal and Forward was on his fourth whisky. On the table in front of Forward was a partly opened box, gift-wrapped, that contained a handsome set of crystal glasses. These had been presented to Forward by Fred Bright, and their presentation had been preceded by a long speech in which Fred had extolled Forward's virtues as a director. Everyone agreed that the play had been an overwhelming success and a magical experience. Now, most of the cast and stage management were celebrating downstairs at the disco. Amongst them were several officers from East Yorkshire CID whom Forward had invited.

"How did I know they played Bridge?" mused Forward. "I have the play to thank for that, as well as a great deal more."

"*The Cherry Orchard*?" said Marjorie.

Forward took another sip of his whisky. "Yes. You see, I'd intuitively felt that Lady Fernshawe had some connection with this case, but I couldn't see what it could possibly be. Funny as it might seem, I had an odd notion that the play was trying to tell me what this connection actually was. Then, in the early hours of this morning, I read parts of it again, and, bugger me, if I didn't get all the answers."

"Like what?" asked Wilmott, reaching for a cigarette and then remembering he'd given up smoking yet again.

"Well, in the First Act one of the characters gets very sentimental about a bookcase. That reminded me of the bookcase in Lady Fernshawe's library."

"Which one? There were loads of them!"

"Ah, but there was only one that contained modern books. Don't you remember? I took one of them out to look at when we went to question Lady Fernshawe about the twenty thousand in the school account. But it wasn't until I thought about the bookcase in the play that I remembered the connection."

"What connection?"

"The bookcase in Lady Fernshawe's library contained several books on Bridge. How to improve your game and so on. Lady Fernshawe and her husband were obviously keen Bridge players. And so, I remembered, was Coulson."

"It could have been just a coincidence."

"Of course. But then, this morning, Griffiths brought me the search on Finesse Holdings, Cartwright's company, and I realised it was he and Lady Fernshawe who really owned the *Phaeton*."

Wilmott and Marjorie stared at him blankly.

"You don't see it, because you don't play Bridge," said Forward. "Finessing is a Bridge technique. You use it to tease out your opponent's best cards. Only a fanatical Bridge player would name his company after a Bridge technique."

"Finesse Holdings," said Wilmott. "Of course."

"Yes. It was then I understood the hold Lady Fernshawe and her husband had over Coulson and how they'd used him."

"But how did you work out what their motive was?" asked Marjorie, fascinated.

"The play again. And a little joke that your husband made."

She pulled a face. "His jokes are useless," she said, and smiling, playfully tapped Wilmott on the leg.

"On the contrary, this one was very useful indeed."

"Go on then. Tell us."

"He said that Melthorpe Hall had once been on the market and both of you had thought about buying it, but it was a bit too small for your needs."

Marjorie grimaced good humouredly. "And you call that a joke?"

"At the time it struck me as vaguely funny but nothing more. However, then I remembered the scene in Act Three of the play where Lopakhin, the businessman, announces that he's bought the estate; and, of course, the owners are dreadfully upset. That really set me thinking. If Lady Fernshawe and her husband had put Melthorpe Hall and its estate up for sale they must have been desperate for money. But why hadn't some rich businessman like Lopakhin come along and bought it? Why were they still living there? Now in the play, the estate containing the cherry orchard is auctioned. Lady Fernshawe's estate is probably much larger than the one in the play, so presumably it had been auctioned too. Those sort of places aren't sold like my little flat or your three bedroomed semi. They're always auctioned. So, I asked myself, what had happened at the auction? I did some telephoning and found out who the estate agents were. They told me that at the auction, held in March of last year, the estate hadn't even achieved its reserved price."

"What was the reserve price?"

"Two and a half million."

Marjorie whistled.

"So, now I had their motive. Money. A simple motive but one that can lead to all sorts of terrible consequences if pursued ruthlessly, as it was in this case. Like the people in the play, Lady Fernshawe and her husband had a deep attachment to their home and a determination not to lose it. Anyway, the estate agents told me that Melthorpe Hall was taken off the market in late April, a month after the abortive auction. I then learned that in the following month Lady Fernshawe and her husband had purchased the *Phaeton*. That's when everything fell into place."

"Brilliant!" Marjorie exclaimed. She leant towards Forward and planted a wet kiss on his cheek.

Forward blushed. "I'm not the brilliant one," he insisted, pointing at Wilmott. "He is. If your husband hadn't recognised Gibbard in that photofit, a chance in a million, we'd still only have very strong suspicions, not a case."

Wilmott raised his glass. "A triumph of lateral thinking," he said, a shade facetiously.

Forward smiled. "Not quite. At the risk of being thought self-aggrandising, I have to say that the real triumph of lateral thinking was my refusal to accept that Dangerfield had murdered Coulson, simply because Miss Newbiggin told us she'd seen him at Monks Bay on Monday evening." His tone became doleful. "I'm glad of that for his mother's sake."

Wilmott stood up. "I think I need a dance," he said. He took hold of his wife's hand. "Are you coming?"

Marjorie glanced at her watch. "We can't, Graham, there's no time." She turned to Forward. "Our babysitter's got to get home soon."

"You run along then. I'll see you next week."

"I don't like leaving you on your own," said Marjorie.

"Don't you worry. After you've gone someone's bound to come up and talk to me. And even if they don't, I've plenty to think about."

****

After Wilmott and Marjorie had left, Forward sat and attacked his whisky. He was deliberating whether or not he should go downstairs into the disco. Normally, he avoided discos like the plague, but he decided it would do him good to drink some more and perhaps even dance. Despite his success and all the compliments, he felt a bit flat. He always felt that way when a production ended. It left a large vacuum in his life. He'd been expecting to fill it with the Coulson and Dangerfield investigations, but now those too had more or less been concluded. He consoled himself with the fact that both cases had generated enough paperwork between them to fill his days and nights for weeks to come. And, then again, there was always the next Players' production to look forward to. He might even act in that one, as well as direct. Now, there was a thought!

A glamorous couple appeared in the doorway hand in hand. They were both tall and dark haired and appeared to be looking for somebody. Forward was shocked when he suddenly realized that the two unfamiliar lovebirds were Jason Holtby and Doreen Foster. Their physical intimacy was so incongruous and unexpected he hadn't immediately recognized them.

Doreen had spotted Forward now. She was moving towards him, tugging Jason behind her.

Why am I surprised they're an item? Forward asked himself, as they bore down on him. I ought to know that when two people play characters involved in a close, romantic relationship on-stage, the simulated passion often becomes indistinguishable from the real thing; it attains a power and a reality that inevitably obtrudes into every aspect of life. And this can happen to the most unlikely people. He recalled that in his time in the theatre he'd seen many incompatible couples put aside their innate hostility and hop into bed with each other. In some cases, their on-stage romance had propelled them all the way to the altar. And then he remembered: in *The Cherry Orchard*, Yepikhodov's love for Dunyasha was not reciprocated.

Jason and Doreen came up to his table and stood there self-consciously, without saying anything. There was a gleam of sweat on their foreheads and they both looked as though they'd had a lot to drink. There was something else radiating off them too: a kind of hysterical rapture. They stood so close together their bodies were touching, and Forward had the distinct impression they were using their proximity to physically communicate to him the power of their mutual obsession. So that was why Doreen had never ruined Jason's brilliantly funny exit again.

"You two look as though you've been having a good dance," said Forward.

"We were but it got a bit hot," said Jason.

Jason and Doreen admired the glasses that had been presented to Forward, and they all exchanged several banal remarks.

Eventually, Jason and Doreen's real reason for leaving the disco and seeking out Forward was revealed. Doreen was curious to know what his next production for the Players was going to be.

"I'm torn between doing a Coward or an Ayckbourn," he said.

"Which Coward?" Doreen demanded. "I've

always wanted to play Gilda in *Design for Living*."

"I was actually thinking of *Hay Fever*."

"Judith Bliss. That's a marvellous part."

Why does she always want to play the leads, even though she's patently unsuitable for them? Forward asked himself. Then he realized he was being uncharitable. After all, hadn't he always wanted to play the leads? Wasn't that what most actors dreamed of? He said, "Yes, but to play Judith Bliss you need to be quite mature."

Doreen's face fell.

"I love *Hay Fever*," said Jason. "But either Coward or Ayckbourn would be great."

"When will you decide?" asked Doreen.

"Tell you what," said Forward, on a sudden impulse. "Let's decide now." He reached into his pocket and took out a ten pence piece. "Heads for Coward. Tails for Ayckbourn," he said, tossing the coin high into the air.

It fell onto the carpet and landed 'heads'.

"It's Coward!" cried Doreen.

They talked of the characters in *Hay Fever* and various other Coward plays for several minutes. With a transparent lack of subtlety, Doreen and Jason attempted to pump Forward about the Coward roles he considered them suitable for. He would not be drawn.

Eventually Doreen tired of the conversation. "Is it a secret we're doing a Coward next. Or can we tell everybody?"

Forward smiled at her urbanely. "Once you reveal anything to anyone, it's no longer a secret," he said.

"Come on, let's go," said Doreen.

"All right," said Jason, looking at her adoringly.

Doreen took his hand and led him away.

As Forward watched them both go, he was surprised to find himself thinking quite positively about Doreen. Despite her faults, and they were legion, you could never say she lacked enthusiasm. And even though she threw the most embarrassing tantrums, she didn't hold grudges and simply carried on as usual, as though nothing unpleasant had happened. Surely, that was in itself quite admirable? A really uncomfortable thought occurred to him. Could his dislike of her be an example of Jung's shadow effect in operation? Did she irk him so much because she reminded him such a lot of himself when he was younger? Hadn't he been rather boorishly self-centred then? Always determined to dominate in whatever part he'd been given? Always keen to steal the show? Or was it that he'd had too much whisky and it was making him soft in the head?

Forward looked up. DC Griffiths had come up from the disco and was standing in the doorway. She was wearing a tight, black dress and her eyes gleamed with youth and dancing.

She came towards him running a hand back through her long blonde hair as though she were partly embarrassed.

"Hello," said Forward. "No need to ask where you've been."

Drink had made her familiar. "We all thought you'd left, Tony."

"No. I intend to stay on and get a little drunk."

She looked at a loss for words. Then she said, "Why not? You deserve it."

Forward felt the need to stand up. He did so, but, after all the whisky, realised it wasn't such a great idea.

"Look, about this morning," he slurred. "I was very rude to you. I've been meaning to apologise all day but, in the excitement, it slipped my mind."

She smiled and impulsively took his hand. "Oh, don't worry about that. Come and have a dance!"

ABOUT THE AUTHOR

Michael Murray

Michael Murray is an actor, writer and teacher. He was born in London.

BOOKS BY THIS AUTHOR

Magnificent Britain

It is 1971 and Nigel Lush's official biography of First World War hero, Sir Maurice Brearley, is ready for publication. But at the last minute Nigel receives startling allegations about Brearley's conduct which presents him with a terrible dilemma.

Julia's Room

Alan is a young reporter working in the heyday of Fleet Street. A chance encounter with a stranger in a pub destroys his illusions about Julia forever.

Leefdale

A beautiful Yorkshire village is riven by conflict when a group of incomers threatens to jeopardise its chances of winning the

Magnificent Britain Gardening Competition for the fifth consecutive year.

Learning Lines? A Practical Guide For Drama Students And Aspiring Actors

When Michael Murray was a student at R.A.D.A. he was told by his drama tutor, "You do not learn lines, you study a part!"

But how do you study a part?

You can make a start by reading "Learning Lines?"